T0312428

Amy Jordan lives by the sea with her husband and young children in Cork, Ireland. A former tutor at Munster Technological University, she worked in the Irish civil service for a number of years before pursuing her passion for writing crime fiction. Amy is a fan of thrillers and crime novels, and her love of suspense and plot twists flows into her writing.

THE DARK HOURS

AMY JORDAN

ONE PLACE. MANY STORIES

HQ
An imprint of HarperCollins*Publishers* Ltd
1 London Bridge Street
London SE1 9GF

www.harpercollins.co.uk

HarperCollins*Publishers*
Macken House, 39/40 Mayor Street Upper,
Dublin 1, D01 C9W8, Ireland
This edition 2025

1
First published in Great Britain by
HQ, an imprint of HarperCollins*Publishers* Ltd 2025

ISBN: HB: 9780008656980
TPB: 9780008656973

This book contains FSC™ certified paper and other controlled
sources to ensure responsible forest management.

For more information visit: www.harpercollins.co.uk/green

This book is set in 11/14.7 pt. Sabon LT Std by HarperCollins*Publishers* India

Printed and Bound in the UK using 100% Renewable
Electricity at CPI Group (UK) Ltd

To Calum

1

2024

Julia Harte has found the perfect place to disappear: Cuan Beag, a secluded village on the east coast of Ireland. Home to fewer than one thousand residents, a popular day trip for tourists, it has proved to be a scenic corner in which to erase a life.

From her living room window she anxiously watches the night steal the remains of the evening sun, chasing the last of the day until even the shadows evaporate. Under the cover of night, the road beyond her short driveway is a gateway to possibilities, yet only residents' cars travel this far from the village, and she knows the sound of the engines and the routines of the drivers. This corner of the world is so peaceful, at times it feels uninhabited; that's why she chose to disappear here. But Julia knows anything is possible in the dark hours.

She snaps the blinds closed and draws the curtains, turning her back on the outside world, sealing off another day. Moving quickly through the rest of the cottage, she follows her nightly ritual, checking that windows are closed and latched properly, that the alarm system light is blinking as it should. She double-locked the front door when she came inside earlier but pushes against the handle now as she walks past. A flashlight stands ready on the hall table and she flicks it on and off, then brushes her fingers against the cool steel of an old golf club resting against the wall. A golf club and a flashlight ... all anyone needs to keep away the darkness.

Everything is as it should be. Safely locked in for another night inside her fortress, tucked into a corner of the world where her old life doesn't exist.

In the kitchen her eyes rest on a single birthday card on the windowsill. She turned sixty last week; a milestone birthday, spent alone. The card is from an old friend, one of the few that know where to find her. Loneliness accosts her suddenly; sometimes she feels the quiet of Cuan Beag seeping into her soul, a cold chokehold that steals her breath, and wonders if she made the right decision. She shakes herself free of it; isn't that how it goes when you leave your life behind? She imagines Philip rolling his eyes at her in those moments; she was never indecisive. In fact, her stubborn certainty that she was right was one of the things he loved about her in the early days. The solitude of this existence is exactly what she needs now. And if she feels lonely sometimes, well, that's her penance.

In her small living room, Mutt is a tiny ball of white fur waiting patiently on the armchair near the hearth, his ears pricking up when she walks in. She smiles at him, the most ineffective guard dog she has ever met, and now, her only companion.

'All tucked in for the night.' She rubs his head as she walks to the dresser and pours a brandy into the same crystal glass that she has used for decades. It's one of the few remnants of her life before; a wedding present, its twin long ago smashed into shards. She raises the glass to her wedding picture hanging on the wall and dips her head.

'Night, Phil.'

Mutt rises onto his paws and circles to make room for her on the armchair. His age is showing, his movements slow, and she rubs his fur affectionately. She takes her first sip of brandy – it's sharp and sears her throat, but she knows the second swallow will be gentler – and switches on the night-time news.

The newsreader's voice is hypnotic; updates from the White House in America, the stock exchange, a protest about climate change planned for Dublin city centre, no news on a young man who has been missing in Cork city for over a week. Her heart sinks at the last news item, but the woman who would have abandoned everything else to find that young man existed in a different life. Now, she sits with her dog on her lap and a brandy in one hand, happy to have escaped it all.

Her eyelids begin to close. But something startles her into alertness; a name. The newsreader's baritone continues as it had before, but the words cause her to sit up straight. She feels her heart rate spike, a thudding that burns uncomfortably, her pulse sounding loud inside her head. The TV screen is blurring; she blinks rapidly and rests one hand heavier on Mutt's fur, the other gripping the crystal glass like a vice.

'A spokesperson from the psychiatric hospital has

confirmed that Mr Cox died suddenly earlier today. His conviction for several murders in 1994 and his subsequent incarceration in Cork—'

She's breathless, fear tightening around her throat, dread that the news report might show photographs of him or even a film reel. Her heart is still pounding fast and hard, and she knows seeing James Cox again, even just a photograph, will be her undoing. And worse still, *she* might be in that photograph. Julia hadn't intended to reach for the remote and change the channel but now she is watching highlights from a recent football match and beginning to breathe easier.

He's dead.

Mutt stirs and she feels his eyes on her. His mouth twitches, anxious. He knows her moods by now. She pulls his face close and kisses him gently.

'It's all right, my little scruff. We might sleep easier tonight. The monster is dead.'

But she doesn't sleep; she rarely does. With the dog breathing deeply and curled at her feet, she sits at a small desk in the second bedroom, the blue-white glow of the screen lighting up the room. She doesn't feel the cold of the night. Her fingers tap the keys of her laptop, finding news articles, pausing to skim-read, searching for more. It's almost thirty years since his arrest, and as the night passes, she relives that day as if it were yesterday. As the darkness fades into the weak light of dawn, she reads and rereads, then searches again.

He *is* dead.

It's confirmed by all the major news stations; cause of

death is a suspected heart attack, more details to follow. She allows her eyes to rest on the image of his face just once. He was handsome, in a way. A strong jaw, a high forehead, small, light-coloured eyes. He had benefitted from the best mental health care the state could offer, yet he was never released. She has been grateful for that mercy every day for decades.

Her head feels fuzzy. She resists the urge to trawl through archived newspaper articles detailing the worst of James Cox; she doesn't need the words and images on a screen to remember the names of his victims, their faces, their families' grief. Now that he's dead, will those families have peace?

Will she?

Experience has taught her that now is not the time to relax. The media will dredge up the past again, will force the country to relive his crimes in all their gruesome detail. It will be a frenzy, less than it was thirty years ago, perhaps, but it will consume the front pages for a while. Will the articles mention her name? Will they show photographs of her? She can't see why not. She and Cox are forever entwined, even in death.

This chapter of my life is over, she thinks, closing the laptop with a soft click, her eyes on Mutt, who is sleeping soundly, his weight reassuring and warm against her ankles. She just has to keep her head down for the next week while the media run their stories and it will all blow over.

Perhaps then she can finally lay the ghost of James Cox to rest.

Perhaps now she can stop being afraid of the dark.

2

1994

'What do you reckon?'

Garda Adrian Clancy parked the squad car against the kerb and leaned forward, peering into the semi-darkness.

'Turn the engine off,' Julia suggested quietly.

'Okay, boss.' He turned the key and both of them rolled down their windows a couple of inches. They watched the road in front of them for few minutes in silence, noting it undisturbed.

'It's quiet as a mouse,' Adrian murmured and Julia nodded her agreement, angling her head to look all around them, straining to see in the half-light. After a stiflingly hot day, the night was cool and still. She welcomed the chill air yet shuddered as it rolled over her skin.

The housing estate in Douglas had two parallel rows of neatly landscaped semi-detached houses and looked like a postcard for suburban bliss. Cars parked in driveways, the adjacent grass neatly trimmed, low hedges the only permissible demarcation of ownership. A skateboard lay abandoned on the grass nearest to them, its green logo glinting in the glow of an overhead streetlight. True, graffiti marred a nearby electricity box, but it all looked so ordinary.

Still, they were on high alert. Two teenage girls had been reported missing one week ago. Extensive searches had yielded nothing so far, and the frustration of each investigating officer was laced with fear. People had disappeared before, and some of them had never been found. But in this case, that was a reality the chief superintendent, Des Riordan, refused to accept. And it was why Julia and her partner were here; a resident had reported a disturbance that might fit with the disappearance of the two girls.

Or it might all be a total waste of time.

'What's this guy's name again?' she asked, and Adrian pulled a notebook from the glovebox, his eyes flicking over his scrawled notes. He did a bad job of stifling a yawn as he read.

'O'Mahony. Tony. Says he can hear a girl crying for the last few hours inside number thirty-six. The chief is jumpy; he sent word to check it out. Problem with this guy O'Mahony is that last month he made several complaints about someone knocking on his living room window at the crack of dawn, which turned out to be a pair of hooded crows, so you know ...' His voice trailed away and he returned to watching the street in front of them, yawning again.

Julia rolled her window down further. 'I suppose Molloy and Connolly will want an update in case we turn up anything linked to those two missing girls.'

Her lip curled as she spoke their names; one of them was younger than her, she was sure of it, and she hated that he'd been promoted while she felt stifled as a Garda.

'Connolly said to let him know how this turns out. They're in the city at a possible sighting; us lackeys get the grunt work, as per.'

The Garda station had a pressure-cooker feel to it and the chief superintendent was coming under increasing scrutiny. Julia was intrigued by the case, but as a rank-and-file Garda, she'd only been tasked with door-to-door interviews and searches of a football pitch behind the girls' school. She walked past the conference room wistfully every day on her way to the canteen, catching glimpses of the girls' photographs on the noticeboard. Julia knew everything about them – Louise Hynes and Jeanette Coyle were best friends, just sixteen years old, both from loving families that desperately wanted them home. Her hands itched to grab the file reports and study them, to be more involved in it all, but the detective inspectors, especially Jim Connolly, seemed to take great pleasure in shutting her out.

Adrian yawned again, loud and uninhibited.

'Ugh … sorry.'

'Is Audrey still not sleeping?' Julia asked sympathetically.

He rubbed his hands roughly over his face, his stubble rasping against his fingers. 'That child has our hearts broken. Mary says it's bound to be colic. There's no let-up whatsoever.'

Julia smiled weakly; babies and their sleeping habits wasn't something she could advise her work partner on. She cleared her throat.

'Right. So, Tony O'Mahony and his nuisance calls. As I said, what do you reckon?'

'Well, that behaviour isn't unusual for crows actually, they were probably pecking at their own reflection. I told him to close the bloody curtains, or failing that, to hang a few CDs on a string to confuse the birds, and lo and behold—'

Julia suppressed an exasperated groan. 'Not the birds, Adrian, the crying from the house next door. Do we know who owns the house?'

'Oh, right, yeah.' He sounded sheepish. 'O'Mahony said the house is between tenants at the moment; the owners live in Dublin. Says he tried knocking at the door but got no response. He *also* said we're not to disturb him and his wife any further but to do the job the taxpayers are paying us for and make the noise stop.'

'He sounds like a charmer.' She grinned at him.

Adrian knocked his knuckles on the dashboard and sighed; neither of them relished the thought of wasting their time on yet another false lead. Julia peered into the stillness of the estate again. 'Come on; this is creeping me out. Let's get it over with.'

She was reaching to the back seat for her jacket when Adrian's whispered 'Holy Christ!' gave her pause. She looked towards the house, her pulse immediately racing. It seemed at first like a streak of white light rushing at their car. Realization came fast – it was a young woman, a girl really, dressed in a white string vest and underwear, running barefoot towards them. Her long dark hair billowed around her face as she ran. Her legs jerked unsteadily but her arms pushed the air at her sides, desperately propelling herself forward.

Away from number thirty-six.

Julia pushed the car door open so hard it bounced back onto her legs as she leapt onto the footpath. She reached the girl within seconds, Adrian at her side, and together they grabbed her as she collapsed into their arms. Her skin felt wet, slick and slippery, and in the semi-light from a nearby streetlight, Julia realized it was blood – the girl's arms and legs were covered in blood.

The young girl staggered against Adrian's chest and he gripped her around the waist, trying to keep her upright. 'I've got you, pet; I've got you.'

Panic thickened his voice and Julia's eyes met his; she could see he felt the same dread she did.

'Ambulance,' Adrian said, nodding at Julia. Then, to the girl, 'Can you stand?'

She sagged further against him. Julia's eyes roamed over her arms and legs, her torso, looking for wounds. All that blood and no obvious sign of any injury … as though the blood wasn't hers. When her eyes reached the girl's face she gasped; it was one of the two missing teenagers.

'Louise? It's Louise, isn't it? We're here to help you.'

The girl's eyes were rolling in her head as she slumped against Adrian's chest. Julia gripped her arm. 'Are there others inside the house?' she asked, leaning closer. 'Is there anyone else inside? Is Jeanette in there?' She wanted to tell Louise that she was safe now, that whatever ordeal she had endured was over, but she couldn't get the words out. The girl nodded and gasped, half-collapsing again. Heaving with the effort, Adrian scooped her into his arms and turned to the car.

'We need to get her to hospital, we can't wait. Can you get the radio and … where are you going?'

'She nodded; just now she nodded! There's someone else in the house,' Julia said, backing away from them. 'It could be Jeanette Coyle, Adrian! All that blood … I have to get to her!'

He looked frantic, his eyes bulging in his face. His mouth opened and closed while he staggered a little with the girl in his arms. 'Jesus, Jules, no!' he cried, aghast. 'Don't you dare!'

'Stay with her.' Louise Hynes was unconscious now, her head lolling back, dark hair swinging in the air. 'Call for help! But I have to, Adrian. If Jeanette's in there, or anyone else, they could be bleeding out.'

'Are you *mad*? We have to wait! *Jules!*'

She knew it was reckless, to go into number thirty-six alone, but adrenaline fired inside her; she had no choice. Adrian was still shouting but his voice was muffled, easy to drown out. She crossed the road in a quick jog and crouched a little lower to the ground as she ran up the driveway, her eyes alert for movement. The front door of the house was still open. Julia pushed it wider with one hand, the fingers of her other hand flexing behind her back, feeling nothing there. She thought of her baton on the back seat of the car with her jacket and closed her eyes, cursing under her breath. But she couldn't turn back – she could hear it. Weeping, followed by loud, anguished wails; someone inside this house was terrified, crying for help, *begging* for help.

Gritting her teeth she stepped inside.

3

1994

The hall light was on, the narrow space illuminated by a bulb that hung limply from the ceiling, a short magnolia-coloured corridor in front of her. Julia moved forward, shoes squeaking on a plastic carpet runner. The hallway was piled with old newspapers and boxes, stacked against the walls. She stood still to listen, to figure out where the crying was coming from. Downstairs: she was sure of it. But it was difficult to pinpoint exactly from where; it seemed to be coming from all around her. It sounded like a woman was crying from inside the very walls, the sound engulfing the whole house. And she was hugely distressed, begging and sobbing.

Julia placed one hand on the wall, trying to ground herself – the instinct to help this person was so strong she felt light-headed. She wondered if she should shout out but abandoned the idea. There was every chance the perpetrator was inside this house and without her baton, all Julia had was the element of surprise and some self-defence manoeuvres she had been shown during her training. She was sure Jeanette Coyle was in here … but where?

She would have to search the whole house.

She gripped the handle of the nearest door and pushed it open, her fingers flicking on the light. The room was stripped bare of all furniture except a bookcase, every shelf piled with books in haphazard stacks, some piles threatening to fall over. A worn, faded red carpet showed indents where chair legs had once pressed into it. But the room was otherwise empty.

Moving on, heading further down the hallway, Julia stepped into the next room and found it a mirror of the first; the same red carpet but no furniture save for a floor-to-ceiling bookcase that was full of candelabras, framed photographs and stacks of paperwork. There was a radiator against the wall and she rested a hand on it; it was freezing cold to touch. She shuddered; the house had an emptiness about it, as though it was stripped of life except for the loud cries of someone trapped inside.

She moved to the kitchen at the back of the house and turned on the light. The room was empty. Leaving the light on, better to banish the dark, she moved back to the staircase. Panic was rising further inside her, the incessant cries for help pulsating inside her head. The cries reminded her of training videos at the Garda college, of drug addicts in interview rooms, of distressed parents being given bad news. Moaning and weeping; it was the sound of desperation. She felt an urge again to call out *I'm here!*, to scream *Where are you?*

But she carried on in silence.

Back in the hallway, she wiped her damp palms on her

thighs before gripping the wooden banister and hoisting herself up the stairs. The landing was a small, narrow rectangle, set in darkness. She felt along the wall and flicked the switch – nothing. Perhaps the bulb had gone, or had been removed. She stepped towards the nearest door and pushed it open; the air inside the room reeked of something she couldn't bear to think about. She reached for the light switch and exhaled in relief as a bright glare filled the small bathroom. Blinking in the stark light, she could see immediately that the room was empty.

The sound of crying seemed as strong here as it did downstairs. Julia turned in a full circle, confusion and fear making her heart thrash inside her chest. She had to keep searching.

There were three bedrooms, all with working bulbs in the light fittings, harsh glares that made Julia squint as she took in the emptiness. The first bedroom was dominated by a double bed in the centre of the room, while the others had single beds pushed against one wall, all lying like wooden skeletons stripped bare. There were bedside lockers and small wooden wardrobes; Julia rushed through each room, pulling open cupboard doors, checking under beds, quickly establishing each bedroom was empty.

If Jeanette Coyle was crying inside this house, where was she?

She raced back down the stairs, not caring about making any noise, just about getting out of here. A thought struck her suddenly – where was all the blood? The girl outside with Adrian had been covered in it, but the house was clean. Fear was a cold hand at her throat – she was not safe in this house.

But the cries were still loud and she couldn't abandon whoever needed her. She moved quickly to the kitchen again – was there a utility room she hadn't noticed earlier or a downstairs toilet maybe? She reached for the kitchen counter, to lean against it for a moment, but stopped, her hand suspended in mid-air.

This was all wrong.

No matter where she was in the house, the sound of the cries was the same and it was coming from *everywhere*. The same thing, over and over, as though it was on a loop.

Suddenly, the sound and the light seemed to surge and then everything stopped. Julia found herself standing in complete darkness and absolute silence, plunging her into heart-stopping terror. And she understood – the electricity had been cut. The light, the *sound*, cut off. Realization was a stranglehold. It hadn't been a crying woman she was listening to. It had been a *recording* of a crying woman, playing throughout the house.

She gasped for air, fearing that the dark might suffocate her. She had to get out! The hallway beyond the kitchen seemed longer, the partially open front door frustratingly close yet still so far away. Saliva pooled in her mouth, the familiar warning sign before throwing up, and she swallowed hard. The only sound now was of her own heart in her ears, thudding a warning drill. She stood still, willing her eyes to adjust to the near-complete darkness around her, straining to hear any sound, anything at all. Any indication she wasn't alone.

The silence was a deafening pressure in her head as her fingers twitched, wishing she were holding her baton, her flashlight, anything. But then she remembered where she was; kitchens were full of weapons. She and Adrian had attended enough domestic disturbance call-outs to know that.

She reached out cautiously. Her fingers connected with the metal lip of a drawer and pulled on it slowly; it slid open with a soft sigh. Barely breathing, she dipped her fingers inside, touching metal. A thick shaft with a sharp blade at the top ... a box cutter, perhaps? It was enough. She pulled it out and gripped the handle, then forced her legs forward. With her hands stretched out in front of her, the box cutter hit the kitchen door with a soft tap. Julia moved around it, leaned against the wall briefly, steadying herself; now it was just the hallway to walk through, then the front door. To Adrian, to safety.

The darkness was less dense as she moved through the hallway, the streetlights outside, and the moonlight, offering a lighter shade of night. Her eyes found the shadows made by the piles of newspapers and she stepped carefully around them. Her shoes squeaked on the plastic carpet runner and she groaned inwardly, moving forward with a sense that someone was behind her, anticipating a touch on her shoulder at any moment.

Once she stepped over the threshold and her foot hit concrete, Julia sprinted from the house. The cold air stung her face and her vision clouded with tears. She blinked them away; the road was as quiet and still as before, mocking her, as though the terror of the last ten minutes hadn't happened.

The Garda car was still in situ, Adrian now in the driver's seat. She focused on that as she ran. But something wasn't right; he sat still and straight, staring at her through the windscreen. What was wrong with him? Why hadn't he come to help her? He needed to know it was a trap, that whoever had hurt the girl was inside the house. They needed to get out of here!

As Julia yanked open the driver's door, the car's interior light flooded it and she stopped still, the box cutter slipping from her hand. Adrian gasped, a sickening wet gurgle, and his body began to shake. She watched as his hands clutched at a large slash at his throat, his fingers desperately trying to quell the pulsing dark blood that flowed onto his neck. His eyes met hers and a sob escaped her lips.

'No!' She crouched down and pressed her hands to his throat over his own weak fingers. Her face was close to his, close enough to see the fear in his eyes, pleading with her silently to save him. 'Adrian!' she whispered. Tearing her eyes away from his, Julia looked left and right, to the empty street, the dark houses. 'Help me! *Please!*' she screamed, but the only answer was a wretched gasping as Adrian struggled to breathe. He began to convulse violently and then, all too quickly, he stopped. In the backseat, the young girl lay on her front, her face hidden by her hair. In the weak light, Julia could see patches of fresh blood on her back and dark liquid dripping from her wrists onto the carpeted footwell.

Julia stood up. Her hands felt wet now, her palms soaked in Adrian's blood. In the still and quiet street, in the semi-darkness, while she had been inside number thirty-six, someone had cut the power to the house and killed her partner and the girl they were trying to save. The night pressed in on her from all sides as she scanned the street, certain she wasn't alone.

4

2024

Julia watches the sun rise, feeling calmer as hues of rust and fire hang low on the horizon, edging out the night. Warmth washes over her skin and she smiles; they are safer in the light of a new day. She hates the night, never sleeping more than a few hours. If she were to try to explain it to someone, she would say that the dead, the victims she didn't save, come for her during the dark hours. When the sun goes down, the failures of those cases morph from bad luck into blame, and Julia always finds herself to be at fault. A sound night's sleep with a clear conscience is a luxury she doesn't believe she deserves.

Mutt barks a soft greeting, stopping in front of her chair by the window. He's used to waking in her bedroom to find her gone.

'Good morning.' She bends to rub his snow-white fur. 'Let's get you some fresh air.'

They move together through the cottage and she keys in the alarm code and unlocks the back door, pulling it open for him. As Mutt darts between her legs and onto the grass, Julia looks around their small garden, at the six-foot-high fence behind thick Griselinia hedging, at the large metal padlock on the side gate. Everything is in its place and looks the way it should; there are no holes or gaps, no sign of attempted entry. Three weeks ago, she would have stepped outside with a golf club in her hand and pulled on the padlock, just to be sure. For the last thirty years she has lived in fear that a madman had escaped or been released from his hospital prison; but now he's dead and she's beginning to feel safe at last.

As she fills the kettle at the sink her eyes rest on a white and pink card propped up against the window; an invitation her neighbours had delivered a fortnight ago. Ger and Veronica Walsh are hosting their granddaughter's christening party this afternoon, and they said they would love Julia to join them. Since she moved to Cuan Beag she's largely kept to herself. But now she can feel herself evolve from a woman who wanted to disappear into one who just might consider the company of strangers to pass an afternoon.

The Walshes are Julia's closest neighbours, and still a five-minute drive away. The heat of the summer is slowly fading as the cool breath of autumn approaches, but the afternoon sun is hotter than she had expected; as she stops at their entrance gate she pulls her blouse from under her arms where it has stuck unpleasantly to her skin. At the front door, a young boy in his teens greets her, his glinting smile showing shiny metal braces. He grins broadly at Mutt. 'Aw, he's so cute! I love dogs! Come on in.' He adds Julia's gift to a pile on the hall table and leads her through the house to glass doors that open outward onto the garden. 'Everyone's back here.'

Julia looks at the crowd of people standing and sitting

in clusters, chatting and smiling with each other with ease. Butterflies flutter in her stomach – it's been so long since she's been around this many people. Mutt wriggles in her arms, keen to be let loose on the grass, but she holds him close a little longer, the fur on the top of his head tickling her chin.

'Mrs Harte!' A woman steps towards her, a small bundle in pink nestled in her arms. 'Welcome!'

'Oh, please call me Julia.' Julia thinks she and Veronica Walsh must be of similar age, but the other woman has kept the colour in her hair, a light blonde that offsets the fan of wrinkles around her eyes. They've nodded in greeting a few times, but never properly spoken. It's an unsettling reality that she knows nothing about most of the people that live in Cuan Beag.

'Thank you for coming! This is my daughter Nicole's baby, Megan.' She dips her head towards the baby shrouded in a pink blanket. 'Would you like to hold her?'

Veronica's eyes rest on Mutt in Julia's arms and her mouth wobbles, as if she wishes to retract her offer. Julia squeezes Mutt gently in gratitude. 'Oh, I'm probably covered in little dog hairs; best not.'

Veronica visibly relaxes, her smile returning. 'Well, I'll just get this one inside for a nap. Ger is over there at the barbecue, and my other daughter Colleen is at the drinks table – quelle surprise! She'll sort you out.'

As Veronica steps into the house, the teenage boy with the braces returns and guides Julia to a deckchair in a shady part of the garden, offering her a drink. She opts for a lemonade, finally lowering Mutt to the ground once she's seated. The drink is cool, the glass filled with ice, and she's glad of it. Her blouse is sticking to her back now, and the elastic waistband of her trousers feels suctioned to the deep scar above her hip. The boy returns with a bowl of water for Mutt and she thanks him again, watching him dash to and fro among the guests.

'I see you've met my son.' Julia shades her eyes as she looks up at the woman standing in front of her. 'I'm Colleen Walsh, that's my Bailey. So you're Julia Harte, living in the old Pearson cottage.'

'That's me.' Julia half stands to shake her hand, marvelling that though she's tried to keep to herself, this stranger knows who she is and where she lives. 'It's nice to meet you. Bailey is a lovely young man, you must be proud of him.'

'He's a good boy.' Colleen remains standing, despite a cluster of empty deckchairs beside Julia, a full glass of wine in her hand. 'I see you from time to time in the village.' The statement hangs between them, almost an accusation. The low set of Colleen's eyebrows belies an earlier tension or argument she's still ruminating on; Julia learned to read people a long time ago. Colleen gulps two swallows of wine, her eyes on Julia. 'Word is you used to be a detective.'

Julia licks her lips, her heart beating fast.

'I guess that's why McGuire never made a fuss when you took his dog. He had a lot more to hide than a neglected animal, according to my dad. If you ask me, you did the poor thing a favour.' She bends and ruffles Mutt's ear, almost tipping her wine onto the grass.

'You seem to know a lot about me.' Julia tries to keep her tone light-hearted. Cuan Beag is a small place; she knew a new resident would draw curiosity. But the extent of what they know about her comes as a surprise.

'Yeah well, people here need something to talk about.

It's secluded here, dead boring for a teenager. That's why I moved Bailey closer to the city.' She waves the wine glass in the air. 'I'm hoping to open up a florist in the village, actually. The rent on a place is half what it is in town.'

'Oh, yes?' Small talk … Julia hasn't missed this.

'Mum says I'm mad, that we just don't have the population here. But she's forgetting about the internet. People will order online. I keep telling her – you can find *anything* on the internet, isn't that right?'

Julia sips from her lemonade, the glass slippery with condensation, wondering if that's a loaded question. Colleen doesn't wait long for an answer.

'Anyway, I'd better go and help Bailey. Nicole doesn't have to do a thing, seeing as she "just gave birth" seven months ago.' The exaggerated air quotes betray her sarcasm and disgust at not getting to sit down and relax like her sister; Julia marvels at how the woman didn't spill a drop of wine in the process. She watches her disappear inside the house with a sigh of relief and leans back in the deckchair, watching the people around her. Noting features and watching body language are things she did before, in her career. It doesn't surprise her that she's still doing it now; old habits are hard to break.

There are two couples standing together, the women chatting and laughing in a carefree way. But the stiff-shouldered posture of the men beside them makes Julia smile; they don't want to be here, beside each other, making small talk. There's tension between them; in such a rural setting, she's not surprised. The fallout over land kept her busy many years ago as a Garda. She and Adrian were well versed in such disputes and she can spot the signs. Another couple stand with a small child, a little apart from the others. They appear to be arguing in low voices, the man fighting to keep his expression neutral, small angry hand gestures punching the space between them.

Though people-watching can be morbid in a way, she regrets the interruption when a number of guests decide to sit near her, seeking shade under a cluster of large trees.

'Hello.' A man takes the deckchair beside her and leans forward, offering his hand. 'I'm Dale Robinson, I live over past the dock road.'

'Hello.' Julia returns his handshake, clearing her throat. 'I'm Julia Harte. Call me Julia.'

'I've seen you in the café in town.' She smiles at him referring to the tiny village of Cuan Beag as a town. 'The wife and myself are here five years, over from London. Lovely little place. We moved here to retire; the wife was born and raised in Wicklow.'

Julia wonders if 'the wife' has a name and if she's here today. It doesn't look like it – Dale seems to be alone and keen to talk.

'He's a cute little fellow.' He gestures towards Mutt, who is lapping water at Julia's feet. 'Very well behaved. I'm not sure what Ger and Veronica will make of him to be honest – Ger can be a bit uptight about his garden. Still, as long as he doesn't sh—'

'So, how do you like retirement, Dale?' she interrupts. 'Is the quiet peace of Cuan Beag suiting you and your wife?'

He looks around the garden, at the neighbours who inhabit his life now in this new home. 'It's, as you Irish say, *grand*. The kids visit now and then, keep us busy. Much quieter than my previous life, let me tell you! I used to be a reporter.'

'Oh yes?'

'Crime and punishment, that was my bread and butter. Solid living out of it too – people never tire of breaking the law. In fact ...' He raises his sunglasses to the top of his head, his eyes squinting at her. Julia swallows a bolt of sour-tasting dread, feeling it settle in the pit of her stomach. '... I could swear I've met you before.' Suddenly he sits up straight and clicks his fingers. 'I *knew* you looked familiar!'

She closes her eyes; she knows there's no way to deny who she is ... *was*. This is her worst nightmare, the very thing she has tried to avoid for five years.

'Julia Harte! Detective Inspector, no less!' Dale lowers his voice, resting his elbow on the arm of the deckchair, leaning closer. 'My daughter Karen is a big fan of yours. She studied a textbook you wrote like it was the bloody bible. She's a senior detective with the Met Police, a great girl. She'll be delighted I met you!'

Julia forces herself to smile. Her book, an academic project she dedicated her first two years of retirement to, had been a resounding success. It had been intended to be an academic textbook for trainee detectives and students of criminal psychology and procedure. Julia had been intrigued by the idea of documenting the skills she had learned over the course of her career. Books were something she had devoured in her early days as a Garda when she'd been hungry for promotion. She had fought hard for her position in the force, and the team she had worked with had helped a lot of people. The book had been her way to try to give something back. Julia had made sure to keep the cases she chose to feature behind a veil of anonymity – no dates were used, the victims' and perpetrators' names changed, and only scant facts given to allow introduction to the weightier procedural text in each chapter.

But it had catapulted her into the public eye in a way she had neither anticipated nor wanted. Her dreams of the book becoming a beacon for aspiring detectives shrivelled into a nightmare, as ghoulish true crime enthusiasts proclaimed it their 'book of the year' and it became a multi-genre bestseller. Among the online forums, podcasts and magazine articles praising the book, some dedicated their efforts to decoding the pseudonyms she had used in the book's case studies. Her horror and notoriety grew in tandem and she was acutely aware that as each alias was deciphered and announced online, families were retraumatized, their pain fodder for profit, their loved ones reduced to ink on a page. The limelight shamed her; the book remains one of her biggest regrets.

She sits up straighter and smooths out the fabric on her trousers, avoiding the man's eyes.

'I'm retired. Or at least I'm trying to be. That all feels like another life. I hope you can understand that.' She smiles at him, but hopes her words convey how strongly she does not want to discuss this.

'Of course I understand! I'm sure it was a very exciting career though.' He leans closer still, lowering his voice to a conspiratorial murmur. 'That fellow that died a few weeks ago – Cox, wasn't it? Karen asked me about that when she rang home last weekend. She was fascinated; she mentioned reading about the crimes and capture of James Cox when she was in college in London.'

Julia blinks several times; it takes her a moment to absorb the words. James Cox is still a topic of conversation and suddenly, she feels lightheaded. Even hearing Cox's name spoken aloud is jarring, the casualness of how Dale says it unsettling.

'Christ, the things he did! Sickening stuff! Did you work on that case?' Dale's eyes are wide, his gaze intense. He's treating one of the worst periods of her life like an entertaining story, a piece of gossip he can share with his daughter. The stifling heat of the afternoon has quickly vanished; she shivers, feeling queasy.

The crimes and capture of James Cox didn't feature in Julia's book. She couldn't do it. There was no way to shroud the facts of what he did in pseudonyms – Cox was one of the most infamous killers in Ireland at the time. The details of his arrest remain a memory she finds too painful to relive. Though her editor all but threatened to pull the book if she didn't include it, Julia held firm; she owed it to Philip to never revisit that night.

A cool breeze lifts the hair at the nape of her neck. It's a welcome breath of air that startles her out of the dazzling panic brought on by speaking about Cox, at being fully identified by the man beside her. She stands up and gathers Mutt into her arms.

'I'll have to go now; so sorry. It was lovely to meet you, Dale.'

'Well … when my daughter visits can I bring her to your house? She'd love to pick your brains! Or buy you lunch in town?'

His voice is fading as she moves through the garden and steps inside the house. Out of the corner of her eye she can see Veronica watching her open-mouthed, a tray of cooked sausages in her hands. Her grandson Bailey asks, 'Are you okay, Mrs Harte?' as she passes him, but she keeps going, her eyes on the front door. Mutt licks her arms gently as she walks to her car; she blinks tears from her eyes and kisses his head.

'Let's go home.'

The postman has been while she was out; a postcard, the bright blues and dazzling whites of southern Spain on the front, the neat handwriting of Mary Clancy on the back.

Dearest Julia — sending you love and best wishes from the beach! All my love, Mary

She leans her head against the wall in the hallway as she reads. Mary Clancy lives with her daughter Audrey now. Adrian's family became Julia's too, after his death. She misses them. A cup of tea with someone who understands her feels like the most wonderful thing in the world right now.

A little while later, sipping her second brandy and sitting in her armchair, Julia's hands have stopped shaking. The setting sun angles on the handle of a golf club resting against the wall beside the TV. She sighs. Her eyes find Philip's face, frozen in happiness on their wedding day. What would he say if he could see her now? Exhausted after barely thirty minutes with her neighbours in this little village where she is a stranger. Emotional after being confronted with her career, something she had fought for, something everything once came second to. And still so scared that later, before it gets dark, she'll spend almost an hour checking and rechecking that her home is a fortress.

It seems her penance is to live in fear after all.

5

2024

Warm midday sunlight glistens on the swell of the sea as Julia pulls into the car park at Cuan Beag and selects a space. She ruffles the white fur on Mutt's head as he sits in the passenger seat beside her.

'Ready, my love?'

Scooping him up, she climbs out of the car and locks it, checks it twice. She bends to snap on his lead and they set off at their usual brisk pace. The sun is warm on the back of her neck where it touches her skin around the pink silk scarf that was a gift from Mary. She feels calmer today, relaxed in the heat. There's a busload of tourists disembarking at the stop near the car park entrance; Julia smiles at them as they admire the boats moored by the pier. Cuan Beag needs tourists; it depends on the income they generate in the summer and early autumn. Julia knows the guides' routine and is glad they never venture away from the main village into the more secluded residential areas; the fewer people in her life, the better.

Her favourite coffee shop, Annie's Corner, quickly became a staple in her life, despite her intentions not to settle into anything resembling real life here; after all, Cuan Beag was where she was supposed to disappear. She deposits Mutt in the courtyard at the back, calling a greeting to Annie as she walks to her usual spot near the window overlooking the main street.

'Hello there, Annie!'

'Hello, Julia, how are you today? Will you have the usual?'

Julia smiles her thanks and settles herself on the chair, pulling off her cardigan and draping it over the wooden backrest. There are only three other patrons inside the café; a local widower, Mick, who comes in every morning with his newspaper and pen, hunched over the crossword while he slowly sips every cooling drop of tea poured from a single teapot into a patterned cup. There's a much younger man in a crisp blue shirt, scrolling on his mobile phone while he waits for his order – she thinks he's probably a rep visiting the guesthouse in the centre of the village. And a young woman, a mug of coffee on the table beside a thick book, her head bent over the words.

Julia smiles gratefully as Annie places a still-warm scone and pot of tea in front of her, followed by a cup, jam and a little bowl of cream. She breathes in the aroma and closes her eyes … *Relax*, she tells herself.

When she opens her eyes again, Julia realizes the young woman is watching her with a shy smile on her face. The look in the woman's eyes is familiar; it's one Julia thought she had left behind five years ago.

Curiosity.

The look of someone who thinks they know her, who thinks they might recognize her from the news, or from the author profile photo on the back of a book they're reading. 'Are you ...?' The voice was laced with uncertainty.

'Fecking Dale,' she mutters, shaking her head.

The melodic ring of her mobile phone startles her and she pulls it out, expecting it to be Mary Clancy. Anxiety races along her skin in tiny pinpricks as she checks the caller ID, feeling the hairs standing to attention at the back of her neck. It's not Mary ...

Why is *he* calling?

She lets it ring out. Not answering is the easiest thing to do. She ponders how a ringing phone could make a person feel so claustrophobic, and finally pours her tea. The sun is shining, her scone is delicious, and she will not allow anyone to ruin this day.

But before two minutes have passed, the phone rings again, vibrating hard on the wooden table in front of her, and she jumps as if someone has grabbed her from behind. She licks salty sweat from her lips and answers the call, twirling the small metal teaspoon over and back to stop her hand shaking.

'Des. It's been a long time.'

'Julia. We need to talk.'

'Is everything all right?' The politest way of asking 'what do you want?'. He hasn't called her in years. His voice sounds firm and deep, the way she remembers it, even though he must be in his mid-seventies now. The few words he's spoken hint at his broad Northern Irish accent. She hears him breathe in sharply before he answers. 'It's happening again.'

She blinks in confusion. 'What's that now?'

'Cox. It's happening again.'

The teaspoon hits the table with a loud clang. For the last thirty years, that name and the madness he wrought have been their binding ties, her and Des's. He respected her decision to retire here – he understood – and he has never called her, even though they had been friends. That he's calling her now means she knows it's serious. But the words he just said don't make sense.

'That can't be right. He's dead.'

'I can send you some crime scene photos.'

'No, I can't … Why do you think it's him? He's *dead*!' Her voice is soft, but inside her head she is screaming at herself to hang up. But she sits still, waiting, touching her hip, a reflex she makes involuntarily. Her fingertips slip underneath the elastic of her skirt and trace the long scar there. No! It can't be that. It can't be him.

'Two college students. Killed in the same way. And Julia, they were *marked* first, just like the other girls in '94.'

She closes her eyes and listens to the silence as he gathers himself to continue.

'The young women were found this morning and probably killed just before their bodies were placed.'

'Placed?'

'The position of their bodies was staged. When they were found, they were arranged in almost the exact same way as Cox's victims, the two girls. God forgive me, I can't remember their names just now, so I can't.'

'Louise and Jeanette,' she whispers; time won't let her forget.

'Yes; one girl was face down, half sitting, half leaning

away.' With her eyes closed Julia can easily recall the memory of Louise Hynes in the back of her and Adrian's squad car, dark patches of blood on her back visible in the dim light. 'And one girl was curled into a ball on the ground.' Just like Jeanette Coyle had been when her body was found.

'Could it be—'

'It's not a coincidence,' he says gruffly. 'Come on, Julia. These women were stabbed to death, and the wounds match his old victims'. Even the wrists.'

She swallows hard. 'Well that … that could be—'

'Your book was found at the scene. It was in one of the victims' bags. I want you to come and have a look for yourself. I'd like your take on this.'

Her eyes open in shock and she pulls the phone away from her ear, staring at it. Her book was found at the scene … and Des wants her to go back to Cork. Riordan is still talking; she brings the phone back to her ear. Her mouth feels full of sand and grit. She reaches for her tea and gulps a mouthful, her hands shaking.

'This all points to Cox – the wounds to kill, the positioning of the bodies. …We need to—'

She squeezes her eyes shut – there is no *we*, not any more. 'He's *dead*!' Her voice is loud and she feels heat from the gaze of the other diners. Annie too has stopped what she was doing behind the counter to stare at her. Julia lowers her voice as she continues. 'He died three weeks ago. You *must* have seen it in the press.'

'I'm well aware he's dead and it doesn't matter. It may not be Cox's work but it's certainly inspired by him.'

'You said the girls were found only this morning – how do you even know about this already? You're retired, Des –

why are you involved?'

She can hear his sharp intake of breath before he speaks. 'I'm always involved, Julia. So are you, really. Hiding away doesn't change that. I keep my ears open and my hand in. I don't like the positioning of the victims and that your book – *your* book – was there. This has Cox's stamp all over it.'

Julia's heart sinks; Des is right. She remembers him as a chief superintendent worthy of respect – a fair man, one whose head was ruled by logic, a man who believed in her and would have died for his co-workers. In the time they worked together, his word was always good enough for her. And so it is now. She understands why, after years without contact, he's calling to tell her this.

'All right. I can see why you're concerned. It does sound like a copycat.' She rubs her temple with her fingertips, trying to think. Why would someone do this? Could this be the work of a deranged James Cox fan? Her mind is racing, trying to sort through everything he's said. It must be significant that her book is at the crime scene …

Des pauses, choosing his words carefully. It's no less than what she'd expect from him and her heart is hammering unsteadily as she waits for him to speak.

'I'm conscious we're both retired but once I made an approach to the current chief, she agreed it's too similar to the Cox killings to ignore. So soon after his death, it seems there must be a connection. I want you to come back to Cork and work with me and the city personnel on this.'

'But *why*?'

'You were the best investigator we had, it's as simple as that. We made a good team. And you were … close to him.'

33

Julia closes her eyes again. She feels feverish, sweaty in the cool café. 'Please, Des,' she whispers, '*I can't.*'

'But Julia, this is *Cox*, for heaven's sake! You know that if this escalates like it did the last time, more people will die! Give me two days. Look over the case with me. I'm an old man, Julia. I can't let this sit on my conscience if I turn my back and another girl dies. Can you? Look, have you the same email address?'

'What? Yes, I—'

'I'll send you the photographs I have. The young women are scheduled for autopsy tomorrow morning. I need you with me, Julia; will you come back and look at the evidence? We'll consult from the sidelines. You were good at this – the best. I'll email you.'

Riordan ends the call. Julia swallows a bitter taste that lurks in her throat and pushes the plate and cup away from her across the small table, needing space, feeling a suffocating pressure on her chest. Her legs feel weak but she stands up anyway, hearing the wooden legs of her chair scrape on the tiles of the café floor. The walls rush at her so fast she feels giddy.

This cannot be happening.

She steps away from the table and walks briskly to the back of the café to retrieve Mutt, not meeting Annie's inquisitive stare. Her hands tremble as she clips on his lead again and she lifts him into her arms, pressing the heat of him to her chest. Mutt licks her chin and she rubs his neck, so grateful to him. He grounds her every time she needs it, but right now, sadly, he's not going to be enough.

'I'm afraid it's time we head back.'

As she's about to leave the café she looks at her own

reflection in the window, touching the white hair at the nape of her neck, suddenly very conscious of the wrinkles around her eyes and mouth. She was a young woman when she faced James Cox. Young and hungry for promotion, keen to prove herself. Now ... for the last five years she has hidden herself away from life, trying to find contentment.

Riordan said he needs her. That would have made her heart soar once when all she wanted was approval and endorsement, the chance to rise through the ranks. Now she wants nothing more than to disappear all over again. But she knows that if this *does* have anything to do with James Cox, then the clock is ticking ...

6

1994

Julia stared at Adrian, the horror of his death frozen on his face. Dark spots of colour danced in front of her eyes and she steadied herself against the car door, her chest jerking uncomfortably, fighting to breathe. She blinked quickly, clearing her vision as a name screamed inside her head … *Louise*! She turned and pulled open the back door of the car. Louise's body looked so small on the backseat. A choking sob escaped Julia's lips with the certainty there was nothing she could do. They were both dead.

As she stood in the empty street, she became aware of the sound of her own breathing, of the slick coating of blood on her hands. A chill stole over her skin – was the killer watching her from the shadows?

The houses to her left and right were dark, unwelcoming voids. She should wake someone, ask them to call for help … she needed help. She thought of the radio in the car and turned back, closer to Adrian and Louise again. Her vision blurred with tears and she swiped them away; Adrian's bloodied hands rested in his lap, his feet were splayed apart in the footwell. Beside one of his shiny black shoes lay the dark shape of the radio. Gingerly leaning her hand on his leg, Julia reached into the footwell and grasped the small device. He must have been about to call for support when he was attacked; the realization of this, and the absolute violence of his – and Louise's – deaths, hit her with such force then that it felt almost impossible to speak. But she pressed the button and mumbled the words she needed to say, then dropped the radio and ran to the grass verge beside the car, vomiting until only water came up in painful heaves.

On her knees on the grass, as her breathing steadied, she felt her skin prickle with the certainty that she was being watched. With one last look at the squad car she sprinted to the nearest house, pounding her fists on the front door.

News spread quickly through the estate, the double-murder drawing people from their beds into the cold street. The residents formed a kerb-side audience as Julia returned to stand beside Adrian and Louise. She felt safer with the watchful gaze of the men and women nearby, craning their necks to see into the car, whispering together, watching the young Garda standing beside the driver's door.

Within minutes, the blue lights and wailing sirens that had always made her feel proud to be among the ranks of the cavalry were now *her* saviours, and relief made her whole body weak. A Garda put gentle hands on her shoulders and guided her away from the car. She told him everything she could remember, watching his pen fly across his notebook, checking he had written every detail. One of the paramedics hovered beside him, waiting to examine her. Julia turned, allowed a thin light to be shone into her eyes, her hands cleaned. Someone draped a blanket over her shoulders, someone else pressed a cup of sweet tea into her hands.

After a while, she sat on the kerb, her legs too weak to stand any longer. People spoke – she saw their mouths move – but their words didn't reach her.

The estate, quiet and peaceful earlier, was now an active crime scene. She watched as a forensics tent was erected around the Garda car that she kept thinking of as a tomb. Lights flashed in every direction she looked and the number of people on the street seemed to have increased tenfold; ambulance crews, Garda personnel, faces she recognized but their names wouldn't form in her mind. Men and women in uniform and in the protective gear of the forensics team moved slowly around her, as though wading through water.

As dawn broke, and a chorus of birds announced a new day, the tea was long-since cold. Julia shivered as she watched her colleagues work around the shrouded car, around Adrian, refusing to look away for long. Protecting him, maybe. It was stupid but she couldn't make herself stop.

'Jesus H. Christ!'

She heard the chief superintendent's voice penetrate the noise around her but she didn't raise her eyes. She remained on the concrete kerb; her chin resting on her knees, her body too heavy to move. But soon she became aware of someone in front of her, standing over her. She had expected to see her own sergeant, and she was sure he was here somewhere. But Des Riordan stood before her instead. He was so far up the ladder of command, she wasn't sure if she'd ever spoken to him before, but she knew who he was. Of course he was here – a Garda was dead. She inhaled sharply; she knew she should stand up but she didn't think her knees could unbend without tremendous pain, so she stayed where she was.

For a brief moment, the man looked unrecognizable. Julia blinked until his features returned to their normal place; his square jaw off-centre, his eyes red-rimmed and bulging. His nose bent crookedly to the left, and she remembered hearing about an assault during a raid on a bar in Donegal … word was he'd been lucky to get out of that one alive. These days he was mostly confined to his office, and she'd sometimes wondered if the stories of his wild youth in the force had been embellished over the years. He looked both furious and shell-shocked now, unable to stand still, rocking onto his toes and back onto his heels again, over and over, running one hand over his tightly cut greying hair.

'Garda Harte, are you all right?' His voice sounded far away. 'One of our men … what in God's name!' He pinched the bridge of his nose, fighting for composure, then reached out a hand to help her stand. His grip was tight and she anchored herself against him, forcing her body upright. The blanket fell to the ground; without it around her shoulders she felt the sting of the cold morning air and she clamped her jaw tight to avoid her teeth rattling.

'I really …' Her voice died; she didn't quite know where, or *how*, to begin.

Riordan towered over her. He had his arms folded across his chest, biceps bulging under his jacket sleeves. There was a menacing quality about him, physically – too tall, too broad, eyebrows knotted together, altogether too *big*. She felt a sudden need to be taller when they spoke

39

and she stepped up onto the kerb behind her. She knew it was ridiculous carrying this chip around on her shoulder, this resentment, and was surprised that even now, she instinctively wanted to be at eye level with the men she was working with. To never have them looking down on her, as if that might somehow stop them from *talking* down to her. Not that Adrian ever had. Adrian … She swallowed hard, trying to lubricate her throat.

'Run through for me what happened here, Garda Harte, right from the start. I need to know what to say to Dublin, and God knows how I'm going to explain this to Mary Clancy.'

Hearing the name of Adrian's wife, and remembering their conversation about baby Audrey, the youngest of their five children, Julia swallowed a fresh wave of vomit. Keeping all emotion from her voice she told him everything, from Adrian being at the station and getting the details of the call-out, to the girl running onto the street in front of them, from her search of the house to her certainty that the sound of a crying woman had been recorded and played throughout the house, and that someone had cut the power.

'Jesus H. Christ,' he repeated, whispering now. With his hands on his hips, he shook his head roughly, his face red with emotion. 'Did you see anyone when you ran out of the house? Anyone near the car? There must have been someone nearby, whoever did this can't have been far away! *Anything?*'

'No, nothing,' she said, remembering the feeling of being watched as she stood beside Adrian at the open car door. 'I didn't see anyone.'

'Have you given a statement?'

'Yes, I—'

A man appeared beside them, only his face visible from beneath a white jumpsuit, hood and gloves.

'We've a small update; we're certain the power was cut from inside the house. The amp fuse was pulled from the fuse board inside the back door. We're looking into it further. But it was definitely deliberate.'

The power was cut from inside the house ... Julia wrapped her arms around herself. Whoever had orchestrated this hadn't been too far away. Had he been inside the house the whole time? Or perhaps he killed Adrian and Louise Hynes and then came inside and cut the power. He had chosen to watch her in the dark rather than attack her too ... *Why?*

'And the sound of crying? Was it a recording?' the chief superintendent demanded.

'It was. So far we've counted six tape recorders placed throughout the house. Four downstairs and two upstairs.'

'The downstairs ones, were they on the bookshelves and in the kitchen?' Julia interrupted; how had she not seen them? This was so disturbing, so planned. They had been set up.

The man turned tired eyes towards her. 'One plugged in behind a bookshelf in the living room near the front of the house, another in the next room, one in the kitchen and one concealed behind a stack of newspapers in the hall.'

'So it was a trap. A set-up.' Riordan read her thoughts and was back rocking on his heels again. The man moved away, and Riordan raised an arm, beckoning an inspector closer. It was Steven Molloy, one of the detectives searching for the missing girls. His face was pale and his hands shook as he folded a small notebook and stuffed it into his pocket, the task of slotting it into place taking far longer than it should. His eyes found Julia's and they both nodded, solidarity at the horror of this night binding them together.

'Get this guy Tony O'Mahony in for questioning,' Riordan hissed, and as his eyes observed the swarm of neighbours and reporters near the crime-scene tape, he gritted his teeth and spoke in lower tones. 'The man that called it in. I want him questioned.'

Steven Molloy cleared his throat. 'Already done, chief, but I'd wager he's not our man. Too old, too frail, and sound asleep in bed with the missus when Gardaí arrived on the scene. They'd taken a sleeping tablet to nod off, seeing as the sound of crying was keeping them awake. So they say. We'll check it all out, but I guarantee he's not who we're looking for.'

'For the love of God.' Riordan exhaled heavily and looked at Julia again, his eyes clouded with something she couldn't read. 'You could have been killed!' He cleared his throat. 'Right. Well a man is dead; a *Garda* is dead. And the young girl,' he turned to Molloy again, 'any ID on her yet?'

'Nothing can be confirmed until her parents can identify her but it's Louise Hynes. Matches the description, age, hair colour and so on. And the slash wound on her back looks about a week old, just like her parents said. We'll know for sure soon.'

The three of them stood silently, the workings of the crime scene continuing around them. Despair swirled in the morning air, pressing into Julia as though she were being squeezed in a vice. After a few seconds more, and without another word to either of them, Riordan turned and walked into the thick of bodies near the tent shrouding the Garda car. Molloy reached a hand towards Julia and dropped it again, changing his mind.

'Are you all right?'

'Yeah, I'm fine,' she answered quickly.

'I'll get someone to drive you home, okay?'

Julia ignored that. 'What's the next step? There's still one girl missing. Is there any update?'

Molloy shook his head. 'Look, I know you've already given your statement, and now you really should get home. As long as the medics are happy of course.'

'Don't shut me out, Molloy! I'm Adrian's partner, I was *here* when he died, so don't push me out of this!' she snarled, not caring what he thought, not willing to put up with him and the others' usual tactics, not this time.

He sighed, lowering his eyes, his shoulders slumped. 'I get it. Jesus, poor Adrian, it's just awful. And what you've suffered here is very hard to imagine. Come into the station tomorrow, okay? Or today, I mean. Later. We'll need to go over everything again. But only if you can manage it.'

This was pointless; Julia stepped off the kerb, walking away from him. Though he was dismissing her, the kindness in Molloy's voice was laced with tiredness and something else, something akin to pity. She couldn't bear to listen to him any longer. The more she stood beside him, the more he spoke about what she had suffered and how she needed to go over her statement, the more she felt like a victim. She was a *Garda,* for heaven's sake! Somehow, she was on the other side of the crime; perhaps not a victim, not really, but a useless bystander while her partner had bled out beside her.

Her legs felt jittery as she walked across the street, stopping when she was closer to Riordan again. He stood amid a cluster of people and she hovered at the edge of it, able to overhear their conversation.

'Is there any doubt?'

'No, chief. It's her. Jeanette Coyle.'

'Where was she found?'

'On some wasteland behind the estate, about five hundred metres away.'

'Absolute madness … do you know the cause of death?'

'Too early to put it down on paper but the poor girl almost certainly died from multiple stab wounds. Plenty of them, all on her back. Nasty way to go. And her wrists seem to have been cut, but I don't know the sequence of … of events, if you like. The pathologist will tell us all that.'

'And the mark?'

'On her lower back, right-hand side. About four inches long. Doc guesses it's about a week old. It was the same on both of them, same injuries … do you think it's significant?'

Julia stopped moving, just stood still, buffered by the rising wind. Two best friends who had disappeared on a warm summer's evening, were both dead. It hadn't been her case. She was too junior, too rank-and-file for such crimes. Yet still she felt she had failed them somehow. They should have protected these girls. And Adrian … *Adrian.*

'I want to see Jeanette,' she said, her voice louder than she had expected it to be. Riordan looked at her in surprise. Julia cleared her throat. 'I'd like to see Jeanette Coyle's body.'

The chief stepped towards her, his eyes impossible to read. 'There's no need for that. You should go home. This has been rough enough on you, just—'

'I was so close to the killer. He or she was in the house

with me. And I was first on the scene to Adrian's and Louise Hynes's deaths. I should go. I might be able to spot something significant.'

The man that had briefed Des Riordan guffawed, clearly doubting Julia could spot something he hadn't. But after a moment's pause, Riordan nodded and turned to the man.

'Lead the way. And we'll need shoe covers.' His tone allowed no room for discussion.

A laneway between two sets of semi-detached houses led to a narrow path, and just beyond that, a low, untamed hedge. Julia had seen these forgotten spaces in housing estates all over Cork; places the building contractors had abandoned, spots that irked parents but thrilled their teenagers. Two members of the forensics staff were crouched low, bagging cigarette butts and empty beer bottles. The detective Julia now recognized as Jim Connolly led them through a gap in the hedge and across a patch of wasteland, the grass scorched dry by the recent hot weather. A forensic team surrounded an area a short distance in; Julia's eyes found a small bundle on the ground and saliva flooded her mouth. She swallowed and kept moving.

Jeanette Coyle's body was curled around itself, as though she had wanted to make her already tiny body smaller still. Her hands were clasped in prayer, her knees pressed to her chest. Julia heard Riordan gasp and curse beside her as her eyes found wounds that matched the ones on Louise's body – cuts on Jeanette's wrists, puncture wounds in her back. Her blonde hair sprayed around her head like a crown.

'Have you seen enough?' Riordan asked softly beside her.

Without a word, Julia turned and walked away.

The lights and sounds of the estate were startling after the quiet of the area where Jeanette lay. The residents of the housing estate flanked the Garda cordon separating them from the crime scene, wrapped in coats, raising cups to their lips, watching the misery unfold. There was something chilling about their determination to stay until forced to move away. She looked at their faces, noted their features, hating the curiosity that lit them, all standing on tiptoe or stretching their necks for a better view. Suddenly they began to blur; they were the decorative walls of her nightmare, and they were swirling too fast. She staggered to the left, away from Steven Molloy, from Des Riordan and the group around him, away from the house and the car where Adrian had died, watching the concrete road rise to meet her as her knee banged painfully against it.

Pressure at her elbow guided her to standing again. She looked into green eyes, set deep under thick eyebrows in a face dusted with freckles. A young man, a stranger in a Garda uniform.

'Garda Harte? Come with me. DI Molloy says I'm to drive you home.'

7

1994

The Garda beside her drove steadily through the throng of onlookers, building up speed as soon as the crowd allowed. Julia sensed he was desperate to get away. He was tall, his head almost cresting the ceiling of the car, and his hands on the steering wheel clenched it tightly, squeezing the leather hard. She watched the street fade slowly from view in the wing mirror as they drove away from everything, away from Adrian. The lump in her throat felt so big she feared it might choke her.

The man beside her spoke in a sudden rush.

'I'm Shay Foley, not long in. I did a short stint in Mallow, Waterford city before that. Glad to be back in Cork to be honest; well, my mam is glad to have me back anyway. I'm living out near Ballyvourney.'

She appreciated that he had introduced himself but she felt exhausted now, too tired to rouse the effort of conversation. Their eyes met. 'Desperate thing that happened to Adrian Clancy ... just awful.'

She nodded and turned to face the road ahead, hoping he wasn't one of those people that felt compelled to fill any silence with conversation. He was pale, his freckles standing out, his eyes huge. Perhaps he was a bit shell-shocked, like every other member of the force they had left behind at the scene. She couldn't believe he had a couple of years under his belt already; a smattering of bright red spots on his chin and at his tight hairline lent a teenage hue to his face. He was freshly shaved, something Adrian hadn't managed since baby Audrey had been born, and his uniform looked pristine. She'd already noted the shine from his black shoes and the sharp crease in his trouser legs when he'd escorted her to the car. She could imagine Shay Foley's mammy taking good care of him.

'Actually, Garda Harte, we've met before, in the station. I—'

She looked at him, confused; she had no memory of meeting him before. He looked familiar, but she was certain they hadn't been introduced. There were often new recruits rambling around the station, assigned to different divisions, rarely overlapping with her and Adrian's duties.

'I'm sorry, I … you can call me Julia, by the way. I'm sorry I don't remember meeting you before.'

Shay smiled sheepishly, embarrassed, and turned back to watch the road. Julia could feel anxiety radiating from him as he gripped the steering wheel.

'I'm sorry,' she began again, 'I've had such a shock and I just don't—'

'Don't worry about it,' he said quickly. 'And I'm sorry about Adrian Clancy.' He appeared committed to filling the silence. 'I knew him a little, played a few games of pool with

48

him over pints after work once. Nice man. A family man.'

Julia nodded again, still struggling for words. A family man ...

'I heard what happened ... and ... for what it's worth, I would have done the exact same as you. I would have gone into that house as well, considering you thought a young girl was in danger.'

She turned to him and their eyes met; his forehead was creased with tension, his eyes earnest, and when he turned to watch the road again, she noticed the harsh clench of his jaw. 'Right ... so ... where do you live?'

Julia didn't answer just yet. She couldn't imagine going home, carrying on as normal. When Philip asked her how her night shift had been, how could she find the words? Shay had the heating on in the car yet she shivered and huddled against the door. She felt so cold, so tired ... and realized that home was exactly what she needed.

'Knockchapel. And thanks, Shay, I really appreciate the lift.'

Julia closed her front door and leaned against it, letting it support her body. Philip was in the kitchen, where she knew he would be, readying to leave for work. She could hear him moving and humming along to something as he cooked; something classical, his favourite. Her body felt drained and weak. She sagged against the door, knowing she couldn't tell him what had happened yet. Instead she kicked off her shoes and mounted the stairs quietly, heading for the bathroom. Leaving her uniform in a heap on the floor, she stepped under the shower, praying absolution might come from the heat of the water.

When she made her way back downstairs, she stood in the kitchen doorway and closed her eyes. The hiss of frying bacon competed with the radio, the sounds of her home soothing her. The smell of breakfast enveloped her and she opened her eyes, blinking tears from them, wiping her cheeks dry.

Philip's dark hair was gelled back, his pale blue shirt covered in an apron – a jokey Christmas gift adorned with reindeer and elves – his shirtsleeves rolled up. He was standing at the stove, his brow creased in concentration, and as Julia watched him flip bacon and eggs carefully, her heart swelled with the comforting familiarity of him.

'Hi, love.' He turned to her and grinned. 'I missed you last night!' He crossed the kitchen and pulled her into a hug. Julia felt his kiss against her wet hair as she wrapped her arms around him.

'You've showered already? I didn't hear you come in. I'm just about to brew up here if you're ready to eat.'

She moved to the table and sat down, realizing he didn't know what had happened to Adrian yet; no one from the station had called him, and he must not have listened to the news bulletin on the radio. She felt dizzy with relief; she had a few more minutes of normality before she had to tell him that Adrian had been murdered but the killer had let her walk away.

He placed a plate of food in front of her and turned away to make a pot of tea, his citrus freshly showered scent lingering behind him, and Julia pushed the plate away, sure she couldn't stomach the salty grease she normally devoured after each night shift.

'Are you all right, love?' he asked from the other side of

50

the room. When Julia spoke her voice sounded alien to her, too calm, too soft.

'Come upstairs with me.'

Philip laughed and poured boiling water into the teapot. 'Is my sexy apron turning you on?'

'I'm serious. Take me to bed.'

He looked at her quizzically and a soft laugh escaped his lips. 'I'd love to but I can't, Julia, I'll be late for work.'

'You won't be *that* late.'

'Cheeky!' A wide grin creased his cheeks. 'Are you sure you're okay?'

She stood up, crossed the kitchen and took his hand, leading him out the kitchen door and upstairs. Let his patients wait a bit longer for the doctor, let the practice receptionist make up an excuse. Julia needed him now; his gentle touch, his familiar movements, the heat of his body to banish the cold of Adrian's skin. She needed to feel something other than the deep hollowness that was spreading inside her, the fear that was clouding her brain. For just a few minutes more she needed to pretend that everything was normal. And most of all, she needed to push the question, the one that wouldn't quit, out of her mind.

Why had she been allowed to survive the night?

8

2024

Insomnia is a relentless plague, even more so after Des Riordan's call. Julia stares into the dark while Mutt breathes deeply on the foot of her bed, one paw twitching, dreaming about a tennis ball, she suspects. Her body aches, every joint heavy against the mattress, but her mind races, making sleep impossible.

After she left the café, she knew she couldn't return to the cottage quite yet; instead, she'd walked the length and breadth of Cuan Beag far quicker than she ever had before. She couldn't recall any coherent thoughts as she pounded the narrow streets, and for the rest of the afternoon her mind had been agitated, ruminating on possibilities. Eventually she stopped at the newsagent's to buy a bottle of water for Mutt, pouring it into the cupped palm of her hand to let him lap up as much as he needed, then carried him the rest of the way back to the car, where he curled up on the passenger seat and fell asleep.

'Sorry.' She'd nuzzled his fur before starting the engine

and heading for home.

The evening passed in almost complete silence, save for the noise inside the cottage, the ticking clock and settling creaks that always penetrated her consciousness. As she cooked dinner, as she pushed around her food before eventually passing the remains of her meal to Mutt, and as she cleaned up, she raged against an idea that was taking shape – she should go back. She had years of experience and she could help Riordan, help the victims' families, do what she could to prevent this happening again.

Part of her, the sane, rational part that wants to stay alive, can't help fighting against the idea. She is sixty years old – retired! James Cox almost killed her, so why is the thought of this new case searing itself into her mind and refusing to let go? She feels drawn to this – and she hates herself for it.

Now, as night settles around her, the need to know more about the murdered students has her in its grip. Throwing back the covers she pads softly to the living room and lifts the decanter of brandy, pouring a generous measure into her wedding-gift glass, her eyes on her husband, forever smiling and happy in the photograph on the wall. Her thumb rubs the gold of her wedding ring and she moves to the living room window and parts the curtains, raising the blind a little. Cox always attacked in the dark …

'I can't let it rest, Phil. It could be dangerous but maybe I can help.' Her own heavy sigh is loud in her ears. 'I have to do this, don't I?'

Philip never answers; that, at least, is something she's grateful for. It's one thing speaking to him in the empty cottage, imagining he's still with her. It'd be quite another to hear him speak back. Although she knows what he'd say if he did answer. He'd tell her to leave this to the detectives in Cork, to stay out of it. He'd remind her how vicious James Cox was, and how dangerous this might be. And she knows she wouldn't listen, even now.

Moving to the second bedroom she sits down at her computer. Riordan emailed her earlier; she clicks into her account and opens it before she can change her mind. Along with the names and ages of the two students, he has sent an attachment with photographs. She writes the victims' names on a notepad beside her now; Elena Kehoe and Hannah Miller. According to Riordan, both were nineteen years old and first-year students at a city-centre college, studying criminal psychology.

Taking a steadying breath, she opens the photographs. Her years of retirement are shedding as she readies herself to scan the images for detail and learn all she can. The grief of their deaths will come, but to be effective she needs to stay detached for now.

It is as Riordan described. Elena Kehoe was found lying in a half-seated position, her face to one side and covered with her long dark hair, her upper torso flat against a surface that looks like a mound of earth and debris. She is wearing a white vest and underwear. On her back, a dark mass of jelly-like blood indicates where she was stabbed; it looks fresh to Julia, as if she was killed just before being moved into position. Another photograph shows her wrists, both with vertical slits. She scrolls the mouse to zoom in closer – each looks like a shallow cut. So it's superficial, done to replicate Cox's kills rather than to cause serious injury. A third photograph shows a partially healed cut on the young woman's lower back, on the right-hand side, pink against

54

her white skin.

Julia exhales slowly and continues to click through the photographs; Hannah Miller is shown as she was found, curled into a C-shape. Her injuries are identical to Elena Kehoe's. Their handbags and belongings are strewn on the ground beside them; wallets, mobile phones, make-up. And one other item, visible inside one of the victims' bags … the familiar dark grey and red-lettered cover of a textbook … her book. Seeing it there makes Julia feel sick; she clicks out of the image and clasps her shaking hands together on her lap, leaning away from the computer into the back of the chair. It's as macabre as she had feared.

Picking up her glass, Julia swallows the brandy in one gulp and rolls the cool crystal across her forehead. Why? Why would someone do this …? Has Cox's death inspired someone into madness? Could it be some crazed fan of his work that is doing this in tribute to him now that he's dead? Did Cox have any visitors in the psychiatric hospital over the last few years? Was he close to anyone on the outside, or any member of staff perhaps? Is anyone currently researching his life for a podcast or book, delving so deep they have become obsessed? There are so many *whys,* but she knows that *who* is the most important question. Once they figure that out, the rest always falls into place. She's already inserting herself into this, thinking about how the detectives in Cork need to investigate. She leans forward again, keen to know more.

The national newspapers yield little so far so she focuses on local papers in Cork city and county, scrolling quickly past any articles on James Cox's death. Her fingers tap quickly, the click-clack filling the silence, the familiar act of research calming her.

Once she has learned everything she can from the online news sites, which isn't much at this early stage in the investigation, she checks in on social media. She created several profiles when this first became a useful search tool in her line of work. Julia finds their profile pages quickly, glad they're not set to private. She needs to know everything she can about Elena and Hannah; their feeds will give her their habits, their likes, where they socialized, who their friends were. It's not unheard of for major cases to be solved based on detailed evidence recovered from social media accounts.

She decides to focus on Elena Kehoe's page first.

Her most recent post, just days ago, is linked to the case. There's a photograph of a young woman from a side angle, twisting her back so that she's looking straight at the camera, a frown on her heavily made-up face. Her long, purple-painted nails are clamped around dark-coloured leggings, which she has pulled down to reveal the line of a lacy black thong. It's the thin red slash just over the band of the thong that Julia squints at to see better, before zooming in with the mouse; it's a fresh, angry cut, made with a sharp blade, about six inches long. Her heart begins to thud faster in her chest, the chair creaking softly as she sits up straighter, one hand reaching reflexively to her back, rubbing the old scar through her dressing gown.

The photograph is captioned **WTAF** in bold lettering, with a long line of exclamation marks filling the remaining space underneath. She reads through the comments quickly.

OMG! What happened?

Some creepy weirdo slashed me in Rebellion at the fancy dress party. Avoid this club!! Bouncers couldn't care less!

There are many more comments, sympathetic and outraged in equal measure, urging her to go to the Gardaí, but one comment, from the account of Hannah Miller, causes Julia to suck in her breath.

Me too! What the actual f*ck!! Cork city IS NOT SAFE! Did you go to the guards girl???

No one cares!

Julia puts her head in her hands. Both girls were slashed in a similar way, *marked* the way James Cox did to his victims.

At some point over the next few minutes Mutt wanders into the room and lies across her feet, dozing; Julia keeps writing, keeps searching. Elena was more active online, but not as obsessively as some of the people Julia has profiled in the past. An obvious fan of music events, she had posted multiple images of festivals and concerts around Ireland and in the UK. In those photographs she grinned broadly at the camera, wearing bohemian-style floaty skirts and headbands over her dark hair, her arms wrapped around her friends' waists. Her college campus photographs were more muted, where her favoured style was blazers and tight jeans, usually with a cardboard coffee cup in hand.

Hannah Miller loved nature and animals; in almost every photograph she posted online, she was immersed in the outdoors. Early morning sunrises and dips in the sea, walks in woodlands with a German shepherd, she was always smiling for an anonymous photographer. A partner, perhaps? She shared competitions online for airline vouchers and followed several bloggers who detailed their backpacking adventures; she had wanted to travel.

Innocent, vibrant young women with their lives ahead of them. It was always the same for Julia – sadness at the senselessness of it, then anger and resolve to put this right.

This doesn't feel any different, and that scares her.

The glass of brandy rests on the table beside her hand, empty. Julia eyes it; if she has another, she can't get into the car and drive to Cork. But if she chases it away with tea and a decent breakfast, she can leave before the sun is up. Walking through to the kitchen, with a sleepy Mutt at her heels, she fills his water bowl, lowering it to the ground. He gazes up at her, adoring brown eyes shining.

'We're going on a trip, my love. Just a short one – we'll be back soon.'

She knows it will be dangerous, that they'll be hunting someone who won't hesitate to harm them if they get too close. That they'll be putting their lives at risk to stop this person taking anyone else's. She remembers the cold blade of Cox's knife on her skin, his lips whispering in her ear. She can't deny the dread building inside her chest but if there is even a sliver of hope that she can help, then she must try. All that matters is finding whoever killed Elena and Hannah before he takes another life. She built her reputation on such dogged determination. Ultimately, it cost her everything back then.

The only difference now is that she has nothing left to lose.

9

1994

Philip left for his practice while Julia sat in the scalding heat of a full bath; she had watched him get dressed again, smiling and chatting about his day ahead, without telling him anything of the horror she had experienced overnight. She couldn't find the words. He would have stayed at home and comforted her if she'd have let him. The doctor in him would have made her rest, and the loving husband he had been for almost five years wouldn't have left her side. But to speak of Adrian's death would be to shatter something inside her and Julia stayed quiet.

The shower earlier had proved to be an ineffectual salve to the sensation that flecks of Adrian's blood remained on her skin. Squirting more shower gel into her hands, she rubbed them together for a long time, pushing the gel between her fingers and under her fingernails. When she was done, and when the water was growing cold, she hugged her knees to her chest, resting her forehead against them.

Inside her mind she was back there, moving through the

house, searching for a crying girl that could never be found. He, whoever he was, had been nearby then. Julia wondered about the sequence of death – was Jeanette already dead when she'd entered the house? When had he slit Adrian's throat? When had he killed Louise Hynes? How long was he inside the house with her, ready to cut the power? It must have been an exciting game for him, watching a Garda frantically search for a young girl in distress, knowing it was a recording of crying she could hear, knowing that the real victims were dying outside. The idea of him lurking in the house, deciding her fate, made her angry. She punched her fists into the water but the answering splash was unsatisfactory, doing nothing to stem her frustration.

She reached for a towel that was resting over the sink beside the bath and dried her face. There was no use in crying; that wouldn't change anything and it wouldn't catch the person who had done this. She got out of the bath and dried her whole body roughly, pulling on her dressing gown. Without Philip and his classical music playing on the radio, the silence of the house rushed at her, and she gripped the sink. Not telling him had been a mistake – suddenly she felt completely alone.

'Jules!' She heard Adrian again, in her mind. He always called her that. They had been assigned to work together eight years ago, and in their first week, he had stopped using her full name. She'd liked it; it felt familiar, something only he did, and somehow it made her feel even safer around him. She straightened up and wiped the steam from the mirror in front of her face. Looking at herself in the hazy glass, she was surprised not to find a stranger's face staring back at her – she felt like an entirely different person. *Still the same old me,* she thought. *Skin a little too red, perhaps, from being scrubbed too hard, but still Jules.*

'I'll find him Adrian,' she whispered, 'I promise you that.'

Downstairs she gulped fresh tea and chewed cold bacon as she dialled the number for the station. The idea of sitting around the house all day, alone and with nothing to distract her, filled her with panic. She stood at the hall table, listening to the call ringing, her heart beating loudly in her ears, wishing she had left the radio on to fill the silence of the house.

'Hello, this is—'

'Liz!' Julia interrupted, recognizing the voice immediately. She'd worked with Liz Begley for almost her whole tenure in the city station. In such a male-dominated job the women tended to stick together, and it was easy to stick with Liz. Bubbly, outgoing, she was one of those people who had that rare quality of lighting up every room she stepped into and lifted the spirits of everyone in it. Not today though, Julia imagined, not with the loss of Adrian and the girls they had all been so intent on finding alive.

'Oh, Julia! Jesus, girl, what happened last night? This whole place is in a heap. Adrian ... I can't take it in!'

Julia heard Liz sniffing and her stomach lurched. The station was not a place she wanted to be right now. Not yet.

'Can you send a car out for me, Liz? Phil's taken our car to work and I need to be somewhere.'

'Are ... are you serious? Surely you need to take it easy.' Liz lowered her voice to a whisper. 'A couple of the lads that were there this morning have been sent home; one of them kept throwing up, and the other, Colm Levis, he couldn't

61

stop crying. Poor Adrian. And his poor wife … I can't even imagine how you're feeling … and I heard you could have been killed, like!'

'Please, Liz!'

'Grand, grand.' She inhaled loudly. 'I'll send one of the new fellas out to you; there's only room for experienced hands in here today. But promise me you'll take it easy.'

Julia hung up without promising anything.

Thirty minutes later, a squad car parked outside her house. Julia pulled her front door closed, noting her neighbour Kathleen was tending to her garden out front. She waved quickly when the woman called a greeting and climbed into the passenger seat of the Garda car.

'Hello again,' Shay Foley said, an uncomfortable grimace twisting his face. He seemed less pale than before, or perhaps he was blushing again. She smiled at him.

'Hello, Shay – thank you for this. Sorry you got stuck driving me around twice in one morning. And sorry about earlier; to say I was a little shocked is a massive understatement.' Her eyes filled with tears and she blinked them away furiously, biting hard on her lower lip. *This is ridiculous*, she thought, *you can cry after whoever did this is caught!*

'Not a bother.' Shay turned away from her to concentrate on reversing the car into her driveway to turn it around. 'To tell you the truth, I was glad of an excuse to get out of the station. It's as quiet as a morgue in there … *Christ*, sorry.'

She looked at him sympathetically as even his ears burned red with embarrassment.

'Knockchapel is a nice place,' he said, still keen to fill the quiet with conversation. 'Like a postcard with the boats on the way in. I imagine it was named after the big church on the hill. *Cnoc* becoming knock and *séipéal* becoming chapel. I'm a *gaeilgeoir*,' he explained with a smile. Shay was fluent in Irish – something he had in common with Adrian. 'So,' he cleared his throat, 'where do you need to be?'

Julia rubbed her palms on the smooth denim of her jeans and took a deep breath.

'Adrian Clancy's house.'

10

1994

Adrian and Mary Clancy's house was set on a small farm on a back road on the north side of Cork city. Any further north, Adrian used to say, and they'd stray into the enemy territory of Limerick; a Gaelic Games rivalry he never let lie. On approaching the house it looked as though there wasn't another for miles around, but cars littered the laneway to the farmyard, and when Julia and Shay stepped inside the front door, the house was full of people. It was mid-morning, and Adrian had been dead less than twelve hours, but that was long enough for the small community to drop what they were doing and offer their support. Bad news spread like racing fire in rural villages like this – one phone call was enough to call the residents to arms. Mary could lean on her neighbours now and Julia was glad of that.

The hallway and nearby living room were filled with men cradling cups in their hands, talking in hushed tones. Everyone fell silent and stood still when they entered the house, taking in the pale woman and a uniformed Garda.

She felt respectful eyes on them, curious eyes too. Shay hovered behind her, shifting from foot to foot, fiddling with his hat in his hands, and she reached out and tapped his arm.

'Mary will be in the kitchen; I'll go on through. Why don't you wait outside.'

'What do I say if anyone asks me for details?' he whispered, his eyes darting about the faces in the living room. She realized this must be his first time in such a situation as a Garda; she touched his arm again, hoping to focus his attention on her face.

'Tell them the investigation is ongoing and we'll do everything in our power to catch whoever did this and bring them to justice.' Her voice broke and she left him there, still looking ill at ease.

She found Adrian's wife, now widow, sitting at the kitchen table, a cup and a plate of biscuits in front of her. Three other women busied themselves at the sink and the counter, buttering bread, washing cups. A pot bubbled on the stove. Julia felt a swell of emotion, of gratitude for these women and their attempts to alleviate some of the stress on Mary Clancy. She knew her neighbours and family would be a silent, comforting presence in the house until the funeral was over, running the home and catering to the well-wishers until Mary closed her door on the last sympathizer and tried to get on with her life. It was the way things were in every town and village across Ireland. She hoped the community spirit would rally around Adrian's family long past that time, because she knew it would be then, when the dust had settled, that they would truly need it.

'Mary,' she said softly from the doorway to the tiny

figure, red hair scraped off her face into a ponytail, rounded shoulders shrouded in a brown wool cardigan. All eyes turned towards Julia and she sat quickly beside the woman she barely knew. In the eight years she had been partnered with Adrian she had rarely met Mary, and each time she had, the other woman had been pregnant. Her swollen belly and glowing face, radiating happiness, had repelled Julia in a way she could never explain and which she had been deeply ashamed of. While she and Adrian had shared an easy camaraderie, every time she met his wife she had been reminded that what she and Philip desired the most wasn't happening, and subconsciously, it had dimmed her otherwise friendly nature. She couldn't talk to Mary without seeing her baby bump, she couldn't ignore the joy in her voice as she stroked her belly and complained good-naturedly about her swollen ankles and heartburn. Julia's heart had broken a little bit every time they'd seen each other; now she felt a desperate need to protect the other woman.

'Oh, Julia!' Mary gulped and reached across the table for Julia's hands, gripping them tightly.

'I'm so sorry, Mary, so sorry,' she whispered. What else was there to say?

'You were with him. Tell me, tell me what happened!'

'What have you been told already?' Julia asked softly. Her voice was steady and calm, the one she used in difficult situations at work. Her training was kicking in and she was grateful for it.

'They told me he was stabbed in—' Her hands waved aimlessly in the air in front of her own throat. 'But why would anyone do that? Sure, Adrian never harmed anyone, it doesn't make sense! He's just a *guard*, like, how could he … how could this …? Tell me what happened!'

Her voice was shrill, and Julia could sense the movement of the other women in the room stop. She turned as Shay came into her peripheral vision, hovering by the kitchen door. She'd told him to go and wait outside, but it seemed he wanted to stay close. She understood that feeling; the need to offer support, the feeling that the burden of the harder parts of the job could be shared better between two. She met his eyes, grateful he was there, then tilted her head in the direction of the ladies standing beside the stove and sink.

'Let's give Mrs Clancy and Garda Harte a few moments please, ladies,' he said softly, but with enough authority that everyone moved like herded sheep, some touching Mary on the shoulder as they passed. Shay shut the door behind them and it was just Mary and Julia in the kitchen, sitting at the table, their joined hands resting on the wax tablecloth. Julia imagined Shay was standing sentinel outside and felt herself relax a little, used to having a partner, to never working alone. Mary sniffed loudly and when she spoke again her voice was a whisper, her eyes cast down on the tabletop.

'My poor Adrian … I just don't understand. Oh Julia, I don't know … I don't know what to do!' She wept softly.

'I wish I could say it's all a big mistake. You've no idea how much I wish this weren't happening,' Julia whispered.

Mary sobbed harder.

'He died quickly.' Julia desperately hoped this might bring consolation. The panic in Adrian's eyes, the frantic grip of his hand, the wet gurgling sounds he had made were things she would keep to herself. She looked at her own hands; only hours earlier they had been stained by Adrian's

67

blood and then scrubbed raw in the bath. Now, holding his wife's hands, she had a sudden, lurching, out-of-body feeling. How was this really happening?

Mary continued to cry but it subsided into sniffing again and an occasional hiccup before ceasing altogether. She gripped Julia's hands tightly; perhaps they anchored her. Julia felt pain form at her temples, as though her head was being compressed. After a few minutes Mary spoke again. 'What were ye doing when he was killed? Will you tell me, Julia? I need to know.'

Julia felt her body slump under the weight of it all. She quickly decided Mary needed to know as much detail as she could give her – she deserved as much truth as Julia could offer.

'We were on a call-out. Someone telephoned to say that they could hear women crying in a house in Douglas. So we went to check it out. It was true – a young girl ran out of the house covered in blood. While Adrian tried to help her I went into the house to see if there was anyone else inside.'

Mary looked into Julia's eyes, her hands trembling.

'The house was empty,' she didn't elaborate on the crying inside number thirty-six, the terrible darkness, but she shuddered as she continued speaking, 'but when I got back to the car Adrian and the girl had been attacked. I can't … I'm so sorry. I left him – he asked me not to go!'

Mary's whole body was shaking now, her head bobbing up and down. She pulled her hands away, running them over her hair and then her face, resting them around her throat. 'And you said he died quickly?' she whispered.

'Yes. I was with him at the end.'

'At least he had that; ye were close. I'm glad he wasn't

alone.' Mary's voice was almost impossible to hear over the bubbling sounds from the hob nearby.

'I'm glad I was there too. I tried to help but I … I was too late.' Her voice broke and Mary reached for her hands again, her watery blue eyes meeting Julia's. 'I should have helped him. I should have—'

'Ah stop; Adrian loved working with you, he trusted you. He called you Jules,' Mary said softly, 'and he called me Mare. As though Mary was too many syllables for him. Lazy git.'

Julia wished Mary would stop speaking; the lump in her throat felt like concrete, like it could cut off her airway. She tried to remember her training again, the needs of the woman in front of her, but she was drowning inside herself.

Mary drew in a deep breath as the piercing cry of a baby from somewhere near the front of the house reached them. 'Audrey needs me. Oh God, Julia, what am I going to do?' Her eyes were wide and panic-stricken. 'Five children, and Christ help me, the farm to look after as well. Julia, what on earth am I going to do without him?'

When Julia stepped outside the house and into the driveway, the sun was strong and bright and she welcomed the glare of it. If she could burn the images of this morning from her mind she would welcome the pain. Upon leaving Mary, with promises to call again tomorrow, she had passed men rearranging furniture in the living room at the front of the house. It took a moment to understand what they were doing; when she realized they were making room for Adrian's coffin, in the traditional Irish custom of waking the dead at home before burial, something had unfurled inside her. Something she had never felt before. For the rest of her life she would never be able to put words to the feeling; all she knew, all she understood, was that it was the first time she felt capable of taking a life.

Garda Shay Foley was leaning against the car, his hat back in place over his tightly shaved hair, his arms folded. He stood to attention as she approached.

'Are you okay, Garda Harte?'

'Please, call me Julia. I'll go into the station now, Shay, if you don't mind; I need to speak to the inspectors. And the chief too.'

He nodded his understanding and opened the door for her. Julia sank into the passenger seat as Shay started the car and pulled away in silence. Their journey was decidedly different from the one they had shared a few hours ago, where he had seemed afraid of the silence. Now he was subdued by the grief inside the farmhouse.

'That poor woman,' he said softly after they had driven a few kilometres. 'Five children they have is it? I didn't see any of them except the baby.'

'They're gone to Adrian's sister's house. Better to keep the older ones away from the house for today, let things settle there a bit.' Julia heard the angry rasp in her own voice and forced herself to breathe steadily.

'Of course, of course.' He drove faster, wanting to get as far from the house as he could. 'So what happens now?'

'Now, Shay, every Garda in the country – in all of Ireland – will be on the hunt for this madman.'

'Well let's hope it doesn't take too long to catch him. Do you know when the funeral will be?'

She shook her head. Her thoughts weren't on the funeral but on whoever had cut the power in the house, whoever had killed Adrian and stabbed Louise in the back as she'd lain unconscious in the back of the car. On whoever had left Jeanette lying dead, alone. Her thoughts were on Mary Clancy, at home with five children to raise without her loving husband. Her thoughts were on Molloy and Connolly, on what else they might have learned this morning from the examination of the house and the car, if anything. And her thoughts were on the chief superintendent, Des Riordan, and how she might convince him to let her into the investigation. Because she knew she wouldn't be resting at home, or sitting at her own desk, working on her own cases, wishing her colleagues well in the hunt. She would do everything she could to catch Adrian's killer.

11

1994

Once Shay parked the car at the station and they said goodbye in the lobby, Julia made her way to the desk she and Adrian shared with two other Gardaí. The room was full of men and women in uniform and a few admin assistants, who all fell silent as she walked in; her colleagues stopped what they were doing to stare at her, a few gasped audibly, and some wiped their eyes. She kept her gaze straight ahead, aware of heat flaring in her cheeks. When she reached her desk she gripped the edges of it, the wood a solid pressure between her fingers. A weakness in her legs betrayed an impending need to sit down.

'I'm sorry for your troubles.' A male Garda crossed the room and gripped her hand roughly before turning away again. Her vision blurred, her weak legs begging her to sink into the chair.

'Don't cry here, girl, for God's sake.' Liz Begley was beside her, one firm hand steering her by the elbow towards the exit. 'Not in front of the lads; you'll undo years of showing them we're the ones with the bigger balls. Come on, we'll go to the canteen, I'll make you a cuppa.'

An hour later, Julia had typed out her statement and was poring over it, rereading her own words with the detachment she normally applied to the cases she worked on. She hoped that something might shift in her memory and she might recall more details that could catch whoever had murdered Adrian. The reality – that she had been there, just not when it mattered – stung and there was nothing more to add to her statement. With a sigh she pushed away from her desk and walked upstairs, adding the bound pages to the pile of others beside a heaving stack of paperwork on Molloy's desk. There was no sign of him, nor of his partner, Jim Connolly. Only one other man was present in the room, hunched low over his desk, so absorbed in a report that he hadn't heard her come in.

'Are any of the others around?' she asked, startling him. He looked up, pushing black-framed glasses back up his nose, his startled eyes magnified.

'Oh, I didn't see you there.' He sounded affronted. Some detective, Julia thought.

'I'm looking for DI Molloy, or Connolly. Actually, I'll just head to the chief's office, never mind.'

'Oh, you won't be able to speak to any of them, they're all in a meeting.'

'Oh, right.' She knew what that meeting was about, and she wanted in. 'Upstairs?'

He stood up, his desk chair creaking. Julia squared her shoulders and set her mouth as he walked towards her, something she now realized was her automatic response lately. She thought his name was McCarthy but couldn't recall anything else about him. He looked at her sympathetically; the sad twist of his thin lips made her want to scream.

'You won't be able to go into that meeting I'm afraid. But I'm sure they'll fill you in. It's Garda Harte, isn't it? I'm sorry about your partner; terrible thing to happen. This place will be in a heap for a while – best to leave the boys to it, eh?'

Back at her desk, Julia stared into the space in front of her, not seeing anything. Someone had placed a fresh cup of tea beside her; she couldn't drink any more tea. The sounds of the office hummed and throbbed, adding to the noise inside her head; it was busy here, but she felt alone, an island amid her colleagues. She chewed on a thumbnail, her eyes moving to the door that led to the stairs, to the meeting room. They were strategizing, regrouping after an attack on one of their own; she could imagine the tension, the testosterone, inside that room. The pumping fury, the certainty that the killer would be caught. But they hadn't invited the person that had been *right there* to contribute anything ...

Picking up her desk phone, Julia dialled the internal extension for Kay Nielson, the woman who could provide access to the chief superintendent. She wasn't sure exactly what Kay did aside from admin duties, but she knew that to get to Des Riordan, everyone had to go through Kay.

'Sorry, Julia, he's not to be disturbed. He was quite insistent on that.'

'Right.'

'In fact, he said to tell you if I saw you, that once you've submitted your statement he recommends you return home and rest. Your own sergeant will be in touch – he's at the Clancy place right now.'

'Yes, I'm aware of that. But—'

'And he agrees with Mr Riordan that you are better off resting at home. Report back in a couple of days.'

Julia hung up. She ran shaking hands over her face, pulling in a deep breath. Go home … rest … stay out of it. Furious hot tears flooded her eyes and she blinked them away quickly, her head spinning. Was this survivor's guilt? This ripping feeling in the pit of her stomach, the need to vomit. Or was it anger at being kept out of the investigation into the death of her partner?

She had to get out of here.

No one commented when she grabbed her jacket and stalked from the room, roughly pushing open the door so hard it cracked against the wall. She descended the staircase quickly, ignoring a handful of Gardaí that stepped aside to let her pass. One of them – he looked like Shay – called her name but she kept moving.

Outside, rain was spitting weakly, the morning sunshine giving way to the dull greyness of a wet afternoon. There was a large group of people near the front entrance, standing in clusters, some with notebooks in their hands. They huddled into turned-up collars and dipped their heads against the rain, but their eyes were watchful, waiting. It took Julia a moment to realize they were journalists hoping for a statement. She turned around and walked quickly back inside, veering to the right to the side entrance, pushing open the heavy fire exit door. She inhaled deeply; the bus station was several streets away and she intended to move fast and keep her eyes down.

When a hand clamped her arm she gasped, her eyes moving from the rough-knuckled meaty grip on her wrist to the deep-red face of a man who she guessed was in his mid-fifties. His eyes bulged alarmingly and the skin on his neck and face was growing a darker red.

'It's you!' he shouted, a falter in his voice giving way to tears. 'You were there when my daughter was murdered!'

Louise Hynes's father, she realized, and groaned inwardly. His grip on her wrist tightened and she didn't protest.

'He killed my little girl while you just stood there!'

'I wasn't …' she whispered but her words faltered and died. His eyes carried the glazed look of someone too long inside their own torment to be able to reason with. She became aware of several journalists on the street nearby turning towards them. 'Please, Mr Hynes, let go of my arm! I wasn't there when Louise was attacked. I'm sorry I wasn't able to—'

'*You useless fucking bitch!*' He yanked her arm and she fell to the ground, her knees slamming hard into the concrete, pain shooting up her back. There was a shout from behind them and Julia exhaled in relief as two female Gardaí reached her side. Their firm commands to the grieving father seemed muted – she watched their mouths move but their voices were far away. They guided her to standing but it all felt as though it was happening to someone else. She let herself be led back inside, squeezing her eyes shut, wishing she could banish the sight of Mr Hynes's cries as he stood, bewildered and helpless outside the city Garda station.

12

1994

'Julia! Wake up!'

She blinked, then squinted, the bedside light too harsh. Philip leaned over her, his face flushed.

'What?' she groaned, pushing up onto her elbows, stunned. She had tossed and turned all night and now felt the queasy tilt of being roughly pulled from a deep sleep.

Philip collapsed back onto his own pillow, his hand on his chest.

'You almost gave me a heart attack! You were having some type of nightmare. Screaming and kicking. God almighty!' With his hand over his heart and his hair wild and tousled, he did look scared and Julia grimaced apologetically. Philip sat forward, reaching one hand across the bed to grip hers. 'Are you all right, love? I suppose it's natural to have nightmares after everything you've been through.'

Julia lay down again, pulling her hand free to cover her face. She couldn't remember any dream … she was barely awake and already the pity in Philip's voice was starting to annoy her. 'What time is it?' she asked, keeping her face covered, shielding her eyes from the light.

'Almost six. Julia, you really should have let me know what happened yesterday, I wouldn't have left you alone. Do you want me to stay home from work today? I can ask Rob Green to cover me.'

'No, no, I'm fine.' She tried to sound reassuring. 'The chief has banned me from going into work so I'll take it easy here at home.'

'Well, that's good.' His fingers brushed her hair from her forehead and Julia lowered her hand, smiling at him. Philip's eyes were clouded in concern; he kissed her lips gently. 'If you're sure you're okay, I'll go in to the surgery. Just take it easy today, doctor's orders.'

'Actually … I might ask Kathleen next door if I can borrow her car later. I want to visit the Clancys.'

'Again?' He frowned. 'Are you sure that's a good idea?'

'It's the right thing to do, Phil. And it beats sitting around here twiddling my thumbs.' She rose quickly and left the room, closing the door firmly behind her, shutting her husband out. It was stifling under Philip's concern and she was happy he was going to work – solitude would allow her the space to think.

Time had raced away from her since yesterday lunchtime, since the encounter with Louise Hynes's father. She had insisted she was fine and had left for her bus home almost immediately, the journalists still preoccupied with the man crying outside the station. But his words had echoed in her mind all the way home. As the bus trundled over potholes and her shoulder jostled against the condensation-covered window, all she could hear was his broken voice …

Useless fucking bitch.

Once she reached home, she'd kicked off her shoes and poured herself a brandy and sat in the most comfortable chair in their living room. Tucking her legs underneath her she'd sipped her drink slowly, willing herself to remember every single breath from that night – every shadow, every detail she might have seen, even in her peripheral vision. She'd tried this at the station, but maybe here, in her home, with a brandy helping to dull the sound of her thudding heart, clarity might come. There *must* be something. Instead, the sounds of her quiet house had invaded her mind – the ticking clocks, the humming fridge – and she hated every second of it.

Philip kissed her cheek as he left for work, making her promise to call his receptionist if she wanted him to come home or needed anything. She watched at the front door until their car was out of sight, then stepped back into the house, closing the door firmly. In the hallway, the telephone rested on top of the antique mahogany hall table her grandmother had bequeathed her in her will. Without really deciding to do it, Julia was suddenly standing beside it, the receiver pressed to her ear, her fingers dialling numbers. When the call was answered, she asked to be put through to Steven Molloy.

'Who's calling?'

'It's Garda Julia Harte.'

'I'm sorry, Inspector Molloy is unavailable right now.'

'Fine ... can I speak to Jim Connolly?'

'He's not free at the moment.'

'Chief Superintendent Riordan?'

'I'm sorry, he's—'

She slammed down the phone, balled up her fists and screamed.

Kathleen Adlington was happy to loan Julia her car but she needed it back to take her husband Brendan to an appointment in a couple of hours. It didn't allow Julia time to go to the station, which was disappointing. But she could briefly call in to Mary Clancy again. She had promised she would visit often, though it felt now like an impending torture she couldn't escape. She tutted to herself as she adjusted the seat – the least she felt she could do was visit Adrian's wife and children.

She was glad the Clancy house remained full of friends and family, thankful for the smell of a hot meal cooking. Still, the torment in the house hung like mist in the air, clouding everything, shrouding them. Mary looked more unkempt than yesterday, her hair clinging greasily to her scalp. Her eyes seemed vacant as she guided Julia to the space made in the living room for Adrian's coffin. The pathologist had released his body back to his family. He was home.

'Jerry – that's Adrian's brother – thinks the coffin should be closed, but I … What do you think?'

Julia stepped closer. Adrian's oldest child, a fifteen-year-old girl named Shauna, shared his dark hair and serious expression. She stood at the foot of his coffin, her eyes wet. Adrian looked just like his usual self, his dark hair brushed to the left like always. It was his hands that bothered Julia – folded over his stomach, the fingers interlinked around a set of rosary beads, the stillness of them so alien. His hands were always, *always* moving. Writing in his notebook, gesturing, drumming at his desk while thinking, flicking the top of a pen … in life, he was a man that had been expressive, had never been still.

'We gave him his favourite scarf.' Shauna spoke suddenly. 'What do you think?'

The red and white of Cork Gaelic football was wrapped around the wound on his neck. Julia smiled at Shauna and looked at Adrian's face just once; she wouldn't look again.

'I think he looks perfect.' She squeezed Mary's hand and strode quickly from the house.

It had been a shorter visit than she'd planned, shorter than they deserved. Julia drove home quickly, realizing as she turned into the Adlingtons's driveway that she had no memory of the journey. Inside her house she stepped over to the hall table and picked up the phone, dialled the station again.

'I'm sorry, Garda Harte, but the chief superintendent is unavailable …'

She tried begging.

Adrian's fingers, and the rosary beads twisted around them, seared her eyes and she squeezed them shut, cradling the receiver beside her ear. There had to be an update by now, a plan in place, more forensic results … she *had* to know.

Her calls never got past Kay Nielson. Not even when she *demanded* to speak to the chief.

So she rifled through a deep drawer until she found the Golden Pages and the telephone directory that came with it. Licking her forefinger and thumb she turned the pages, praying that Riordan's details were contained inside. If he wouldn't take her calls at the station, she would leave a message for him at home. There were several Desmond

Riordans in the telephone directory, but none in Rochestown, where she knew he lived. She ground her teeth together in frustration. And then she remembered his wife ... Julia had met her once, when she'd called into the station at Christmas time, bearing mince pies. A warm, friendly woman, that no-one could believe was married to someone as austere as the chief ... *Síle*. Could their details be listed under *her* name? She ran her finger down the page until she found it; now she had their full address and home telephone number. Perhaps his wife would be better able to convey how important it was that Des Riordan take the Garda that had been beside Adrian when he died seriously. A flutter of caution danced in her chest, but Julia ignored it, gritting her teeth as she dialled.

By shutting her out, Riordan had given her no choice.

13

2024

When Julia drove away from Cork city five years ago, she felt giddy with relief. Leaving Cuan Beag is different; she promises herself she'll be back soon as she passes through the village, still shrouded in darkness. She has everything she needs; a small suitcase with enough essentials for a week, some powerful flashlights and a set of golf clubs that fills the boot of her red Hyundai Tucson, and Mutt, wagging his tail excitedly in the passenger seat.

All that's missing is a sense of certainty that she's doing the right thing.

The journey to Cork passes quickly, the radio loud in her ears. As she approaches the Dunkettle Interchange she experiences her first real moment of doubt; it's so strong she takes her foot off the accelerator and stares ahead, open-mouthed. The approach is like nothing she remembers, and for a moment that feels far too long, she doesn't know which lane to take. Is this a sign of things to come? Perhaps in disappearing from the city so suddenly it has repaid the favour and made its entry unfathomable to her.

'If this were a Hollywood movie, you'd put your paws over your eyes right about now,' she tells Mutt, but he's oblivious to her panic, excitedly watching the trucks and cars to their left and right. She pulls into the next lane, horns blaring. 'Oh to hell with you all!' she cries as she points the car in the direction she is sure is the city centre.

Eventually, the buildings around her start to look familiar. With her window open the smell of the river and sounds of the city reach her on the breeze and her heart skips a beat; she pushes the button to close it again. No point letting nostalgia and the pain of memories derail her. She doesn't want to be here, not really. She parks near Fitzgerald's Park and guides Mutt to the bushes to do what he needs to do, then cleans up and deposits the bag in a nearby wastebin.

'Off we go.' She gently tugs the lead and he trots briskly beside her, happy to be able to stretch his legs again. The pedestrian bridge is near. She remembers reading a news article about the refurbishment of the bridge, but that the 'shake' was kept in by the engineers. It made her laugh at the time – how very like Cork to keep the infamous rumble intact. At least this is the same as when she left it. She takes a deep lungful of air and steps forward; there are memories wrapped around this bridge, all centred around her and Philip. Many times she crossed it with her hand clutching his arm while he laughed at her fear of the bridge's trademark wobble. It feels so long ago it's as though their life together is an old film, faded and dated. 'Get a grip on yourself, girl,' she whispers, stopping at the centre of the bridge and holding the railings, waiting. The River Lee is a grey sheet of glass beneath her, rippling gently.

84

Before long, Des Riordan walks slowly towards her, his hands swinging by his sides, his eyes never leaving her face. He doesn't smile until he reaches her and then it's brief, appraising her with a hint of relief.

'So you came back then.' The Northern Irish lilt wraps around her like a comfort blanket. She hadn't expected to feel so happy to see him.

'I said I would.'

'Good to see you're still alive.'

It's over five years since they stood face to face. Time has blunted the force of him, leaving him thin and frail; the square jaw looks more prominent now that age has stripped his face of its flesh. His nose, still askew, seems more disfigured than before. He is wrapped in layers against a breeze which Julia finds pleasantly mild; a blue woollen hat is pulled low over his ears and his coat hangs stiffly from his broad shoulders. There's no kerb for her to stand on to meet his eyes, but she no longer feels the need to.

'Yes, Des, I'm still alive. I'm surprised *you* are though.'

He grins at her, and he looks younger, closer to the man she remembers. 'Since when do you own a dog?'

'Ah, this is my best friend, Mutt.'

Riordan bends down to stroke the fur on Mutt's back. 'Mutt? That's not a very nice name for your best friend.'

'Well the guy I took him from didn't bother naming him, said he was "just some stupid mutt". The name kind of stuck.'

He straightens up, looking at her quizzically. 'The guy you *took* him from? You do know theft is a crime, don't you, inspector?' He's teasing her – God, she's missed him.

'It's retired *detective* inspector actually, and animal

cruelty is also a crime. I was happy to commit the lesser evil.'

He chuckles and she smiles broadly at him.

'Fair enough. It's good to see you, Julia. It's been too long. So … the Shakey Bridge? Why are we meeting here at this old spot?'

'Ah you know, revisiting memories.'

'Speaking of memories … I read your book.' His voice is so soft she almost misses it.

She looks up at him, into his eyes. 'Don't, Des …'

'Things got a little out of hand with it, didn't they?'

'I was naive. What I intended was a theoretical format – a small introduction to a case we worked on where a technique proved particularly useful, then the academic instruction of that technique. I changed names and dates, I did everything to shield the people we helped! I didn't even include the high-profile cases! The last thing I expected was for podcasters to latch on to it and work out who the cases referred to. It was stupid really, to ever have written it.'

'Is that why you left Cork?' Both his hands grip the railings beside her, his eyes on the river beneath them. She sighs, knowing they need to address this before they move forward.

'Call it penance. Call it whatever you want, but I felt I had to leave. I'm happy in Cuan Beag. I don't answer my phone or return any messages; I only keep the bloody thing so Mary Clancy can call me. The book was a mistake. I never expected it to go the way it did. I never wanted anyone to get hurt by it, but that's what happened anyway. Once the names were revealed I … honestly, I didn't know what to do. And the work we did together – I can't forget! I

86

needed to get away from here.'

'It's the nature of it. I warned you when you went for promotion. I told you there'd never be any rest from it. You think I forget the faces?'

'Do you?'

'No, not really. Unluckily for me, my mind is still sharp as a tack; my body might be letting me down but the memory is still sound, still churning it all out.' He taps his temple with one crooked finger. 'But you have to deal with it and move on.'

Julia stares at him, her arms wrapped around her waist. That's her problem; she can't forget, she's not moving on.

'Well, I'm glad you answered my call. Are you here because you think this will help with laying the past to rest?'

She shrugs. 'This might help me or it might help the girls' families … maybe it's the same thing.'

He nods, flexing his hands on the metal railings. He understands.

'Right; we need to crack on.' He was never one to linger on small talk. He lifts his hands and she notices the shake in them.

'Are you okay, Des?'

'Yeah, aside from a few health complaints. Nothing I can't handle. We'd better head to the Regional. You drive – Síle dropped me off.'

Julia swallows, thinking of the upcoming autopsy on the two victims. She has researched the lives of the two young women so deeply, she almost feels she knows them. Elena Kehoe and Hannah Miller. It's years since she attended an autopsy in person. The laying bare of a victim in every sense was always difficult – the smell, the images, the reality of their suffering. Having fought for her place to be at the centre of an investigation, it was something Julia always made sure she was fully present for; the strain of the experience was always a catalyst to spur her on. The autopsy will take place in the Cork University Hospital, still known as the Regional Hospital to Riordan and his generation.

She feels a sudden anxiety to be off this bridge and get started; the sooner this is over with, the sooner she can get on with disappearing from her old life again. They fall into step beside each other, Mutt trotting alongside.

'So what's the story with these health complaints then? Should I be worried you'll keel over midway through this consult we're doing?'

'Relax,' he answers, so softly she leans closer to hear him, 'it's just a bit of diabetes, a bit of angina, nothing major.'

'Type one or two?' she asks, referring to the diabetes, keeping her eyes on the bridge in front of them.

'Does it matter?'

'I guess not. Are you on meds for your heart?'

'Some pills, a nitroglycerine spray now and again; like I said, nothing major. Let's drop it.'

'Sure.'

She knows he won't want her to make a fuss, so she leaves it.

'So, who are we meeting at the morgue?'

This topic is easier and his voice is strong again.

'A DS named Armstrong. Later, we'll go back to the station and liaise with Sadie Horgan, she's the SIO.'

'So she's leading this.' Julia is certain she's heard the woman's name before, but knows they never worked together. 'And she's happy to have us involved?'

'More than happy. Her chief called me, and she's fully on board. This whole connection to Cox is undeniable – no one knows yet quite what it means and everyone is keen to have the input from the lead investigators on the original case.'

'All right, great. And Des, if we need to take a break, just say so.'

He turns to her, offering his best withering look, and she grins at him. As they reach the car he stops and catches her arm.

'Thank you for coming back, Julia,'

'You were right to call me,' she concedes.

'You know this could be dangerous, don't you? We'll be on the sidelines but still—'

'You don't have to worry about me, Des. I'm a big girl. Besides, I have my guard dog with me!'

He looks down at the tiny ball of white fur hopping into the passenger seat and scoffs.

'Still ... watch your back, okay? Last time—'

'That was a long time ago.'

'Even so. Promise me you'll be careful.'

She squeezes his hand and smiles. 'I always am, chief.'

14

2024

Riordan is appalled to find himself in the backseat; the passenger seat is Mutt's.

'I've never seen the like of it!' Still, he settles into the seat, resting his head back, finding it comfortable. He rubs his hand across the soft leather. 'Nice car, by the way. Is it an automatic?'

Julia is surprised; perhaps there'll be small talk after all. 'No, but it has all the latest gadgets; technology makes life so much easier, don't you think?'

She catches his grin in the rear-view mirror. 'Who are you and what have you done with Detective Inspector Julia Harte?'

She laughs and it feels good. 'Oh come on, I wasn't that bad!'

'You were allergic to technology! Steven Molloy was put in charge of each new gadget if I recall correctly. I suppose the radio was left to poor Adrian Clancy when ye worked together.'

Her laugh fades at the mention of Adrian; it's been such a long time. Riordan seems more sober now too, his thin face crestfallen. He turns to watch the passing streets and they continue on. After a few minutes he leans forward to point to their left; somewhere across town he and his wife run a guesthouse.

'We can put you up for a few days if you need it? Although, Síle doesn't know there's a dog in tow. Still, I can't see it being an issue. We're having renovations done, and there's no other guests besides us and Rosie.'

Julia interrupts, surprised at his choice of retirement plan. 'Somehow, I can't imagine you serving breakfast in the mornings.' She grins at the look of irritation that crosses his face. 'But I'd be grateful for the room, thank you. It's years since I saw Rosie – the last time, she was five or six?'

'Yes, well, you tend to miss out on kids growing up when you leave.' His matter-of-fact tone silences her.

The city streets are familiar enough that Julia feels as though they are swept along with the traffic until the University Hospital looms large on her right. The sun is high in the sky, the temperature soaring. The steering wheel is hot to touch; the car has felt stifling in the short trip across to the hospital and Riordan has removed his hat.

'What is it about September? Ireland always has some of the best weather when the schools go back.' He gestures to the passenger seat. 'You'll have to find something to do with your dog.'

'I was thinking the exact same thing.'

She doesn't know if it's the rising heat, the dread at seeing two young women on the mortuary table or watching Riordan struggle to climb out of the car, but she can feel her mood plummet. Rubbing the band of her wedding ring with her thumb, she tries to counsel herself against the overwhelming urge to turn the car around and head for Cuan Beag. In her peripheral she sees a squad car parked nearby, a Garda leaning against the bonnet, wearing the uncomfortable look of a man standing too long in the glare of the sun.

'That lad might know where Armstrong is,' Riordan says and they make their way towards him; the Garda doesn't acknowledge them, his eyes on the mobile phone in his hand.

'You two need something?' He doesn't look up from the phone, but pulls at his collar, his balding head shiny with sweat. Julia remembers the burden of wearing the uniform in the heat. She bends to pick Mutt up – he's been in the car too long today, and she wants him to stretch his legs, but sniffing at the trousers of a man that already looks agitated is not a good idea.

The Garda raises small, stone-like eyes towards them, sweat glistening on his upper lip. 'Garda business here.' His eyes rest on Mutt and he frowns. 'If you don't need anything you both need to move along.' He sounds bored and lowers his head again to his mobile phone.

Julia has had enough.

'I'm retired Detective Inspector Julia Harte, and I'm going to give you the benefit of the doubt and assume the sun is frying your brain cells. Otherwise, there's no reasonable excuse for speaking to two senior citizens in such a dismissive manner, especially seeing as we've been requested to attend here by Senior Investigating Officer Sadie Horgan to consult on a murder case.' Her words and her tone have the desired effect. He drops his hands to his sides and his mouth hangs open. 'What's your name and registered number?' she asks.

He blinks at her silently, shocked.

'Start speaking fast before I contact your superiors!'

Julia is aware of Riordan chuckling, not bothering to hide his amusement – the Garda tells her his details, suddenly standing straighter, his hands clasped behind his back.

'Right, Garda Lee Murphy, this is Mutt. He needs a walk – twice around the car park will be enough. Here's a bag if he does his business. After that he'll need a drink; I'll leave that up to you to sort out.'

'Now, hang on!' His Adam's apple bobs as he lubricates his throat. 'I – I can't leave the car.' She glares at him and his eyes move past her to something, or someone, over her shoulder. 'Oh Christ, Small Step is on his way back.' He stands up even straighter, moving away from the car.

Julia turns to follow his gaze. There's a man walking towards them; Small Step she assumes. She has heard some memorable nicknames in her time as a Garda, the worst of them were reserved for the sergeants and those higher up. She appreciates a good joke as much as anyone else, but the man drawing closer is hardly short in stature – if anything, he's the opposite. He's definitely over six feet tall; the muscles in his shoulders bulge slightly inside his white shirt, not enough to make her think of steroids and hours in the gym, but enough to know that he's capable when situations get tricky. The sun glints on his unruly-looking blonde hair. Julia notices a thick beard over his set jaw; beards like that weren't allowed in her time. His eyes are on Julia and Riordan, but he walks past them and pulls open the car door, depositing his jacket inside. When he steps closer he's opening a bottle of water he found in the car.

'Des Riordan and Julia Harte, I assume? DS Neil

Armstrong.' He drains the bottle and passes the empty to the Garda behind him, then rolls up the sleeves of his white shirt. Ah, Julia thinks, *Small Step*. 'You're late.'

'I beg your pardon!' Riordan is affronted. 'We were told half past!'

'Half past what?' Armstrong sounds exasperated. 'Luckily for you two, Dr Moore is going to run through her findings after she's taken a break, which,' he angles his wristwatch to check the time, 'should be over now. Murphy – why are you holding a dog?'

Lee Murphy looks at Julia with a quick, panicked glance.

'I gave him a job to do,' she says, extending her hand to shake Armstrong's. 'Julia Harte.'

Armstrong's grip is tight. His eyes squint against the sun and she can't read him. 'I know who you are.' He shakes Riordan's hand too. After a pause he steps away from them and towards the mortuary entrance, and after a brief moment, they follow.

'I guess we follow him then. By the way, cheers for calling me a senior citizen!' She can hear the amusement in Riordan's voice.

'Any time.'

'Not exactly the welcoming committee, is he?' Riordan mutters. 'I hope you know that story about getting the Garda to walk your dog will be doing the rounds in the station before we step inside this building!'

Armstrong has let the door slam shut behind him. Julia sighs heavily, yanking it open.

'Don't Des!' she groans. 'Just don't!'

* * *

94

This section of the hospital is the cavernous bubble of disinfectant and hushed voices Julia remembers. They follow Armstrong to an office, where she assumes the pathologist is waiting for them. It's the smell that gets her; it's sterile and cloying at the same time, morphing from an odour into a taste within a few minutes of breathing it in.

There's a waiting area outside the autopsy room proper, with cushioned chairs beside a glass-panelled door. A young female Garda in uniform stands up as they approach. She looks between Armstrong and Riordan, before her eyes rest on Julia.

'I'm Garda Saoirse O'Reilly.' She extends her hand. 'It's such an honour to meet you! I've read your book, of course, and I absolutely *loved* it.' Julia returns the handshake and murmurs a greeting, stepping back to allow Riordan to shake hands with her too. He sits down and zips his jacket all the way up to his neck; it's cooler here, for obvious reasons.

DS Armstrong doesn't sit but stands with his hands in his pockets, waiting silently, his eyes on the wall. So, not one for conversation, Julia thinks. She steps towards him; her whole career has been spent reading the mood of the men in the room and she didn't get where she wanted to be by waiting for their approval. It's time to get straight to the point.

'I presume you're aware Des and I were asked to consult on this case by the chief superintendent and Sadie Horgan is fully on board?' She smiles, something she learned to do years ago ... *we are on the same side.* Armstrong turns his eyes to her and folds his arms across his chest; she can see sweat patches staining the underarms of his white shirt. 'I hate to use a cliché, but time is against us. So let's work together and get this done.'

'I'm all for that,' he says, his voice a strained rumble through clenched teeth. 'DI Horgan has made it perfectly clear I'm to let you two look over my shoulder. But that's as far as it goes. Let's sort through the ground rules while we're here – this is *my* investigation. You don't interrupt my work, you don't advise witnesses or anyone else, you don't ask the questions. Is that clear? As far as I'm concerned, you're a retired inspector and I'm doing you a courtesy, letting you tag along for God knows what reason, and that's it. Understood?'

'Now hang on a damn minute!' Riordan is on his feet.

'I don't care who you were, how many cases you solved,' Armstrong continues. 'And I really don't care about your book and all the rest of it. I have this under control and I don't need any hangers-on. If we're doing this, stay in the background and be on time. And another thing – keep that fucking dog out of my sight.'

'Neil—'

'It's DS Armstrong!'

'No, it's Neil!' Julia says firmly, taking them both by surprise. She's never been called a 'hanger-on' before – it's a big fall from detective inspector. That doesn't bother her, but Neil does; she's only been in his company for five minutes and it's like trying to hold barbed wire. She doubts the detective's nickname 'Small Step' is ever uttered in an affectionate, jokey way by his colleagues. Aware now that she has drawn herself up to full height, she bristles – she hasn't felt like this in a long time, hasn't felt the need for the kerb of a footpath to stand up on to meet a male colleague's eyes.

'Neil,' she sighs, needing to find the patience to keep this man onside. 'You can call me Julia. I'm sorry if you feel that your investigation is being trodden on. And you're right – you don't need us here; you don't need two consultants looking over your shoulder. But *we* need to be here. *We* need to find whoever killed those girls, because this is very much like James Cox's crimes in 1994, and I'll be damned if I sit on my backside waiting for updates on the nightly news!'

She can feel Riordan watching her. Saoirse O'Reilly seems to be holding her breath and her hands are knotted together in front of her.

'Us being here has nothing to do with you and your colleagues. It's just … I lost my partner to him. James Cox killed him. Adrian Clancy, do you remember his name? I know he was before your time but I hope fallen Gardaí are remembered still in Cork.'

Armstrong meets her eyes again. 'His name and photo are on the wall in the station.'

Julia knows that and likes knowing current detectives pay attention to these things, even if the man in front of her was probably a teenager when it happened. He watches her for a long moment and she meets his eyes, her mouth set in a stiff line. He needs to know she's not leaving, not until she's satisfied history isn't repeating itself here.

'I'm not very familiar with James Cox,' Armstrong admits eventually, his voice more controlled. 'The higher-ups think this is some type of copycat crime.'

'We can't know that for sure. All I know is that if the killer is trying to pay homage to James Cox, then we are dealing with a very dangerous individual.'

'Right.' He nods. 'Look, Mrs Harte—'

'Call me Julia. It'd be wise not to forget that a Garda was

97

murdered in the midst of Cox's killing spree, if you want to call it that. If whoever killed these two girls is copying his methods, who knows why or how far this will go. We need to solve this urgently.'

Because I really want to disappear again.

'Right.' Armstrong pinches his lower lip. 'I need to get my hands on that investigation file.'

'I can tell you everything you need to know,' Julia says; she remembers it like it happened yesterday. But he doesn't seem to have heard her.

'I should be able to access it today. It was 1994, wasn't it?'

'Yes, that's right,' she answers wearily; he seems determined to do this on his own.

Riordan steps forward; he always had her back. 'Julia's right – we need to move fast. Initially, Cox seemed to be acting impulsively. At the time we couldn't find any relationship between him and his first two victims. We now know that his abduction of Louise Hynes and Jeanette Coyle was opportunistic. He didn't plan it out; the girls were in the wrong place at the wrong time. But after that, he changed MO and began to target people.'

The Gardaí are listening intently as Riordan continues; as always, he commands the room. 'Time is in short supply here. Unless you find a motive that proves otherwise, we should assume the two victims were randomly targeted. We need to get ahead of this.'

15

2024

The light is stark and bright inside the pathologist's office. Dr Christina Moore greets them and ushers them inside. She explains she's filling in for the pathologist that normally covers this geographical area and gestures for them to sit while she sorts photographs and files at her desk. Julia guesses the woman is in her late forties; with her hair in a neat bun at the nape of her neck, and dressed in dark trousers and a blue blouse, she has obviously completed her examination of the two victims and freshened up. Clearing her throat, Julia wonders just how late they are.

'I'm sorry we weren't here earlier; we seem to have been given the wrong time.'

Dr Moore nods, her eyes coolly focused. 'DS Armstrong and Garda O'Reilly were present and I will forward all the paperwork on to the detective. There are a number of anomalies that require further testing.'

'When will the results be back? We need them urgently,' Armstrong presses. Saoirse O'Reilly sits beside him with a notebook open in her lap, a pen poised to write down details.

'You said that but as I explained earlier it can take six weeks in some cases. I do understand this is a murder investigation. I'll see what can be done to speed things up.'

The only indication that Armstrong is unhappy with that is the clicking sound as he flexes his jaw under his beard. Dr Moore points a remote control at a screen mounted on the wall beside her desk and the first image flicks into view.

'I examined both victims in situ and I conclude they were not killed where they were found. On examination, there was no evidence of sexual assault and both died in an almost identical manner. We'll start with Elena Kehoe,' she says. 'I understand her identity and age were easily confirmed. I concur with her age. She's nineteen years old, was in good health, with no serious health conditions to note. Typical of her age and gender.'

Julia stares at the young woman's face. Only last night she viewed almost fifty images of her in life from her Instagram account. Vibrant, with glossy black hair, always smiling. Now her hair is slicked off her face, which is so pale it looks almost blue. She looks younger without her make-up and with her smile wiped away. The image of her face disappears and is replaced with one of her upper back, showing three puncture wounds set close together.

'Here we see the injuries that caused death. Wounds were inflicted by a thin, single-edged blade deeply penetrated, severing tissue and blood vessels and perforating both lungs. Considerable force was used here.' She points the remote control again and the image changes. 'The deceased's wrists are also cut in two vertical lines per wrist; this was done post-mortem, and it wouldn't have caused death in any case.'

Julia swallows hard – so far, so like Cox's crimes.

'The next image,' Dr Moore continues, 'shows a laceration on the deceased's lower back, approximately four days old at the time of death. You can see the wound wasn't deep and the skin here is partially healed.'

Again, the way Cox marked his victims before he killed them. Her heart sinks, the last hope that Riordan had got this all wrong dissolving into dust.

'This is interesting.' Dr Moore changes the image again. 'This is the back of the deceased's neck and head, and her upper back. Notice the lacerations on the skin, see the cuts and grazes there? Tiny pebbles were embedded in her skin and were found in the deceased's hair. They will be sent for analysis.'

'What does this mean?' Julia leans forward. This is different.

'It's hard to say conclusively but I think the deceased was dragged prior to being killed. We can see the scratches appear fresh. Both victims were wearing only a white vest and underwear when they were found, and there was dirt and similar small stones in the fabric. Again, it's all being tested, but my theory is they *both* were dragged. I found almost identical wounds and debris on the second victim, Hannah Miller.'

She switches to images of Hannah, the young woman who loved to walk her German shepherd and wanted to travel. Julia grips the cool metal legs of her chair, noting the rising feeling that always accompanied an autopsy report. She equates it to the feeling she had when she first visited the Clancy household after Adrian died, when she first saw him laid out for his wake … it's determination, possibly raw anger, but something so real she knows it will sustain her when the investigation seems impossible to piece together.

'There are no defensive wounds to note, except possibly on one of the deceased, and this in itself leads me to believe they were incapacitated by some type of substance.'

Saoirse O'Reilly finally looks up from her notebook. 'You mean they were drugged?'

'We test for chemicals and any other substances in the body, where possible and necessary. And in this case it's particularly appropriate. Toxicology tests will determine if I'm right, but it's a distinct possibility.'

Julia pinches her lips between her fingers. Cox never drugged his victims. He never dragged their bodies either.

'Results will take a while, but as I said,' she looks at Armstrong, 'I'll request they are given the highest priority.'

'You said there were no defensive wounds except perhaps on one of the deceased?' Riordan prompts.

'Yes.' This time Dr Moore flicks the remote control to show an image of something on a glass slide. 'This is human skin. It was found under the index and middle fingernails of Elena Kehoe's left hand. There's some sort of dye on it. It'll need to be tested of course. And the shape of it is something I don't yet understand – it's not as you'd expect.'

'I need you to elaborate.' Armstrong has steepled his fingers and rests his chin on top.

'Normally the skin deposited under a fingernail in a defensive pattern of movement is ripped, torn off if you like. The skin sample found here is … well, it doesn't conform to that. It has straight, not jagged, edges in a way that's quite unusual. I'll consult with a colleague in Dublin and for now, it needs further testing.'

'So do you think Elena Kehoe fought with her attacker or not?'

Dr Moore frowns at Armstrong's impatience and takes a deep breath. Julia feels a pinprick of anticipation. As Riordan used to say when she worked under his direction, 'the devil is in the detail'. She hears his chair creak as he sits forward.

'Skin under the fingernails of someone that was violently killed would normally lead to that conclusion, yes. But the drag wounds on the deceased's back, and the fact that her fingernails are otherwise intact, don't tie in with that. Firstly, the drag wounds are pretty much a straight line. So it's my conclusion she was dragged while unconscious, or at least, didn't fight it. If she had twisted and turned, it would have altered the pattern of the scratches and grazes. Secondly, fingernails will often break or show some sign of trauma in defensive injuries. I don't see that here.'

'So how did the skin get under her fingernails?' Armstrong asks.

'That's your job, detective. The skin sample found needs further testing. I'll tell you everything I can about the bodies presented to me. Beyond that, I can't help you.'

16

1994

The men leading the investigation into Adrian's murder remained 'unavailable'. If Julia didn't do something other than press redial and ask to be put through to one of them, or continue to leave messages with Des Riordan's wife, she'd soon be fired or arrested for harassment. Spending time with Mary Clancy was excruciating. But even worse was Philip's increasing attempts to diagnose her with some type of post-traumatic disorder – Julia felt he was determined to use this to add to the argument he was making so frequently now, that her job was too dangerous. She felt restless and unproductive, so she made herself useful to the elderly couple next door.

Brendan and Kathleen Adlington were easy company and good neighbours, who needed more support as Brendan fell into ill health. Their houses stood side by side, detached two-storeys built in the 1960s, with a small wooden gate that separated their back gardens. Julia found the distraction of keeping an eye on him while his wife Kathleen ran errands oddly comforting, especially after a difficult shift at work.

On Sunday evening, in the warmth of the Adlingtons's living room, she listened to stories of Brendan's career in the navy; she'd heard them all before. Her eyes strayed to the mantel clock, wondering if she should have left a message for Riordan to contact her here.

Brendan's watery green eyes glazed in memory. 'It was the lights, you see. Always look to the flashing lights! Great way to communicate when you're out at sea.'

Julia felt her eyelids droop.

'It was the Morse code that saved *him*.' Brendan paused, his eyes finding Julia and she sat up straighter.

'Who? Who was saved?' She wasn't sure if this was still a maritime memory or if he had moved on to something else. She felt very close to falling asleep. 'Will I make you a cup of tea, Brendan?'

'Eh?' He looked up at her and confusion crossed his face. 'Where's Kathleen?'

'She's popped out. She won't be too long more. Will I put the kettle on?'

He relaxed again. 'Ah, you're the guard. The doctor's wife. When are you going to have some babies, eh?'

Julia smiled at him. 'How about that cup of tea?'

In the kitchen she opened the window, noticing it had begun to rain heavily. She slumped against the counter. Adrian is being buried tomorrow, she thought. Aged thirty-seven, he was gone forever, leaving five children behind, while in the next room, a ninety-year-old man was still living in the past. How was any of this fair?

Kathleen pushed open the back door before the kettle finished boiling, shaking raindrops from her fringe.

'Hello, Julia. Thanks so much, love. How's he been?' She

peeled off her jacket.

'He's been fine really.' Julia pulled another cup from the cupboard overhead. 'We're just about to have a cup of tea.'

'I think you'd best head on home. There's a Garda car outside your house.'

'There is?' Julia rushed to the kitchen window. She couldn't see anything from here; the car must be parked in the driveway, obscured by the hedge. Her heart rate jumped – who was at her house, and why? Feeling Kathleen's curious eyes on her, she forced a smile, hoping she didn't look as panicked as she felt.

Sheets of rain lashed her face as Julia crossed the two gardens. She had a better view of the squad car from the side of her house and could see a uniformed Garda in the driver's seat. As she walked towards it she saw the stiff-backed figure of Des Riordan waiting at her front door.

Oh hell, she thought, *he's come to fire me.*

The gravel crunched underfoot as she stepped onto the driveway and he turned to look at her, his eyes cold. Her mouth felt suddenly bone dry; she swallowed a few times before she could speak.

'Chief Superintendent. Um … what—'

'I'll come inside. We're overdue a serious conversation.'

She chewed her lower lip – she had pushed him too far. So much insubordination … what could she do now but let him come in and take her punishment?

'Of course. You'll have to follow me around to the back.' She never locked the door, not then; no one around here did. Knockchapel was a peaceful, sleepy village near the sea where nothing much ever happened. But her front door could only be opened with a key from the outside, so she led the way to the back door, conscious of Riordan's heavy tread behind her, feeling the frostiness off him so strong she shivered. Her fingers slipped on the metal handle of the door twice before she managed to push it open, and she stepped aside, gesturing for him to enter in front of her.

'Shall we …?' She wasn't sure what she might have said – shall we go through to a more formal room, the good sitting room perhaps, so you can fire me in a more appropriate setting? But she never got to finish the sentence. Riordan pulled out a kitchen chair and sat down heavily, folding his hands in his lap, raindrops dripping onto her linoleum floor.

'Would you like some tea? Or maybe you prefer coffee?'

'Sit.'

Such a command would normally have been like a red rag to a very agitated bull. Julia didn't suffer idiots issuing orders; but this was the chief superintendent, a man who, up until recently, she'd known by reputation only. She fought to steady her breathing and remain calm.

'Well, I'm gasping for a cup of tea, and my mother brought me up too well to drink mine while a guest goes dry, so if you don't mind …' She moved across the kitchen on jerky legs, pushing her wet hair out of her eyes. She filled and boiled the kettle, arranged a tray with two cups, sugar and a little jug of milk, all while keeping her back to him. How on earth would she explain getting fired to Philip? Although, come to think of it, maybe he'd be delighted …

When she finally sat opposite Riordan he was as stony-faced as before.

'Milk?' she enquired, trying to keep her voice light. His face looked even harsher when he was angry; she focused

107

on the raindrops on the shoulders of his jacket instead.

'Enough of this,' he said quietly and she looked up at him. His eyes fixed on hers in a way that made her even more uncomfortable.

'Sorry?'

'Enough calling my office, calling my home. My wife has had enough, *I* have had enough – it's harassment so it is! Look, I get it – you don't like being told to stay out of things and rest. But I'm telling you now, it has to stop!'

'Is that why you're here?'

'Why else would I call to your house?'

'You could have just … So there's no updates then? No arrest warrant? Adrian is ready to be buried and still no—'

He slammed one open palm onto the table, making her jump. 'ENOUGH! How I conduct this investigation is—'

Suddenly Julia was on her feet, her finger pointing at Riordan, her body almost bent in half, leaning across the table as she screamed away her pent-up frustration.

'No, *you* enough! I'm *not* staying at home another minute while you ignore my calls and order me away from my job! I was *there*, Des. I was there when the life bled out of Adrian. If you don't let me into this investigation I swear to God I'll do it myself!'

As quickly as it had flared inside her the rage dissipated, but it left her whole body trembling. She sat down and pressed her elbows into the table, needing the pain of it. She pushed the fingertips of both hands hard into her lips, as though forcing her mouth shut. Tears betrayed her and slipped down her cheeks but she dared not move her hands to wipe them. Riordan was breathing hard, the only sound she could hear. She wouldn't look at him. Her thoughts spiralled uncomfortably inside her head, her anger growing again. He might fire her or he might not, either way, she was tired of waiting around. She'd find a way to move on this on her own.

'Look at me please, Julia. You're a solid Garda; you and Adrian worked well together. I don't doubt you'll move heaven and earth to find whoever killed him. But you're *not* a detective.'

'Not yet,' she corrected in a whisper and thought she saw his mouth twitch at the corners. She blinked tears away, her lips quivering beneath her fingers.

'Report back tomorrow morning.'

'But the funeral—'

'If you'd let me speak for one damn second!' A flash of temper, that for some reason made her smile. 'The funeral is at eleven. Come in to the station first thing – in *uniform*, you're still a Garda! Molloy will catch you up and we can take it from there.'

'You'll let me be involved?'

'To a point. Molloy will get you up to speed tomorrow morning and you do what he says, is that clear? *Exactly* what he says. I've lost one man, I've no intention of losing another.'

She scrubbed at her eyes with the heels of her hands and nodded. He stood up; there was nothing else to say.

When Julia opened the kitchen door to show Riordan out at the front of the house, Philip was standing in the hallway, his leather doctor's bag on the carpet beside him, hands stuffed into his pockets. She hadn't heard him come home. The look on his face betrayed that he had heard every word and he wasn't happy. Under the heat of Philip's eyes she said goodbye to Riordan, feeling the elation of his visit dissolve inside her.

17

1994

Once the front door clicked behind her boss, Julia turned to her husband.

'All right, say it.'

'Say what?'

'Say what's written all over your face! That you heard our conversation and you don't want me to get involved in the investigation.'

'What's the point in saying anything? It's not like you'll listen.'

He walked away from her, into the living room, to the mahogany liquor cabinet in the corner. He pulled out the bottle of whiskey she'd given him for Christmas and sloshed a large measure into one of their wedding-present crystal glasses. With his eyes closed he swallowed half the liquid, wincing around the heat of it.

'Philip,' she said from the doorway. 'Talk to me.'

'All right.' He opened his eyes. 'First of all – what were you thinking? Phoning the man's wife? It sounds very like harassment, Julia, you could have been fired! Have you gone mad?'

'I know! Believe me, I *know!* But he wouldn't listen, he—'

'That doesn't matter! This is very atypical behaviour … this isn't like you, Julia. Have you even cried for Adrian?'

She didn't answer but moved into the room, sitting opposite him on the armchair.

'It's my fault, I shouldn't have left you alone. I'll take some time off; you've had an awful shock, and the loss of Adrian, it's—'

'Oh for goodness' sake! Stop trying to diagnose me with something, Philip! I'm not having a breakdown!'

'But you're not acting like a sane person! And … look, I don't want you to be involved in the investigation. There – I said it! It's too dangerous.' The words rushed out, leaving him deflated. His hand shook as he raised the glass to his lips again, swallowing hard.

Julia felt any remnants of her elation from mere minutes ago fizzle and die – Philip looked both worried and angry, his lips a thin slash in his face. Anxiety danced inside her.

'Phil, what's wrong? I mean – what's *really* wrong? Adrian was my partner for the last eight years; he was more than that, he was like a brother, for God's sake! How can I do nothing? Surely there's some merit in helping myself to heal from the trauma, as you call it, by staying busy and doing something constructive with my time!'

His eyes were on the carpet now; he would no longer look at her. Julia knew his mannerisms, the familiar territory of their arguments. They were fighting more lately, and he often complained afterwards that her logical, coolheadedness would further wind him up. While she could remain calm, he would get too emotional in the heat of the moment and lose his train of thought. And that was always *her* fault.

He puffed out his cheeks, rubbing the back of his neck with one hand. 'It's too bloody dangerous. Adrian's throat was slit by a madman! And you want to run out into that, to put yourself back in the line of fire! Why do *you* have to be front and centre? It's not … it's just … *fuck!*'

Julia waited quietly while he composed himself, feeling tearful at how upset he was.

'You could have been killed, Julia.' When he spoke it was through gritted teeth.

'But I wasn't.'

His eyes bulged in shock. 'That's just … I don't know how to respond to that. That's just such a ridiculous thing to say!'

'*Adrian* was killed. *I* wasn't.'

'Oh for God's sake, Julia! We both know it's just pure luck you weren't murdered too. The person you're looking to arrest is depraved! So please, can you just—'

'Look, I know you're upset. But do you really expect me to sit back while Adrian's killer is still out there?'

He laughed, a mocking sound which caused her to sit up taller, her eyes to blaze with anger. 'Listen to yourself! You're not some vigilante! You're a fucking beat Garda, you know, thieves and punch-ups and car crashes. Not killers! Not chasing down men that stab people. I mean, for God's sake, you're—' He stopped himself and looked away, running a hand through his hair.

'I'm what? A *woman*, is that it?' Julia was on her feet and shouting now. 'Is that what this is about?'

'Oh for fuck's sake!'

'Say what you mean, Phil. I can take it, I'm a big girl!'

He swallowed more whiskey, then spoke calmly and slowly, as though to a child. 'Julia … I'm sorry for swearing! I don't want to lose you. Isn't that reason enough to stop this? And how much longer are we going to wait before we try for a baby again? However long this investigation takes? Or the next one? Are you ever going to be ready? Because this feels very much like an excuse.'

She was stunned into silence; how was this in any way connected to their attempts to start a family? 'This isn't about that,' she finally said softly.

'Of course it is! Look … all I'm saying is, shouldn't we both decide this?'

'But it's my career. My life.'

'No – it's *our* life!'

She held his gaze for a long time; Philip was the first to look away. In the early days of their relationship, he used to tell her proudly that he had never met anyone more determined. Recently, he had accused her of being stubborn in a tone that made her think he didn't like that side to her any more. He drained the last of the whiskey, his shoulders rounded, the fight leaving his body.

'I said nothing when you applied for promotion, twice.' He spoke softly now. 'I know you didn't get it, but if you're involved in this and it's successful, you'll be a shoo-in next time. I deserve to know – are you still looking for a promotion at work, and are you saying we're done with trying for a family? Because I don't think both lives can intersect.'

She looked into his eyes, stunned. 'I can't believe you're

making this about trying for a baby. I'm only thirty – there's plenty of time!'

Lately, everything came back to this. If she were to be promoted, what options did she have if she fell pregnant? There were more and more women in her position within the Garda force, and she knew she could take maternity leave and return to work – there was precedent for that already. But it was possible she'd be confined to desk duty and that wasn't something she wanted. It was a push-pull situation her husband didn't have to weigh up, and she was weary of thinking about it.

'Adrian's funeral is tomorrow. I'll be going back to work in the morning, but I could meet you at the church if—'

Philip shook his head, his mouth twisted in anger. He turned to leave, banging the crystal glass hard onto the mantel. It was too close to the edge. For a moment it wobbled, suspended between the wooden tip and the air, then toppled onto the tiled fireplace and smashed. They both flinched; he paused, tense, then strode from the room, leaving Julia alone, her hands shaking.

The sound of the slamming front door brought her to her senses; in the kitchen she fetched the brush and pan and returned to the living room, sweeping up the shards of broken glass, her hands working on autopilot. This would all be fine – once Adrian's killer was caught she and Philip could talk about trying again for a baby. They could make a joint decision about whether she tried to progress her career if that's what he wanted. He just needed to understand that, for now, the investigation was the only thing she could focus on.

Standing to return to the kitchen she paused at the living room window. Her eyes found flickering lights coming from the upstairs bedroom window of the Adlingtons. She could see the silhouette of Brendan, standing in the dark room, flashing a beam of light into the darkness.

18

2024

Being back at the city station is the last thing Julia ever wanted. She and Riordan want no tour of the building, no fuss. There isn't time for fanfare over the returning chief and his favourite inspector. After leaving Mutt at reception with two adoring trainee clerical support staff, they are escorted upstairs by Neil Armstrong and Saoirse O'Reilly. Julia notes the changes to the floorplan, the updated decor and seating arrangements. It's like an entirely different building. She knows it isn't possible that the walls inside are closer together, it's just that they seem that way. O'Reilly chats continuously as they move; Julia guesses she's in her late twenties, although she could easily pass for younger. Her short brown layered bob and wide eyes lend her a delicate appearance, but she moves confidently, striding ahead of them.

'I expect you'll find a lot has changed since you were last here. Is it ten years since you retired?'

'It's a while.' Julia walks quickly. The faster they get to

the incident room, the sooner she can leave. The solitude and anonymity of Cuan Beag have never felt more appealing.

'Your career progressed incredibly fast once you started to get promoted. I don't know if there's anyone else to compare it to. I hope this doesn't sound weird or anything, but you've been an inspiration to me.'

'Why don't you get her to sign your yearbook?' Armstrong mutters, walking around them to a coffee station outside the door of the incident room.

'Can I get you a tea or a coffee?' O'Reilly ignores him and gestures to the kettle and cups stacked beside it.

'Not right now, thank you,' Julia answers. 'But I'd love you to introduce me to Sadie Horgan.'

The incident room in the city Garda station isn't where it was when Julia worked here; it has moved up a floor, and the equipment has been upgraded. She focuses on that, noting the changes, fighting the feeling that she's slowly suffocating. The room is hot; the windows are open but the air inside the room doesn't stir.

They find seats right at the back and she watches the room fill with Gardaí and plain-clothes detectives she doesn't recognize. Garda Lee Murphy walks into the room and keeps his eyes straight ahead as he selects a seat nearby. Julia notices a couple of his colleagues chuckle as he sits down; when Riordan elbows her and says, 'Told you!' into her ear, she feels a twinge of guilt.

It isn't possible to be introduced to Sadie Horgan as she's deep in conversation with Neil Armstrong. They stand together at the side of the room. DI Horgan is willowy with short blonde hair and is the same rank as Julia was when she retired. It's clear she and Armstrong are arguing. Her hands gesture expressively in the air between them; as Julia settles herself in her seat, she catches a little of their discussion.

'Now look! I knew you'd hate someone looking over your shoulder but for Christ's sake can't you just get on with it? It's a personal favour to the chief, and by all accounts, the woman was something of an expert! Granted she was before our time but maybe you could learn a thing or two. Right now I need you to focus on the case, not some petty resentment at working with someone else.'

Armstrong would be rubbish at poker, Julia thinks, his every emotion is stamped on his face as soon as he feels it. Right now, that feeling is outrage. He walks away without another word and sits at the top of the room, blowing air onto his coffee, keeping his eyes down. Sadie Horgan isn't wasting any further time on the topic either and walks to the front of the room;

'All right, folks, now that we're all here, we'll get started. A word of welcome to retired Chief Super Riordan and DI Harte ...' She nods towards them at the back of the room. The assembled crowd turn and nod or murmur their greeting, then turn back to face the front. 'They have agreed to consult with us on this case because it bears striking similarities to the James Cox murders in 1994, one of which was a Garda. Adrian Clancy.'

Julia can feel Armstrong's eyes on her. She doesn't meet them.

'So, if anyone can offer insight into catching the person responsible for Elena Kehoe and Hannah Miller's murders, it will be the two people at the back of the room. Thank you both.' She dips her head and Des returns the gesture.

Julia can feel sweat trickling softly down her back and sits forward.

'Dan West is your coordinator and will assign the job book duties; all updates are to go through him,' Sadie continues, 'Dan, a recap please.'

The room is respectfully silent as a tall, heavy-set man near the front stands up and turns to face them, nods in greeting, then sits down again, keeping his focus on the computer in front of him. He's young for this gig, Julia thinks, taking in the slight blush that's colouring his face. But then, she's underestimated young people before. He pushes glasses up his nose, a nervous tic that he repeats several times over the next few minutes. A white screen at the front of the room flicks to life.

'So … eh … I'd appreciate it if you pass all documentation to me; anything you want to pin to the noticeboard, I'll do it. So … our victims – both aged nineteen, Elena Kehoe on the left and Hannah Miller on the right. Both college students, living together in student accommodation in the city. Their bodies were found yesterday morning at 6.40 a.m. on a section of The Marina not too far from the Atlantic Pond. It's marked on the map here.' He hovers the cursor over that area of the city. 'Their ID was found, along with their mobile phones.'

'Any intel on how they got there?'

'Not yet. But they weren't *carried* to the spot, they were driven there, and it was some time overnight. We've put out an appeal for dashcam footage. CCTV and street cameras are being examined but so far, it's early days. We have a partial on a black SUV that was in the area at the time that's being followed up. There was very little blood near the victims and the pathologist confirmed they were killed elsewhere. But whoever did this needed time to stage their bodies – someone may have seen a vehicle parked up.'

Julia remembers the area; popular with dog walkers and joggers, it's not exactly secluded. The killer must have known the women would be found quickly.

'The victims were clubbing with friends before they were killed, and there's a period of time where they're unaccounted for. One of their housemates described what they were wearing when they left the house, but those clothes weren't at the scene. She didn't have a chance to report the victims missing before their bodies turned up.'

'Any update to report from the club?' Sadie Horgan asks. A young female Garda stands up.

'Myself and Garda Roche viewed CCTV footage at the nightclub this morning and it was sent to our IT unit an hour ago. It's being further examined. We identified the girls. They had some drinks, they danced, they left with a group of others, mixed genders, at 1 a.m. Two minutes past, to be precise. We're following up on that; we're trying to ID who they left with and where they went. We've requested street cameras and nearby CCTV from buildings and that, but that'll take time. Their housemate doesn't know who they were with, but she thinks it was a class party.'

'So, sometime after they left the club, they were killed and their bodies arranged in a place where early-morning walkers would find them.' Horgan motions to Dan West to continue. Julia can feel her heart rate rising. Every one of that group needs to be identified and located. Every step Elena Kehoe and Hannah Miller took needs to be accounted for.

'Moving on …' Dan West clicks on the mouse and crime scene images flash onto the screen. 'The victims were both first-year college students studying criminal psychology. DS Harper and DS Ring are on campus right now, interviewing their lecturers. They'll go back again tomorrow if they don't get to speak to everyone today.'

Julia looks at the images of Elena Kehoe and Hannah Miller; their names will forever be linked by how their lives were so brutally ended. She thinks of their parents … she's witnessed that pain over the years, the heartbreak of burying a child, the unnatural order of it. She hasn't met them yet but she can imagine how proud they were of their daughters; Elena and Hannah must have done well in their school exams to earn a place in college, and they had both chosen to study an area that could make a really positive impact on society. She looks at their faces on the noticeboard at the front of the room … their bodies are crime scenes now, places to collect evidence from, but they were much more than that. There was life in their eyes, there were smiles on their faces. Now there are empty beds in their homes, and their smiles exist only in memories and photographs.

'Any boyfriends? Any issues with friends?'

'The families don't know about any boyfriends, and neither do the friends we've spoken to. Our lads are on their social media now, so if anything shows up there, we'll have it in an hour or so.'

'Good. What about the cut on their backs. They reported that here, didn't they?'

'They did.' West continues, 'There was a delay accessing CCTV footage from the club they were in when that happened, but it will be here within the hour. Who can I put on that? We need to get someone out to interview the manageress of that club.'

Several hands are raised and he assigns the task of viewing the footage and interviewing the staff at the club where the victims were marked. When he's finished he clicks on the images from where the young women were discovered.

'The scene of crime officers are still on site. The victims were positioned … thus,' he moves the images from Elena to Hannah, 'and thus.'

Julia can't look at the bodies again and lowers her eyes. She listens to Riordan inhale, watches his hands fold over each other, banishing the discomfort these images evoke.

Sadie Horgan is addressing the room once more.

'The staging of the scene and the injuries inflicted on these women are very similar to crimes committed in 1994 and it's reasonable that we give those crimes our attention now. James Cox, as you all know, is dead.' She rests her eyes on Julia. 'Do we know if Cox has any living family?'

'We don't believe so but verify this for your own case notes. He was estranged from his father, and the man died in 2002. He killed the only other living relative we knew of.'

'The press had fun with that one,' Riordan says, 'I can still remember the headlines. *Killer's mother his final victim.*'

Horgan frowns. 'All right. We need to find out who has been in Cox's life for the last thirty years and cross-reference that with anyone that knows either of the two victims. Mrs Harte?'

Julia takes a deep breath. 'Call me Julia, please. I'd start with the staff in the psychiatric hospital Cox was in, anyone who grew close to him, any visitors he had. And cross-reference all the names you get with the victims' lives. There could be a common denominator.'

Horgan looks around the room expectantly until two hands raise; Dan West writes down their names.

'And we need to know more than that,' Julia continues. 'I've been thinking about how the victims were cut on their backs a few days before they were killed. We know it was an MO of Cox, and back in 1994, he moved quickly, from one person to another. It all happened within a few days. So, can you check with the hospitals to see if anyone has presented with a similar injury? And find out if anyone reported anything like that at Garda stations across the city. It might have slipped through before we knew how significant it was. As for the book in Elena Kehoe's bag ...'

'We've been wondering about that,' Sadie Horgan answers. 'We've lifted several usable prints off it and none of them are in the system. Having it there seems a good way to get your attention.'

'If the victims were studying criminal psychology then it's not a huge leap that my book was on Elena's radar; perhaps a friend loaned her a copy and gave it to her in the club or afterwards. Or, as you say, it was placed with the victims as a way to draw me out.'

'Exactly. We should explore the theory that whoever did this placed the book at the scene for us to find.' Horgan's eyes are on Julia.

There's a burst of noise as jobs are assigned. Horgan calls on DS Armstrong to talk the group through the autopsy findings. Julia watches him swallow more coffee before he stands up; with the images of Elena and Hannah on the screen behind him, he runs through everything Dr Moore

123

spoke about earlier. To Julia, his words grow muffled and distant. She can feel the sweat on her back migrate now to her torso, pooling under her arms and at her throat. She needs to get air. She whispers to Riordan that she'll be back and slips out, closing the door softly, leaning against it, squeezing her eyes shut.

When she opens them she sees that the door to the office across the hall is ajar, and more importantly, the window is open as far as it will go. While that isn't very far, it will offer cooler air, and she moves towards it. Resting her forehead against the cool metal of the frame helps. The street below is busy and she watches the people moving underneath her, like tiny ants scurrying to the important parts of their day. One of them could be the killer, she muses, or perhaps the next victim. She sighs and sits down heavily at the desk, noticing a set of keys. Julia knows what those keys are for … Fingering the cool metal she looks around her, finding the weapons lockbox in a corner of the room. It's a quick, easy decision. She unlocks it and pulls out two small canisters of pepper spray.

'Didn't I tell you earlier that stealing is a crime?' Riordan is leaning against the door frame. 'I also said, "Who are you and what have you done with Detective Inspector Julia Harte?" Are you feeling okay?'

Julia runs her hands through her hair, letting them rest on the back of her neck; her head feels light and heavy all at once. 'I'm fine, Des. But being back here wasn't high on my bucket list, you know?'

'Are you leaving again?' he asks softly.

Her eyes find his. 'You know I won't.'

'You're overwhelmed, so you are. I get it. I'm thinking

about asking for some protection outside the guesthouse while you're back.'

'Des! There's no need! As you said, we'll stay on the sidelines and look over things.'

He holds up his hands, his face ruddy with annoyance. 'Now look! I remember how you hated that idea before but hear me out. Someone murdered two young women and your goddamned book was right in the middle of it! I asked you to come back and I'm going to make bloody sure you're safe while you're here. Let me do this!'

Julia smiles. The years fade away and they are back in this building, standing face to face, arguing about some element of a case, and she knows she will have no choice but to do as she's told.

'Yes, chief.' She drops the keys back onto the table and holds out one of the canisters to him. 'And just in case you're right, and I'm not saying you are, put this in your pocket and let's play it extra safe.'

He weighs the small canister in his hand before slipping it into the pocket of his jacket. Philip used to call her stubborn; Riordan said it was determination. They both know she won't stop until this is done.

'Come on. There's a lot to sift through; we have a day of it in front of us.'

She follows him back to the others feeling as though Cuan Beag doesn't exist, her solitude was just a dream, and nothing at all has changed.

19

2024

It's dusk when they arrive back at the guesthouse on the Western Road; Julia parks in the wide, paved driveway, gazing up at the three-storey house. Though there is a cement mixer near the front door and two ladders lying in the narrow strip of grass beside the driveway, the house is beautiful, with colourful hanging baskets that remind her of Cuan Beag. Riordan exits the car ahead of her, walking into the house. Julia watches his stiff gait and feels immeasurably sad. She pushes open the car door and turns to look at Mutt, who is rousing himself from a short nap.

'We'll give this until the end of the week and then it's back home, I promise.' He whimpers and rests his chin on his front paws. 'Yeah, I wouldn't believe me either if I were you. But I don't want to be here – it's too hard seeing Des so frail and it's too hard doing this work again. So the end of the week, okay?'

At the front door, Riordan's wife, Síle, greets her enthusiastically, pulling Julia closer for a quick kiss on the cheek. They've met many times socially over the years, at Christmas parties and memorial services.

'It's so wonderful to see you again! It's been far too long!'

Riordan kisses Síle's cheek lightly and walks away towards the back of the house, tiredness draining the colour from his face, making the lines more haggard. 'Be back in a little while, ladies. I must say hello to my Rosie.'

'He needs to take it easier, I keep telling him! You'll keep an eye on him for me through all this, won't you, Julia?' Síle whispers, her eyes following him down the hallway and into the living room. She's shorter than Julia, and gazes up at her warmly, before running her hands over her own neat bob, seeming concerned that every hair is in place. She's a little breathless, almost as though she wants to make a good impression. Julia's fingers trail the end of her white hair at the nape of her neck; her growing-out pixie cut seems much less elegant. She's glad she's worn one of the silk scarves Mary Clancy always sends her on her birthday; smiling at the other woman, she wonders why she feels ill at ease. They stand in an awkward silence that feels too big and empty not to fill with words.

'I'm very grateful to you for giving me a room at such short notice. Especially considering I have this little fellow in tow. Mutt is very well behaved, I promise!'

Síle waves away her thanks and smiles at the dog.

'It's no trouble; he's a cutie! It's late now, and the builders are gone, but they'll be back in the morning. I'm putting an extension on at the back, so apologies in advance for the noise! We're expanding the kitchen – it's all sealed in, the walls are plastered, but it's still such a mess! The alarm system is down – some electrical fault the lads will sort – but here's your front door key, come on through.'

Julia allows herself to be escorted through the house to the kitchen at the back, her small suitcase under Síle's arm. It looks like a room that's normally off-limits to the other guests, with folded laundry in a heap beside a half-prepped meal on the island counter. At the back of the room, large plastic sheets hang where she imagines a wall once stood; they stir in a slight breeze.

'Des and I sleep down here on the ground floor and all the guests are upstairs. We love having the house full of students; it gives a great buzz to the place. Your room is on the first floor, just up one flight of stairs if that's all right?' She pauses, her eyes resting on Mutt at Julia's feet. 'I'm sure I have a treat around here somewhere for this handsome little fellow!' Síle bends down and fusses over him, calling to Rosie to come and see him. 'Rosie's staying with us for a few days while her parents are abroad. A cruise, if you don't mind, and right when school starts back.' She conveys her displeasure with an eyeroll. 'Rosie – look, isn't he cute! Check the press to see if we've any treats for him.'

A young girl steps into the kitchen, pocketing a mobile phone with an expectant smile. The child Julia remembers has grown into a pre-teen who seems content in her grandparents' company. She kneels on the floor beside Mutt, her long brown hair sweeping over him, and ruffles the fur on his back vigorously, laughing as his tongue licks her face and neck. 'Could I take him for a walk?' she asks shyly. Julia smiles in relief. The poor animal has been indoors for far too long. 'Is that okay, Nan?'

'It's fine with me if it's fine with Mrs Harte. But only for five minutes, it's getting dark.'

'Is that okay with you, Mrs Harte?'

'Julia, please.' She smiles at the girl and hands her Mutt's lead and a little pouch of dog treats from her pocket. 'Mutt will be thrilled to stretch his legs. In fact, I've to pop in and out of town while I'm here. I'd be happy to pay you to watch him for me after school, perhaps take him for a walk? Only if you approve, Síle?'

Síle has moved to the island counter, returning to the half-completed task of chopping vegetables. 'Certainly. Rosie is a good girl. Her homework is done already and she was getting bored. You can leave Mutt in the garden while she's in school, he'll be quite safe. The builders will take a shine to him, they're two lovely lads. So, Julia, Des tells me you left Cork a few years ago and you lost touch. Where do you live now?'

Julia blinks, trying to keep up with the speed of the conversation. She's tired, the day spent reading notes and watching CCTV has strained her eyes and she just wants to rest. But how can she dodge the question without being rude?

'I live along the east coast, in a little fishing village called Cuan Beag.'

'Oh, I've heard of it! One of those blink-and-you-miss-it places. Whatever drew you there?'

She tries to suppress a sigh. 'Well, I guess I needed a change of scenery.'

'Did you bring Mutt with you from Cork?'

'Hmm? Mutt? No, no, I found him in Cuan Beag.'

She found him on the day she called to a local man, Jed McGuire, to enquire about a cottage she might be able to rent. As he and Julia were discussing things, standing in his

129

driveway, she spotted a frayed blue rope trailing around the side of the house, and on the end of it, a thin-looking dog. He had no collar, just rope pinching his fur. He had looked at her with sad brown eyes and when she had approached, he had attempted to stand up weakly. Even now she can recall the fiery anger she'd felt when he'd licked her hands and whimpered.

'I'll give you your asking price if you throw in the dog,' she'd said, and the man had laughed.

'Him? What do you want him for, he's just some stupid mutt.'

She refused to rent his house – there would be other cottages. On that very same night, she left her B&B and walked in the rain, with her old flashlight in one hand and a new hunting knife in the other, back to the property. She found the dog curled in a shaking ball on the grass as wind and rain lashed his tiny body. She cut the rope and picked him up. 'You're coming with me.' Opening her raincoat she secured him inside, held against her dry clothes, and fastened the buttons up around him. It was awkward to walk back like that, but his fur dried and he stayed warm, licking her neck from time to time. No one in the B&B noticed him by night and she found Annie's café, where he could rest safely in the courtyard by day. McGuire never came looking for his dog – Colleen helped Julia to understand why at the recent garden party.

'He's my best friend now,' she says with a shrug.

'I'd *love* a best friend like Mutt,' Rosie says, and Síle laughs. 'I'm sure you would. Will you join us for supper, Julia? I've read your book and I'd love to hear more about the adventures you and Des got up to!' Her eyes shine brightly with excitement. 'I must root out my copy and get you to sign it, actually.'

Julia's breath catches in her throat, the bright and airy kitchen suddenly feeling too small.

'Thanks for the offer, Síle, but I'm exhausted. I have a very early start. I think I'll just head upstairs.'

'Not to worry! Tomorrow then, at breakfast?' Síle smiles broadly. 'Rosie will deliver Mutt up to your room after his walk, won't you, Rosie?'

Julia forces her mouth into a smile and nods; it would be nothing short of time spent in hell to sit and discuss the cases of her career again. She's promised herself those days are over. In the morning, she'll make her excuses.

20

2024

In her bedroom, Julia unpacks before she freshens up, setting her framed wedding photograph on the bedside locker. The bed is much the same height as her own in Cuan Beag, and she spreads Mutt's blanket across the end of it, ready for later. She even brought her favourite brandy and her wedding-present crystal glass and arranges them on a dresser with her cosmetics; if she has to be here, Cork might as well feel like home again. After a moment's hesitation she pours some brandy into the glass, about a quarter full, just to taste the familiarity of it, and sits on the bed to drink, one hand caressing the soft yellow blanket beside her. She blinks back sudden tears.

'Get a grip on yourself, girl.' She looks at their wedding photograph, focusing on Philip's face. 'It's just being back in Cork, that's all. Just get this done and go back to the blank slate.' She raises the glass to Philip and swallows the brandy in one searing gulp. This guesthouse on the Western Road is neutral ground. She should be able to sleep here unless the ghosts of the past have followed her back.

She jerks upright in the bed, aware now that she did, in fact, sleep for a little while. Her subconscious must have been working to process being back here, surrounded by the accent and the smells of the city, because old memories penetrated her sleep, weaving into her mind like images in vibrant colour. A hand gripping her arm while teeth bared – '*You useless fucking bitch!*' – and another, a woman, ghostly pale, with pools of white saliva forming at the corners of her mouth, approaching her after a criminology lecture at the university in Cork. She'd gripped Julia's arm too, like the dead clasping at the heels of the living; '*How dare you use my son's death in your book! Everyone knows it was him. Using my boy for profit ... shame on you!*'

Julia's hands are clutching at her chest; she can feel her heart pounding against her fingers. Her whole body feels clammy with sweat. Breathing deeply, she waits for the panic attack to stop. She switches on the bedside light and focuses on Mutt, his curled-up little body enough to steady her.

The guesthouse is like any other old house – it makes noise, even when everybody is asleep. Creaking floorboards, humming electrics, rumbling pipes, as though the house is relaxing into itself as the night ticks on. There's a digital clock on her bedside locker; she finds it irritating, a reminder that day two is turning into day three in the investigation without any viable lead. She turns the clock the other way, its blue-lit numbers facing the wall. The clock isn't the problem. Feeling a little stronger now, she rises and pulls on her cardigan, laying a hand on Mutt's back as she stands beside him. His body rises and falls rhythmically but it's still not enough to fully calm her. Something is bothering her that she can't put her finger on. It's not the dreams, she's used to them, it's more of a thought process that won't form.

She moves to the long, rectangular window that overlooks the Western Road, parting the curtains. Everything is as it should be in the middle of the night, just the way it appeared on the night Adrian was killed. She doesn't trust the dark; the eeriness of a quiet street still has the power to unnerve her, knowing that if she pulled back the veneer of peace, anything could be lurking underneath. She contemplates another small glass of brandy but quickly decides it won't help. She needs to sit a while with the memories she usually banishes to the corner of her mind.

There are so many ghosts in Cork. Victims saved and lost. Cases that turned on a few seconds, a hunch ignored or picked apart. Sitting now in the dark, Julia realizes she has no hunches this time, no idea why this is happening, and that reality winds around her throat like a tightening rope. Every hour that passes without a viable lead turns the case to sand, pouring through the hourglass too fast. Ghostly shadows creep from the walls and she closes her eyes.

Think, Julia.

Truth will come from the most innocuous place; body language, an atypical reaction, a lingering look, a stranger in a graveyard. All clues lead to something, and some present a fork in the road of the investigation – Julia learned that the trick is following *all* the roads, not choosing which one to take. She forces herself to remember the successful cases: a man saved from a serious assault after detectives observed the woman walking behind him slip a knife from her pocket;

a teenager returned to her family as her body language towards the man she was shopping with raised suspicion; a child rescued from a predator, because her neighbour saw a childless man buying little girls' underwear and reported it.

Julia exhales and breathes easier. The breakthrough will come. Until then, she has to be prepared.

Turning on the torch on her phone and pocketing her car key, she opens the bedroom door gently and steps into the hallway. She knows she's alone on the first floor, and that everyone else is asleep downstairs; she treads as lightly as she can on her way to the front door.

Outside, she shivers. The street around her is cast in shadow, shapes of denser darkness that invite a range of unwelcome thoughts. She can't allow her mind to wander. There's enough illumination from the streetlights to see into the driveway, but she uses the light on her phone to find the bag of flashlights in the boot of her car. She hauls them out with the golf clubs. Once inside again, she closes the door softly and listens – all is as it was before. Everyone is still asleep.

Using one of the more powerful lights from her bag she sets about doing what she should have done hours ago. She hides one golf club and flashlight inside the hall closet, pushed to the back behind a thick bundle of coats. She places another set just behind a bookshelf in the living room, another behind the plastic sheeting separating the house from the new extension at the back. She works for fifteen minutes to find hiding places that are within easy reach yet out of sight. She'll explain to Des in the morning – she knows he'll understand. They might be planning to keep a low profile, to keep out of the way, but she and Riordan were the primary officers in the James Cox investigation.

Riordan has requested protection, but in the midst of a murder investigation, it's considered a low priority. Julia isn't fazed – she learned how to protect herself a long time ago. She's fit, only sixty years old, and so used to being underestimated that she understands how to turn it to her advantage. Still, it's better to arm the house she's staying in, for her protection and for the others. She learned that lesson the hard way almost thirty years ago.

The night crawls slowly towards dawn. Julia sits at the window and watches the street outside the guesthouse, listening to Mutt's soft snores, rereading the notes she has made since she received Des's phone call in Annie's café in Cuan Beag. As much as she hates to, it's necessary to remember everything about what James Cox did. If someone is copying his methods, knowing every detail of that time is crucial now. Armstrong had ignored her offer to fill him in, preferring to request the case files and delve into the detail himself. Julia checks her phone – it's 5.45, an acceptable time to check if the detective has familiarized himself sufficiently.

Neil Armstrong answers his mobile phone on the third ring. 'Yeah?' His voice is the groggy croak of a man who had been sleeping soundly; lucky him.

'Neil? It's Julia.'

She can hear the sound of rustling, muffled words she can't quite decipher, and then, 'I need to take this sweetheart, it's work. Go back to sleep.'

Ah! She cringes. He has company. A few seconds later he speaks again, tension and anger vying for dominance in his tone. 'Mrs Harte. How did you get my number?'

'Call me Julia.' *How many times!* She takes a deep breath.

'Sadie Horgan gave it to me.' *Which you should have done!* 'I'm sorry to disturb you, especially as you have company.'

'That's my daughter,' he answers gruffly. 'She had trouble sleeping so she was in bed with us.' Julia blinks, silent for a moment. *Us.* So he has a family. Good for him.

'Well I won't keep you. I'd like to discuss something with you, and it's better we talk now. It's so busy at the station, we might not get a chance later. I hope you don't mind being disturbed?'

'Why would I mind?' A rough rasping sound makes her imagine he's running one hand over his beard. 'I mean, it's the crack of dawn. What else would I be doing except waiting on your call to *discuss* something?'

'You know, Neil, sarcasm isn't a form of intelligence, despite popular opinion.'

'What is it you want, Mrs Harte?'

'Call me Julia, for heaven's sake!'

She can't know, of course, that he's smiling at her exasperation, but she thinks he is. The end of the week, the length of time she's promised herself and Mutt that she'll give to this case, can't come soon enough.

'I've been thinking over something Sadie said earlier. I really feel that my book at the crime scene might have been left there deliberately and I think it's significant. What I can't understand is why someone would do that.'

He sighs loudly. 'You and me both.'

'I don't have unfinished business, Neil. I don't have any enemies out there. The people I arrested are either in jail or they're dead.'

There's a pause while he digests her words. 'Do you think this is personal to you?'

137

'I can't help it. With Cox, we thought it was random but it wasn't. It was personal to Adrian and me. But as I said, I have no unfinished business. This is *all* about the crime scene. It wouldn't be hard to find out details of the murders in 1994 – it was documented by the press at the time, and a lot of it was reprinted recently when Cox died. The current crime scene seems a little *too* precise to me. I think we should try to find out if anyone tried to access the old case files from the coroner's office. It's a long shot, but it might be a lead. We might get a name.'

Armstrong yawns loudly. 'You don't have much faith in me, do you?'

'I beg your pardon?'

'I submitted that request to the coroner's office yesterday evening. I read the file. What happened in '94 is too similar to this to be written off as coincidence. I understand why you came back here – I would do the same if my partner had been killed. And if my husband had been—'

'How long do you think it'll take to get the information?' She doesn't want to talk about this part of the past.

'It won't take long. I'll push on it this morning.'

'All right, good. Good job … and thanks for answering my call. I hope your daughter gets back to sleep.'

After he ends the call Julia holds the phone for a few minutes, thinking. She's impressed and a little stunned at the speed he's moving. Perhaps this will be wrapped up by the end of the week after all. She wishes he had kept her and Riordan, the people asked to consult with him on this, informed of the steps he had taken, but she's glad their minds are in sync. And she's grateful he has read the notes from 1994.

21

1994

On the morning of Adrian's funeral, Julia had convinced herself she was glad Philip wasn't joining her. It was better to attend as a Garda, not a grieving friend, and as such she was planning to be fully on duty, watching everyone and everything. She didn't have time to play the dutiful wife as well.

Philip had slept in the spare bedroom after their argument. She had felt cold and restless all night, unable to sleep without him; she couldn't remember the last time they had slept apart. He had gone to work before sunrise, not enquiring if she needed to be dropped off at the station. He had left her stranded at home on the day of Adrian's funeral ... one phone call to request a car in the area to drive by her house was all it took to alleviate the problem, but the sting of Philip's lack of concern ran deep.

Either it was too early for the journalists to fill the area outside the station or they had decided to set up camp at the graveyard instead. Julia was relieved to be able to walk freely into work without questions and camera flashes going off in her face. No grieving parents grabbed her on the way either; not that she could blame them if they were angry with her, she just didn't think she could cope with another stark reminder of how she had failed.

Useless fucking bitch.

She didn't bother checking in with her sergeant or seek any updates on her current cases. Instead she made her way straight to the cluster of desks where the inspectors sat, frowning at finding it empty; Riordan had said Steven Molloy would meet her and get her up to speed on the progress of the investigation. She spied several brown manila folders in the centre of his desk, and as her hand reached forward to pull one closer, she heard the door open behind her.

'Ah, she's here, the eager beaver. Now, now, step away from those files, no one likes a snoop!'

Jim Connolly, with an edge of a warning in his voice, strode quickly towards her, a cup in hand. He didn't make eye contact when he reached her, but sat down, dragging his chair forward, one large hand protectively on the stack of folders, ignoring her. The message was clear – this was *his* territory, and as far as he was concerned, she wasn't welcome.

'Julia!' Steven Molloy called from the doorway; he carried two steaming cups of what smelled like strong coffee, and he used one leg to push the door closed behind him. 'I brought you a coffee, I wasn't sure if you wanted sugar.'

'I'm sure Garda Harte is sweet enough,' Connolly said, his eyes on her. When she met his gaze he winked. She could hear Adrian's sarcastic response as if he were still here …

'Something wrong with your eye, Connolly?'

She swallowed hard, having no time for the sudden lump of emotion in her throat as she remembered that casual sexism was something Adrian had never failed to challenge. He'd never wanted to play the role of her protector, but he'd done it subtly anyway. Today was about *him*, about finally having a chance to be on the inner circle of the people tasked with catching his killer – so she would ignore Connolly. She wasn't going to waste this precious time giving him the reaction he was looking for.

'Cheers, Steven.' She reached for the coffee, deciding not to mention she only drank tea. She appreciated the gesture and would appreciate even more being kept up with the progress in the investigation. 'And thanks for this. The chief said you'd get me up to speed on things.'

Steven Molloy pulled his chair out quickly for her to sit down while he sat on the edge of the desk, facing her. 'I'm glad you'll be working on this with us, to be honest. I'll fill you in on everything now and you can meet the rest of the team this afternoon. We've an update scheduled with Riordan at two-thirty, after the funeral. How're you holding up? I can only imagine how you feel, having been there when Clancy was killed; it must be hard to sleep.'

'Yes, it is,' she said, surprised by his insight. She had barely slept more than a few hours since the night of the attack. Had he suffered something similar to this? She tried to recall what she knew about him but realized it was very little. 'Adrian died on my watch and I'll do whatever I can to catch his killer.'

He rubbed a hand over his face and nodded, his eyes clouded, troubled.

'I get that. I don't know if you know this, but we've very little to go on. The examination at the house last Thursday morning was pretty full-on. There's a bunch of fingerprints there and on the squad car but most of them have been identified and eliminated—'

'Including *yours*.' Connolly tut-tutted sarcastically. Molloy looked at him sternly, but the other man kept his eyes down.

'And the rest of the prints,' Molloy continued with exaggerated patience, 'are unidentified, but could be from any number of people that have been in and out of the house. The previous tenants have been located and questioned, and to be honest, there's no way they're involved in this.'

'All right … but we know the person that killed Adrian was inside the house with me, at least for some of the time. So his or her fingerprints are definitely there.'

'Unless he was wearing gloves,' Connolly turned back to the file in front of him, 'and believe me, it was definitely a *he*. Clancy was a big fella. There's no way a woman got one over on him.'

'Right.' Julia didn't waste time arguing with him; despite the obvious and absolute sexism of the comment, a good detective should consider all possibilities until the evidence pointed in a particular direction. 'Well, we know the power was cut from the inside, so someone was inside the house while I was there. I know as well that there weren't any crying girls in the house. What do you know about the tape recorders?'

Molloy slurped from his coffee, closing his eyes in what looked like relief as he swallowed, and it was then Julia really looked at him. His appearance was unkempt, his trousers wrinkled and stained with drops of coffee or something greasy, and there were dark sweat patches under the arms of his light blue shirt. It was almost nine in the morning – he carried the look of a man that hadn't showered or changed his clothes in a few days. Perhaps he hadn't been home, she thought, and felt a rush of gratitude towards him for working so hard to catch the person responsible for this nightmare.

'The tape recorders are standard models, readily available in any electrical shop. An awful lot of fingerprints and partials showed up on them, and they're being tested further but we don't expect anything usable.'

'Nothing at all?' Julia was beginning to understand the aura of gloom about the man. There was so little evidence ... He swallowed more coffee and shook his head.

'Did the neighbours see anything? It would be really helpful if one of them had trouble sleeping and went downstairs for a cup of hot milk or something.'

'No such luck.' Connolly sounded a little bored now. This was obviously old ground being covered, even though it had only happened days ago. 'The only vehicle reported on the street was the squad car. And then, of course, the estate was full of Garda cars. But nothing else unusual.'

'So the killer was on foot?'

'In theory.' Molloy clearly didn't want to jump to any conclusions. 'For all we know, the person responsible lives two doors up and walked back inside their house afterwards.'

'Do you really think—'

'No, not really, but we're open to anything. All the neighbouring houses, and the ones running parallel behind

143

number thirty-six are being forensically searched, and the surrounding area as well.'

'And?'

He shook his head. 'Nothing.'

'What about the man that reported the crying ... Tony O'Mahony, isn't it? What did he have to say?'

'He said he heard it, reported it, took two sleeping tablets and fell asleep. End of story.' Connolly licked his forefinger and flicked a page over in the file, keeping his eyes down. 'Another dead end.'

'The murder weapon?'

'Unaccounted for. Thankfully for *you*, it's not the box cutter that had your prints all over it!' he said, earning a rebuke from Molloy: 'Jesus, man, shut up, will you!'

Julia ignored Connolly; she had a list of questions ready and rehearsed, and she wouldn't let him derail that.

'What do we know about the girls? Louise Hynes and Jeanette Coyle. I know they were stabbed.' She closed her eyes, remembering the shock she'd felt as she'd watched Louise Hynes run towards their squad car, covered in blood. She could still see Adrian supporting Louise as she'd slipped in and out of consciousness. And poor Jeanette – she had been completely alone when she died. 'Was there any useful evidence where Jeanette's body was found?'

'Nothing.' Molloy shifted his weight on the desk. 'No tyre tracks in the area, no fibres on the body. Whoever did this is practically invisible! But get this – the stab wounds on both girls were identical. Three wounds, right in the centre of their backs, and so close they almost joined into one big wound.' He traced the shape in the air with one finger, stabbing three dots into the space between them, his eyes unfocused. Julia shuddered. 'And it gets weirder; both victims had their wrists slit. But that wasn't what killed them. It was all a bit clumsy – the coroner's words, not mine – but like, why slit someone's wrists *after* you'd stabbed a big hole in their back?'

Jim Connolly stopped flicking through his file and sat back heavily into his chair, his eyes on Julia. She felt a strange sensation steal over her face, almost as though the blood was draining away from it, leaving her cold and clammy. The cup of coffee in her hands was beginning to wobble and she placed it carefully onto the desk.

'Um … that's … very disturbing, to say the least. But Adrian wasn't killed that way.'

'Clancy suffered what you might call a "rage" kill,' Connolly said, showing none of the horror that was lingering on his colleague's face. 'I'm guessing he was in the way. Wrong place, wrong time.'

'And Louise and Jeanette?' Julia asked. 'Were they in the wrong place and wrong time too?'

Connolly shrugged. 'All we know is they were on a sleepover together in Louise's house. Her parents went to the pub for a few hours and when they came back the girls were gone. You know what teenagers are like – who knows where they went or how they got into this mess.'

Julia stared at him for a moment, anger coiling inside her. 'Are you serious?' she demanded, her voice rising. 'They were sixteen-year-old kids – they should have been safe!'

'Those girls—' Connolly began, but she cut him off.

'Their *names* are Louise Hynes and Jeanette Coyle!'

In the moment of tense silence that followed, Steven Molloy swallowed another mouthful of coffee loudly, his eyes on the wall behind Julia's head.

'If we could focus …' he said softly. 'There was no sign of forced entry into the house and no sign of a struggle. The first anyone knew they were missing was when Louise's parents came home to find them gone.'

Heat flooded Julia's face and she felt a little ashamed of her outburst. Connolly was getting to her after all. 'Didn't Louise have a younger sister?'

'Two of them. And they were sound asleep in bed; they hadn't heard a thing.'

'So there's no evidence there was a struggle to take the girls?'

'Nothing enough to wake her sisters anyway. It's more likely the girls left the house to meet someone. That's the theory we're working on for now. As we expected, there was nothing of use at their house and we've uniforms doing door-to-door interviews, but no one saw a thing. The girls' clothes have been sent to Dublin for further tests. We're doing what we can.'

She cleared her throat. 'Was there evidence of …'

'No sexual assault. It's as though he didn't even touch them – there's not a mark on them, aside from the injuries that killed them. Not including the previous cuts to their backs, obviously.'

'What's the story on that? When did they get those cuts?'

'A couple of days prior to going missing. Our only theory is that the guy's a weirdo.' Connolly rose to his feet.

'Did they talk to their friends about it? Have you—'

'You know all we know. This guy gets his kicks cutting and stabbing young girls, and Adrian Clancy got himself murdered. You're bloody lucky it's not your funeral we're going to today as well; a two-for-one special. Now come on; I'm driving and I want to get a good parking spot.'

'Sorry, lads?' Liz Begley stood at the door to the room, her eyes on Julia for a brief moment before she addressed Jim Connolly. 'The parents of the two girls are downstairs. They're causing a bit of a fuss. Thought you should know …'

As Connolly sighed in exasperation she shifted her attention to Steven Molloy. He smiled, one hand running the length of his tie, rising from his perch on the desk.

'Show them into the conference room, will you, thanks, Liz. Offer them a cup of tea; we'll be down in a minute.'

Jim Connolly's eyes found Julia's and a smirk lit up his face.

'Off you go now, Garda; you wanted to be involved!'

Julia felt as though her body were moving on autopilot as she followed Steven Molloy into the conference room and took her seat. The adults before them sat as two distinct pairs, an empty chair between them, anguish and exhaustion mirrored across their faces. The men rose in unison, their voices loud and demanding. Molloy urged them to sit, to listen, and reluctantly, they did. As he told them everything he could, every plan that was in place and every resource that was being utilized, his words faded for Julia, the sound overtaken by her loud heartbeat.

The man sitting directly across from her was the man that had grabbed her yesterday – Louise's father. The look in his eyes had terrified her then. Now his jaw trembled as he listened, and he made no attempt to stem the tears that poured from his eyes; he seemed a faded ghost of the man who had frightened her. The woman beside him, Louise's mother, pressed a tissue to her mouth, unable to raise her eyes from the table. The other woman – blonde like her daughter, Jeanette – rocked gently in her chair while her husband leaned forward, staring at the detective's mouth as though to memorize every word he spoke.

'So if there's anything else we can do in the meantime, please don't hesitate to phone me,' Molloy said quietly; the meeting was over.

'Tell me about Louise.' Julia spoke softly to the couple across the table. 'What did she like to do; what were her interests?'

Louise's father looked at his wife; her eyes met Julia's and she lowered the tissue with a trembling hand. 'She ... she loved music.' Her voice was barely a whisper. 'Take That especially. Her bedroom walls were covered in posters.'

'Who was her favourite?' Julia pressed gently.

'Hmm?'

'Which member of the band was her favourite?'

Mrs Hynes smiled and it softened her face. 'Jason Orange. I think she felt sorry for him because he's not as popular as Robbie or Mark, you know? She wrote to him, well to his fan club. And he wrote back too. I know it was probably just an office girl that typed up the letter but you should have heard the screams when she opened it.' Her smile crumpled and her husband pulled her close.

Julia turned to Jeanette's parents, aware of Molloy's eyes on the side of her face.

'Was Jeanette a fan too?'

'Not really,' her father answered. His voice broke. 'All Jeanette wanted was a horse. We got her a young colt only last month. She loved him. He was jet black. We thought she'd call him Black Beauty, like the book.'

'But she didn't?'

'No.' His eyes met hers and Julia saw defiance there. He was proud of his daughter. 'She called him Casper.'

Julia smiled and closed her eyes for a moment, picturing Jeanette in the photographs she had seen of the girl in life. 'That's clever. A play on words. I like that.'

'So what happens now?' Mrs Coyle spoke suddenly, her body finally still. 'Are you going to catch the man that took my Jeanette?'

Julia looked into her eyes. 'I promise you – we'll do everything we can. My partner was killed too and I won't rest until whoever did this is caught.'

Outside the conference room, Molloy touched Julia's elbow gently and she turned to him.

'You were brilliant in there, Julia. But take my advice – be careful what you promise a grieving family. We don't close every case, and even when we do, it can take a long time. So just … don't make promises you can't keep.'

'I fully intend to keep my word,' she answered.

He smiled at her sadly and nodded before turning to go. They walked towards the exit, pausing briefly in the lobby where Connolly was exchanging a few words with the Garda at the reception desk. Julia exhaled, feeling the pressure of tears behind her eyes. She blinked quickly and looked up into the freckled face of Garda Shay Foley.

'Garda Harte.' He smiled warmly when she automatically murmured 'call me Julia', looking at his shoes and back to her face again. 'How are you holding up?'

She shrugged, resisting the urge to say she was 'grand', the empty platitude designed to relieve the other person of bearing witness to any genuinely alarming emotion. Shay nodded as though he understood.

'I'm better than Mary Clancy anyway,' she finally said. 'It's Adrian's funeral this morning. Are you going?'

His face coloured. 'I wish I could but I'm in court with that hit-and-run thing. You know, the young lad by Parnell Place?'

Julia nodded, impressed; the fact that Shay was actively involved in this high-profile case was testament to his maturity and skill in the job. She found herself remembering the argument with Philip and his concern that she was interested in going for promotion again. Right then she knew that she was, and she would look forward to working with Gardaí like Shay Foley if she were successful. The realization that she had her mind made up about her future winded her suddenly – this, here, was what she wanted. Not a desk job, not pushing paper around while her colleagues solved serious crime. She really needed to have a conversation with her husband.

'Not to worry, I understand. I'll catch up with you later today. Good luck in court.'

'Ah, I'm only doing security really. See you later.' He smiled at her again and turned to go.

'If you're finished with the love-in, we might crack on?' Connolly's voice was heavy with sarcasm and he pushed past her, letting the glass door swing shut behind him. Taking a deep, temper-steadying breath, Julia followed him out to the car on weighted legs. They drove out of the city, leaving the winding River Lee behind them, its water a swirling grey, and Julia felt anxiety creeping over her skin, squeezing the air from her lungs.

22

1994

Only three of Adrian Clancy's children stood beside their mother, the toddler and baby Audrey considered too young to be immersed in the misery of the next few hours. Julia hugged them at the front of the church and found each of them as limp and disinterested as the other. Shauna kept one hand on her mother's back protectively as she greeted mourners and accepted their sympathy. Julia watched her sadly, thinking Adrian's child was fast becoming an adult.

She nodded at Des Riordan, who returned her greeting with a stiff tilt of his head, and then she moved away to the back of the church, where she took her place among her uniformed colleagues, alert to everyone around her. She had one objective for the duration of the funeral mass – find anyone who didn't belong here, anyone who looked out of place.

What if the killer was here? She had been in close proximity to him or her before – would a gut feeling tell her that person was in this packed church? Adrian would have scoffed at that theory, but she'd read a lot of criminology books when she'd been preparing for her interviews and assessments for promotion. Sometimes killers returned to the scene of the crime or watched their victim's families, wanting to remain close to the thrill of the kill. And sometimes they didn't … She was grasping at any theory she could think of. It was better than letting her thoughts shift into memory. And better than her constant deliberation on why she had been allowed to live. All she had were questions, rolling on top of one another, without a chink of light in the darkness of this case. Questions and stupid theories from academic textbooks and no idea what she was doing. This was a case without any leads and she was growing desperate.

An hour passed, an hour in which Julia sat stiff-backed, her hands folded in her lap, her body numb. She stood when the congregation stood, sat down again and knelt at the appropriate times. She took her position outside the church as Adrian's coffin was carried out, a sea of navy paying their respects, honouring their fallen colleague. She could have been anywhere; the wind buffered her but all she truly felt was the dryness inside her mouth and pain on the sides of her face from clamping her teeth together.

Soon the crowd was moving gradually behind Adrian's coffin to the adjoining graveyard. Julia stopped, feeling no need to be part of this final goodbye. This was where grief peaked, this last part of the ritual, and her body wouldn't bring her closer. She felt eyes on her and looked up to find Steven Molloy had turned back, mouthing 'are you okay?' She nodded and gestured for him to go on, holding her position on the gravel, letting the crowd of mourners move forward around her. The peal of church bells disturbed the air, scattering nearby birds skyward. Julia bent forward, her hands on her knees, longing for Philip's arms around her.

She saw the man when she straightened up, her breath coming fast as her heart began to knock hard against her ribcage. He stood on the grass verge to the right of the crowd, an unmoving statue amid the rippling river of mourners. His hands were hidden inside the pockets of a padded dark jacket, a grey woollen peaked cap pulled low over his forehead, casting his face into shadow. He hadn't been inside the church – she was certain of that, and he stared at the funeral procession now, his head tilted a little to one side, his attention absorbed by the crowd of mourners.

Suddenly, he looked in her direction. Though Julia couldn't see his eyes, she would swear later, when she regained consciousness, that he'd looked right at her. The lower half of his face stretched into a broad grin. For a brief moment she was rendered powerless, unable to move a single muscle in her body. The soundtrack of the graveyard – the crunch of gravel underfoot, the soft cries, the muted chatter as people moved around her – grew silent as suddenly as the silence inside the house had descended last Wednesday night when this man had cut the power.

She reached to her belt – her baton and flashlight were in place. She pulled the baton out, the weight of it in her hand giving her confidence. It seemed to her that his smile grew wider. The man turned and walked away quickly, and she began to run, to break the distance between them.

Julia was fast; she had always been the one to catch up with a thief or a runaway brawler, Adrian puffing loudly as he followed. Her quick strides turned to sprints as the man

153

began to run through the gates of the church and onto the main road, racing along the grass verge ahead of her.

'Stop!' she shouted, hoping to gain the attention of any of her colleagues near the church entrance, but she couldn't hear anyone, and she couldn't see anyone but the man in front of her. He kept a fast pace, the distance between them never closing.

About a hundred feet from the church there was a weathered-looking wall to her left, approximately ten feet high, with rusting metal gates amid stone pillars set in the centre, falcons perched imposingly on top. The Carmichael Estate; the long-ago abandoned country manor of an English lord. She and Adrian had been there once or twice when they'd assisted the local station; the overgrown gardens were a popular hang-out for teenagers from the nearest village, to drink and smoke and do other things that made them pray fervently for forgiveness every Sunday morning in the church nearby. Her heart sank when the man in front of her ran to the gates and scaled one of them easily, disappearing from view.

She stopped at the entrance to the old property, hands on her hips, breathing heavily, her pulse a loud thud in her ears as she tried to think. He could hide in here or he could escape while she ran back to her colleagues for help. He was guilty – why else had he run? She couldn't let him escape, not a second time. She shook her head, the words of Louise Hynes's grieving father ringing loud in her ears; *'You useless fucking bitch!'*

She had no choice but to climb over the gate and follow him.

Remembering the last time she was here, she quickly

tried to picture the area beyond. A narrow lane ran between the trees towards the big house, mostly covered in grass and weeds. It wound like a curling river, pitted with potholes and flanked by tall hawthorn trees on either side. She remembered that they cast shadows on the driveway, their branches meeting overhead to partially block the sky. Her heart sank but she sheathed her baton and put one foot on the lowest rung of the metal gate, reaching upward.

She scaled the gate easily and dropped onto the grassy lane, staying low, pulling the baton from her belt again. Everything was silent except for her own breath; she clamped her lips shut, quieting herself. Jogging forward, she gripped the baton tight, staying in the middle of the lane, her eyes straining to see in the shadowy gloom. The air seemed thicker in here, the haze reducing her vision. She pulled out her flashlight, swinging it around slowly in front of her and moved further up the lane, deeper into the property than she had ever been before.

She noticed a crumbling concrete wall running alongside her at shoulder height, covered in some type of creeping plant. On the top of it were metal spiked railings, once painted green but now mostly rust-brown, the old trees visible behind them in the half-light. The walled garden. She remembered Adrian talking about it, about how the lady of the house had once had such a vibrant array of flowers and plants that it was featured in the local newspaper. But that had been a generation ago, and its beauty was lost to overgrown weeds and trees now. She stopped still, unsure where the wall had begun or even how to get inside it.

She had no idea what to do and the uncertainty of the terrain and the semi-darkness was chilling; she was too deep

155

inside the property now, too far away from anyone that might help her. A sense of déjà vu was stark – just like the night Adrian had died, she was vulnerable and alone in this dark, quiet place. And just like that night, she suddenly felt desperate to get to the light.

As she turned to run back the way she had come, she saw the shape of him; a man's outline, a peaked cap, broad shoulders. He stood in front of her inside the walled garden; only the crumbling concrete and the rusted railings separated them. He was staring at her and standing so close she could reach out and touch him if she pushed her fingers through the gaps in the railings.

'Julia,' he whispered, piercing the silence.

Her heart skipped and she turned and ran back towards the entrance, as fast as the uneven lane would allow. Her flashlight arced wildly in front of her, the bouncing light disorientating her even more. Initially, her panicked breathing was so loud in her ears she could hear nothing else, but she became aware of another sound – thrashing and grunting. He was running parallel beside her, roughly pushing branches aside, crashing through the garden, keeping pace with her, a dark blurred mass in her peripheral vision. Ahead she saw only trees beside her – but the realization that the concrete wall was ending, or beginning, came too late. All of a sudden he was in front of her and pain exploded in the centre of her face. Her feet lifted off the ground and she flew backwards through the air, landing with a heavy thud in the middle of the lane.

For a moment everything was dark. Though her eyes were open she couldn't see anything. She swallowed and licked her lips, tasting blood. Moving caused every nerve ending in her left shoulder to protest, pushing all the air from her lungs. Her right hand twitched and flexed, empty. She had no weapon now. She felt so much pain, and a desperate, frantic need to get away from here.

'Julia.'

She felt fingers on her face, the pressure on her cheek gentler than she'd expected. He was here, beside her. Bile burned in the back of her throat. His hands moved to her waist, roughly pulling at her clothes, lifting her shirt free from where she had tucked it in earlier. The air was cold on the bare skin of her back.

'No!' she tried to scream, but it was a stifled whimper. She couldn't move. The fear was paralyzing, her body refusing to cooperate; she thought of Adrian, and of the girls, and wondered had they felt this fear in their final moments. Her eyes focused now in the half-light; a glint of silver in front of her face, the cold kiss of metal against her cheek, her neck, and then suddenly, searing pain as the skin on her back was slashed, wide and deep. She could sense his face close to her, feel his breath on her neck.

'Hurts, doesn't it? Feel it, Julia. This is what you both deserve – all of it. Fucking Clancy and you, you deserve *everything*! I'll see you again. I'll find you in the dark.'

Before she could reply, she felt his hands clamp around the sides of her head, and pain exploded again before darkness engulfed her.

23

2024

From her chair by the window, Julia turns to Mutt as he barks softly and hops from the bed. She pulls him into her arms, running her fingers through his short white fur while he licks whatever part of her skin he can reach.

'We've another busy day ahead of us, my boy,' she says softly. 'Well, at least I do. Síle said you can stay in the garden while I check in with Neil and the others. Be good!'

She hopes their telephone call might have thawed things between her and Neil. Yesterday afternoon, after his conversation with Sadie Horgan in the incident room, he was cooperative, albeit a little cold, towards them. It's as much as she can expect from a detective sergeant who suddenly has two retirees looking over his shoulder. She knows how it goes; she remembers the early days, the never-ending need to prove herself and the sense that she was always on the back foot. She's not sure how she would have taken to two people shadowing her as she worked, especially if one of them called her up at dawn to suggest she do something she'd already done. Still, Armstrong's ego isn't her problem.

Pulling on her dressing gown she leads Mutt downstairs to the back of the house. Opening the back door to let him run outside, she smiles as he races around, sniffing the builder's paraphernalia and stretching his legs.

'Good morning!' Síle's sing-song voice behind her makes her jump. 'I hope you slept well! We've a full Irish for breakfast, of course, and continental too if you fancy it. I get beautiful fresh croissants every day from a lady in the English Market. They get snapped up but with no one else here, there's plenty. Until the builders arrive at least!'

'Oh!' Julia tightens the rope of her dressing gown self-consciously. 'Um, yes, that'd be lovely. I'll just have a shower and get dressed.' She smiles, turning to go.

'And don't forget – you promised to sign your book this morning!' Síle smiles expectantly. A copy of the book rests on the kitchen counter. Julia touches the raised red lettering on the cover and her stomach clenches. She turns over the book; the small photograph of her on the back – arms folded, glossy brown hair framing a no-nonsense expression on her face – still makes her cringe. She stopped dyeing her hair when she moved away, letting grey weave through the brown until it eventually turned to white, and she cut it shorter. It had felt like a rebirth of sorts. Seeing herself *then* makes her stomach flip unsettlingly.

'I'd love to talk to you about my book club too if you can spare the time?'

'Really?' Julia asks, surprised. 'It's an academic book – I wouldn't have thought it was read in book clubs!'

'Oh you'd be surprised, there's a huge appetite for true crime these days. And I told the girls you used to work with

Des. They'd just *love* to meet you! We've about a thousand questions for you!' Síle is chuckling to herself as Julia increases her pace to the staircase. Once she reaches her bedroom she locks the door and leans against it exhaling, wondering again why she ever wrote that damn book.

Garda Lee Murphy still hasn't lived it down. Several times this morning someone has barked at him like a dog. Yesterday, some newbie, who really should know his place, shouted 'Here, boy, walkies!' when he stepped inside the canteen. Everyone knows that old lady instructed him to walk her dog and that he had complied, twice around the hospital car park like some lackey. He can't believe he actually did what he was told – even if she *is* that one who wrote that book. Six years in the job and now he's become the butt of everyone's joke.

He sits at his desk, a game of solitaire open on his phone, his fourth since he sat down. There's no point playing really, he never wins; it doesn't even beat the boredom any more. He knows he should be doing something productive but he can't muster the enthusiasm, and just wants to keep his head down.

Garda Ritchie Kelly saunters past, deliberately shunting his chair as he goes, and sits down opposite him, leaning forward. 'Solitaire again?'

Kelly is among the worst offenders, barking and howling at an imaginary moon since he clocked in this morning. Lee won't be giving him more than a grunt of acknowledgement.

'Got any treats on you? I hear there's a guide dog in reception.'

Murphy narrows his eyes and raises his middle finger

over the partition separating their desks. 'Drop dead Kelly!'

'Oh real mature!' The other man laughs heartily before lowering his voice. 'Have you heard? There's progress on whoever murdered those young students. Something about a backpack. Although no one can make head nor tail of it.'

'Oh yeah?' This has Murphy's attention. A bit of gossip is better than losing at solitaire.

'Here, check this out.' Kelly flings an A4 page into the air between them and Murphy reaches forward to grab it. It's a CCTV image, grainy and near useless, of what looks like a bag. Or a backpack. It has a distinctive swirling symbol on the front pocket. He could swear he's seen it before.

Kelly continues, 'So the two victims were attacked in a nightclub earlier this week and whoever did it checked *this* into the cloakroom. No one recognizes that symbol though.'

'Can I keep this?' Kelly doesn't answer, already absorbed in something on his computer screen.

Lee Murphy pushes his mobile phone away and sits still, rubbing his fingertips along the palms of his hands. He's *definitely* seen that backpack before. Maybe he can do something more useful than walking a dog. He opens up a search engine, diving down an online rabbit hole.

In the incident room, the aroma of freshly brewed coffee is plunging Julia back into the past. Riordan used to drink cup after cup when they were working a case, going through the details in a room similar to this, one floor down. She notes he has switched to tea now; he's on his second cup since they arrived, hands clasped around it. He looks brighter today, and she's glad of it. There's more colour in his face and the tremble in his hands seems to have disappeared, and though he confessed to getting little sleep, he definitely looks more like his old self.

'I've been awake half the night. It could have been you stashing weapons around the house,' he smiles at her, teasing her about what she told him on the way here, 'or it could be that I can't figure out why the young women were dragged.' His eyes focus on the wall where images from the autopsy and the crime scene are pinned to the noticeboard. 'It's been on my mind all night. Cox never did that. I think it's significant.'

DS Armstrong has been holding a thin silver pen, flicking it on and off continuously for over five minutes, his face twisted into a sour scowl. He's beginning to grate on Julia's nerves. While Riordan appears revived since yesterday, Armstrong looks like he's disintegrating. His appearance is more unkempt; his light blonde hair stands on end, as though he's spent the morning pushing his hands through it, and there are dark bruise-like circles under his eyes. She notices one leg bouncing continuously. Between his daughter's restless night and Julia's early morning phone call, she's certain he had very little sleep. He tuts now as Riordan finishes speaking.

'You don't agree with Des?' she asks, hearing the challenge in her voice.

He glares at her. 'I don't think you should place too much emphasis on what Cox did or didn't do.' He speaks slowly, as though exasperated to have to explain this. 'Yes, this killer is copying elements of his work but it's a completely different person – Cox is dead. So I don't think we should look too deeply at everything Cox did. This is a *separate* crime.'

'Separate, yes, but with too many similarities to ignore. You said so yourself yesterday! The person we're looking for copied Cox's methods. You've read the file, Neil – you know what he did in '94. James Cox is the reason Des and I are back here,' Julia argues. If the detective doesn't factor Cox into his investigation, she's certain he's making a mistake. Which means her time here will be dragged out even longer. This morning, it seemed like they were on the same page – what's changed?

'I didn't invite you to come back.' He shrugs. 'And I *have* read the case file but we're not looking for Cox. We're looking for someone else. Getting obsessed about Cox isn't going to help – we should keep that in mind is all I'm saying. Yes, the crime scene is very similar, and yes, the killer seems to be inspired by Cox, but there could be ten different reasons why the victims were dragged, and James Cox amounts to none of them.'

Julia squares her shoulders; she's been accused of being obsessed about Cox before. Armstrong stands up and crosses to the noticeboard where earlier, images from a nightclub three streets away were pinned alongside the other photographs. Several days before they were murdered, Elena Kehoe and Hannah Miller had attended a fancy dress party; their housemate had told investigators what they were wearing, and they had been easy to find on the CCTV footage. Elena had been dressed as a cat, in black leather trousers, a strapless black top and a hairband with cat ears. Hannah wore a short white skirt with a white top with angel wings. Their features are difficult to make out in the images but they are satisfied it's them; their bodies are captured swaying unsteadily, arms stretched upward, moving to a beat no one can hear. And the next image – Hannah has arched her back, shock and pain making her mouth a wide O shape. This is the moment she was attacked, her back cut. There's a person standing behind her, pressed close to her back, with both arms stretched towards her – one hand to pull up her top, another to cut her, it seems. In another image, Hannah is clutching her back and turning to look behind her; the other person is taller, a baseball cap pulled low, wearing dark clothing; totally useless images that were tracked by CCTV along the street until the person disappeared into the darkness of the city. Frustration is a thick fog permeating the air inside the room.

'*Fuck!*' Armstrong hisses between his teeth, cracking the knuckles of one hand inside the palm of the other. 'It's impossible! Just impossible to make anything out at all! It's actually useless!'

'Well we have the backpack,' Sadie Horgan says from a desk nearby; she's been sifting through paperwork since they arrived, her head down. Julia had assumed she wasn't paying attention but realizes the woman doesn't miss a single thread of conversation inside this room. 'That's a strong lead, and we're interviewing the cloakroom attendant later today. Hopefully she can give us a description of whoever checked it in. Most people don't check a backpack in at a nightclub. I want to know was it heavy or light, was it searched, how did the person seem when it was collected. Don't worry; we'll get something from that soon.'

'I bloody hope so.' Armstrong continues to flick the pen in his hand, his shoulders tense. 'Was there anything useful from the on-street CCTV after the women left the club?'

Horgan shakes her head. 'Not yet. We're still trying to

identify who the victims were with; a group of seven left the club together. Five of the group broke off at Singers Corner and walked towards Washington Street, while Elena and Hannah continued along Grand Parade.'

'They should have been safe.' Julia feels heat rushing through her.

Sadie Horgan meets her eyes. 'Indeed. Don't worry, we're piecing together their movements. The girls cut down by Bishop Lucey Park and onto South Main Street, and on towards Barrack Street, at which point they got into a dark SUV. Because some asshole parked his truck half across the opposite lane, we only have a partial on the plate. We don't have enough to tell us if it's the same vehicle that was in the area where their bodies were found. But we're closing in.'

Armstrong turns away from the noticeboard. 'The street cameras will pick it up. Who's on that?'

'Saoirse O'Reilly is on it now; it takes time unfortunately, it's painstaking work. I'm expecting a full report from the college interviews this morning. So far it seems that the victims were quiet students who attended their lectures and tutorials and handed their first assignment in on time – basically, the young women didn't draw any undue attention to themselves.' She sighs, and pushes away from her desk, rolling back the chair. 'I really need a coffee – anyone else?'

Julia shakes her head and Riordan raises his cup of tea, still half-full. Armstrong doesn't answer but turns back to the noticeboard. He raises his hand and traces one finger along the image of the red track lines along Elena Kehoe's upper back and neck.

'You really think we should focus on this?'

'At the very least it tells us they were dragged over

165

ground with small stones. The *why* we can figure out later. But it might help to pinpoint a location.' Julia stands up and walks towards him. 'I've learned the hard way that every single detail is worth focusing on. We should check back today with the pathologist, see if those tests results are back.'

Armstrong turns and rests his gaze on her face. His lips are pressed tight into a thin line – she can't tell which annoys him more, the lack of progress on this, or her and Des sharing this investigation with him. He exhales loudly through his nose and mutters, 'Right.'

'Sarge?' A uniformed Garda steps into the room, his round face flushed. 'I have an update on the information you requested yesterday evening from the coroner's office.'

The pen-clicking finally stops. 'And?'

'Well, the coroner that worked on the Cox case is retired since 1997. So all his closed files were sent to the County Registrar for Cork; only, seeing as that office only holds on to them for twenty-five years, they will have been sent to the National Archives. That's standard procedure.'

'Meaning? Come on, Cahalane, spit it out!'

'Meaning anyone could have accessed the coroner's reports from the National Archives. We're on it.'

Armstrong swears under his breath and throws the pen onto a nearby desk.

'But here's the thing,' Garda Cahalane continues, a smile breaking across his face, 'I'm not the first person the coroner's office explained that process to lately. Someone else enquired about accessing old case files and how to go about it. He didn't mention the Cox case by name, but he *did* mention the year. He asked how it might be possible to access a coroner's report from 1994.'

There's a moment of stunned silence; this means something.

'That's one hell of a coincidence,' Riordan remarks.

'We don't believe in coincidences, remember?' Julia grips her hands together, feeling a little breathless. The first piece of the puzzle is about to slot into place, she can feel it.

'Did you get a name?' Armstrong demands.

'Yes. The request came through email; he said it was for work purposes. Maybe it was.' He shrugs and lifts a notebook to read his notes. 'Ian Daunt. Works for a publisher here in the city. Said it was for a book he's working on, that he needed to access visuals from an old case. I have his email and work address. What do you think?'

Julia frowns; she knows that name. Her fingers rest on the wall behind her and she pushes her weight into it. The publishers ... *her* publishers. Her book was found at the scene ...

'We'll have to talk to him!' Riordan's voice is strong. 'We'll have to at least talk to the man!'

Cahalane steps aside as another Garda rushes into the room. Julia focuses on his face; Lee Murphy, the one she lost her temper with yesterday.

'Jesus, Murphy, you took your time!' Cahalane grumbles; they share a pointed look.

'Sorry, I was checking something.' All eyes in the room turn to him and he licks his lips. Armstrong glares at him; the expectant atmosphere in the room propels him forward and he hands Armstrong an A4 sheet of paper with the backpack logo on it.

'My cousin has a backpack just like this. And a hoodie

167

too. The symbol is the same, I got him to send me a photo of it.'

'Don't keep us in suspense, Lee.' Julia ignores the heightened anxiety that flashes across the younger man's face. 'Where did your cousin get his backpack?'

'He said he bought it online. There's a guy who designs anything you need, logos and artwork and whatnot, and he has his own logos as well. He can print stuff on backpacks and T-shirts, mugs, whatever. So I looked up his company. He's based here in Cork; it's run by a guy called Shane Boyd.'

'Let's get him in then.' Sadie Horgan is at the doorway, coffee in hand, her eyes narrowed. 'Let's see what he has to say.'

'Not possible,' Cahalane answers. 'Murphy and I already checked. He's in Australia, his mother says he emigrated last June. His company has been all but wound up.'

'So it's a dead end,' Horgan sighs.

'Well, this is what I was checking,' Lee Murphy continues. 'Shane Boyd studied graphic design with Ian Daunt; the design company was a joint enterprise. Boyd's social media has pictures of the two of them out on the town. They were friends as well as business partners.'

Riordan hops up from his seat faster than Julia has seen him move since they met yesterday, spilling tea onto the carpet. She steps toward Armstrong and he nods, almost to himself.

'Good work. Let's have a chat with Ian Daunt.'

24

2024

There is something unsettling about the level of adrenaline firing in her blood. Julia waits with Riordan in the viewing room, staring at the screen showing the still-empty interview room, her mouth dry. In a few minutes Armstrong will escort Ian Daunt inside and quiz him about the email he sent and the backpack he may have printed. He's their first possible suspect, the first chink of light in this case.

Long ago she decided nothing could be explained by coincidence, not in a criminal investigation anyway. The request for images in a coroner's report in 1994, along with once owning a graphic design company that produced the backpack checked into the nightclub by the person that slashed the victims' backs, is too far over the line of circumstantial to be discounted.

Riordan felt weak and needed to eat again and Julia requested someone bring filled rolls into the room along with more tea. He sits beside her now, eating slowly and quietly, neither of them able to speak to the other. He was always comfortable in silence, and Julia learned to respect that when working with him; she grew to know his moods, and he was always quietest when something was about to break. Sadie Horgan, Lee Murphy, Dan West and several other detectives and Gardaí are present in the room but no one speaks. The air is heavy with anticipation.

Ian Daunt is escorted into the interview room by two Gardaí; one offers him a drink and he asks for water, as casually as ordering in a bar. He's left alone with a Garda who stands against the wall while Daunt sits in a black plastic chair, an amiable tilt to his mouth, like a man enjoying a new experience. When the other Garda returns with his drink, he accepts it with a smile and sips it casually. He is a man completely at ease.

Julia leans toward the screen and studies his features; it's probably eight years since she last saw him, and time hasn't dealt him a flattering hand. When Daunt consulted with her on the cover design for her book, he had seemed like an eager young man, not long out of college, trim and fit, with wiry red hair and chunky-framed glasses that lent him a trendy, arty vibe. She remembers he'd said the word 'deadly' a lot during their discussions. He'd been charming and sure of himself.

He still carries the aura of a man with nothing to worry about, but his appearance is very different; now his look is more teacher than trendy student. His stomach stretches his light pink T-shirt to the point that he can no longer tuck it fully into his low-slung jeans; it hangs out in places, making him look dishevelled. His hair has receded from his forehead and his glasses are frameless and too tight; she can see indents where the legs of them are digging into the flesh

170

at the sides of his face. Her eyes take in every feature, every movement in case it betrays his thoughts, noting everything; *old habits ...*

'What do you think?' Riordan asks, his voice soft. He throws the end of his bread roll into a nearby wastebin.

'Daunt doesn't seem like a man with much to worry about.'

'That's true. He still works for your old publishers then.'

'Looks that way.' Julia focuses on the screen. With his ankles crossed under the table and his hands folded in his lap, Daunt couldn't look more nonchalant if he tried.

Armstrong enters the room, bringing Garda Saoirse O'Reilly along with him and the two uniformed Gardaí step outside. She busies herself with setting up a voice recorder and switches it on, saying the date and time and the names of everyone present in the room.

As she mentions Armstrong's name, Daunt smiles broadly, and says, 'Ah, like that guy on the moon!'

Behind Julia, Lee Murphy laughs before disguising it in a forced cough; Sadie Horgan turns to glare at him. Julia smiles to herself, her eyes on the screen again; some of the lightest moments of her career happened when the pressure was high.

Armstrong has kept his eyes focused on a thin cardboard file on the desk, his hands resting on the paperwork inside; when he raises his eyes to Daunt's his face is expressionless, blank. Saoirse O'Reilly holds her hand steady over a notebook, pen poised and ready. Julia watches, feeling the cold breath of tension blowing on the back of her neck. She's missed this.

'Ian Daunt, we've asked you to come in to answer a

number of questions in relation to a murder investigation; I believe this was made clear to you already.'

'Yes, the guards said. I would have come in, you know, if you'd called me on the phone. There was no need to come to my workplace, like. Do I need a solicitor?'

'You are certainly entitled to legal representation. Would you like to arrange that before we continue?'

'No, no. Like I told the lads, I didn't kill anyone, so there's no hassle there. But I've a deadline at work and I wouldn't mind getting this over with. What do you want to know?'

A pause while Armstrong looks at him for a few moments, appraising him. Julia imagines she can feel the heat of his stare; it's somewhat admirable that Daunt doesn't flinch. Armstrong slides a sheet of paper across the desk.

'For the benefit of the recording, I am showing Ian Daunt a copy of an email sent to the coroner's office, requesting information on how to access an autopsy report from 1994. Can you confirm this is from your email address and that you sent this email on the date in the top left corner?'

Daunt reaches out and pulls the sheet of paper towards him, taking a few moments to read it.

'Ah yes. I remember sending that. Yes, that's correct.'

'Which case were you referring to?'

'I was going to ask them about the old James Cox case; do you know it? He died about a month ago, but he killed a bunch of people in Cork back in 1994.'

Julia jerks backwards as though his words have leapt through the screen and slapped her in the face. Beside her, Riordan takes something from his trouser pocket; she can hear a soft hiss as he sprays from the nitroglycerine bottle into his mouth. She turns to him, her eyes seeking reassurance he's okay, but he hasn't stopped watching the screen.

'And why were you interested in the coroner's report on James Cox's crimes?' Armstrong continues inside the interview room. He doesn't make eye contact, and he has a casual way of asking questions, Julia notes, as though he's a very lazy spider slowly weaving a tight-knit web around the man sitting opposite him.

'My employer is working on a new book about his crimes. I mean, with his death, the time is ripe. In my opinion, we should have had something ready to go, but I guess he wasn't exactly old or anything. Mid-fifties, I think.'

Julia wishes she could sink deeper into the chair.

'Whose idea was it to request the coroner's report?' Armstrong continues.

'Well, mine. I need good graphics. All the images surrounding his victims have been available online for years. People are interested in the finer details – the man is a legend in some circles, if you know what I mean.' He leans forward, as though trying to draw the investigators into his confidence. Julia and Riordan turn to each other; they've seen this before. It doesn't always mean guilt, but it's definitely something to pay close attention to. 'He's been spoken about on true crime podcasts, his motives examined by psychologists in criminology courses – it's all out there already and people lap this sort of stuff up. We need something *different*, you know? Something to set the book apart. The visuals are my responsibility and I thought having the *actual* crime-scene photos and autopsy reports would add that certain something.'

'Have you spoken to the victims' families?'

Finally, a bit of emotion reveals itself in Daunt's unflappable veneer; his mouth turns down and he uncrosses his ankles, one leg kicking at the air as he straightens in the chair.

'That was a total waste of time – they were closed shops, the lot of them. Even the Garda's wife, and I had expected a bit of understanding from her to be honest.'

Julia's fists close, her fingernails pressing half-moon crescents in the flesh of the palms of her hands. So he approached Mary Clancy looking for graphic images of Adrian's death ... her distaste at everything her book drew from the past is lurking like a sour wedge in the back of her throat. How did she ever think it would be a good idea? Shame and anger twist in her gut.

'So anyway,' Ian Daunt continues, 'I got nowhere, and I had the idea of going straight to the source.'

'Have you requested the information from the National Archives?'

'Not yet ... look, what's this all about? What is it to you that I looked for the images? That's not illegal you know!'

Armstrong ignores that, pushing another sheet of paper across the desk.

'For the purpose of the recording, I am now presenting an image of a backpack taken from CCTV in Rebellion nightclub. You can see the date and time printed on the bottom right there. This backpack – you and your friend designed these. Your graphic design company has been operational for seven years now and this is your own logo?'

Daunt picks up the page and studies the images.

'No, that's my mate's company. We set it up together back in the day, but he bought me out when I got too busy to be involved. Not that it was worth much. Where did you get that?' He licks his lips, a quick dart of the tongue, and wipes at his upper lip so quickly Julia almost misses it. He's beginning to worry, the skin on his neck turning as pink as his T-shirt. More pages are passed across the table; he snatches up each one in turn. 'Who is this? What is this?'

'At this point I want to remind you, Mr Daunt, of your right to counsel.'

'What? Fuck that, I want to get this over with. What's this? What's going on here? I want to know exactly what you think I did!'

Finally, Armstrong fixes his eyes on Daunt's face. 'Two young women were violently murdered and their bodies dumped in the city. The injuries on their bodies exactly match the injuries inflicted by James Cox on two of his victims in 1994 – injuries you admit to being interested in. Furthermore, the deceased were attacked in Rebellion nightclub prior to their murder by someone that checked *this* backpack into the cloakroom. A backpack bearing a logo you, or your friend, designed and sold via your online graphic design company.'

Daunt is frozen, his hands raised from the table as though to push the detective's words away, his mouth hanging slack. The assembled group in the viewing room wait silently.

'Where were you on the night of September twenty-first, Mr Daunt?' Armstrong closes the thin file and folds his hands on top of it. 'And on the twenty-fifth – where were you?'

'I … you …' Daunt is struggling to compose himself. He swallows several times, the noise loud. Pulling off his glasses, he pinches the bridge of his nose and closes his eyes. After a moment he replaces his glasses and looks at Armstrong; the expression on his face is markedly different from the one when he first walked into the room.

'I was in Amsterdam. I flew out for a friend's stag – there are about eighteen lads who will vouch for me. I wasn't anywhere near here!'

'You flew back on the twenty-fifth?'

'Yes, but into Dublin! You have the wrong man for this!'

'But can you see how everything points to you?' Armstrong speaks gently, an invitation for the other man to see it from his point of view.

'That could have been *anyone* in that club – Shane sold about a hundred backpacks a year!'

'We'll need to see his records,' Saoirse O'Reilly interjects.

'Ask him then! But I'm telling you now I *wasn't there*!'

'Do you own a vehicle, Mr Daunt?'

'What? Yes. A blue Audi. Why?'

The interview winds up, a few details clarified, Daunt warned not to go anywhere and to make himself available for further questioning, and the screen in the viewing room goes blank. Julia turns away from it and stands up, keen to stretch her legs.

'What do ye think?' Sadie Horgan turns to Julia and Riordan. She sounds defeated, her voice reflecting how they all feel. 'I think our first lead just hit a wall. I was hopeful this would go somewhere but if his alibi checks out, we're back to nothing.'

'Daunt's involved,' Riordan answers confidently. 'His hands are all over this. Just because he was out of the country doesn't mean he didn't do anything. He's linked to this.'

'You think? Any decent solicitor will tear this apart. Cork is a small place in many ways. The backpack ...' Horgan crosses her arms angrily, 'that's completely circumstantial. Shane Boyd sold them; we've nothing to prove he wore his own merchandise, and in any case, he's out of the country. Anyone could have gifted the bag or stolen it; Ian Daunt's link to the backpack is questionable at best. We need to get that cloakroom attendant interviewed – Dan, get Daunt's photo to the detectives out with her now. And verify that Shane Boyd didn't return for any length of time.'

'On it.' He hops up and leaves the room.

'Mrs Harte, you've experience with the publishers Ian Daunt works for; Wyse Publishing House. Does what he said about needing better graphics for the book sound legit to you?'

'Call me Julia, please.' She shrugs in answer to the question. 'I don't know anything about them to be honest, except they did a good job on my own book. But it makes sense to me that anyone producing a book on Cox would want crime-scene photos.' Her stomach flips at the thought of it. The stakes are high that photographs of thirty-years-younger Julia Harte will feature too. 'It all needs to be verified with the publisher, obviously.'

Horgan turns away as the door to the viewing room bangs open. Armstrong fills the frame, his eyes on her. 'Well that was a waste of time!' she prompts. 'Good interview but he's confident, although he has every reason to be with that alibi. Your thoughts?'

'Ian Daunt has an answer for everything and I don't like it. He's too cocky by half and I still think he may be involved somehow, alibi or not.'

'Actually I agree. Keep an eye on him,' she instructs. 'But we don't have enough right now to hold him.'

'Solid interview.' Riordan addresses Armstrong, standing up as a loud ringing from his trouser pocket signals an incoming call. 'Very thorough.' He puts the phone to his ear, stepping away. Armstrong turns to Horgan again. 'Hannah Miller's parents are downstairs. They want to speak to both of us.'

'Sure,' she sighs and follows him from the room.

'All right ... all right, let me ask her.' Riordan holds the phone away from his mouth and looks at Julia. 'It's Síle. She said to tell you Mutt is being a dream dog and the two lads that are there to finish the plastering are spoiling him rotten. Also, she wants to know if we're having dinner with her and Rosie later, and to tell you that you received a lovely fruit basket.'

Julia's stomach clenches tight; that last part doesn't make sense. 'Why would I receive a fruit basket? No one knows I'm here. Ask Síle if there's a card. Does it say who it's from?'

She can see her fear reflected in his eyes. He's about to speak but stops to listen instead; Síle has heard Julia's question and is already answering.

'Yes, there's a card,' he says, his face growing paler, 'it says "Welcome back". No name or anything.'

Julia is aware of a sudden tightness in her chest, a restrictive, rigid grip. She forces herself to breathe through it.

'No one knows I'm back, Des. No one except the people in this station and your wife and granddaughter.'

He lowers the phone a little and she watches it rock from side to side in his hand. 'So someone is watching you.' His

178

words, and the absolute certainty that he's right, make her draw her arms protectively around herself. She looks at Lee Murphy, who is studying her closely.

'You might do me another favour please, Lee.' She's glad her voice remains steady. 'I need you to go to Des's home on the Western Road and retrieve that fruit basket. Handle it forensically now.'

He nods, shoulders back, eager to get going, looking a lot more enthusiastic than when she told him to walk her dog.

'And you'll need to take a statement from the homeowner, Síle. Find out what time it was delivered, by whom, and who handled it once it was received, all right? Get it to the forensics unit ASAP.'

Riordan has ended the call and pockets his phone again, his hand fumbling; Julia notices he seems more stooped than before, paler too. She wishes he would sit out the rest of the day and go home but knows better than to suggest it.

'What are you thinking, Des?'

'I'm thinking I should warn Síle to get Rosie and herself out of that house,' he growls, angrily shaking his head. 'I *knew* protection was a good idea!'

Before Julia can answer, Dan West is back at the door, poking his head around it.

'We've had a call from the CUH – a young woman went to A & E claiming to have been stabbed on her lower back while walking to her car late at night.'

'When was this?'

'Three nights ago. It was a superficial cut, so initially it didn't raise any alarm bells with the hospital staff. She was

179

treated and advised to contact the guards and sent on her way.'

'And did she? Contact the guards?'

'No and I can't get an answer on her mobile phone. It's in North Cork, a place called the Carmichael Estate. Are you familiar with it?'

Suddenly, Julia is back there, thirty years ago, watching Cox easily climb over the gate, running after him up the winding, narrow lane, the trees on either side closing overhead to seal them into the crumbling estate together. The waistband of her trousers feels tight now against the long-healed slash wound on her lower back. A twinge of pain in her left shoulder reminds her of that injury too; she flexes her shoulder now, her eyes on Riordan, who is standing taller again.

'I'll tell Lee Murphy to stick around with Síle and Rosie for a while; you and I are going back to the Carmichael Estate. Are you up for this, Julia?'

Part of her wants to say no. But another young woman has been marked; how long will it take before she ends up dead too, her face added to the board in the incident room? She can't allow this woman to join the ghosts that haunt her in the dark.

'Let's go.'

25

1994

Julia experienced brief moments of awareness, flashes of light through the trees, the gentle push of the wind, thrusts of pain from her left shoulder and the wound on her back. But mostly, as she lay in the lane beside the dense hawthorn trees inside the old Carmichael Estate, she was shrouded in darkness. Time passed and she had no idea how long the cold ground had pressed against her. When consciousness returned, only one thought formed, repeating on a loop in her mind: why had he let her live again?

She drifted between light and darkness, between fear and pain. When she felt the soft pressure of fingers at her wrist she opened her eyes, blinking in the harsh glare of a bright light. It was the distinct brightness of a doctor's light, similar to the one in Philip's rooms. Sounds reached her, male voices, speaking quietly. Familiar voices; she was safe.

A clock on the wall read six-fifteen ... she had lost hours of what she hoped was the same day. A nurse stood nearby but with her back turned away, writing on a sheet of paper on a clipboard. Steven Molloy and Des Riordan were in conversation at the end of her hospital bed, their heads bent together, Molloy pinching his lips anxiously. There was no other bed in her room, just three black plastic chairs against a white-painted radiator. The evening sun slanted into the room through slatted blinds; Julia watched dust motes float in the air beside the window as full consciousness returned and the men spoke in hushed whispers. Her left shoulder ached – she noticed a dense pain in her left arm and couldn't move it. She lifted her right hand and tried to feel her back. Someone had dressed her in a hospital gown and she could feel a padded dressing through the thin cotton; she squeezed her eyes shut again.

It had really happened.

Her eyes flew open when Des Riordan shouted, 'She's awake!'

The nurse turned to him with a start, a rebuke on her lips, but the two men had already moved to the bed, one on either side of Julia, and the nurse found herself edged out to the back of the room. 'I'll go and fetch the doctor then,' she muttered with a scowl.

It was the first time Julia had seen her chief superintendent smile. Relief washed over his face and she couldn't help but return it, though she groaned in pain as her lips throbbed.

'Careful!' he said. 'Although that smile is a sight for sore eyes, so it is! I believe you've some stitches in your top lip.'

Gingerly she touched her lips with her fingertips, finding them swollen, the hard ridge of thread in the centre. She exhaled slowly, worry spiking inside her – exactly how badly injured was she?

'Before we go any further, I need to know …' Riordan was

watching her closely, his voice harsh after the momentary warmth. 'Is this it? Are you done being reckless? Just in case you need reminding, we don't put ourselves in the line of fire the way you did today and last Wednesday night. I don't need another Garda death on my service record. Is that clear?'

His familiar severity was comforting. Steven Molloy's eyes were ringed with dark circles, his arms folded tightly across his chest as he stepped forward. 'Give her a break, chief! Can't the lecture wait? We're very glad to see you're awake. We weren't sure how long you'd be out.'

She tilted her head at Riordan; it was the closest he was going to get to agreement that she was done being 'reckless' as he'd called it. Even that movement was painful ... she needed to know what the man she had followed had done to her.

'Is it very bad?' Her voice was an agonising croak. Molloy grimaced before he answered.

'I'll give it to you straight. You've a split lip, a fractured collarbone, a deep cut on your back just over your right hip, and a bump on the head where the back of it bounced off the ground. So, yeah, it's bad enough.'

Julia closed her eyes to stop the room spinning, to quiet the rushing sound in her head as she took it all in. 'So the cut on my back,' she swallowed, her throat aching and dry, 'are there stitches?'

'Ten or twelve, I think.'

'Right. Could someone ... help me sit up?'

Wanting to be the same height as the men she worked with was bad enough – there was no way she was going to lie down in bed any longer while they spoke to her. The two men fiddled with the mechanics of the bed and Julia suppressed jolts of nausea as the top half jerked a few times, Riordan muttering and cursing as he pressed every button like a character in a bad comedy sketch. Eventually they had her sitting upright, a pile of pillows behind her head. Molloy poured her a glass of water and popped a straw into it; he tried to hold it while she drank but she resolutely refused his offer, holding out her right hand for the plastic cup. Her wrist shook and for one brief, alarming second, she wasn't sure she had the strength to hold it. But she managed to bring it to her lips and drink, grateful when Molloy took it back from her as soon as she was ready.

'Right.' Riordan sank heavily onto one of the chairs on her right-hand side. 'Now that we know you're going to live we need to know what happened. Tell me everything.'

'If you can manage it, of course,' Molloy interjected, his eyes sympathetic.

'Of course, of course.' Riordan shifted his weight, uncomfortable on the narrow chair. 'But we need to get men on the ground on this. We've searched the Carmichael Estate with a fine-tooth comb but he's vanished again. So what can you tell us?'

'Wait … how did I get here? Who found me?'

The door to the room was kicked open with a rough bang; Jim Connolly stepped inside, balancing three polystyrene cups stacked on top of each other, a chocolate bar packet hanging from his teeth.

'He did.' Molloy nodded towards him, earning a quizzical look.

Connolly opened his mouth and dropped the packet onto the end of the bed. 'What? What did I do?'

'We were just filling Julia in on how she was found earlier.'

'Oh yeah.' He passed around the cups of tea to the other men before settling himself into a chair by the end of the bed. 'Sorry, no tea for you, doctor's orders.' He looked at her face and grimaced. 'Christ, he really did a number on you. Lucky I came to the rescue!'

They all waited while he lifted the lid, blew on the hot liquid, and slurped his first mouthful. He seemed to be enjoying letting the tension build, resting back in the chair and crossing his legs casually, one foot balanced on his knee. She refused to say anything to prompt him, but Riordan had had enough; 'Jesus H. Christ, will you get on with it!'

'Right, right,' Connolly said with a grin. 'I saw you running out of the church gate like a mad thing. So I followed. Found you lying in the middle of the lane inside the old Carmichael Estate, looking like hell.' He shrugged and slurped more tea. 'There was no sign of anyone else, but to be honest, the guy could have been anywhere. There isn't much light in there; running after him was a pretty stupid thing to do if you ask me. We don't put ourselves in danger like that, not when you're not armed or when you don't have back-up. But like I said, you were lucky I was around.' He looked at her again and pointed at her face, his eyes on her lips. 'You can thank me when the swelling's gone down.'

'Jesus, Jim,' Molloy muttered and shook his head in disgust.

'What?' Connolly asked innocently, but he couldn't hide a smirk of amusement. 'Oh come on! You've a sick mind, that's your problem!'

Riordan glared at him in stunned silence. Julia watched

185

the muscles clench at the side of his face; it steadied her, somehow, to know Connolly's vulgarity bothered him. As he opened his mouth to speak, no doubt some furious rebuke that Connolly would find amusing, she cut him off, forcing strength into her voice. She had to take it slow to speak around the pain in her lip.

'No, that's not right. You weren't there; I looked for you all and there was no one around. You couldn't have seen me run out the church gate because you *weren't there*!'

Her mouth ached from the effort of speaking but it was worth it to see Connolly's cheeks quivering and blushing a deep purple. 'I was in the fucking jacks, is that allowed? I saw you when I walked out!'

'Why didn't you call for anyone to go with you?' she pressed.

'What? What is this?' Connolly's anger mounted to fury.

'Where did you search for the guy? Well? How far into the estate did you go? He could have gone anywhere!' Julia continued, ignoring the pain it caused to speak.

Connolly rose from his seat, his cup toppling to the ground, pale brown liquid pooling onto the lino. Riordan jumped to his feet. '*Enough!* Connolly, clean that up, now!'

Connolly didn't take his eyes off Julia's; they glared at each other until Riordan barked something unintelligible, then the other man stormed from the room, letting the door slam loudly behind him.

'Jesus H. Christ!' Riordan growled again, running a hand over his hair. He sat down, cursing under his breath, while Molloy stepped into the adjoining bathroom for some paper hand towels. He kept his eyes on the ground as he mopped up. 'Connolly may be an uncivilized ape at times

186

but we're all part of the same team. He found you and raised the alarm – we shouldn't turn on each other, Julia. There's someone out there that's already killed one of us.' He looked up at her. 'If you can remember what happened, now is a good time to tell us.'

She stared at the white blanket; he was right. And though she hated to have to relive what had happened, she tried to remember as much as she could. It was all there, imprinted behind her eyes like images viewed in a folder at work. The man's face partially hidden by his hat, the smile that stretched his mouth wide, his speed when he ran away from her, how he had whispered her name, how he had said she deserved the attack. What on earth could that mean? Taking a steadying breath, she told them everything she could think of.

'*Deserved* it? I don't get it.' Molloy's confusion was mirrored on Des Riordan's face. 'And you didn't get a clear view of him?' His disappointment was palpable.

'No. But there are things that stood out.' She was growing used to speaking around the wound in her lip, the words tumbling more quickly. 'He's fast, really fast. *I'm* fast and he was well ahead of me. He's fit with a slim build.'

'That rules Connolly out then,' Molloy muttered.

'He wore a peaked cap, a wool one; like a cockney hat, do you know what I mean? He … he knew my name. He said it. And the thing about deserving it … could it be someone we arrested? Me and Adrian?'

'I don't know.' Molloy sat down on the edge of the bed again, seeming to favour it over the plastic chairs, his tea going untouched on the nearby table. 'The press has been all over this and every detail they can get is out in public for everyone to read. Your name is out there and everyone knows you were there when Clancy was killed.' His eyes found hers and he winced. 'Sorry. But it's true. And as for deserving it – lots of people carry grudges against us. Law enforcement riles up certain civilians; that's just the way it's always been. But the man who attacked you said he'd see you again. I don't like that.'

'Agreed. The things this man said to you are a lot more concerning when you add in the fact that he slashed your back,' Riordan said quietly.

Both men stared at Julia until she looked away, uncomfortable.

'You know what this means,' Riordan continued, his voice firm now. 'You're out of work until a doctor clears you and until I say so. And if and when I can get the resources for it, I'm arranging a Garda presence outside your house. Saying he'd see you again wasn't an empty threat, and I'm not taking any chances.'

Julia opened her mouth to protest but he leaned forward in the chair. 'And this time, I *will* fire you if you don't do what you're told!'

26

1994

The only good part of all of this for Julia was that Philip was speaking to her again, even if it was only perfunctory phrases without eye contact. His mouth dropped in shock when he first saw her in the hospital room, then he stared at her coldly for several minutes, grim-faced, his silent I-told-you-so hanging between them. He had worked with Julia's doctor before and hid his horror well when the man outlined the extent of her injuries. Philip read her charts and spoke to her doctor with the cool detachment he'd perfected as a general practitioner. Julia was advised to stay in hospital, but she begged Philip to take her home. He convinced the medics she was in safe hands, and they drove home in silence.

But when they stepped inside the front door of their home and he wrapped his arms around her, burying his face in her hair, she could feel the depth of his upset in his trembling body. His grip around her was tight, his arms in the middle of her back, careful to avoid the cut at her side.

She hugged him back with one arm, the other still secured to her chest with a sling.

'He could have killed you,' he whispered, holding her face in his hands. They were the same height – it was one of the things she loved about him. She could look straight into his eyes, always equal. Now his eyes were squeezed shut, tears leaking gently from underneath his eyelashes. 'I fucking told you! You could have died … that's the second time in less than a week!' He covered her face in gentle kisses, avoiding her lips.

'I know,' she whispered, feeling truly lucky and grateful to be safely back in her own home. 'I know.'

'This is it now, okay? Tell me this is the end of the line for you in this investigation; I don't want you obsessing over this any more! Please, Julia! I can't take another phone call like the one I got this afternoon.'

She nodded her agreement and hugged him again. She didn't have the energy to argue with him, or with Riordan who was so adamant she was to stay out of her colleagues' way while they hunted for this man. Right then, she was so tired she just needed to sleep. Most importantly, though, she needed Philip's love and support; at that moment she would have agreed to anything he might have asked of her.

He pulled back from her and gripped her chin gently, his eyes serious. 'If – when – you *do* go back to work, I want you to get a mobile phone.'

'What? Are you kidding?' She couldn't believe he was saying this – they had laughed together whenever they saw someone shouting into the devices in the street. 'We hate those things!'

'Come on, Julia – you'd be safer with one! Especially if

you go running off on your own chasing suspects into the woods.'

'But they're so expensive and I've heard the signal is really patchy around here. Not to mention I'd look like an idiot!' She groaned. 'I don't think so, Phil.'

'Fine.' He held up his hands. 'You and technology ... If you'd give it a chance it would make your life easier, you know. And if you insist on continuing on with—'

He stopped himself, and she was glad he hadn't ruined the moment. She sagged against him and he led her towards the stairs, to bed. Perhaps he was right; she could step away from this now, leave it to the others and return to cosy nights with Philip, sipping wine with him on the sofa in the living room, snuggling into his chest, catching up on their day. But then she remembered Mary Clancy at the front of the church, and the sound of the man's heavy breathing as he'd cut her skin. Turning away from this wasn't an option. Not yet.

Julia slept for almost twenty-four hours. She blamed the pain medication and Philip said it was the shock of the assault on her body. She had needed every minute of it – since Adrian had died, she had barely slept at all. When she woke, mid-afternoon the following day, Philip was sitting on the end of their bed, watching her.

'Hey.' Her tongue felt stuck to the roof of her mouth. It was hot under the quilt; the afternoon sunshine was bright, rendering the bedroom curtains ineffective against the glare.

'How are you feeling?' he asked, leaning over her, peering into her eyes, touching her lip. She groaned and pushed his hand away. Philip laughed. 'You'll live! It's a relief to see you're getting back to your stubborn self.' He kissed her forehead. 'I'm sorry about this but I've to go into the surgery later; I can't get out of it, it's a meeting we scheduled ages ago. Some of your colleagues are parked up outside, so I don't feel quite so bad about leaving you alone.'

'They are?' Julia groaned, pushing the covers back with her right hand, needing to cool down. Riordan hadn't wasted any time arranging protection outside the house. Philip helped her to stand up. She groaned as she moved her left arm to allow him to slot the sling back into place.

'How's the pain? Give me a number; one is mild, ten is unbearable.'

'It's about a three,' she said, closing her eyes against a fresh wave of it and reaching for his arm, steadying herself against him.

'Liar.' He stepped to her side and lifted her T-shirt gently, his fingers on the dressing on her back.

'How does it look?' She could remember the cool steel of the knife pressed against her face and the shock when it had pierced the flesh on her back. An image of Adrian gasping for life came to her and she shivered – this attack on her could have been so much worse. It was probably better not to dwell on that.

'Well, it's not bleeding through the dressing, so that's a start. I'll check it for infection.'

Julia tried to smile her gratitude as he got to work but it hurt her lips. Instead she whispered her thanks as she watched him in their bedroom mirror, watched his serious eyes and his gentle fingers, and felt relief at being enveloped in his love again.

Thirty minutes later, she was sitting at their kitchen table, nibbling a slice of toast and sipping tea through a straw. Her pain medication was lined up on the wooden table, waiting for Philip to decide she had eaten enough. 'It'll rip your stomach apart if you don't have something decent to eat!'

'Yes, doctor,' she muttered, but winked at him when he narrowed his eyes at her.

She'd managed to avoid looking in a mirror since she'd come home. Philip had gently washed her and pulled her dark brown hair into a ponytail, helping her dress in jogging pants, T-shirt and loose hoodie. She was cold; she'd have loved a blanket, but he was already doing so much for her that she decided not to ask.

'I've asked Kathleen to pop over and keep an eye on you while I go in to work later. The meeting should be wrapped up in a couple of hours. I hope that's okay?'

'What?' She spluttered tea onto her chin. 'No way, Phil! The woman has enough to do with Brendan. Absolutely not!' It was bad enough to be a victim without draining the energy of her elderly neighbour as well.

With a tea towel wrapped around his hands Phil pulled a casserole from the oven, dropping it hard onto the countertop, before tossing the towel towards her to clean herself up. He didn't look at her as he spoke. 'Come on, Julia, I'm tired of arguing with you about everything! Will you just agree with me on this?'

She stared at him, her eyes wide, feeling even colder in the midst of his sudden anger. Where was the loving husband who had tended to her wounds, who had made her feel safe?

'I don't argue with you about everything,' she said in a tiny voice, wiping the tea from her chin.

193

Philip pinched the bridge of his nose. 'You do realize you're now arguing with me about the fact that you don't argue with me?' She tried to smile at him but her lips hurt too much, and she realized there was no humour in his eyes anyway. With a sigh he moved across the kitchen and sat down beside her, winding his fingers around hers, his other hand tucking a loose strand of hair behind her ear. 'I miss you. When have we last gone out on the boat together? You never want to, it seems like you're always working.'

Where was this coming from? 'I'd love to go out on the boat and I will. There's just been a lot of overtime and now this investigation ... I will, Philip, I said I would.'

His eyes met hers and she held his gaze, knowing for sure that what was on his mind had nothing to do with the small fishing boat his grandfather had left him.

'All right. Well, Kathleen said she's happy to come over – we do enough for her. She doesn't actually have to *do* anything; dinner is here, just eat it when it's cool enough. All I want is for someone to make sure you haven't fainted or anything. She said she'd pop in a couple of times, that's all. She won't stay long. I'll only be gone for a couple of hours.'

'Are you ... are you checking up on me? Making sure I don't go in to work?'

He looked into her eyes. 'Are you planning to?'

'No! I can hardly move!'

'Good! And don't go ringing your boss again either. We could do without you getting fired. Just be nice to Kathleen when she comes over and try to get some rest.' His tone carried the finality that his mind was made up, the plan was decided, and therefore she should agree.

Julia's voice rose in frustration. 'Look, Phil, I'd really rather Kathleen didn't call!'

He released her hand and clenched his teeth together in annoyance. 'Well you can't stay here on your own. And I can't get anyone else at this short notice.'

Julia pulled the corner off the slice of toast and popped it into her mouth, chewing slowly. There was one place she could go – it wasn't that far from his surgery and it would mean keeping her promise to call in as often as she could.

'How about you drop me to Mary Clancy's?'

27

1994

The upheaval of their loss inside the Clancy household was evident in how the children watched their mother, how she moved too slowly and never seemed to focus on anything for long. As soon as she arrived, Julia wanted to leave, to cocoon herself away from the sadness inside his home, but she knew she'd never turn away from Adrian's family. She didn't know why she was alive while he was dead – so she would sit here amid their pain and take her penance.

Useless fucking bitch.

When Mary opened the front door to them, the baby on her hip and two younger children beside her, her relief at greeting another adult was quickly replaced by horror at seeing Julia's face. She told the children she'd fallen over; they readily believed her, even fifteen-year-old Shauna, who flicked through a magazine with only scant interest in her father's work colleague. Philip had wrapped the casserole in towels to keep it warm and he brought it to the Clancys's kitchen table before he said goodbye. But as they all sat around the table, enjoying the food, Mary watched her carefully, her expression fearful. Julia knew she was wondering if her injuries had something to do with Adrian's killer.

After dinner, Shauna left to babysit for a neighbour. While Julia read the younger children bedtime stories and tucked them in, Mary had a bath, bringing the baby with her to sit in her bouncy chair in the bathroom. Once the other children were settled, Julia made her way back downstairs and into the small living room. Everything was now back in its proper place after Adrian's wake, except nothing seemed right inside the house.

'Are you all right, Julia?'

Mary had returned with baby Audrey on her hip. Julia realized she had one hand over her mouth, her eyes cast down, thinking about the earlier argument with Philip; she straightened on the sofa and smiled as best she could around the cut on her lip.

'Thanks, Mary, I'm grand. Just tired. Are you okay?'

Mary didn't answer, but settled herself onto the sofa beside Julia, adjusting the buttons on her blouse. Her hair was still wet, wound into a bun at the nape of her neck, soaking a half-moon sliver on her pale blue blouse. She brought the baby to her breast; Julia watched one tiny hand rubbing her mother's skin as she suckled. She turned her head away, unable to look at them for too long before feeling a surging anger at what Adrian had been denied – this family, this future.

'So, can you tell me what really happened to your face and your arm?'

Julia rubbed the soft material of her sling with her

fingertips; did this woman need any further horror in her life? But at least if Julia told her what had happened, she would know the Gardaí were doing everything they could to catch Adrian's killer. It might be a comfort. She decided to tell Mary everything.

'Nothing surprises me any more,' Mary said angrily, shaking her head. 'There are some terrible people in this world and for some reason, we're all caught up in this saga with one of them. You could have been killed, Jules!'

Julia wished everyone would stop saying that. And she wished Mary wouldn't use the nickname Adrian had given her; it made her uncomfortable. She shifted in her seat, the heat of the fire making her feel sleepy; as the baby dozed at her mother's breast, and Mary stared silently into the flames in the hearth, Julia felt her eyelids droop.

'Do you mind if I open the door, Mary? The pain meds I'm on are knocking me out and I could do with some air.'

Julia pulled the door open, sticking her head into the hallway for some cooler air, straining an ear for the other children upstairs. Everyone was silent, hopefully asleep. She walked back to the sofa and sat down gingerly; she could feel the pain of her injuries flare to life again, letting her know it was almost time for more medication. If Philip were to ask her now for a number on the pain scale, it would be a solid nine. Mary winced sympathetically as Julia settled back against the cushions.

'It must be so painful – whatever is the point of slashing someone's skin?'

'We think it's some kind of ritual thing he does, like, to mark his victims before taking them. He cut the two girls he killed a few days before they disappeared.' Just saying this aloud, for the first time, sent a ripple of fear over her skin. Yesterday, she had been … *marked*.

Mary's eyes were wide; the baby whimpered and she adjusted her to the other breast.

'Julia, that's horrific!'

'I know.'

'What does this mean for you?'

'It means I get Garda protection at my house, which is just mortifying. I can imagine the comments at the station.'

'This person is obviously crazy!' Mary was crying suddenly, tears spilling fast down her cheeks. 'Take your protection, Julia. My poor Adrian didn't stand a chance! Why did he have to—'

She started up in the seat at the sound of a firm knock at the front door.

'Oh that'll be Shauna. She doesn't have a key.' She wiped her eyes roughly with the back of one hand.

'Or it might be Philip. I'll go.' Julia shuffled forward, suppressing a moan of pain as she rose from the sofa. In the hallway she pulled open the front door, confusion mounting as the man in front of her asked if he could come inside. He carried a hat in one hand and he tapped it against his thigh as he waited for her to pull open the door fully. He was agitated, impatient, his eyes roaming over her bruised and cut face, over her sling.

'Look, I need to speak to Mary.'

'Is that you, John?' Mary called from behind Julia, appearing with the baby over her shoulder, rubbing her back in circles. 'What are you doing here?'

'Can I come in?' he appealed to her.

'Of course!' Mary nodded to Julia, who stepped aside to

allow the man into the hall. Mary led the way back into the living room. 'Is everything all right?'

John – a neighbour Julia now recognized from his presence in the house after Adrian's death – looked uncomfortable. They all stood in a little circle inside the living room, no one moving to sit.

'Look this is awkward, Mary,' her neighbour started, just as she interrupted to ask, 'Is Shauna not with you?'

'It's about Shauna that I'm here,' John said, his neck and face blotchy and red. 'Look, I know you've had a terrible time of it. And poor Shauna too. But she can't just up and leave, not until we come back! The little ones were hysterical, alone in the house! Claire has been trying to settle them for the last fifteen minutes!'

'What? What do you mean "up and leave"?' Mary looked at him, confusion drawing her eyebrows together.

'Shauna! She left early. Like, I mean, she has to wait for us to get back!'

'No ... she'd never do that!'

Suddenly Mary thrust the baby at Julia and ran from the room, her footsteps thudding loudly on the carpeted stairs. With her left arm bound in a sling, Julia clutched Audrey to her tightly with her right arm. The baby gazed up at her with the same pale green eyes as her father's. John didn't say anything, just continued to tap his hat against his thigh, looking around him awkwardly.

In less than a minute Mary rushed back into the room, taking the baby again, her face flushed.

'She's not in the house! But we'd have heard her come back ... I don't understand! She'd never leave your kids alone, she loves them! She'd never let any harm come to them!'

Julia didn't like this – from chatting to Adrian in the car over the last eight years, she knew a lot about his family. She knew his oldest daughter was conscientious, had babysat for her neighbours for the last six months, and was more mature than her fifteen years. Certainly over the last week she had had to grow up faster. It was so far out of character for Shauna to leave the children in her charge that Julia felt a spike of anxiety. Audrey had begun to cry and Mary rocked her in her arms, pacing.

John scratched the back of his neck, looking embarrassed. 'I'm sorry, Mary – I just assumed she had come home. That maybe she was upset, like.'

'All right, let's stay calm.' Julia heard the strength in her voice, despite her mounting alarm. 'I'm sure Shauna had a reason to step outside, and she probably got delayed. John, could you drive around a bit, have a look out for her? Mary, you stay here in case she comes home. And I'll—'

There was a sound at the living room door; they all turned to find Dermot, Shauna's younger brother, standing in the door frame in his pyjamas, his face streaked with tears.

'What is it, Dermot?' Mary asked, her voice a frantic cry.

'I heard you. I heard what you said about Shauna.' He sniffed and wiped his face with the sleeve of his pyjama top. Julia stepped closer to him.

'It's okay, Dermot. Shauna's not in any trouble. We'd just like to find her, that's all. It's not like her to leave her babysitting job before the correct time.' He stared up at her, his eyes wide. 'Do you know where she is?'

Dermot shook his head quickly.

'But do you know something that might help us find her?'

His lips were trembling as he gripped the door frame tightly; Julia placed a hand on his shoulder and crouched down to look into his eyes, silencing a groan of pain. 'Dermot. We're worried. If you know anyth—'

'For God's sake, Dermot!' Mary shouted.

He jumped, whimpering. 'Someone hurt her.' The words tumbled from his mouth as he sobbed loudly. 'Someone followed her and cut her back. It wasn't a bad cut. I put a plaster on it. She made me promise not to tell you! She said you had enough to worry about.'

For a brief moment the room stilled and Julia stared at him open-mouthed; then the loud throb of her pulse in her ears brought her back to her senses. She stepped into the hallway and picked up the phone. Her mind was strangely blank. She dialled the only phone number at the station that she could remember, the phone near her own desk on the ground floor.

'Hello Cork city Gar—'

'This is Garda Julia Harte; I need immediate assistance.'

'Julia? It's Shay. Are you all right?'

She felt weak with relief, thinking, *Thank God!*

She explained to him everything that was happening and everything that she needed, while behind her, Mary screamed her anguish, over and over.

28

1994

After the initial hours spent in the Clancy home supporting Mary while the detectives asked their questions, Julia was told to step back from the investigation yet again. Riordan had directed her to return home and heal; Philip was delighted to have overheard the instruction. He refused to drive her back to Mary's or anywhere else, insisting she needed time to rest and recover. She stopped speaking to him, and with little choice but to rest and ruminate, the void between them grew deeper.

She hated each second that passed; there were too many clocks in their house, each one ticking louder than the other. If she had been physically able to she would have removed them all. But the cut on her back had reached the itchy healing stage and the pain in her shoulder returned whenever she moved her left arm. Her mind raced day and night; Shauna Clancy was missing, suffering God knows what, and Julia could do nothing to help her.

The guilt gnawed at her, a painful burning sensation that

rushed up her throat; each dart of physical discomfort was her punishment. At night she couldn't sleep but lay beside Philip, listening to his steady breathing, ignoring the sleeping tablets he had insisted she take, the vial resting untouched on her bedside locker. Instead, she moved downstairs to sit and listen to the clocks, to look out the living room window and watch Brendan Adlington aim his flashlight into the dark, to try to think her way into making sense of all this.

This was personal, it *felt* personal. But why?

By day, she called the station. Sometimes Des Riordan took her calls, but only to assure her that everything that could be done *was* being done. Every Garda, and as many civilians as they could gather, was searching for Shauna Clancy. There was a press conference. There were calls for all citizens in Cork city and county to search their garages and outhouses. He was 'turning over every stone' but she was still missing, vanished without trace.

He had secured permission and resources to keep a Garda car stationed outside her house. Julia hated the sight of the car parked near her gate, hated the crushing embarrassment of a Garda needing protection. From time to time she walked to the car with fresh cups of tea, an offer to use the bathroom and a mumbled apology at the inconvenience of it all. The young men in the car could never offer any updates on the case. And Philip watched it all with the quiet stoicism of a man who knew that as every second passed he was being proved right.

Julia felt she could explode with rage and frustration.

Late in the evening of the second day after Shauna's disappearance, she heard Philip's key in the front door lock and sat up straighter on the sofa, the rug she had placed over her knees earlier falling to the ground. As she bent down to pick it up, moaning with the pain of stretching the skin on her lower back, she stopped – she could hear two male voices. Philip was greeting someone, letting him inside. She recognized that voice. When he pushed open the living room door her mouth was curled into a sour twist.

'You've a visitor. Julia, are you all right?'

'Connolly,' she said coldly, her eyes narrowed. 'What do you want?'

Philip's eyebrows rose in surprise but he didn't say anything. She ignored him, ignored the fact that he was probably thinking this was more of what he called her 'atypical' behaviour. She'd never told him about the subtle ways that Connolly made her feel uncomfortable. Some of it was so understated, she wondered if she could even put it into words.

Jim Connolly stood in the doorway, an awkward grimace on his face. 'Hey, Julia.' His voice was cautious. Was he nervous? 'Mind if we have a chat?'

She half shrugged, only able to move her right shoulder. Philip gestured for the other man to take a seat and offered him a drink, a cup of tea or something stronger. Connolly shook his head as he settled into the armchair. *He's definitely nervous*, Julia thought with a rush of pleasure that quickly turned into panic. Why was he here? Was there news of Shauna Clancy?

Her fear must have been apparent because Connolly quickly raised both hands as if to ward off her unspoken questions. 'First of all, everyone's fine and I've no news. Nothing to report.'

She exhaled. 'So what are you doing here? I mean, why *you*?'

Philip was staring at her open-mouthed now from the corner of the room; she was pretty sure he'd never heard her speak like this to anyone before. She continued to ignore him. Connolly sat back against the cushions and she studied his face, realizing she'd spent so much of her time in his company lately trying to block him out that she didn't know much about him at all. She guessed now that he was in his mid-fifties. He was quite overweight; flesh pooled over the neck of his shirt and his stomach hung over his dark suit trousers and protruded in gaps between the buttons of his shirt. She wasn't surprised he hadn't been able to catch up with her outside the church – if he had been telling the truth about that. His eyes followed her gaze and he folded his suit jacket across his stomach.

'I'm here because Riordan asked me to check in on you.' His eyes tracked over her face. 'You're looking better.' She knew she looked awful; the swelling was reduced but dark purple bruises discoloured her face.

'Well you can tell him I'm fine. *And* that I'll be back at work soon!' She ignored Philip's incredulous stare. 'How's Mary Clancy? I get an engaged tone at the house any time I telephone.'

'The phone's being kept off the hook.'

'Why? That doesn't make any sense! Surely—'

'She's been getting some prank calls; heavy breathing and so on. Some sicko getting his kicks.'

'But what if Shauna calls! What if—'

'It's been decided that's unlikely to happen. There's a team down from Dublin now and they've effectively taken

206

this out of our hands.' He puffed out his cheeks. 'You're better off here to be honest.'

'I've been saying that for days, but—'

She cut Philip off mid-sentence with a glare. 'How am I better off here doing nothing?'

Connolly shuffled forward in the armchair again, his eyes finding Julia's. 'Well, that's why I came. Riordan thinks you could start making yourself useful.'

Philip stepped forward, about to protest. Julia wished he weren't here right now; the doctor and the husband in him wasn't helping. 'Go on,' she urged Connolly, adrenaline jump-starting her heart. If Riordan wanted her checked up on, he could have had someone telephone the house. Sending Connolly was a strange move. 'Where's Steven Molloy, by the way?'

'He's at the Clancy house. The rest of the children are staying with relatives. Mary's lost her mind, poor woman. She's shouting and crying all day long, refusing to take anything her doctor prescribed.' He shook his head, as though disappointed in her. 'Apparently, Molloy has a gentler bedside manner, so he got to stay there while I drew this particularly short straw.'

Julia snorted; *there you are, Connolly*, she thought. She stared at him, willing him to get to the point.

'Anyway, Riordan is convinced this is personal to the Gardaí. Specifically, personal to you and Adrian Clancy. We're pretty certain now that the supposed sighting of Louise Hynes and Jeanette Coyle in the city was a prank. There were no witnesses who could remember seeing anyone like the girls, and no one would admit to phoning the station about it. Molloy and myself were all set to go check out the report about girls crying in a house, only the sighting at the hostel was deemed priority. But it was a fake.'

'So, let me get this straight,' Philip interrupted, sitting down beside Julia, his arms folded tightly. 'You think this was a set-up? But they sent Julia and Adrian because the guy who called about the crying had previously made crank calls, right?'

'Right,' Connolly confirmed. 'It seemed likely that this latest call was more of the same. So it was assigned to you two. Ye were the only other guards in the area at the time.'

'But who would have known that?'

'Any number of people really.' Connolly spread his hands wide and shrugged.

'What are you saying?' Julia sat forward, pain stealing her breath. She felt Philip's hand on her arm but brushed it off. 'Do you mean Adrian and I were sent there deliberately? That someone was waiting for us? But that would mean one of our own sent us there, knowing that—'

Connolly raised his hands again, pushing against the air. 'Hold on! Hold on! No one's saying that this was a set-up from inside the station. There were actually four reported sightings of the girls called in that night. So there were five sites that Gardaí would have been present. If the killer was looking to kill a guard then that's a pretty good way to go about it, but he couldn't have known which ones would be sent where. This is all new information, for you, I get that. We're unravelling this, but too slowly for Riordan's liking.'

Julia stared at him, stunned.

'So he, whoever did this, was planning to kill a Garda and lured us out? Do you think that's why he took the girls in the first place?'

'It's certainly possible. It's been a theory in the station the whole time.'

'But why do you think this is specific to me and Adrian?'

'I'm not sure that I do. It's just an idea. The man that slashed your back – he said you deserved it, "you both" deserved it. Are you sure it was that? Could it have been "you *all*" do?'

Julia blinked, trying to think. 'No, I'm pretty sure it was *both*. Why?' Philip was staring at her so hard she imagined she could feel hot flecks of anger bounce onto her skin. She hadn't told him about that part of the night she was attacked.

'Riordan and the team from Dublin are considering whether this is a targeted attack against the guards in general or something particular to you and Clancy. Which is why I'm here.' He sighed, looking as exhausted as she felt. 'You need to think back over all your old cases, everything you and Clancy worked on.'

'Oh come on!' She laughed incredulously. 'Adrian and I worked together for eight years! Do you know how many different incidents we worked on? It must run into hundreds! This will be impossible!'

'Well you'd better make it possible because this is all we have to go on. It could help find Shauna Clancy, and to be frank, time is in short supply here. If the pattern repeats, she has two days before her body turns up.'

'But … we did the grunt work. That's what Adrian called it. The run-of-the-mill stuff. Nothing we worked on could be related to this, I'm sure of it!'

'Maybe you're right, I don't know.' He patted his pockets and pulled out a packet of cigarettes.

'Don't think about lighting up in here,' Philip said coldly, and Connolly scowled, muttering under his breath as he put the packet away again.

'Look, Clancy is dead, you were attacked, and now Clancy's daughter is taken. If we can't figure out the common denominator in this that girl will be dead soon. I don't care if it's bike theft, some domestic dispute ye got stuck into the middle of, even some drunken lunatic ye arrested – you'll have to try to find something that stands out.'

'Well, if Riordan would let me back in to the station—'

'Absolutely not!' Philip said at the same time as Connolly frowned, saying, 'I really wouldn't cross Riordan right now. That man is a walking coronary. Maybe if you think of something, come on in, but for now, he says you're to stay put here so that's what you'll do.'

Pressure wrapped around Julia's chest like a tightening belt. Eight years of Garda work meant an awful lot of cases had been opened, closed and filed away. Connolly was saying Shauna's life could depend on it, but how on earth could she remember each incident she and Adrian had worked on?

'It might help to write things down.' He seemed to be reading her mind. 'Plus, it'd be worth remembering that this guy seems a little obsessed with you. You walked away from him twice, but only because he let you. If I were you I'd assume you'll meet him a third time and things might end differently.'

Philip jumped to his feet. 'This is absolutely ridiculous!' He stalked to the mantelpiece and leaned against it, his eyes blazing, his face burning with anger. 'This is too dangerous! Look at her – look at her face! Look at what he's already done to her, and now you're saying it'll happen again? What are you lot going to do about protecting my wife?'

Connolly pointed to the window. The Garda car was still parked outside, two silhouettes visible in the gloomy darkness of evening turning to night.

'Two fucking young fellas in uniform?' Philip blustered. 'That's it?'

'Best we can do. Talk to the boss if you're not happy; it's nothing to do with me!'

'I'll have to stay off work – Julia, why the hell didn't you tell me this man had threatened you? This is just unbelievable!'

Julia had never expected to feel anything but disdain in Jim Connolly's company, but when he stood up and stepped towards her husband, she began to suspect she might feel grateful for his forthrightness.

'No disrespect, but this is a high-stress situation already. Can we not add your hysterics into the mix?'

In the end, he stayed for dinner. The evening was spent around the dining table, her husband and her least-favourite work colleague discussing the All-Ireland Hurling Championship and whether the Cork team had a chance of coming back next year. She watched them silently, chewing her food but tasting nothing; the pain in her head was strong enough to pull her from the conversation often and she excused herself to get more painkillers midway through the meal. She wasn't sure either man noticed she had left and she didn't hurry back.

Leaning over the sink in the kitchen, she hoped to vomit, praying for relief. But nothing happened – it was as though her body was refusing to heal and let her get on with living.

Turning on the cold tap she held her right wrist underneath it, letting the icy water pound onto her veins. She imagined Shauna Clancy, scared and alone, being held somewhere in the dark. Waiting to die.

'I'm going to head back,' Connolly said from the kitchen doorway, making her jump. She turned off the tap and dried her wrist on her jumper. 'Okay. Listen, tell Mary I'm thinking of her, will you?'

He nodded, muttering, 'If she will listen to a word anyone says,' as they walked towards the front door.

The cold air of the night invaded the house as Julia and Philip stood at the front door, Connolly on the step outside. The squad car was parked conspicuously outside the gate, Connolly's car behind it.

'So, what's the actual plan here?' Philip nodded towards the car where the two Gardaí were sitting stiffly inside. 'They just sit there all day and all night?'

'That's it, they sit tight.' Connolly pulled the packet of cigarettes from his jacket pocket again, drew one out and lit it, cupping his hand around the lighter against the wind. A small moan of pleasure escaped as he exhaled. He plucked a stray piece of tobacco from his tongue as he continued. 'Unless they see anything suspicious, in which case they do something about it.' He shrugged. 'Not a gig I'd fancy.'

'It's very … obvious,' Julia said, shivering.

'That's the whole point.' He blew smoke into the air again, his face angled towards the night sky. His head turned to the right, his attention caught by something. 'What's that?' He pointed to the Adlingtons's house, one finger crooked around his cigarette.

Julia looked towards her neighbours's house with a

212

pang of guilt – she hadn't been over there since she'd been attacked. 'That's our neighbours, the Adlingtons. Brendan was in the navy; he flashes lights at night.'

'Isn't that Morse code?' Connolly pulled deeply on the cigarette again. She shrugged; he had taken up enough of her time. She just wanted him to go.

'Right,' Connolly turned to look at her again, 'I'll leave you to it. Try to remember everything you can. Maybe write it all down, like I said – I find that always helps.'

The last thing she would do was take advice from *him*, she thought sourly as she turned to go back inside.

Philip went straight to bed, alone, too angry with her to speak. Julia cleared away the dishes and tidied up as best she could with one hand. In the kitchen she leaned against the counter, shoulders slumped – whoever this guy was, he had really done a number on her, as Connolly had said. He had reduced her to a shell of the woman that had sprinted after him. She shook her head to stop imagining what Shauna Clancy might be suffering.

In the living room she half-filled a crystal glass with brandy; their one remaining wedding-present glass. The first swallow was the hardest and stung her lip, the second spread fire into her chest. Pushing two cushions behind her back, she opened a notebook, selecting a blank page.

'Right, help me out here, Adrian. I don't think this has anything to do with a car theft or a parking fine. What else did we get up to?'

29

2024

'Armstrong should really have waited for us,' Riordan grumbles as Julia pulls out of the Garda car park and onto the main road; they're keen to catch up with Armstrong and the others on their way to the Carmichael Estate. She can't decide if the claustrophobic catch in her throat is the growing familiarity of the city or the escalation in the case.

Riordan leans back in the seat, not waiting for an answer; Julia doesn't care whether Armstrong is going to keep them in the loop or not. They've built enough of a rapport with the rest of the team not to let his bruised ego worry them. What does concern her is that another young woman was *marked* and is not answering her phone, and worse, her home is in a place called the Carmichael Estate. Julia doesn't believe in coincidences and she's not about to start, but there seem to be an awful lot of them in this case already.

The hospital has been able to provide only scant

information; the young woman is a twenty-year-old named Grace York. She told the nurse who tended to her that she had met friends in the city and parked her car by the quay near Morrison's Island. Just after one in the morning, as she walked back to her car, she was attacked. There are street cameras in the area and those are being examined now back at the station. Julia is confident they will find answers; she just hopes they can find them quickly enough to save her life.

'Can you look up the Carmichael Estate, Des?' she asks, her eyes on his in the rear-view mirror. 'I know where it is, of course, but what's the story with it? All I know is that it was a run-down, hundreds-of-years-old English manor that was overgrown and in disrepair.'

'I remember it. It's not like any of us could forget what happened there!' he says, pulling out his mobile phone.

Everyone that worked on the Cox case remembers that place. After a minute spent tapping on his phone, Riordan speaks again. 'Okay, according to this website, the construction on the old Carmichael Estate commenced in 2005 after a sale agreement was reached between a Dublin property developer and the only living descendant of Lord Carmichael. Forty properties were constructed on the estate, in three distinctive styles, around a rectangular-shaped green area, which was not as large as was hoped, owing to the discovery of a fairy ring fort on the grounds.' He looks up. 'Best not to disturb the energy there.'

'There's enough bad energy in that place already,' Julia murmurs. The pain in her shoulder is a weak whimper, but strong enough to remind her it's still there. She's carried that day for thirty years.

215

'Anyway, the houses are described as being of exclusive design and having all mod-cons and sold for well over the asking price for newly built homes in the area.' He whistles loudly. 'There's money here.'

'Well it's not Grace York's money, she was a baby at the time. But someone owns the house and must be missing her.'

He doesn't answer and she flexes her foot on the accelerator.

The Carmichael Estate used to sit behind imposing stone pillars that had crumbled over time, the whole place shrouded in darkness and shadow. Now, what was once an overgrown ruin is manicured and restored into something that looks like a feature in a property magazine. As Julia drives through the entrance she feels nothing being back here apart from the anticipation of discovering how far this might go.

She parks behind a squad car; the York house is ahead on the right-hand side, in a row of identical detached houses with near-identical driveways in front. Rows of shrubs and plants flank every driveway in such a uniform way, she assumes a gardening contractor looks after it all. That'll need to be checked in case the gardeners have anything of value to add to the investigation. Assuming there will be an investigation and Grace York is missing; every muscle in her body vibrates with the anticipatory certainty that the house in front of them is about to be declared a crime scene.

She climbs out of the car and walks beside Riordan, approaching the house. Armstrong is at the front door, Saoirse O'Reilly and two uniformed Gardaí hanging back by the cars. Though there's a car parked in the driveway, it's clear Armstrong isn't getting an answer; he cups his hands around his eyes and peers through the window of a room at the front of the house. Julia spots an elderly man watching them from his front door, two doors up.

'Good morning, sir,' she calls to him and walks halfway up his driveway. His expression isn't welcoming but isn't so hostile she rethinks approaching him. 'I'm with the Gardaí. We're looking for your neighbour, Grace York; have you seen her today or over the last few days?'

The man doesn't look inclined to answer, pursing his lips and turning his head back into the house, closing the door slowly. Wearing a light parka, he's dressed to go out but appears to have changed his mind. When Julia spots a thin brown lead hanging from his hand she whistles softly, and sure enough, a brown-and-white Jack Russell darts from behind the man's legs. She hunkers down to catch the dog, rubbing his back, surreptitiously pulling one of Mutt's treats from her pocket, and lets him lick it from her hand. The man will have to engage with her now, one way or another.

'Oscar!' he shouts, demanding the dog return, but Julia holds tight to his collar. 'Oscar, get back here right now!' He steps out onto the driveway so he and Julia are within touching distance. She can see the anger in his face.

'Sir? We need to locate Grace York.' She gestures to Armstrong and the others outside her front door. 'We're investigating the murder of two young women and we need to check on the safety of your neighbour. Can you help us or should I consider it interesting that you won't?'

She straightens up and lets the dog go; Oscar sits down

beside her, earning a frown from his master, who looks like a man backed into a corner.

'I want nothing to do with that family!' He speaks so low, Julia has to lean forward to hear him. 'Parties non-stop, day and bloody night! She's one of those "party girls". Joan and I want nothing to do with them!'

'Is Joan your wife?'

He sighs, knowing he has no choice but to answer her questions. 'Yes, Joan and Richard Bradbury. We moved here in 2006, we were one of the first families to move in. Paid an arm and a leg for it, and we didn't mind because it's far enough away from the city, you know? And then *that* family moved in.'

'When was this?'

'In 2010. She was small then, a pleasant little thing, very quiet. She seemed afraid of me, if I'm honest, although I never gave her reason. She has two older brothers and they were an absolute—' He stops himself from finishing the sentence. 'Anyway, the parents upped and left a few years after that and—'

'What do you mean they left?'

His cheeks grow red and his eyes flick back towards his front door. 'Look – I don't want to be involved. All I know is, her mother is running some type of catering company in London and by Christ did her brothers make full use of the empty house! Things have calmed down a bit now, but the guards have been here a few times. Joan had to call it in, we had no choice. Noise pollution is what it was!'

Julia holds up her hands, trying to calm Richard Bradbury down. The insight he's giving her into Grace York and her family is interesting, but not her pressing concern.

'Mr Bradbury, have you seen Grace York this week?'

'No I have not!' he blusters. 'I notice her car is in the drive – brand new, nothing is too expensive for Daddy's little rich girl – but if you can't get inside, Joan has a key.'

'She does?'

'Mrs York gave it to us for emergencies. Although, to be quite honest ...' His voice fades as Julia glares at him; he's wasting her time. 'The key?'

A few minutes later, with the jagged metal edges of the York's front door key pressing into her hand, Julia jogs across to the driveway. Riordan and Armstrong are standing opposite each other, the Gardaí nearby looking anywhere but at the two men. Riordan is speaking, his voice the low growl she remembers from the past, his Northern Irish accent always strongest when he was angry.

'Whether you respect me or not, Armstrong, I'm giving you solid advice here and it was learned the hard way. I know you're unhappy that we're here, that your superintendent told you to include us. You don't have to like it, but you can stop acting like a brat and keep us informed.'

'I hate to interrupt, gentlemen, but I have a key to the door, so if you wouldn't mind stepping aside?'

Riordan wipes at spittle that has gathered on his lips; Armstrong turns away, his hands on his hips, muttering too low for her to hear. Shaking her head, Julia steps forward, her hand outstretched; with a gasp she stops, her legs unable to move further. She hasn't seen the front door until now. The key trembles in her hand as she looks at the deep burnt-orange painted door, with the number of the house illustrated by calligraphic figures painted in black on the left-hand side. It's number thirty-six. She feels like the two numbers, one lower than the other, stencilled in thick paint, are burning through her flesh.

'Des,' she whispers. When he's standing beside her she drags her eyes away from the door and looks at him, shaking. 'The house in Douglas where we found Louise Hynes. Where Adrian was killed while I was inside ... it was number thirty-six ...'

He presses his lips together, all the blood draining from his face.

'He's copying everything, Des ...'

'Armstrong!' he bellows, making Julia jump, 'Call it in and ask for back-up.' The confidence of decades of experience is ingrained in his voice. The other man takes only a second to decide to cooperate; he pulls out his phone and steps a little to the left, away from the door.

'We'll need shoe covers, hair covers, gloves, the lot,' Riordan continues, turning to the nearby Gardaí. 'You know the drill, folks. Look with your eyes only unless absolutely necessary and be thorough! We are looking for Grace York, preferably alive.'

Julia forces herself to push the key into the lock and open the door, bracing for the wail of a security alarm. Nothing, which is unusual in a house like this, a house with 'all mod-cons'. Gloves and shoe covers are passed to her and she pulls them on, reaching inside to flick on a hall light.

'The power is out,' she says to Riordan, who is pulling on his own set of shoe covers.

As her foot crosses the threshold of number thirty-six her heart thuds hard in her chest. The last time she stepped into a house in these circumstances, Adrian's life ended and her own changed forever. The same house number, the power cut, two girls slashed on the lower back in the days leading up to their murder … it's all happening again. Julia has no idea why anyone would redo the crimes of someone else. Perhaps the answer lies inside the house of a missing young woman.

30

2024

They quickly establish Grace York is not inside her home. Julia's eyes travel over the space inside the front door; dark wood panels flank the walls and the head of a dead stag is mounted high a few feet away. The nearby staircase is wide, walnut and made for dramatically swooshing down with a drink in hand. This is a house designed for entertaining, for being full of people. But according to Grace York's neighbour, only one person lives here. There's a familiar loneliness to the air inside the house that Julia pushes away.

'In here!' Armstrong calls out. She and Riordan follow his voice into the living room. This area is lighter, the wooden wall panelling painted cream with matching leather furniture. A wooden drinks cabinet stands in one corner, a bookshelf in another. A spray of red mist stains one wall – blood. A crystal decanter lies broken on the floor, the alcohol it once contained spilled onto a cream wool rug. Armstrong removes one glove and rubs the wool with his fingertips.

'It's dry.'

'Shit!' Julia stoops down, noting a dry red stain on a shard of crystal that lies on the floor. 'She was attacked here.'

She stands up, takes a deep breath, feeling a tightening urgency to find this young woman alive.

'I presume you've taken DNA samples from Daunt?' Riordan asks, as though reading her mind.

'Obviously,' Armstrong answers, 'but he has an alibi, remember?'

'Doesn't mean he's not behind this. You should search his property right now.'

Armstrong strides from the room without a word, loudly snapping a fresh glove onto his hand. Julia follows him out, but he's moving purposely to the back of the house, his shoulders stiff. He doesn't seem like a man in the mood for a conversation, so she detours to the stairs.

Sunlight streams through large rectangular windows, casting long shadows onto the wooden steps and the cream walls around her. This house is light and airy, filled with the voices of other Gardaí. It's a world away from the other number thirty-six that she searched thirty years ago, listening to the cries of a young girl, terrified and alone in the dark. On the landing, she decides to start on the left and work her way round to the right. It's easy to identify which bedroom is Grace's parents', namely due to the male and female clothing in the closet – trouser suits, evening dresses, leather shoes and handbags, expensive jewellery. The clothes are pristine, as though they are kept here for rare and special occasions but otherwise seldom used. Two other bedrooms are soulless voids which could belong to sons who rarely return home or could be designated as guest bedrooms; cream bedding, en-suite bathrooms with high-end toiletries, closets containing blankets and extra pillows but nothing else. She makes a mental note to find out where every member of this family lives and why Grace lives here completely alone. She realizes there's a noticeable lack of photographs inside this house, as though the people it belongs to don't care to remember the past, or each other. Anything decorating the walls is artwork, nothing personal. It strikes her as incredibly sad. As Riordan said earlier, there's money here, but it seems there's not much love.

Grace's bedroom is the only room that appears lived in. Her curtains are drawn and the quilt on her bed is pushed back, as though she got out of bed and never returned to straighten up. There's enough light from the hallway for Julia to look around with ease; her closet is full of clothes and shoes, nothing unusual. Trainers with mud on the soles rest on the wooden floor beside the bed; these will be bagged up and examined, to see if they can identify where she might have been over the last few days. A mobile phone rests on the bedside locker; Julia touches one gloved finger to the screen and it lights up, showing a photograph of two young women with their faces pressed together, grinning for a selfie. The screen shows forty-one missed calls. Julia's heart sinks. A framed photo collage on the wall shows the same blonde woman with dark brown eyes in a variety of poses with friends, most of which appear to be at a party or club. This must be Grace; none of these photos will be suitable for the public appeal Sadie Horgan will launch soon. They need to search the house for some proper photographs.

'I think she was disturbed overnight,' Riordan says from the doorway, 'but which night is the question. She hasn't been seen in days.' She can hear the effort of climbing the stairs in his voice. Perhaps it's the argument with Armstrong earlier, but he looks more tired than before. She knows better than to ask him if he's all right.

'It certainly looks that way,' she answers, stepping towards a cluttered desk near the bed. An open laptop, the screen blank, has several sticky notes on the edges.

Call mum

PSYC ESSAY 1/10

'She's a student,' she says, looking at a stack of books on the desk. 'Was she studying straight psychology?'

'Criminal psychology.' Armstrong turns into the room, his eyes on Riordan. His lips twitch in what could be construed as an apology or maybe just acknowledgement; Riordan nods. Armstrong looks around the room as he continues. 'I'm just off the phone from Horgan. Grace York hasn't attended her lectures over the last three days. She's on the same course as Elena Kehoe and Hannah Miller.'

'She's twenty years old; is that old these days to be in first year?' Riordan asks. Armstrong doesn't answer. 'At least we have a link!'

'Possibly. Every day on the calendar in the kitchen is ticked off except for the last three – so Grace has been missing since the day before Elena and Hannah's bodies were found.'

'Do you think she's still alive?'

'It's impossible to say.' Armstrong doesn't make eye contact with either of them, preferring to look around the room as he speaks. 'Nothing seems random about this case. A lot of things relate back to the file I read on Cox. Like the house number; number thirty-six. That links back to his first kill in 1994. That and the power cut, plus how the two women died, it all plays into the theory that this is a copycat. He took another girl back then, didn't he?'

'Yes, Shauna Clancy. Adrian's daughter.'

'And that was personal to Cox, wasn't it? So it's got me wondering two things; one – is there a link between these three victims? And two – what makes *this* personal? They all attend the same course in the same college. Is that where they met their killer? Or were they chosen from that course purely because of the link to crime and punishment, and then ultimately to Cox? Or are *you* the link?' He looks pointedly at Julia. 'The more I think about it, the more I think your book being at the scene doesn't make any sense except to draw us to you and ultimately James Cox.'

Julia feels relief that Armstrong is coming around to her way of thinking on this. Focusing on Cox is the only thing that makes sense now. She turns her back to him, her eyes on a stack of books on the small desk.

'That's a distinct possibility. It looks like Grace is *very* interested in crime and punishment. This stack of books makes for some frightening bedtime reading – my book is third from the bottom, there's one here on Bundy, Shipman, the Golden State Killer ... could her interests have drawn the wrong type of attention?'

No one has any answers. They continue on with searching the rest of the house, anxious to leave it as they found it. At the back of the property is a small wooden garden shed, set back behind rows of potted plants that stand on slabs of rose-coloured concrete. It's the most low-maintenance garden Julia has ever seen.

'We need to know who looks after the garden,' she says to Armstrong. 'And I'd wager a housekeeper is employed as well. There was no forced entry. So your team need to compile a list of everyone that has a key.'

He doesn't answer but moves away and angles a flashlight into the shed; sweeping torchlight illuminates the small area inside, showing tins of paint with brushes resting on top, a ladder against one wall, and a small lawnmower, a can of fuel beside it. Nothing unusual. His brows furrow low over his eyes as he stands with his hands tight around the flashlight.

Julia crouches down, running one gloved hand over small pebbles nestled between the slabs of concrete, feeling their hard, sharp edges through the forensic gloves. She walks to the side of the house, where there is a path about two metres wide leading back around to the front of the property.

'Des ... Neil!' she calls.

They find her crouched down again, running both hands over the pebbles. She scoops up a handful and holds one up to the light.

'These pebbles look sharp enough to leave tiny track marks on a person's skin. Especially if they were dragged over enough of them. What do you think, Des?'

He squints to look closer. 'Well ... the pathologist was certain the two women were dragged before they died.' He looks at the pebbles beneath his feet. 'I think we may have just found out *where*.'

31

2024

The afternoon passes in the Carmichael Estate.

The place where James Cox attacked her, this gateway to hell she has built up in her mind, is reduced to just another housing estate swarming with Gardaí as a further case file opens. Grace York's house is the tomb now, even though no body was found inside it. Julia can't shake the feeling it's only a matter of time before they find her dead with injuries matching Hannah's and Elena's. One more homage to James Cox.

Sadie Horgan and several other Gardaí move quietly around the exterior of the property, gathering intel and staying out of the way of the forensics team. She and Armstrong stand together, their heads close, eyes on the house. There's nothing further Julia can do here. As she pulls off her gloves she notices Riordan, sitting on the concrete kerb, his phone in his hand.

'All okay, Des?'

He looks up at her, his eyes red-rimmed and wet from the

cool afternoon breeze.

'I was talking to Síle. Just checking in. They're safe.'

She can see his energy dissolving, the tremor in his hands more pronounced. Garda Saoirse O'Reilly has noticed it too.

'I don't know about you both, but I could really use a break. Can you give me a lift back to the station? Armstrong told me to head back and update Dan West.'

Riordan pushes off the kerb with a muffled grunt and extends his arm to her. 'Your chariot awaits, my dear.'

At the station, he makes his way to the canteen, Saoirse O'Reilly linking his arm. She proclaims a dire need for coffee, Dan West's update forgotten. Julia winks at the young Garda as they go. If Riordan realizes Saoirse is keeping an eye on him and bypassing each coffee dock on each floor, he'll freak out; Julia is happy Riordan is taking an hour out.

She makes her way to the incident room, where Dan West is commanding the influx of information with an authority that surprises Julia; when she'd first met him yesterday, she'd thought him too young for the role of coordinator. Now, as he assigns tasks and accepts documents, the look of deep concentration on his face gives her relief. The room is busy, several Gardaí and detectives in discussion, awaiting updates. A photograph of Grace York has been added to the noticeboard. Julia steps closer; she looks younger than twenty. Her skin is clear, her eyes and eyebrows dark brown, her hair light blonde. There's still life in her eyes, and Julia plans to find her before that changes.

'We got this from the college admin office.' Garda Lee Murphy stands beside Julia. 'And Miss York's mother and stepfather are on their way back from London.'

'Stepfather?'

He blushes a little as Julia turns to face him. 'Er … yes. Mr York is not Grace's dad. He had two sons and her mum already had Grace when they got married.'

'I see.' Julia turns back to the photograph. Blended families are common and usually don't make a difference. But everything is relevant in a case where nothing makes sense.

'Anything else?'

'Um … well, I spoke to a few of Grace's classmates. She seems to have been a bit of a loner. There was one guy claimed to be her ex-boyfriend, who said, and I quote, he was "well shot of her". Whatever that means. I also spoke to Grace's GP. Just in case there's anything we should know, like is she diabetic and in need of insulin or anything like that.'

Julia nods. He's more competent than she gave him credit for.

'And he told me it might be important for us to know that Grace York spent some time in a psychiatric unit when she was seventeen. He wouldn't say any more than that.'

'That's certainly interesting.' She folds her arms. 'But I think her disappearance is linked to Elena and Hannah's murders, rather than to anything in Grace's history or personal life. Take that information to Neil, certainly, but for now, our focus is on finding her alive.'

'Yes, ma'am,' Murphy says with such deference she almost expects a military salute.

'You can call me Julia. How did you get on with the fruit basket?'

She notices he has drawn himself up to his full height. 'It's gone for analysis now. It was hand-delivered; I've sent a file to my sergeant and I recommend we look for home security cameras on the street and see what we find. Mr Riordan's family have been advised to stay with a neighbour for the rest of the evening. And … um … they've taken the dog with them.'

Julia appraises him; she definitely wrote Lee Murphy off too quickly.

'That's fine work, Lee, thank you.'

He blushes again and steps away. Julia can't help a small smile which slips as Armstrong approaches with Sadie Horgan; they must have left the Carmichael Estate just after she did. He's removed his jacket and rolled up the sleeves of his shirt; the way the collar is askew, she imagines he's pulled at it as though it was choking him. She remembers that feeling. His case has escalated from two murdered women to a third potential victim, he has no idea why this is happening and there are more questions than leads. This is the point at which investigators become desperate for a lucky break.

'Mrs Harte.' Armstrong stands beside her, focusing on the image of Grace York.

'I prefer Julia.'

'Is Riordan all right? He seemed a bit weak before.'

'He'll be fine. If he was any younger he'd have pinned you to the wall outside Grace York's house, not given you a talking-to.'

Armstrong turns to face her. 'Is there something you'd like to say, Mrs Harte?'

Julia looks him in the eye for a few seconds and then

sighs. 'There is actually. I've spent my career dealing with the male ego; you, Neil, are very predictable. I really couldn't care less if you don't like me or if you don't want us around. All I'll say is, lives are at risk here, and you really should get over yourself and take all the help you can get. Des and I will be here until this is done. I suggest you deal with that and get on with doing your job. Keep us informed. Take my advice and grow up.'

He lowers his eyes to the floor, his hands on his hips. When he looks at Julia again, his anger is replaced by something else; she can't quite name it but she knows he's heard her words.

'All right. Let's move on. We're searching Ian Daunt's property right now and he has appointed a solicitor. He's our only lead but I don't think it's him. Forensic officers are still at the York house and Grace's family are on their way back. We're going to re-interview everyone from the college and I think at this point, it's a good idea to suspend lectures until we can establish if the other students are in danger. Sadie Horgan has arranged a press conference.'

'When?'

'In thirty minutes. We need to get Grace's face out there.'

'Agreed. Anything else?'

'No, that's it for now.'

'Any update from the pathologist? The pebbles at Grace's house need to be compared to—'

Armstrong holds up his hands. 'It's done. Samples have been sent over. And I've pushed for results on toxicology and results from the skin under Elena Kehoe's nails. Dr Moore is hoping for something tomorrow morning.'

They stand beside each other silently, watching Dan West

pin more sheets to the noticeboard.

'It's not a coincidence, you know.' Julia breaks the silence. 'The Carmichael Estate. Number thirty-six. The power cut. It's like whoever is doing this is studying the file on James Cox and treating it like an instruction manual.'

'I believe you,' Armstrong says quietly. 'Which means at some point, he'll come for you.'

Julia inhales sharply; that very thought has been playing on her mind. She's glad Riordan isn't in the room for this part of the conversation. 'I don't think so, not this time. James Cox blamed me and Adrian for his troubles. I'm not connected to this. The fruit basket and note delivered earlier might not actually be sinister at all; after all, it said, "Welcome back". That's a bit creepy but not actually threatening.' She almost believes her words; in truth, she hasn't had time to think this through properly. She'd rather they focus on finding Grace York before it's too late.

'Are you sure? As I said, I've read the file. That night Cox was captured ... the things that happened to you. And your husband ...'

Sadie Horgan clears her throat at the other end of the room and calls for quiet; Julia takes a seat, glad of the interruption, hating that Philip is being brought into this. She wonders how that night is detailed in the file ...

She can't revisit it; it's too difficult to think about.

32

1994

Julia jerked awake to the sound of the ringing telephone. Her mouth was dry and her neck ached; she looked around her, startled for a moment to find herself on the sofa in the living room. Then she found the notebook resting on her chest and the pen in her lap, and she remembered Connolly's visit and the task he had left her. She glanced at the notebook – the page was blank save for some bullet points she had optimistically drawn in a vertical line. It seemed she had remained uninspired overnight and her heart sank.

How could she remember eight years of Garda work? She would never be able to complete this task without Adrian, not unless she went into the station and searched through their files. But Riordan had been firm – stay at home.

Philip's thundering footsteps on the stairs told her the phone call had woken him too. She heard him speak to the caller, his voice still thick with sleep.

'Yes, hello? Okay ... right, thank you very much. Well that's good, at least. Yes, I'll tell her.'

She stepped into the hallway, her right arm cradling her left elbow; she needed her pain meds. 'Who was that? Was it about Shauna Clancy?'

Philip looked at her in surprise and ran his hands over his face, blinking away sleep. 'That was the guards; just letting us know the lads outside are leaving for the morning. Nothing to report. Someone will be back to replace them in an hour. He didn't mention Shauna.'

'Oh.' She stepped towards him cautiously, hopeful his anger might have eased overnight.

After a moment's hesitation he wrapped his arms around her. 'Did you not go to bed? You need to rest, Julia!' His voice was soft, his hug firm.

She leaned into him, relieved. 'At some point I fell asleep, but I've no idea what time that was.' She yawned loudly. 'I couldn't remember a single thing, Phil! It's a disaster! None of the people I arrested over the last few years had the makings of a killer, at least not that I know of.'

'Right.' He didn't want to talk about it. 'Come on. I'll make you some breakfast, it might perk you up.'

She followed him into the kitchen and lowered herself gingerly onto a chair. The wound on her back ached and she frowned in annoyance – she wasn't used to being incapacitated and she hated it. She wanted, *needed*, to get back to work. At least Philip seemed less angry with her.

'Are you going into the surgery today?' she asked as he pulled a carton of eggs from the fridge.

'Absolutely not! Not when we know that madman has targeted you. How could you not tell me what he said when he attacked you? I thought that might have been the end of it, but now … I wish you weren't shutting me out of this!'

Julia watched him whisk eggs with quick, violent thrusts, realizing he was in fact still as angry as ever. She wanted to tell him that if he wasn't so unsupportive of her career lately, she might have felt able to trust him with that information. This was becoming a habit; Julia sitting, vulnerable and in pain, while Philip prepared a meal, venting his anger and frustration. It seemed to be the sum of their time spent together recently, and it wasn't fair – she needed his support, not an argument. But she stayed quiet.

'It did strike me as a bit excessive that your chief superintendent put protection outside the house. I mean, I was glad of it, but I wondered was it a bit of an overreaction. Now I understand why.' He glanced across at her. 'I hope you're not planning to go into the station today?'

It sounded like an instruction wrapped innocently in a question.

'I was hoping we might talk, actually,' he continued. 'About our discussion the other day. I would really like to know where your head is at. About the future, I mean. *Our* future. You agreed you'd step away from the investigation and now here you are, back in the middle of it.' There was accusation in his voice, and anger too. She held her breath; there would be no reprieve. She really missed the way they used to be; when had ease been replaced with tension, love with anger?

'That was before Shauna Clancy was taken, Phil. If I can help, I will, that's the bottom line.' She hoped her voice didn't quiver and betray her exasperation, but that's exactly how she felt. She didn't want to have this conversation, not now.

Philip busied himself at the stove, adding cream to the eggs and dunking slices of bread into the mixture.

He added a shake of cinnamon and nutmeg, his twist on French toast, just the way she liked it. He was angry but making her favourite breakfast – she felt her head throb in confusion.

'I get that ... but ... we could head out on the boat. You'd be safe out there, for one thing. I could stop worrying about you getting hurt, which would make a nice change. We could invite Matt and Rhea, we haven't been out with them in ages. What do you say?'

She looked at him aghast, the hope in his eyes enough to break her heart. If she was leaving this house, it was to go and support Mary Clancy, or perhaps to sneak into work and search through the files to help kick-start her memory. If he could just understand, just give her some time ...

Pounding at the back door, the most welcome interruption Julia had ever heard, saved her from having to disagree with him again. Philip pulled the door open to a stricken Kathleen, who stood on the step in the crisp morning air, her lips quivering while she wrung her hands in distress.

'I'm sorry to disturb you both. But if you wouldn't mind ... Bren is having some sort of turn. Please – could you look at him?'

The sweater Philip had worn yesterday still lay across the back of the kitchen chair; he pulled it over his pyjamas and rushed through the door, casting apologetic eyes at Julia. She rose gingerly and crossed the kitchen, turning off the stove. She didn't want French toast and she didn't want to talk about their future. The only thing she could concentrate on right now was the past. She made her way back to the living room and settled on the sofa again, picking up her notebook.

Julia promised herself she would continue the task of trying to remember everything she had worked on with Adrian, but after a cup of tea she succumbed to the pain in her head and the absolute, crushing lack of progress and went upstairs to lie down.

It felt like hours later when Philip returned. She could hear him moving around downstairs but she stayed where she was, the heat and comfort of the bed too difficult to leave. The curtains were still open and the sun was bright – it must only be close to midday, she thought. When she heard footsteps mount the staircase she closed her eyes and pulled the blankets higher over her face. She could not have the conversation he wanted, not today. He called her name softly, but she ignored him, and didn't stir when she heard him open and close the wardrobe and pull on fresh clothes. Eventually, with a small sigh, he left the room. She sensed him watching her quietly from the doorway and she breathed deeply and evenly, relieved when she heard his footsteps on the creaking floorboards on his way back downstairs. Tears stung her eyes and she hated herself for pretending to be asleep – when had she begun to want something other than the life they had dreamt of? The tears leaked onto her pillow. Philip deserved better. When this was over she would show him how much he meant to her.

For the rest of the day she stayed in bed, watching the evening approach, shadows lengthening on the bedroom floor. Sitting against her pillows she tried again to remember everything she had worked on with Adrian. She recalled thefts and brawls, car accidents and helping families through grief. Some things stood out; a domestic assault that had left a woman hospitalized with several broken bones was one case she remembered quickly. The level of brutality she had seen there was unforgettable. But why would that prompt these revenge attacks? As far as Julia knew, the husband in that case was living in England now and the woman and her children were getting on with their lives. Trying to recall it all, her head felt fuzzy, her skin clammy as her frustration grew. Why couldn't she remember anything significant?

She wasn't hungry, even hours later, when the sun had set and she finally made her way downstairs. Philip was in the living room, watching the evening news bulletin on the television. He didn't look away from the screen.

'You slept?'

'Yes, thankfully. How's Brendan?'

'He's settled. Will you have some food? I can reheat dinner.' His eyes were still on the news but at least he was being polite.

'No, I don't feel hungry, but thanks.'

He sighed with forced patience. 'Your acid reflux won't improve if you keep taking medication on an empty stomach.' The doctor in him couldn't help lecturing her, but his tone was flat, disinterested. She stayed quiet; minutes passed where Philip ignored her and she didn't step further into the room, the void between them widening every second.

'I think I'll pop next door,' she said finally.

At last he looked towards her, surprise and disappointment in his eyes. 'If that's what you want.'

She hesitated – they should talk, or perhaps sit together in silence and hope time spent side by side might blur the distance between them – but she went into the hall and pushed her right arm into her jacket, flicking the rest of it over her other shoulder.

'See you later then!' she called, but he didn't answer.

Outside, the Garda squad car was clearly visible; she couldn't help but cringe. She walked towards it, knocking on the window, smiling when it was rolled down.

'Shay! It's good to see you!'

Garda Shay Foley flicked on the car's interior light. He looked as pristine as ever, his uniform jacket creased sharply down the arms. But his mouth dropped open in shock.

'Julia … Christ, your face! Sorry! It's just, I haven't seen you since—'

'Oh I'm fine.' She waved her hand dismissively. 'I've always bruised like a peach.'

He laughed at that and she felt her shoulders loosen; it was good to see a friendly face.

'Aren't there supposed to be two of you?'

'There was; Cathy Flynn was supposed to be with me but she had some sort of emergency.' He shrugged. 'It's fine. There's a replacement coming by in a while.'

'Have you heard anything about Shauna Clancy?' she asked, hope leaving her when he shook his head.

'Not a thing. Only that her mam is in a bad way.'

'I heard that too.'

Shay reached out and touched her hand, quickly pulling his own back, seeming embarrassed. He cleared his throat. 'So, where are you off to then?' he asked, before grimacing and biting his lip. 'God, sorry! I just heard how that sounded. Ignore me!'

Julia grinned. 'Don't worry about it. I'm going next door

to visit my neighbour if that's okay with you, Garda Foley!'
He laughed, and she wished him a good night and said
goodbye.

Kathleen Adlington was as grateful for company as Julia
knew she would be, her face lighting up when Julia pushed
open their back door. She'd been crying; now she blinked
water from her eyes and insisted on making tea for them,
busying herself by filling a tray with cups and milk, adding
a small plate of biscuits. The rattle and clank of crockery
against crockery betrayed her upset, both her hands shaking
as she carried the tray into the living room.

Brendan was sitting in his armchair beside the fire, his
head resting back against the cushions, his eyelids drooping.
Julia and Kathleen sat together on the sofa, cups of tea
balancing on their knees, watching him. Julia ate the biscuits
she was offered, finally hungry.

'He seems more settled,' Kathleen said sadly, speaking
quietly. 'Thank God for Philip! Without him we'd probably
be still waiting on a trolley in A&E.'

'Yes, Philip is a wonderful doctor. I suppose Brendan will
have to go for tests now?'

'That's right; it looks like we can't ignore this any more.
I've never understood that phrase about the elephant in the
room until now. Philip said he'll send a message to Bren's
GP and I guess all we can do now is wait for a referral.'

'I suppose so.' Julia was sympathetic, knowing how long
an appointment with a specialist could take. 'Well look, I'm
feeling much better already, so I'll be able to help out more.
I'm sorry I was a bit missing in action these last few days.'

'Not at all, love; you don't need to apologize. Are you

healing well? Philip mentioned your injuries were pretty bad.' Her eyes moved over Julia, from her face to her shoulder and then downwards, towards her side where the wound on her back was now an irritating healing-itch begging to be scratched.

She shifted in her seat, feeling embarrassed. 'Well, I'm in good hands.'

'That's true; you're in the *best* hands! But to slash a person's back! What kind of monster does that? It's very strange, don't you think? It's a funny place to cut someone. It seems quite specific if you ask me.'

Julia stared into the flames in the hearth a few feet in front of her and nodded slowly, feeling the heat against her face. Kathleen was right ... it *was* an odd spot to cut someone. She had thought it was something done to mark out a victim, but right then, feeling Kathleen's eyes on her, she wondered if it meant something that everyone was cut in roughly the same place.

'... do you know what I mean?' Kathleen was speaking again, turning to stare at Julia, expecting an answer.

She blinked. 'What? Sorry, Kathleen, I was miles away for a second there.'

'It's just that, well, you can ignore me if you like now, sure what would I know, but it's like what Bren says. He never stops talking these days about lights and Morse code and sending a message through signals. And it seems to me that anyone that would choose that same spot to cut each person is trying to send a message, aren't they?'

Suddenly, Julia sat upright in the armchair, not even registering the pain in her shoulder and back as she moved. She lowered her cup of tea to the ground beside her, sloshing liquid onto the carpet, barely breathing, lost in the memory of Adrian pulling a screaming toddler from her mother's arms, his eyes wide as he realized the back of the child's vest was covered in blood. She remembered him crying, 'Jesus Christ, Jules!' as he lifted the child's vest, and how his hands fumbled as he wrapped a towel around the wound, trying to stem the flow of blood from a long, deep cut just above the top of the child's nappy. And while, across the room, Brendan began to mutter softly about lights in the dark, and while the fire spat and crackled nearby, Julia could hear again the screams of the child's mother as she restrained her while Adrian carried the bloodied toddler to a waiting ambulance outside.

'Kathleen!' she whispered. 'Thank you for the tea but I have to go! Can I borrow your car?'

'Of course, love!' Kathleen's papery skin was pale and her hands shook as she pushed against the armrests of her chair to stand up. 'Is everything all right?'

'Yes. It's just that I've remembered something. I need to go.'

Kathleen stepped to a nearby shelf and returned with her car key, pressing it into Julia's hand. With a nod of thanks she rose to her feet, scooping up her jacket and rushed through the back door into the cold night.

33

1994

After the heat of the Adlingtons's living room, the night air felt like a cold slap against her skin. She stood on their back doorstep, clutching their car key tightly in her hand, suddenly unsure. Should she run back home and tell Philip she had to drive in to work to check on something? Maybe he'd understand, he might even drive her himself. She laughed at that thought, a brittle sound that was swallowed by the wind. Maybe two years ago Philip would have helped her, would have understood her obsession with finding Adrian's killer. But things between them had changed. Now she knew he'd be angry and would remind her she was to stay at home and let the others get on with it; he didn't understand her any more.

She was on her own.

She jogged quickly to the car in the driveway, noting the squad car parked in front of her house. Shay Foley was still inside, the silhouette of his shoulders a darker shape in the car. As far as she could tell, he was still alone. She could really do without any questions from him either, she decided as she opened the driver's side door and lowered herself into the seat. She pulled her jacket hood up over her hair; she would be turning left and driving away from Shay to leave their road, but if he looked in his rear-view mirror when he saw the car's headlights, she didn't want him to recognize her.

Hunching slightly forward to ease the throbbing in her back, Julia started the car and realized immediately that she had a problem. Her left arm was still bound in a sling and her shoulder continued to ache whenever she moved it. But Shauna Clancy didn't have time for Julia to figure out a solution. Accepting she'd have to drive solely with her right hand, using her knees to steady the steering wheel whenever she needed to change gear, she pushed the stick into first and eased out of the Adlingtons's driveway.

What Kathleen Adlington had said about the marks on each victim's back being some type of signal, some way of trying to send a message, had prompted the memory she was sure was the key to finding the killer. Thinking about it now, remembering her and Adrian rushing to the scene, she flinched – they had had no idea what they were walking into. The child, a toddler, had been seriously injured, a deep cut low on her back. Remembering that child and the screaming young woman who didn't speak much English, who had fought the fact that they were taking her baby away from her, Julia began to shiver. It was cold in the car, and the memory of that night was flooding through her, the adrenaline of that call-out like a muscle memory, making her grip the wheel harder.

It was all so clear in her mind now. A dark stairwell, its

light fixture broken, a sense that her baton was better in her hand than on her belt as she'd run to the flat. The front door had been open; the only light from the streetlights outside. The air had been frigid. And in one corner, screaming in animalistic, primal howls, was a little girl, her vest stained red with blood.

She recalled her shock that a mother could inflict such wounds on her own child. She had restrained her to allow Adrian to remove the child to an ambulance; it had been easy, the woman had been angry but weak and thin, like a little bird. They had filed their reports afterwards and moved on to the next incident. They were busy, their station short-staffed, and she had forgotten about it. Had that night somehow led to this?

She was suddenly floored by the realization that the most likely thing she would find at the station was a dead-end. She only had access to the reports she had compiled herself and filed away, and at that time, they hadn't known anything about the family. Once the child was safe and the woman had been detained, the case had been passed over to other officers higher up the chain. The finer details of the case, the final outcome and all the personal information of the people involved, would be in a report written by someone else, and it was likely to be in files she couldn't access.

She slapped the steering wheel in frustration; the mobile phone Philip wanted her to get would be very useful right about now, she thought, deciding that what she needed to do was call the station and find out where the senior officers were, and if any of them could get her what she needed. The clerical staff would all have gone home hours ago – could there be anyone at all in the station overnight who'd be able

246

to find the information? Perhaps this journey was a waste of time and the only thing she would gain would be another argument with her husband when she eventually returned home.

She was about to turn the car around when she remembered something else … Des Riordan's address. She'd found that in the public phone book alongside his home number when she had embarked on her campaign to be allowed to work on the case. He lived less than ten minutes from her current position. Her eyes flicked to the clock again … ten forty-five … he might be at work. If he were, she would apologize to his wife for disturbing her, continue on with her journey and meet him there. If he were at home, he could help her find what she needed to know – it was his request that she think back over the previous cases with Adrian, after all.

She pressed her foot on the accelerator, thinking of Shauna Clancy.

Des Riordan's home was a semi-detached house, with a neat row of shrubs in the front garden, his short driveway lit up by two powerful security lights. Everything was carefully ordered, the grass trimmed and weeds pulled, the car parked in a perfectly straight line. She pulled to a stop behind his car and climbed out, breathing in the chill air deeply; it steadied her somewhat. She gripped the car key, pushing the flesh of her palm around the metal, welcoming the jarring sharpness.

Ringing the doorbell, apprehension flared in her gut; was this pushing Riordan too far again? Did it matter? If she was right, and what she had remembered would help to understand all this, this small act of insubordination could lead to locating Shauna Clancy by morning.

The lights were on at the front of the house, and she thought she could hear the faint rumbling sound of a television. She rang the bell again, barely ten seconds after the first time, and stood back to wait, gripping the key tighter.

A small dark shape approached the front door, fuzzy in the frosted glass. It was Riordan's wife. She pulled the door open a fraction and peered out.

'Yes?'

'Mrs Riordan, I'm sorry to disturb you. I need to speak to—'

'Jesus H. Christ!' Riordan yanked the door open; he towered over his wife, and as Julia looked up at him, her heart fluttered in her chest. He looked furious, and somehow, even bigger than he did at work.

'Des!' his wife admonished, her eyes roaming over Julia. She gasped as they rested on her bruised face.

'Have I not warned you before?' he hissed, his eyes bulging. 'Do you have any idea what time it is?'

The front door was pulled wide now; the heat from the house hit Julia and she shivered. She decided to get straight to the point, and spoke in a rush, her teeth rattling around the speech she had rehearsed over the last five minutes driving here.

'You sent Jim Connolly to my house to ask me to think through the cases I worked on with Adrian, to see if there was anything that might link to *this* case. And there is. I've remembered a child we removed from her mother about two years ago, but I can't remember more than the child's

248

name – it was Camille. I need to see the files the investigators worked on, but I don't know who followed up on it; I need help. I was passing near here on my way in to the station and I wondered if you might be here, and if *you* could help me. I don't know what else to do.'

Startled at the panic in her voice, she stopped and reached for the wall in front of her, resting her hand on the rough red brick. He looked at her for a long moment. Finally he rubbed a hand over his face and sighed.

'You could have rung the station before you left home. You could have rung *me!* God knows you have my number!'

She knew she could have done those things, but she hadn't; not wanting to confront Philip, and not thinking before rushing headlong into something were habits she really needed to break.

'I could have. But with respect, chief, you barely take my calls.'

Riordan nodded, acknowledging that he'd shut her out, pushed her into a corner. 'Right. Come on then. Pass me my coat, Síle.'

'But you've only just got home!' his wife protested behind him, but then seemed to think better of it. She offered Julia a sympathetic smile and reached behind her, retrieving her husband's coat from a hook behind the door and passing it to him before walking back into the house without another word. A dissatisfied spouse is the price of doing this job well, Julia thought. Riordan stepped outside and pulled the door shut behind him.

'Let's hope you're right about this, because we've nothing else to go on.'

34

1994

Riordan insisted on driving, and seeing as Julia had blocked in his car with the Adlingtons's Fiesta, he decided they would take that, holding his hands out wordlessly for the key.

She felt adrenaline swell inside her at the certainty they were close to a breakthrough. The pain in her back and shoulder had dissipated, dampened by the rush of anticipation that made her heart race and made it difficult to steady her breath. But she did manage a smile as Riordan comically tried to adjust the driver's seat to accommodate his size; he grunted and muttered under his breath as he shunted the seat forward and back with a string of Jesus H. Christs. When he was ready to go, after adjusting the rear-view mirror upwards to meet his eyes, he turned to her.

'I'm going to assume it was sheer desperation to get to the station that made you forget the rules of the road and actually drive in your condition.' His eyes met hers. The light from the streetlamps outside his house glanced off his face, making his strong jaw and broken nose appear more twisted and menacing, but his voice was kind. 'You need to be in control of a vehicle and there's no way you can be with one arm in a sling!'

'Yes, chief,' she murmured. He glanced at her again, unsure if she was being sarcastic, but decided not to press it further, and reversed carefully out of his driveway. 'Look – I've had a very long day with very little to show for it. Mary Clancy is close to a breakdown and the commissioner gave me a dressing-down this morning. So I'll take any hope you can offer me. Tell me what you remember.'

Julia rubbed at her eyes, tired and yet fully alert. The fingers of her right hand played with the metal edge of the zipper on her jacket as she told Riordan everything she could recall.

An elderly woman living in a flat off Barrack Street in Cork city had called the station to request help for an injured child. Julia and Adrian had been nearby and were assigned to the call, arriving on the scene minutes later. The woman who had called the Gardaí met them in the hallway and led them inside the flat, which was dark and smelled of stale water and soiled nappies. Julia remembered pinching her nose to stop her gag reflex as soon as they'd stepped inside. But it was the sound she remembered the most; the high-pitched, hysterical cry of someone in terrible pain. When it became clear that it was a young child, all she felt was an urgency to soothe the pain. Adrian reached the child first. The lower half of her white vest was stained red, and when he lifted it gently they saw a cut on her lower back. There was so much blood ... Julia found a towel on a nearby chair and Adrian wound it around the cut, while the child clung to him with tiny, frantic fingers.

The neighbour, an elderly woman whose name Julia couldn't remember later when it came to writing up her report, hovered at the doorway, running her hands through short white hair that by then was standing on end wildly. Julia had told her to go wait outside for the ambulance. Then she had turned her attention to the other woman in the room, trying to calm her mounting anger.

This woman had been young, much younger than Julia and Adrian; she'd looked like a teenager. She was dressed in tight-fitting jeans and a dark T-shirt and she sat on the floor, her shoulders pressed against a worn armchair, blood-stained hands pressed against her forehead in fists. She had muttered to herself repeatedly. Julia had knelt beside the young woman and asked her name. She hadn't looked up. It was only when the blare of the ambulance siren was loud outside the apartment and Adrian had scooped the moaning child up in his arms, that the young woman had rushed to her feet and begun to scream. Her momentum had knocked Julia to one side and she'd quickly scrambled to standing, grabbing the woman as she'd rushed at Adrian, screaming.

'Non! Non! Camille!'

Julia had gripped the woman's upper arms while she twisted her body left and right, screaming and spitting on the floor; she had eventually sunk onto the carpet, coiled as though to protect herself. A paramedic had entered the flat then and though Julia knew she should stay, she'd moved quickly into the hallway, needing fresher air, needing to be away from her.

A sob caught in her throat as she remembered the child's screams from that night.

'So the child's name was Camille?' Riordan's deep voice

252

dragged her back to the present and she was grateful.

'Yes, but that's all I know. All I can remember anyway. I think it was two years ago.'

'Three, I think. I remember the case. The woman ended up in a psych ward for a while.'

'Do you think it's her? Do you think she's the killer?'

'No. If my memory serves me right, she's dead.'

Julia sat back into the passenger seat, stunned.

'And besides, you were attacked by a man in the Carmichael Estate, not a woman. We're here.' He parked carefully in the staff car park at the front of the station and climbed out, grunting with the effort of extricating his body from the small car. 'Let's get this done.'

He was gone, slamming the driver's door, striding quickly away from the car while Julia was still pushing open the passenger door with her right arm. As she watched him rush ahead of her into the foyer, her heart swelled in relief. He believed this was important, just as she did. She quickened her pace, thinking of Adrian, thinking of his daughter, and of the man that had slashed her back. After days of sitting around doing nothing, willing her body to heal so she could get back to finding whoever had brought this madness into her life, she was finally helping. Despite everything that had happened she couldn't keep the smile off her face.

Riordan was sitting behind his desk when she caught up with him, in a room she had never been inside before. It was smaller than she'd imagined it would be, and more cluttered than she had expected the man to tolerate. He was rifling through a stack of files on his desk when she entered.

'Anything?' she asked, sitting on a chair opposite his desk.

253

He didn't answer, but kept searching, discarding files into another pile as he worked. She wondered if he might search through the computer system but it didn't look as though he had even turned the machine on.

'Would you not check on the computer?' she couldn't help but ask, feeling the pressure of every second that passed. Shauna needed them to figure this out.

'That's Kay Nielson's area of expertise. Ah, here we are!' He sat up straight in the chair, his face red and glistening from exertion, but he look relieved. As he opened the file and his eyes scanned the pages in front of him, Julia fought the urge to stand at his shoulder and read for herself. She rubbed her hand on her jeans, leaning forward, waiting.

'Okay, this is everything. And I was right, it was three years ago, 1991. Gardaí Clancy and Harte responded to a call from a concerned citizen about a child that appeared to be injured and in a high level of distress. Gardaí arrived on scene at eleven fifty-five p.m., twenty-ninth of October. Ambulance was requested and arrived at four minutes past midnight. Child, female, aged approximately two years, appeared to have suffered a deep laceration to her lower back, was removed by Garda Clancy to the ambulance and accompanied to hospital. One female at the scene was agitated, distressed, and had to be restrained by Garda Harte when the child was being removed.'

Julia exhaled. It was as she'd remembered it. 'And the rest? What happened after that?'

Riordan's eyes continued down the page.

'The child's mother was identified as Léa Baudelaire, nineteen years old, living in Cork for an unspecified number of years, originally from Limoges in France. It's unclear when she moved to Ireland. Miss Baudelaire was held overnight in hospital and was transferred to a psychiatric unit the following day.' He pinched the bridge of his nose with one hand and pushed the file away with the other. Julia stared at him, waiting.

After a moment he looked at her; there was something in his gaze she couldn't read.

'Our men never got to interview the young woman. To make a long story very short, Miss Baudelaire was treated in hospital for a number of days and released into the care of her doctor. I don't have any information on what her treatment plan was, obviously, or what her doctors decided. Two of our lads were scheduled to interview her on the second of November, but the poor girl was dead.'

'Suicide?'

'Yes, sadly.'

'Let me guess … she slit her wrists.'

Riordan sat back into his seat, their eyes locked, both remembering the injuries inflicted on Louise Hynes and Jeanette Coyle.

'This is connected, this has to be it!' Julia exclaimed. 'He cuts his victims on their back first, just like the little girl, Camille. Then, after he's killed them, he slits their wrists just like Léa did. That's what he did to Louise and Jeanette. And Adrian and I were the guards that answered the call-out.'

'Okay … all right.' He squeezed his hands into fists, flexing his fingers in and out, agitated. 'So he's targeting you. And Louise Hynes and Jeanette Coyle were used to bait you out.'

Julia swallowed and looked away, feeling sick. 'So how do we find him? How is he connected to Léa and Camille?'

Riordan stabbed the front of the file with one finger. 'This contains nothing that points in that direction. All I know is that after Léa died, her daughter was placed temporarily into foster care. I can follow this up but probably not until the morning.'

'But there must be something we can do tonight!' Julia rose quickly to her feet. She could feel tears behind her eyes and a tight feeling winding around her chest. Her fantasy of finding Shauna Clancy by dawn was fading. 'Shauna is in danger!'

'And so are you!' he growled, his tone inviting no argument. 'Go home – unfortunately, I'll have to let you drive yourself. I'm going to call to the address in Barrack Street—'

'But—'

'... to the neighbour that made the initial call back in 1991. Let's hope she still lives there and that she remembers her neighbours. Although, I doubt that's something she could forget.'

'It must be the child's father! Can we get her birth certificate, I know it's almost the middle of the night now, but can't we—'

'I'm going to wake some people, yes. Now go home please and let me do my job.' He looked at her sternly. 'That's an order. I'm not discussing this any further. You've done well. We have a lead. But I need you to go be safe while I follow it, understood?'

When Julia reached home again, she was thankful the traffic had been light because she knew for sure she hadn't been concentrating on the roads. All she could think about was that night, and about how it had ended so tragically. That a young woman had been in such a state of mental anguish she had harmed her own child, and then taken her own life, made her incredibly sad. Someone close to Léa Baudelaire was blaming them, her and Adrian. She tried to understand the mindset of whoever was doing this, but she couldn't imagine the depth of pain that could drive a person to take life so violently. All she could think was that somehow it must be their only recourse to feeling that justice was being served for Léa.

As she turned onto her road she decided not to bother with stealth, not to dim the headlights and sneak back. She parked in the Adlingtons's driveway and popped the key through the letterbox, hoping it landed on the soft mat and didn't wake anyone up. Then she quickly made her way to her own house. It was past midnight – unless Philip was asleep, he'd be worried about where she had been. She took a deep, calming breath, not relishing another argument.

In her front garden she stopped, confused, feeling the moisture of the grass seep through the soles of her shoes. The interior of the squad car parked in front of her house was in darkness and it looked as though no one was inside it. She walked towards it and pulled open the door. It was empty. Julia stood in the road, in the almost complete darkness of a starless sky, her skin prickling with the familiar, suffocating feeling that she was being watched.

35

1994

The front door was ajar. Julia stepped inside and pushed it closed with a bang.

'Phil?'

Hanging up her jacket in the hall she walked through to the living room. It was empty, the TV still on, a rerun of an old movie playing to an empty room. She stepped towards it and flicked it off, a chill running over her in the still silence.

'Phil? Shay? Are you in here?'

Nothing. Her house was strangely quiet, but then the steady tick of the mantel clock reached her, the hum of something electric in the kitchen, the sounds of the house settling for the night. Things seemed normal, except that there was no sign of her husband. And wherever he'd gone, he'd left the front door open and everything turned on. That wasn't like him; wasting electricity really annoyed him. Had he gone somewhere with Shay? Julia walked back into the hallway and to the foot of the staircase.

'Philip? Are you up there?' she shouted loudly, taking

a moment to listen for any noise, any indication he was upstairs.

Silence. Where was he?

Something familiar crept over her, a panic that started at her toes and rushed up her body, rippling over her skin until it was cold hands at her throat, choking her. Her stomach clenched, her hand moving to the cut at her back. This wasn't right. She needed to do something. Turning to the hall table she snatched up the phone, keying in the station number, relieved to hear a friendly voice.

'Julia! How are you, girl? And here I was feeling sorry for myself getting caught on the night shift. Talking to you will cheer me up no end.'

'Liz!' Julia exhaled, feeling skittish and a little foolish, not quite sure what to say. She and Liz were friends, yet she found herself hesitating. *I had a scary realization earlier and, oh yeah, now I can't find my husband* seemed more than a little crazy.

'Is it true you were in here with Riordan earlier? One of the lads—'

'Is Riordan still there?' Julia interrupted.

'You're not calling Riordan again, are you? 'Cos I can tell you now, if you start that shit again, he'll flippin' freak *out!* Will you ever learn, girl?'

'No, no, it's nothing like that.' Julia cradled the phone between her neck and her chin and rested her right hand against the wall, steadying herself. 'Could you check up on something for me? Shay Foley is meant to be outside my house tonight but he's—'

'Oh yeah, the protection thing? Poor fella got the overnight shift?'

'He was there earlier but now he's gone. He's not in the car and he's not in the house. Do you know what's going on?'

'What did you say his name is? Shay who?' Liz said, in a tone that caused a vein at Julia's temple to throb in confusion.

'Shay Foley.' Her voice rose. 'New in, Waterford and then Mallow, or maybe the other way around. He was working on the hit-and-run case recently. He drove me home from Douglas after Adrian was killed. Actually – you sent him out to pick me up last week.' She drummed her fingers on the wall; the station wasn't that big. How could Liz not be familiar with him?

'Adrian, God rest him, may the Lord have mercy on his soul,' Liz said quietly, then, 'Julia, I haven't the foggiest who you're on about, girl. Hang on a sec, let me go over to Helen's desk. Will you wait while I transfer the call?'

Julia sighed, frustrated. She waited while a clicking sound, as rhythmic and tension-inducing as the mantel clock, filled her ears. After a minute Liz picked up again.

'All right, are you there? Christ, there's a million files … okay, where do I find this …'

Julia turned the receiver away from her mouth and groaned. Liz grumbled and sighed for several more minutes and Julia suffered through each second with bated breath. With a jolt she wondered if she'd got Shay's name wrong when they'd first met. She'd been in shock – had she misheard him then and now he was too polite to correct her?

'Here we go! Transferred in, you said? Oh yeah, yeah, in from Mallow and before that an eight-month stint in Waterford. That was straight after training college … yeah,

I have him.'

Julia released her pent-up breath and sagged against the wall, pressing her forehead into the cold surface.

'But you said Shay? Did I hear that right? Because he's not Shay here, unless he's shortening the Gaelic version of his name. So yeah, *Seamus* is here, but he's down as James in the files. And he's not Foley either, although that must have been his mammy's maiden name.'

'Liz! What are you saying?'

'Sorry, girl! We have a James transferred in from Mallow, but he's got one of those double-barrelled names. James, Seamus in brackets, Foley-Cox was assigned to your house tonight. And you're saying he's not outside any more?'

Julia stared at the table in front of her, at the swirling knots in the wood, the shiny plastic body of the red phone, the ceramic bowl of keys, the framed wedding photograph. Things were in their rightful place, but nothing was as it should be. Shay Foley hadn't given her his full name. Did that mean anything? And where was he? Where was her husband?

The sound of Liz on the other end of the line calling her name, asking if she was still there, was muffled by the loud pounding of Julia's heart in her ears. And suddenly the house went from light to dark as the power surged and then cut out.

The reality of her situation poured over Julia like ice water. She was inside her house with the killer, in the dark, exactly as he'd said he would find her.

36

1994

Julia was aware of each tiny, fragmented breath she took, of pools of cold sweat on her upper lip and between her shoulder blades, making her T-shirt cling to her back beneath her hoodie. She could feel the still-damp soles of her shoes and the solid floor underneath her feet. She could feel her heart thumping, a frightened drum, feel the blood rush inside her veins. She wasn't ready to die yet. Not like this. Not in her own house.

'Liz! I need help! Get someone to my house, quick! He's here!'

'Who? Are you all right, Julia? What's going on?'

'He's here! The killer!'

'Get out, Julia! Get outside!'

Julia dropped the receiver, yanked off her sling and straightened out her left arm, closing her eyes against the rush of pain. Pain was good, she told herself, it meant she was aware and alert, and despite her fear, her body was still capable of doing what it should. Her arm might be useless to her, but her balance was off while she used the sling, and she needed to have as much control as she could.

She looked around the dark hallway. Dark, but not completely devoid of light. Maybe it was because she knew every inch of the house that the darkness felt less complete. She opened the deep drawer in the wooden table and her fingers flexed around the hard metal shaft of a flashlight. Pulling it out she flicked it on, pushing light into the corners of her hallway. It was empty; she was alone. The front door was less than four strides away. Liz would send help – the nearest car – and Julia would wait in the safety of the Adlingtons. Perhaps Philip was there, attending to Brendan again. Riordan would be pleased she was being less reckless, she thought ruefully as she stepped through the hallway towards the front door.

She pulled it open, gasping cold air into her lungs. She wanted to slam the door behind her, let him know she had left the house, that she wasn't playing his games. She looked around her, finding the front garden empty, the Garda car still in situ, the night as calm as it should be. Fourteen steps, she told herself, and she would be at the Adlingtons's front door. Relief was a fleeting thing; as she stepped outside her house she heard him.

Philip. He was close. He was behind her, somewhere *inside* the house. It sounded like he was upstairs.

'Jul ... JULIA! Help me, Julia!'

She stopped, dropping the flashlight to the ground, killing the light. Her eyes darted to her front garden, to the house beside hers ... *Move! Get out of here!* ... but then she heard him again, coughing, retching loudly. One fist pressed

263

against her temple, her fingernails digging into the palm of her hand.

Bending to pick up the flashlight, she tapped it against her thigh until the light returned. Then she swept the hallway with it again, searching for weapons. There was nothing. Philip moaned again, the sound reaching her, making her gasp. He was gurgling and choking now, so loud she could hear him downstairs – there was no time. She rushed through the hallway and ran, taking the stairs two at a time, following the sounds of her husband struggling to survive. She would barricade them into a room and pray Liz would send someone out to the house – it was the only plan she had.

Philip lay on their bedroom floor, curled into a ball; the curtains were open and she saw the shape of him in the wedge of moonlight that carved up the darkness of the room. She closed the door behind her and turned the key, then knelt beside him, reaching for him. She felt moisture on her hands and looked down; the carpet was stained darker around him. She was kneeling in his blood.

'Philip!' she whispered, touching his head and face, her fingers frantic. 'Philip, it's me! What has he done to you?'

He coughed again, a liquid gurgling sound that filled her with fear; the exertion of calling for help had been too much. She angled the light over him and gasped. Puncture wounds in his back stained his shirt, the blood pouring so heavily it was black and thick. Her fingers roamed his throat, his wrists. There weren't any further stab wounds, but she could feel areas of his face that yielded softly where there should have been hard bone – he'd been badly beaten. And she was certain he was bleeding to death.

Jumping to her feet, she pulled a blanket from the end of their bed and pressed it against his back. He hissed in pain. She stood up again, moving to the oak chest of drawers, pulling one open in search of a belt or scarf, anything to wrap around the wounds.

She became aware of a light outside the house flashing in her peripheral vision, to the right, across from her bedroom window. It took her a moment to realize Brendan Adlington was at his window again, flashing light into the dark, lost in his memories of the past. She looked at the flashlight in her hand and remembered Connolly on her doorstep, dragging on his cigarette, watching the lights. *'Isn't that Morse code?'*

Trying to remember if there had been a pattern to the lights was futile – she had never paid attention to that. She hated herself in that moment, for dismissing an elderly man and his memories, for never asking him to show her the SOS signal. The sound of Philip struggling to breathe, to stay alive, grew louder behind her. She stepped towards the window and aimed her flashlight high, flicking it on and off several times towards the Adlingtons. The light in the dark was all she had now.

And then she heard it.

Footsteps, on the stairs, pressing on the familiar creak on the fourth step, then the seventh. Noises she knew in her own house. Someone, *he*, was coming.

She crossed the room again and stood in front of her husband, her flashlight raised and pointed at the locked bedroom door. Willing herself to breathe, she could do nothing but wait. When the chrome door handle was pushed down, she pressed one fist to her mouth to stifle the building scream. But when he began to kick at the lock, she yelped.

In the beam of light she watched the bedroom door splinter and crack. He kicked hard, screaming in rage. She stepped from foot to foot, waiting, her breath coming in short pants, feeling suddenly freezing cold, wondering if this was what it felt like to go into shock. With one final grunt the door was kicked in and a man filled the frame.

'If you're trying to dazzle me with that, you're wasting your time.'

Julia wavered on her feet – she recognized the voice, but she needed to see him to believe it. Shay, or James, stood in front of her. Everything about him was familiar – his tightly cut hair, his freckles, the spots on his chin. But the killer in front of her was a complete stranger; the man she thought she knew had been waiting for this moment, building to it. In each fist he gripped the handle of a large knife. She looked at the blades, shining in the beam of her flashlight – one was still wet with blood. Philip's blood. A hissing sound, as he fought to breathe through his injuries, jolted her. He was still alive … there was still time.

'Liz Begley knows you're here. And she knows that my power was cut, she's sending help, so—'

'Liz Begley is a stupid cow that nobody pays any attention to. No one is coming; it's just us, *Jules*.' He stepped closer. The hatred in his voice terrified her.

'Is this about Camille? And Léa?' He recoiled as though she'd hit him. 'We had to protect Camille! You know this!'

Anger ravaged his face. His hands rocked, his arms jerking, as though he was itching to lash out. Julia couldn't move back; Philip still lay curled on the floor behind her. She pulled herself up to her full height.

'I'm sorry it ended the way it did. I'm sorry Léa took her own life. But you can't think it was because Adrian and I did our duty?'

His eyes closed, screwed up against her words, and his breath was coming fast and hard. He was close to losing control.

'Camille was your daughter,' Julia whispered as the realization dawned. 'I'm sorry for what you lost, Shay. But it wasn't our fault. What did Louise and Jeanette have to do with this?' She knew she was rambling but she had to delay him. *Please, Liz!*

'Nothing at all. But once I had them, I knew I would get you alone eventually. Garda Julia Harte, always so reliable.'

'Where's Shauna Clancy?'

He opened his eyes and smiled. 'You'll never find her.'

The sound of him breathing in front of her and Philip groaning behind her was like a drill inside her head.

'You can't—'

'Shh.' The gentleness of his voice unnerved her. He stepped closer, breathing deeply, inhaling her terror. If she reached out her hand she could touch him. If she swung the flashlight she could hit him. But the glint on the metal edge of the knives in his balled fists stalled her. He stood so close she could smell his sweat. 'Don't you want children, Julia? I've been watching you ... you'd make a good mother. But I'll never give you the chance! You took my child away, you and Clancy ruined my life! He knew why he was dying. Now so do you.' He spat on the ground at her feet.

The walls around her seemed to swell and pulse as she watched him enjoy this moment. She remembered Adrian's face as he died, and the panic in his eyes ... Louise's and

Jeanette's parents in the conference room … Mary Clancy's screams.

'I'm going to fucking destroy you,' she said quietly, looking into his eyes.

He laughed, his breath hot on her face, and pressed his lips to her ear. 'You'll beg me to end it soon.' Julia shivered as he traced the blade of each knife from her navel to her throat, the steel cold and sharp against the skin at her neck. One blade pierced her flesh and she stifled a gasp of pain.

He stopped, turned his head to the right, at the sound of a creak on the stairs. Julia didn't hesitate; with the flashlight clutched tightly in both hands she swung as hard as she could. It landed with a satisfying crack against his temple as a dam of pain burst open in her shoulder. She dropped it onto the ground, gasping.

Shay staggered but stayed on his feet. He touched a deep cut above his eyebrow. Anger ravaged his face, twisting his features into something non-human. He lunged at her but seemed to stop midway. Blood sprayed like mist onto her face as he crumpled onto the ground at her feet. Julia wiped her face with both hands and looked up into the eyes of Brendan Adlington. A golf club hung from his hand and he leaned against it, pushing it into the carpet.

'Brendan!' she gasped. He had seen the flashlight.

'Kathleen will be looking for me.' He reached out for her. 'You're Julia, aren't you, the doctor's wife? Will you help me back home?'

37

1994

Julia clung to hope as the hours turned to days, as Philip was rushed to surgery the first time, then a second time to deal with an unexpected further bleed. Blood clots, a punctured lung, blood transfusions, percentages given on whether he was expected to make it through the first night and then the next ... all familiar words now, the sporadic updates never offering any certainty of his future.

She hadn't seen him since he was removed from the house by the ambulance personnel; he was clinging to life and she had to wait. She watched the clock, hating the long second hand that ticked, ticked, ticked ... Sometimes she ate, sometimes she slept, all in a hard plastic chair in the waiting room. She refused to leave. Steven Molloy kept her company and so did Liz Begley, but neither for very long. There was still so much to do in the investigation, and for the first time, she found she didn't want any part of it.

When Philip's parents and sister arrived, she couldn't form the words to explain to them what had happened.

After Molloy filled in the blanks, they turned reproachful eyes towards her and stepped away, forming their own group to wait for news. She didn't blame them. They left the hospital and checked into a bed and breakfast nearby, asking a nurse at the desk to phone the lady of the house if there was any news.

She had never felt more alone.

'Julia.' She felt a hand on her shoulder, the weight of it a comforting pressure, and she looked into the eyes of Des Riordan. She hadn't seen him since the aftermath of Cox's attack two nights ago. Then he'd been a large figure moving swiftly in the dark, his Northern Irish accent stronger as he shouted orders and directed people into action. Her home was now a crime scene and Riordan was in charge. She hadn't been back to the house; she didn't want to go back there, not without Philip.

His hand on her shoulder moved to her elbow and guided her to standing. They embraced, his hug warm and firm, though careful of her wounds, her arm bound against her chest again. When he pulled away she felt cold and unsteady.

'Let's sit,' he commanded, sliding a second chair closer to Julia's. She wanted to hold his hand suddenly, just to feel the warmth of somebody beside her. But she would never have reached for it, and he kept his hands inside the pockets of his dark jacket. 'How are you holding up?'

'I'm fine. As good as I can be. How's Shauna Clancy? I've tried phoning Mary but no one ever answers.'

He smiled, his face relaxing for a brief moment. 'She's surprisingly good considering everything. Maybe it's youth acting in her favour, I don't know. It could perhaps be the fact that she wasn't harmed physically ... who knows? But she's at home with her mother where she belongs. How's Philip? Do you know anything? Molloy said you're pretty much being kept in the dark.'

Tears pooled in her eyes and she couldn't stem them. She was so glad Adrian's daughter was safe at home with her family. She'd been easy to find once the Gardaí knew where to look. James Foley-Cox had hidden her inside his house, bound and gagged, all while his mother lay dead on the living room floor. Julia wondered if Shauna would carry psychological scars from her ordeal, but for now, knowing she was safe and unharmed was a huge relief. It meant all she had to worry about right now was Philip. She wiped at her eyes with the sleeve of her jumper.

'He survived surgery, thankfully. But one lung was punctured and there's been damage to the soft tissue in his back. It really doesn't sound good.' She looked into Riordan's eyes. 'Can you update me on what's going on? I could do with the distraction.'

He pulled his hands out of his pockets and scrubbed his face with them, dragging the puffy bags under his eyes. He cradled his head in his hands for a moment, blinking quickly, before finally looking at her. 'In my whole career I've never worked on anything like this. James Foley-Cox is one of us, which has been the most shocking part of this for me, to be honest. But he's a very sick man. Inside his head, somehow this is all our fault. You and Adrian were his prime targets because of your involvement with Léa and Camille Baudelaire.'

'I just …' Julia had no words, no way to understand this.

Riordan looked at her sadly. 'It's all over the papers, of course. People talk. Even our own. There's a lot of money to

271

be made from leaking information to the highest bidder. The press have it all – the details of Adrian's death, the attack on you in the Carmichael Estate, everything. That's another problem to add to the list, and let me tell you, heads will roll when I find out who's behind it!'

'So is that his name? James Cox?'

'The media are going with the English version of his name, and apparently a double-barrelled surname takes up too much space on a newspaper headline.'

'Right … and he did all this because he lost his child?'

'And his partner. It's a sad story, really. His devout Catholic mammy refused to allow his name to be put on the child's birth certificate because Shay and Léa weren't married. Shay planned to marry Léa once he'd completed his training, once he had means. His mother allowed Léa and the child to live with her but according to neighbours, the woman was difficult, and didn't treat Léa kindly while Shay was in the Garda college. Léa left Shay and moved to the city when the little girl was about eighteen months old. And shortly after that, she was dead. The list of people Shay blamed was long.'

'Why wait until now?'

Riordan shrugged. 'Maybe he was building up to it. Or maybe he found a way to read the full details of the investigation in the files. Who knows? Shay had his whole life planned out. In his eyes, his mother ruined that and so did we. That doesn't give him the right to kill, though!'

'What happened to Camille afterwards?' This was an element of the job Julia often thought about – what happened when the people sent in to help moved on to the next problem? Who helped the victims recover?

'We're still gathering the facts, but it seems that, unfortunately, after Léa took her own life, the little girl was taken to live abroad with her maternal grandmother. Shay has no idea where she is.'

Julia grimaced; Shay had truly lost everything. The life he had planned, the people he had loved, had all been taken away from him. But it would never excuse the pain he had caused.

Riordan rubbed his palms over the legs of his trousers, slumping a little in the chair. They watched nurses walk to and fro for a few minutes. What else was there to say? It was over; they had the killer in custody and had saved his latest victim. Shauna was recovering well, and hopefully, Philip would survive. They even knew Shay's motive. But the sadness and horror of it all hung over them, preventing any sense of relief or satisfaction from lifting the weight.

'Is it always this bad?' Julia asked softly, trying to read the emotion on his face. 'The hard cases, I mean. I've wanted to be more directly involved for such a long time, but I don't know how I could shake this off and move on to the next thing. How does anyone sit at a desk and open the next file after a case like this?'

Riordan stood up and looked down at her.

'All cases are this hard; we are right in the middle of the worst of humanity. Whether there are two dead girls or a man beating the shit out of his neighbour, it's all the same to us. We deal with it as best we can and move on to the next.'

Julia looked past him at the doctor who seemed to be walking her way. She focused on Riordan again; 'I don't know if I could do that.'

'Well, make up your mind. I heard you've been unlucky

with your bids for promotion. If you decide to apply again, I'll be recommending you.'

'Pardon?' She stared at his face, her mouth hanging open in shock. She had dreamt of hearing a superior officer say those words for years.

'You've earned it, *more* than earned it. I know this isn't the time or the place to discuss it but if you want it, I'll do all I can.'

The young doctor standing beside them cleared his throat. His white coat hung over tiny wrists and off narrow shoulders; he seemed too young to Julia. She had thought that about Shay – James – too. She knew now that outward appearances betrayed nothing of the person underneath. She wiped at her face again and stood up, nodding in greeting.

'Mrs Harte? I'm Dr Martin Leonard, I've been treating your husband. We spoke briefly yesterday.'

'Dr Leonard, yes. How is he?'

The doctor turned and walked down the corridor, expecting to be followed. Riordan waved her away with one hand and turned to go. Julia felt a pang of sadness watching him walk away, feeling that everything was irrevocably different now.

The doctor was speaking as he walked, too busy, it seemed, to stop for a moment. She could hear the soles of her shoes squelching on the damp floor as she tried to keep up with him and his words, as she struggled to concentrate.

'Your husband is still dependent on support to breathe.' Julia's whole body felt rigid with tension. 'The bones in his face will heal, as will his ribs and so on. But really, it's his spine and lungs that are our main concern. We remain unsure about whether there's some nerve damage, but as

274

we've told you, we need time to really determine that.'

They stopped at the door to Philip's room. For the first time since greeting her, Dr Leonard looked at Julia properly. 'We've done all we can. Only time will truly tell how well your husband might recover.'

'I understand,' she whispered, wishing to go back in time, to sipping a brandy on the sofa with Philip after a long day. Dr Leonard walked ahead of her into Philip's room. Julia followed, preparing herself to see him for the first time.

He was almost unrecognizable. His face was swollen and dark patches of colour stained his skin. Tubes protruded from his neck and arms and his body seemed twisted under the bedsheet. As she swayed and struggled to stay on her feet, the doctor was speaking again.

'He *is* stable, but as I said, we have a long way to go. You can sit with him if you like, but not for too long.'

He left and Julia stayed, sitting in another hard plastic chair, rain teeming down outside, bouncing on the windowsill. She watched her husband, his chest rise and fall, his soft eyelashes on his cheeks, his dark hair pushed back from his forehead; hair she had run her fingers through, hair she had nagged him that needed a trim, hair he pulled when he was frustrated. The doctor had said this was a waiting game – well she would wait with him, as long as it took.

Three weeks later, when she stepped inside his room, Philip was awake. He watched her settle into the chair, listened to her tell him that James Foley-Cox had been sent for psychiatric assessment after stabbing a fellow prisoner while on remand, and stayed quiet while she promised him she had lined up the best physical therapist in the province of Munster to take over his care.

When Philip finally spoke to her, she didn't recognize the coldness in his voice.

'I won't be coming home, Julia.'

'Well, of course not yet! You'll be in rehab for a while, I know that. I've had a guy come to look at the house – I think we'll have to consider selling it, to be honest. There's only so much they can do to adapt it for your wheelchair. And yes, I know they said the chair will probably be temporary, but maybe we should move anyway? Change is good. We'd be better off buying a bungalow and maybe we can stay in Knockchapel. Or we could move a little farther out – there are a lot of new estates being built in Carrigaline and that's not too far away. What do you think?'

'I won't be coming home,' he repeated slowly, 'to live with you.' It was obvious that his throat still ached from the breathing tubes, and speaking was a huge effort for him, but his voice was clear and strong. He was determined to say what was on his mind.

She looked at him, blinking quickly, wondering if she'd misheard.

'This has been a wake-up call. I almost died. I've had a lot of time to think. I don't know what my future holds, but I do know that we have grown apart. We want different things.'

'Phil—'

'We've ignored the obvious for a while, Julia. You just won't listen. You brought James Cox into our lives, and I don't blame you, but this isn't what I want. I *know* you. You want *this* life; catching men like him and locking them up, moving on to the next madman. You need it.'

'Philip, no, I—'

'I wanted a family. Isn't it ironic – I'm so fucked up after the attack, I don't even know if that's possible now.'

'Phil – what are you saying? We *love* each other! I don't want to lose you!' He had said those words when he'd pleaded with her to turn away from investigating Adrian's death, but she hadn't listened. Now she couldn't seem to get through to him. The realization that she was losing the love of her life gripped her by the throat. 'I'll give it all up. The job – I don't want it if I can't be with you. We can still try for children, we can—'

'I don't want to, Julia. Not with you.'

She sat back into the chair, winded. He began to cry then, and for the first time since she'd known him, he refused to let her touch him, even to rub his arm while he sobbed violent spasming tears. When he had composed himself enough to speak he asked her to go. She didn't want to upset him any further, so she left.

She gave him time … she lived in hope.

He never came home to their house in Knockchapel. Instead, he moved in with his sister Frances and her family and recuperated there. Julia called to see him every day but he refused to allow her into his sister's living room, his makeshift bedroom. He wouldn't speak to her. She didn't let that deter her – he would change his mind. She drank cups of tea in Frances's kitchen, endured the stony silence of her in-laws' blame, punctured only by Philip's groans of pain from the living room. She was at the house when his physiotherapy commenced, albeit confined to sit outside in the car this time, her sister-in-law weary of it all.

She wanted him to know she wasn't giving up. Philip

had accused her of being stubborn once – now he was the one being obstinate. She convinced herself they would laugh about that in time.

After two months, Frances called to collect the rest of his things. She told Julia she was no longer welcome at the house. Reality and acceptance wound together painfully; she had chosen this, not intentionally, but she had pushed him away.

One month after that, Julia put their home on the market. The small wooden For Sale sign at the front garden was a symbol of all she had lost.

Solace was found in the one thing she had promised Philip she would trade if he came back to her. There were people who needed her; assault victims, lost children, car accidents, drunken brawlers. Des Riordan stood by his promise to support her bid for promotion. She purchased the mobile phone Philip had wanted her to have, left her number with Brendan and Kathleen, hoping that one day he might remember the love they had shared and want to find her.

He never did.

Five years later, when Julia returned to her city-centre apartment from a memorial ceremony commemorating the life and work of Adrian Clancy, she found that Philip had had legal documents delivered; he had begun the process to end their marriage.

38

2024

The press conference, with an update on the murdered college students and the disappearance of Grace York, is running behind schedule.

Julia looks at the images on the large screen that flanks the wall at the front of the room. The three victims are on display, the photographs chosen showing them in the full vibrancy of life. Hannah Miller's smile is broad, her face flushed and happy as she hugs her German shepherd to her cheek. Elena Kehoe's parents provided a photograph of her at her school graduation ball. Her dark hair is curled and swept back from her face, her smile full of anticipation and excitement. Grace York is the only person in the trilogy of young women affected by this who could still be alive. Her smile is less bright; the only image available right now is from her college identification card. Julia stares at the young woman's dark eyes on the screen, her heart beating hard in her chest.

Neil Armstrong and Sadie Horgan are standing at the

top of the packed room, waiting for the go-ahead to begin. Armstrong has put his suit jacket back on and added a tie, but the collar of his shirt remains askew, mainly because he keeps adjusting it. His face is pink. A Garda is handing out sheets of paper bearing bullet-point details of the case; as he walks past Julia he grimaces. 'Small Step looks like he's gonna explode!'

She can empathize; she always hated press conferences and only did them on the instruction of her boss. Riordan is standing beside her now, both of them up near the lecterns but out of sight of the journalists who have taken their seats and are waiting expectantly. She's glad he seems more like himself, revived after some food and a rest in the staff canteen; she has Saoirse O'Reilly to thank for that. Standing here beside him feels natural, despite her trepidation at coming back. It feels like the old days, when they worked as part of a team where the chief was happy to be hands-on and she was happy to learn. His presence beside her is the only thing making this return to Cork bearable.

Riordan seems calmer now, knowing that Síle and Rosie are out of the house while Gardaí investigate whoever delivered the note and basket of fruit to Julia. The more Julia thinks about that, the less she thinks it's threatening. Fruit? That's hardly sinister. If anyone wanted to freak her out, some heavy breathing down the phone would do it. A basket of fruit isn't usually something to worry about. A thought has been vying for attention in her mind for the last thirty minutes, though – could Philip have sent it? It seems unlikely, but perhaps he knows she's back in Cork and wanted to reach out. Then she remembers the note wasn't signed, and that wasn't something he'd do. Not that she really knows him any more, not after thirty years ...

Sadie Horgan calls for attention and the room grows silent. Julia looks at the journalists and news reporters. They'll want sound bites as well as visuals and details. It's a useful, though often fractious relationship; now she remembers the journalists who camped outside the station after Adrian was murdered, and how afraid she felt of their presence. Over the years she learned how to say she had no answers in a way that didn't give away too much truth. She wonders how Neil Armstrong will fare.

Sadie Horgan turns and gestures to the images of Elena Kehoe, Hannah Miller and Grace York. She outlines the progress in the two murders and appeals to the public for any information they might have. It's stark listening; the questions heavily outweigh the answers and the sum of their leads points to Ian Daunt, a man with a solid alibi, forcing her to admit they have no suspects at this point in time.

Beside her she notices Riordan step forward slightly, patting his pockets.

'Blast!' he moans, and turns to her. 'Can I have your key? I could do with my nitro spray and I've left it in the car.'

She pulls the key from her pocket. 'Do you want me to come with you?'

He shakes his head. 'I won't be long. Five minutes.' He walks to the door behind them and slips out of the room.

The press conference continues and she leans against the wall behind her, her left shoulder pinching a little. The discomfort of it is beginning to annoy her. Questions are invited from the journalists, and Julia notices that there's been no mention of her book at the crime scene, which means the reporters are unaware of it and its possible significance. There's been no mention of a possible link to James Cox so far either; the chief superintendent has obviously decided there's no need to bring it into the public realm of information yet. She knows this is a good idea, holding something back until they are sure it's really necessary to release the information. It will leak eventually, these things always do, but she agrees with the tactic. Is there any need to mention Cox and the fact that the person they are looking for is probably copying his killing spree? She doesn't think so. He's serving as inspiration to someone, that's for sure, but until they know more …

She steps away from the wall. She can tell that Armstrong has noticed her and is watching, but she can't focus on him.

They've missed something; the sequence doesn't make sense. She remembers what Armstrong said earlier … 'he'll come for you'. Cox came for Julia at the end, but before that he killed two young girls, took another … and killed her partner. By the time Shauna Clancy was taken, Adrian was already dead. So this time, is the killer skipping a step? If he *is* recreating the past and following the blueprint laid out by Cox, why has he decided not to kill the man she's working with?

Unless he hasn't.

Yanking open the door she runs from the room, jarring her shoulder on the wooden door frame but pushing on. The air in the reception area of the station is colder than the heat of the conference room, and the car park outside is colder still; the chill rushes into her lungs. She gasps it in. Someone is calling to her from behind but she keeps moving.

The car park was full when they returned from searching Grace York's house, so she parked on a narrow side street,

282

approximately three hundred metres away from the station. It had been a short walk back; now she runs along the street, her silk scarf whipping about her face, and quickly spots the red Hyundai. The back door behind the passenger side is open, and she can see the silhouette of Riordan sitting inside. She slows to a walk, fear weighing her whole body down.

Maybe she's wrong. Maybe the anxiety and dread she has carried for the last thirty years were all for nothing and she's overreacting now. But as she approaches the car and Riordan's silhouette doesn't move, she knows. When she reaches him, her mobile phone is already pressed to her ear for an ambulance. She doesn't want to see it but she can't look away – Riordan is Adrian, much older and yet the same, wide, frightened eyes staring at her desperately while his hands clutch at the blood seeping from a slash on his neck.

She pulls off her scarf and carefully winds it around the wound, closing her eyes as he gasps a wet, sickening sound. Behind her, Armstrong and Lee Murphy are running towards them; around her, two pedestrians have stopped to stare, a woman to scream. Cameras are angled at them, flashes lighting the air around her. This is no Morse code, this flashing of lights. It's the macabre fascination of death, pointed at them, capturing their pain.

Julia isn't a young Garda in a dark, deserted street, with her partner's blood drying into the lines on her hands. She isn't alone. But the horror she feels is the same, as is the certainty that whoever did this is nearby, watching her, running down the clock until they meet face to face.

39

2024

Riordan's granddaughter, Rosie, has fallen asleep, the young girl's head on Julia's shoulder. She thinks it's a blessing, although she marvels that anyone could sleep on the hard plastic chairs of the hospital waiting room. Síle is in a treatment room with Des. He's conscious, for now, and Julia hopes that's a good sign.

She hates being here. The smell of disinfectant rests like a taste in her throat. The sight of nurses and doctors in uniforms and soft shoes is setting her teeth on edge. It all reminds her of Philip; this is the same hospital she waited in for him to come home, but he never did. His doctors weren't sure if he'd survive James Cox's attack, but he defied the odds night after night.

Ultimately, she lost him anyway.

She thinks of her old house in Knockchapel, the home they shared before she let everything that mattered to her slip away and replaced it with things she thought were important. What a fool she has been. She often wonders if he would have ended their marriage eventually, or if they would have plodded along like so many couples do, honouring their vows and settling for companionship, for someone familiar to grow old with. But she would have gladly accepted a faded love, an aged version of him, rather than losing him.

She'll never know.

She filled the gap he left with work. There were relationships with new colleagues to forge, mostly men, but that was something she was used to. She earned their respect – even Jim Connolly's. Her bond with Des Riordan deepened. But she never recreated what she had with Adrian Clancy, the soft jibes, the trust, eventually sharing each other's thoughts. No one ever called her Jules again. She never met anyone outside of her professional life that she had any interest in. She has remained alone, and busy, for thirty years.

A lonely life.

There was more money than she knew what to do with, first from the sale of the house in Knockchapel, and then from her increased salary when she was promoted. She bought an apartment in the city to be nearer her job, but the amount of money sitting in her bank account freaked her out. People like her didn't have this much money, she hadn't grown up with it and she had no idea what to do with it.

Until unexpectedly she did; on an afternoon in Mary Clancy's house, when Shauna and her mother were sitting at the kitchen table with a sheet of paper and a pen, trying to figure out how to pay for Shauna to study medicine. She had worked hard at her exams, had earned her place in college, but she had four younger siblings and there was never enough money to go around. Julia had an idea then and it had felt like the most wonderful idea she'd ever had. At first Mary and Shauna protested. Eventually she wore them down, just like she'd worn down Des Riordan a few years earlier, and Shauna studied medicine. Julia had felt proud she could do this for Adrian's child.

She shifts her weight on the chair, thinking there's nothing quite like a hospital waiting room to make a person relive their past. She begins to shiver, her teeth clattering together inside her mouth, feeling exhausted.

She doesn't hear anyone approach, but when she opens her eyes, Dr Shauna Clancy is standing in front of them. She smiles at Julia and sits down beside her. Shauna looks so like her father that Julia feels close to tears.

'Julia! When I heard the name of the patient I wondered if I'd see you.' She clasps Julia's hands in hers. 'You should have called me! How long have you been back in Cork?'

'Just a few days. I thought you might be on holidays with Mary – I got her postcard.' Was that only days ago? 'Des and I are consulting on a case.'

A shadow crosses Shauna's face and she blinks whatever thoughts were intruding into her consciousness away.

'Are you unwell, Julia? You look very pale. You look like you need to rest.'

'What can you tell me about Des? Please, Shauna – his throat was cut and I—'

She stops speaking; how could she have been so insensitive? This is the exact way Shauna's own father was murdered. She must be finding this difficult, to deal with a patient with a similar injury. Julia squeezes her hands harder. 'I'm so sorry. This must be very hard for you.'

'It's okay,' Shauna reassures her with a slight smile. 'I

know it wasn't done by the same person – I saw the news last month. I know that *he* is dead. And while this is very similar to Dad's injury, it isn't enough to kill a person.'

Julia's heart jolts in her chest. 'How do you mean?'

'It wasn't a deep cut and didn't cause enough blood loss to seriously injure Mr Riordan. As deliberate attacks go, and I've seen too many stab wounds in here, this seems almost half-hearted – it's a shallow cut in a straight line. Nothing significant was severed. But it's worth considering Mr Riordan's age and heart condition. Time will tell how well he comes back from this.'

Fifteen minutes later, Julia decides that Rosie would be better off at home. Des is sleeping, and Síle doesn't want to leave him, but she's happy for Rosie to return to the guesthouse with Julia. Her car is still behind the Garda tape of a cordoned-off crime scene in the heart of the city. A Garda whose name she doesn't know offers to drive her home and she gratefully accepts. Julia and Rosie hold hands in the back of the squad car and sit silently for most of the short drive home.

'Do you think Gram will be all right?' Rosie asks as they approach the Western Road; the nickname for Riordan isn't something Julia was aware of, and for some reason it makes her feel sad.

'I don't know, love. He's had an awful shock. But the doctors are taking good care of him.'

'Okay,' Rosie says simply. She turns her head away to watch the city lights, raising her hand to wipe at her cheeks every few seconds. Julia holds her other hand tight. When they turn into the driveway of Síle's guesthouse and the squad car pulls to a stop, Rosie runs from the car into the house next door to retrieve Mutt.

Julia leans forward and speaks to the Garda. 'Can you stay here while I make a quick phone call please?' She nods her agreement and turns on the radio, offering Julia a small measure of privacy. Neil Armstrong answers on the first ring.

'Mrs Harte, I was just about to call you. How is Mr Riordan?'

Why the man insists on keeping things so formal by calling her *Mrs Harte* is beyond Julia's comprehension, and not something she cares about any more.

'He's comfortable,' she answers. 'I'm back at the guesthouse with his granddaughter. Until her parents arrive back from a cruise tomorrow morning, I want protection outside the house.'

'Pardon?'

'You heard what I said. Whoever is doing this is definitely copying James Cox, which means Des was in the firing line the whole time, only we didn't consider that until it was too late. So here we are; let's not make any further mistakes. It's too late for Rosie and me to stay anywhere else and the child is exhausted. Her parents' flight lands in the morning – I want a Garda presence outside this house for the night, and tomorrow morning, we'll leave here.'

'I don't think—'

'Síle is going to stay with Des overnight, which is very understandable. Rosie's family are away, so tonight, I'll take care of her. I want someone outside the house. It needs to happen.'

There's silence on the other end of the line while he thinks about what she's said. Eventually he answers, frustration weighing his words.

'I don't know if the chief will go for it; resources are tight.'

'It's a couple of hours, Neil. Make it happen.'

'Leave it with me.'

He hangs up. Julia nods her thanks to the Garda in the front of the car and climbs out.

An hour later, Rosie is asleep in a bedroom at the top of the house, having moved out of her ground-floor room. Julia reasons it's safer for the girl not to be near a window at street level. After she had checked the whole house and made sure they were alone, she prepared buttery toast and hot chocolate for them both and allowed Rosie to watch TV for a while before she suggested bed. Rosie was so tired she complied easily, especially when Julia suggested she bring Mutt with her. He's more comfort blanket than guard dog, but it made Rosie happy to have him by her side.

She checks on them now, the door creaking as she pushes it open. This bedroom is colder than the others, probably because it hasn't been in use while the guesthouse is closed. Julia steps inside and pulls a blanket from the end of the bed onto the bundle on top of Rosie, who is sleeping soundly, one arm wrapped around Mutt.

She walks through the house again, methodically checking all the windows and doors. Peering around the sheeting that separates the new kitchen from the old, she shivers. Outside, the equipment the builders left behind makes hulking shadows on the grass; she turns on the external lights, deciding to leave them on overnight.

At the front of the house, she lifts the living room curtains to examine the street. A Garda car is parked outside as requested. Only one person sits in the driver's seat; it's enough. She remembers her embarrassment at having protection outside her house before but that was when she cared about how things looked. Now, she knows the power of such a deterrent. Tonight, the car parked outside is a symbol of protection. Tomorrow, Rosie's parents will return and take her home, and Julia will check in to a hotel until she can see this through.

She sits down on the sofa, the TV muted in front of her. There will be no sleep tonight. She couldn't even if she wanted to. Every time she closes her eyes she sees Riordan's face, and she fears that if she falls asleep, he'll be in her dreams too. Riordan and Adrian, each one bleeding their life out onto her hands while she stands beside them, letting it happen.

Useless fucking bitch.

Two flashlights rest on the coffee table in front of her, both ready to be used if needed. One golf club is propped up against the nearby armchair. She places the small canister of stolen pepper spray beside the flashlights – she gave one to Riordan too but he never got to use it. On the table, she rests her fully charged mobile phone, her bottle of brandy and the one remaining wedding-present glass. She stares at the liquid for a few minutes ...

Who is doing this?

Why?

She pours the only measure of alcohol she'll allow herself tonight and swallows it quickly, gasping. There are no answers. Only questions. But everything comes to a head eventually; the last thirty years have taught her that.

40

2024

The dawn wind rattles against the windows. Mutt needs to go outside; he peers out at the rain with a small whimper.

'Go on, be quick!' Julia encourages him, watching from the back door. The shapes that worried her last night, the builder's equipment that lies scattered around the grass haphazardly, are getting soaked in this downpour. Pulling her mobile from her pocket she texts Síle, asking her to tell the builders not to come to work today. From now on, she will assume that this house, and anything associated with her here in Cork, is not safe.

Mutt scoots back inside and she dries him off with a towel before filling his breakfast bowl. While he's busy, and while Rosie is still sleeping, she makes her way to her room and begins to pack. She's not sure where she'll stay yet – it needs to be somewhere that allows her dog – but she knows she won't be leaving Cork until this is over.

Noise downstairs jolts her; she picks up one of the golf clubs, running towards the sound. Neil Armstrong, and a woman Julia has never seen before, are standing in the hall being enthusiastically licked by the worst guard dog in the world.

'Mrs Harte.' Armstrong smiles tightly. 'I was outside when I saw Mrs Riordan here arrive at the door.' His eyes rest on the golf club; Julia pushes it into the hall closet.

'I'm Rosie's mum, Elle,' the woman says. Her auburn hair is scraped into a ponytail, her face flushed in annoyance as she shakes her legs, pushing Mutt away and running her hands over her jeans. 'Where is she?'

'Rosie is asleep upstairs,' Julia answers, raising a hand to block the woman from walking past. She could be anyone; she's not about to let a complete stranger walk unchecked through the house, not after what she saw yesterday. The woman in front of her tuts audibly with indignation.

'Excuse me! This is my mother-in-law's house!' She raises one hand, letting a set of keys dangle in the air. 'How do you think we came inside?'

'Mum?' Rosie interrupts, running towards them in pyjamas and bare feet. 'You're back!' Mutt leaps onto her and she pulls him into her arms. 'Have you spoken to Granny? Where's Dad?'

'Your father has gone to the hospital,' Elle answers, her eyes on the dog. 'Remind me where Granny keeps the coffee.' She pockets her keys and strides forward.

'You can't stay here,' Julia says firmly, folding her arms. 'It isn't safe. We can't go into the specifics right now, but you both need to find somewhere else to stay. Just for a few days.'

Elle stops, her eyebrows raised, pink staining her cheeks. 'Is that some sort of joke?' Her shrill tone belies too little time spent on holiday and too little sleep on the journey home. 'Patrick just dropped me off here and went straight to the hospital. Where exactly am I supposed to go? Rosie – for God's sake, put down that bloody dog!'

Armstrong steps forward, his arms spread wide, appealing to Elle to see reason. 'I realize this is a far cry from your Mediterranean cruise but we are investigating a murder.' Julia can't believe a sweet girl like Rosie is in any way related to this woman; the attack on Des seems like nothing more than an inconvenience to her. 'You and Rosie need to go somewhere else. Do you have any other family in Cork?'

The pink on Elle's cheeks is now bright red.

'Rosie and I are not going anywhere!'

Armstrong glares at her; pulling his mobile from his pocket at the sound of an incoming call, he listens, offers agreement, and hangs up.

'Have they found Grace York?' Julia asks.

'No. That was Dr Moore. She has some test results back. I'm going to her office now. Are you coming?'

This is a first. It takes Julia only a moment to nod.

'And what exactly are *we* supposed to do?' Elle demands.

'*Christ!*' Armstrong bellows, making them all jump. He pushes his hands through his hair roughly, before making a fresh call and issuing instructions. When he turns to them again his expression allows for no discussion.

'Garda Lee Murphy will be here in less than three minutes. He'll stay with you in this house until your husband returns. And then you all leave – I don't care where you go. All right?'

As they walk to the squad car outside, Julia looks at the crumpled lines on the back of Armstrong's suit. It's the same suit he was wearing yesterday.

'Rough night?' she asks.

'You could say that,' he mutters, climbing into the driver's seat.

'It was you in the car. You stayed outside all night. Why?' She's stunned. She'd told him to sort out protection; she had no idea he would do it himself.

'You wanted a presence outside the house. I get it. It's a good deterrent. But the chief said we didn't have the resources.' He shrugs as he starts the car. 'It's no big deal. By the way, what's with the golf club?'

Julia ignores that. 'Don't you have a family?'

He blinks in surprise at the change in conversation. 'A daughter, Aria. She's ten.'

'Aria Armstrong … that's a memorable name. Are you still with her mother?' She's never seen him wearing a wedding ring. She doesn't understand why she wants to know, just that she does. For a moment, she thinks he'll tell her it's none of her business. But he nods.

'We're not married, but we've been together for over twenty years.'

'That's good.' Julia turns to watch the road. 'I'm grateful you protected us last night. But take a fool's advice: don't spend too many nights on the job when you could be at home with the people you love.'

As they drive onto the Western Road the nearby paths are already busy with students, some with backpacks, most with headphones, a lot of them walking alone. Elena and Hannah should be among them, Grace too, attending their lectures. How ironically sad, Julia thinks, that three women studying the minds of serious offenders should find

294

themselves suffering at the hands of one.

Armstrong is silently brooding as he drives; when they stop at a red light he rests his wrists on the steering wheel, tapping his fingertips on the dashboard. This case is draining him, she can see that. Julia flexes and rotates her left shoulder in the small space of the passenger seat.

'What's wrong with your arm?'

'Nothing. It's just an old injury playing up.'

'Yesterday was … hard.' He doesn't look at her, keeping his eyes on the road ahead of them as he attempts to merge into the right-hand lane.

Julia inhales sharply. 'It really was. Hopefully, Des will pull through.'

Suddenly, she feels a mounting urge to punch and kick the dashboard, to expel all the anger that's been burning inside her since Des was attacked. She doesn't feel tired, even though she didn't close her eyes all night. Her body feels the jerky pulse of adrenaline and she's in desperate need to expel it. Instead, she rests her head back against the seat and digs her nails into the palms of her hands.

'You must have seen some terrible things over the last thirty years,' Armstrong continues. 'I haven't been a DS long, but I've already seen too much. There's just no reconciling it, is there?'

Julia can tell he's really struggling with this case. Twenty years ago, maybe, Des was in her position and she was the younger investigator, battling to make sense of the horror their chosen career exposed them to. He counselled her then, but she can't remember what he said now.

'How are we ever supposed to get used to this?' Armstrong continues as he turns the car into the hospital car park.

'We're not,' she answers quietly. 'If you ever think any of this is normal then it's time to quit. People do terrible things to each other every day, Neil. You learn to live with it. It gets easier.'

And then the day turns to night and the dark hours arrive, making a liar of her, because nothing is easier at all. Has she ever learned to live with it? If Des dies without justice, can she live with that?

'Come on, let's see what the doctor can tell us.'

41

2024

Dr Moore is waiting for them in her office.

'Christina,' Julia says, 'you have results for us?'

The last time she was here – was it only yesterday? – she told Armstrong she wouldn't step all over his investigation, that she'd let him ask the questions. But that was then, before Riordan was attacked and before she realized this all comes back to her again, just like it did for James Cox. So today, she's first to ask the questions and the detective sergeant can deal with that however he likes.

The doctor smiles at her, and it doesn't reach her eyes.

'Please take a seat.' She gestures to two chairs opposite her desk. 'The results from some of the tests I ordered came in early this morning. We have—'

The phone on her desk rings; Julia rubs her forehead, feeling the dull pain of a headache take hold. As the doctor disagrees with the caller on something and orders more tests, Armstrong checks an incoming text on his phone. Suddenly, Julia feels very alone. Without Riordan beside her she feels like a boat adrift at sea. She wraps her arms around her stomach, pressing them into herself, wishing she could sit beside his hospital bed and be near him.

'Sorry about that.' Christina hangs up the phone. 'As I was saying, some of the tests I ordered came back this morning with results that might be useful to you.'

'Can you tell us if the victims were drugged?' Armstrong gets straight to it. 'A young woman is missing from her home and she had a similar cut on the right side of her back. She was attacked a few days ago. Her home does look like there was an attack of some sort, and it would be helpful to know what we're dealing with here. If the first two victims were drugged perhaps this young woman was too.'

Julia looks at him, startled. He's right. There's hardly any sign of disturbance in Grace York's home, just that one wall with a small area of blood on it, and a drop of blood on a broken decanter. It's not a lot to go on. They really know very little about how she disappeared. It's a good assumption that she was taken from her house – her phone was on the bedside locker, her car in the driveway, she hasn't been seen in days. But there's very little evidence that she left the house by force. Perhaps she knew her kidnapper. Or perhaps he drugged her too and dragged her across the same small stones as he did Elena Kehoe and Hannah Miller.

'No, I can't answer that yet.' Christina looks down at a sheet of paper on her desk, avoiding Armstrong's disappointment. 'This isn't some TV show where I can magic toxicology results overnight, as you well know. If you want my opinion, as I said yesterday, it's that it makes sense to me that the women I examined were incapacitated in some way.

But it could be that they were heavily intoxicated. As soon as I have those results, you'll be the first to know.'

'So what *do* you have?' He doesn't bother to temper his exasperation.

'The skin I removed from under Elena Kehoe's fingernails. I told you it wasn't presented as one would usually expect in defensive wounds; the skin wasn't raggedly torn. It was peeled. Or shaved. At least, that's what it looks like.'

She turns the computer monitor towards them and they lean forward. The image of the skin sample reminds Julia of the little shavings that are left behind after a pencil has been sharpened.

'How could that have happened?' she asks, watching as the woman across the desk shrugs gently.

'I really can't say. It's this part,' she points to an area of the skin that is red in colour, different from the rest, 'that I have information on. I was very intrigued by this, and it's the first result I have. I expect a full report on the skin samples by tomorrow, but I thought you might be interested in these early results.'

She pauses while Armstrong pulls a small notebook from his pocket and flips over to a clean page.

'What we found is a combination of chemicals, including biocides and cuprous oxide.'

'Meaning?' Armstrong asks, his pen poised.

'Meaning a substance was on that person's skin containing those chemicals. I can't speculate about what that means. Both chemicals are found in a variety of products and biocides have a range of uses. My lab contact told me that antifouling paint is one product that contains that chemical mix. Perhaps that's significant.'

'Antifouling paint is used on boats,' Julia says quietly, feeling a heave of anxiety roll in her stomach; this means something, she just needs the pieces to slot together to give her the answer. She and Philip had a boat ... she clasps her shaking hands together.

'Right ... so ... there's skin from another person under one victim's fingernails that contains chemicals found in antifouling paint, but it's probably found in other products as well. Is that the sum of it?' Armstrong snaps his notebook closed and stands up.

'For now, yes.' Christina looks at him coldly. 'The skin sample is being further analysed and I'll know more soon. I'll be in touch.'

With a shake of his head Armstrong turns to go, but Julia has one more question.

'Christina, the sample of pebbles we sent over. Have you had a chance to examine them?'

'I did actually. I compared them to the cuts on the victims. We are testing them – obviously – but I think you've found where they were dragged. Until I can confirm it, it will stay out of my report, but I hope to amend that by tomorrow evening.'

It has stopped raining but the clouds are heavy and dark, threatening to dump a further downpour on them as they jog through the car park. Inside the car, Armstrong broods silently for a few minutes, his hands tight on the steering wheel. Julia stares out the windscreen. There's an idea forming; she's letting it grow, examining it from all angles, turning it three-sixty degrees in her head. Riordan would never have needed these minutes to work it all out – she used to think that was her failing, taking the time to process information, needing to let it ferment in her mind. She long ago stopped comparing herself to the chief. She wishes she could run this past him now though …

Armstrong slaps one hand hard onto the wheel, breaking her thoughts.

'It's never a good idea to get on the wrong side of the pathologist,' Julia says gently. His shoulders are rigid with tension. 'You know by now test results take time.'

'Is that right?' He's seething, losing control of his temper along with this case.

'You know,' she says cautiously, 'you could work on your demeanour a little bit. It's just a suggestion. I've noticed you're a little … shall we call it, *tense*, which is understandable but it's off-putting. You wear your emotions on your sleeve and it'd be better to cultivate a calmer environment. Maybe try out a poker face from time to time.'

She watches him blink in surprise before turning to stare at her, his cheeks red.

'I don't have time to "cultivate a calmer environment"!' The effort to breathe steadily is making his shoulders shake. 'Grace York's parents will arrive at the station soon, demanding answers that I can't give them. Meanwhile, that same twenty-year-old woman is very likely to end up under that doctor's scalpel,' he jerks his thumb towards the office they just left, 'if I don't find her fast – if she's still alive. I got an update from Dan while we were in there; the group of friends Elena Kehoe and Hannah Miller left the club with are all accounted for and all have solid alibis for the rest of the night. One went home and had a late-night cuppa with her mother, another climbed into bed with her flatmate, three are on a taxi rank's CCTV waiting for over an hour to get home. The two girls separated from the others and got into an SUV; at some point in the night they likely ended up in Grace York's house where they were dragged across her garden stones and turned up dead the following morning. York hasn't been seen since then – she's either being kept somewhere or has been dumped somewhere. Nothing to report from the college interviews, no update on the partial of the SUV, a retired chief superintendent with his throat slit in hospital and the bloody pathologist is taking a fucking *age* to find anything worth working with! Whoever is doing this is making fucking fools of us and all our evidence amounts to jack shit!'

He stops, wiping his mouth with the back of his hand, and shakes his head.

'Sorry, Mrs Harte. You don't need to hear that. You didn't come down here to—' He turns his body to face her. 'Are you all right? Look, sorry – I didn't mean to upset you.'

'It's not that … I … it's just …'

She remembers everything Riordan taught her; how to turn over the evidence, to look at it from every angle, how each crime is a puzzle, the pieces all floating in the air. Some will land faster than others, but the trick is to recognize the ones that do. Everything is significant – a choice of drink, a turn of phrase, a look in someone's eye or a shrug in place of an answer. A name, changed from English to Irish and back again.

'What is it, Mrs Harte?'

'Call me Julia, for God's sake!' *How many times!*

'All right … Julia. What is it?'

302

Her face feels very hot, her chest tight. She looks into his eyes.

'You think this is about me, don't you? You've said it before. I didn't want to believe it but ... the book, the attack on Riordan ... you think it's about me and that he will come for me eventually?'

'Yes, I'm afraid I do. I know the file on James Cox inside out now. It's a pattern. What are you thinking?'

'The chemicals on the skin under Elena Kehoe's fingernails ... I don't believe in coincidences, Neil. The doctor said those chemicals are found in many substances, but they *are* found in antifouling paint. Philip and I had a boat; we used to treat it every year with antifouling paint to protect it before we launched it back into the water. I'm wondering if this person has a boat too, or at least *knows* boats.'

'And knows you had one.' His eyes are blazing with the possibility that she's right. 'We'd have to search every port and dock in the county. There must be ... I couldn't even guess the number of boats moored around Cork. It's a huge task and will take a lot of manpower. We'll have to get the whole crew out!' He pulls his mobile phone from his pocket. 'I'll contact the Port of Cork, they'll be able to tell me where to start.'

'I don't think you need to do that.' Julia takes a deep breath. 'I told you – Philip and I had a boat. It was moored in the Knockchapel boatyard. I could guarantee you that if this *is* about me, then that's where we need to go next.'

303

42

2024

Thirty years.

They drive south, every kilometre taking Julia closer to the only place that ever felt like home. She has never been back here; work took her very close a few times, which she found uncomfortable, but she has never been back to Knockchapel.

Brendan Adlington died two years after Julia left. Though she contacted Kathleen to express her sympathy, Julia didn't attend his funeral, citing her caseload as an excuse, knowing it was fear of returning to Knockchapel and seeing Philip again that kept her away. She couldn't face seeing him – she still loved the man who had rejected her.

Her fingers rub the hard band of her wedding ring now as they drive over a humpbacked bridge towards Knockchapel; the familiarity of the journey becomes stifling and she opens the passenger-side window.

'Sadie Horgan won't be there.' She knows this, having listened to Armstrong make arrangements as they drove.

'Grace York's parents have arrived. But she's sending a team down; we won't be on our own.' Julia wonders if he's repeating things out loud for his own benefit.

'I know, Neil,' she says softly.

'It's just, you didn't seem with it there for a while.'

'Ah,' she feels a little embarrassed, 'memories, you know.'

'Yeah well, the trip down memory lane can wait. Open the glovebox, there.' His voice is gruff and impatient again. She opens it and finds two slim, black flashlights. 'Anything else inside?'

'Nothing.' She thinks of the canister of pepper spray in her pocket but decides not to mention it. He's breaking the speed limit but keeps the lights and sirens off.

'Park a little bit up the street,' she suggests, peering out the windscreen at the brightening sky. 'We'll leave the car here and walk to the boatyard. We'll be two friends out for a morning stroll.'

'You don't want to announce that help is here?'

'This guy slits throats quick enough and has no issue stabbing young women in the back. I'd prefer you had an unmarked car and I'd prefer the rest of your colleagues were here already, so yes, let's hang back and take it slow.' Her days of rushing into dark houses and abandoned woodland estates ended long ago.

They drive on silently, following the winding road. Eventually Julia can see the water beside her, the breadth of it widening as they approach the village, the sun breaking through the clouds to glisten on the surface. It's a beautiful, scenic postcard and she feels sick. The boatyard sits beyond a small guesthouse at the entrance to the village. Armstrong pulls the car into the car park there and they climb out, both

305

standing still for a moment, the calm before the storm.

'Right.' Armstrong nods, stuffing one flashlight into his pocket. 'You take the other. I think we should go on ahead of the others. They'll see the car parked here and I have the phone. Are you okay to get going?'

She nods. She's very keen to get this over with.

The marina is to their left as they walk, turning into the entrance with quick strides and eyes focused on their surroundings. They walk past large metal hangers and through a concrete patch of ground where boats are parked up in various states of disrepair. There are two metal containers to the right and several cars parked around the boats; Armstrong nudges Julia. Every container is an enclosed space and that makes it a possibility where a body could be hidden, dead or alive. The jetty is ahead of them, composed of one long wooden boardwalk with six straight lines off it with too many vessels to count moored alongside. A few men walk and work nearby, and one straightens up, his eyes on Armstrong, and makes his way over.

'Here comes the man in charge,' Armstrong says under his breath.

Julia steps onto the jetty. The men are speaking now; she knows the guy will cooperate once Armstrong explains the situation. She walks on, familiar with the scenario and how it goes, so experienced with it that she feels a little suffocated. Or maybe it's the smell of the sea that's closing her airways – she knows that smell will linger in her hair long after she's left and bring with it memories and feelings she'd rather forget.

As she turns to look at the boats her knees buckle and she crashes onto the wood. There's a small yacht moored in the centre, with navy blue lettering on the white paint, the name of the vessel screaming through her mind.

The Léa-Camille.

She doesn't believe in coincidences.

Cox's partner.

His daughter.

This is it.

'Did you slip?' Armstrong is by her side. 'What ...' He follows her gaze and sees it too. He's been reading the file on James Cox, said he knows it inside out. Without a word he runs forward; the rush of air beside her is the jolt she needs. Julia takes a deep breath and sprints after him.

The ground is wet, the wood slippery from the earlier rain. *The Léa-Camille* is six boats in; as they approach a man emerges from the yacht onto the jetty, a small dark bag in his arms. Receding red hair, frameless glasses, a windbreaker straining over his large stomach: Ian Daunt. He turns as they approach – they are only feet apart now – and when he sees them his eyes grow wide, his mouth a startled O.

Daunt looks to the end of the jetty in the opposite direction; it offers nothing but open water. His flight response kicks in anyway – if he was thinking he could dodge past them, his quick decision is entirely flawed. Armstrong grabs him as he barrels past, both men collide and spin and hit the ground hard.

Julia runs forward, leaving the grunts and heaves of their tussle behind her. She hurries onto the boat, opening a small door and stepping into the cabin, immediately slipping to the floor. The ground is slick, and when she rises to her knees and struggles up to standing, she sees that her hands are stained red. There are lines through the blood on her palms, and a memory breaks through her thoughts. A cold night that slowly turned to morning when her hands were covered in Adrian's blood. A sob bubbles in her throat.

The door swings shut behind her and clicks loudly. The light inside is dimmer with the door closed and she can't see any switches on the wall. The yacht tilts; it's not quite dark in here, but the feeling of déjà vu tightens her chest.

Pulling out the flashlight Armstrong gave her she turns it on and sweeps the light around. A sound drives her forward. The cabin inside isn't big; to her right, the area opens into a living space with a sofa, a writing desk and a small double bed. There's a girl on the mattress, sitting upright against the wall. She looks so different to the photos that were in her bedroom, to the photograph the college provided for the missing person press release. This was something Julia grew familiar with; it was always the same when she and the other detectives were successful, that moment of wondering if they had saved the right person. The effects of trauma could change a person's appearance drastically. But she's sure this time – in the centre of the mattress, with her hands tied and her mouth gagged with white rope, is Grace York.

Her eyes are wide, as though she is silently screaming, and after a moment Julia realizes that the young woman is in fact screaming for help, her cries muffled but loud all the same. Shock is dulling her senses; she shakes her head and stares at the girl in front of her. She has bruising around her wide, dark eyes and dried blood on her chin, her pale blonde hair is limp and sticking to her forehead. A gash on her cheek reminds Julia of the broken crystal decanter on her living room floor. It's her – and she's alive.

'Grace? I'm Detective Inspector Julia Harte. Everything is going to be all right.'

43

2024

Armstrong walks into the incident room to a round of applause. He stops, mildly embarrassed, and holds up a hand for the group of colleagues around him to stop. It's been a long day. Though Grace York is in hospital, alive, with her parents by her bedside, he knows this isn't the time to celebrate. Not yet.

'Good result, Neil.' Sadie Horgan is beaming, her face flushed as she strides towards him and pumps his hand. 'Finding a missing person alive is what we do this for. I would congratulate you on some solid detective work but I believe it was a hunch?'

Armstrong doesn't answer but moves away to the top of the room where Dan West is pinning sheets to the noticeboard. This is still an open investigation. Armstrong hands him some images he's just printed out; the other man is too preoccupied to acknowledge him, and keeps moving, his hands in rhythmic motion over and back, desk to noticeboard.

'There's still a lot to do, but you did well. I'm proud of everyone on this team. I need a full report as soon as you can.' Horgan is beside him again, looking at him expectantly.

Armstrong pushes his sleeves up as he turns to her – the heat inside the room feels stifling. 'I agree there's a lot to do but today was good ... the pathologist led us to consider antifouling paint, and Mrs Harte wanted to check out Knockchapel. She used to have a boat, well her husband did. And it was moored there once upon a time. She was right.'

'So it *was* all linked to Julia Harte. And the name on the boat was a relative of James Cox?'

'His partner was named Léa and his daughter Camille.'

Horgan whistles and purses her lips. 'That's creepy to say the least. Ian Daunt at the scene is pretty great. I *knew* he was involved.'

And yet you turned him loose, Armstrong wants to say, but thinks better of it. He knows she had little choice. He turns his attention to Dan West. 'Did anything of interest turn up at the search of the York house?' Early results from the forensic search might be back by now.

'The latest update came in a half hour ago; there's nothing of note so far.' West scrawls notes on a whiteboard now with a thick marker. 'Except perhaps that Grace liked to get high. A small bag of weed was found in her bedside locker.'

'Anything from her laptop?'

'It's still with the tech lads. I'll put a rush on it.'

'Here you go, sarge, you look like you need it!' Saoirse O'Reilly hands Armstrong a coffee, a smile on her face. He accepts it with a grateful nod. 'In case anyone tells you I was bitching about you behind your back, I was, and I'll just say it to your face – I'm pissed you left me out of what happened this morning.'

He stares at her over the rim of the mug, unsure if she's serious.

'But I heard you were at the guesthouse anyway, and it all happened in a rush. Don't leave me out next time, okay?' She punches his arm playfully and moves away, sitting down at a desk and logging on to the system. He gulps the coffee; the adrenaline of the morning has faded and the lack of sleep overnight – and the night before – has caught up with him. He sits down heavily on the chair at Dan West's desk.

'So where's Mrs Harte now?' Horgan asks, perching on the edge of the desk opposite him.

'Gone back to the guesthouse. She's made her statement but she slipped in blood. We had to give her tracksuit pants. Needless to say, she wants to shower and change.'

'Does Grace York have significant injuries?'

'Nothing too serious,' Dan West answers from the noticeboard, back to pinning sheets to it again. 'Four stitches over her eye, lacerations on her wrists, a cut on her arm, bruises and so on. She'll be kept in hospital overnight for observation.'

Armstrong rests back into the chair and closes his eyes for a moment. When he opens them again, West is staring down at him. 'I need my desk.'

The room is growing louder and busier, as more Gardaí arrive for a look at the fresh crime scene photos and to hear first-hand what happened rather than pull titbits together from the gossip at the coffee dock. Armstrong stands slowly, his back protesting from sitting in the car all night and from the tussle with Ian Daunt earlier today. The man ended up with concussion, which has pissed Armstrong off on two counts – he'll have to fill in an extra report and there could be an investigation into his actions, plus it delays getting to interview him until tomorrow at the earliest.

Horgan is less buoyant now. She chews a thumbnail and stares at Armstrong; he knows she's thinking the same thing as him. 'If we can't interview Daunt until tomorrow then we have to look at his movements over the last twenty-four hours. I want to know who he texted, who he spoke to, where he was. He wasn't working alone.'

'I completely agree.' Tiredness is making Armstrong's legs feel weak. The coffee isn't substitute enough for two nights of broken sleep.

'We know he didn't kill the two students because his alibi checks out. He must be working with someone – this isn't over. I want a checkpoint set up on the road into Knockchapel. If Daunt's accomplice doesn't know about this morning yet he may decide to go back to the boatyard; only residents allowed into the area and anyone else is to be detained, got it?'

'On it.' West picks up his desk phone while summoning two nearby Gardaí to his side with his other hand. Despite this morning's result, the gnawing feeling in Armstrong's gut is growing stronger – while whoever killed Elena Kehoe and Hannah Miller is still at large, they should assume he's still active.

'This is weird.' Saoirse O'Reilly turns to them, leaning her arm over the back of the chair. 'I ran a search on *The Léa-Camille*. The information just came in. It's registered to a man named Conrad York.'

'Grace's father?' Horgan asks.

'Stepfather. He bought it back in 2022. Why would she be tied up on their own boat?'

The room has grown quieter, a sense of foreboding stealing the chatter. Standing still, Armstrong pinches his lower lip in between his fingers. 'What month did he buy it, can you find that?' He leans over her as she taps the keyboard.

'June, why?'

'Grace turned eighteen in June that year. The neighbour Mrs Harte spoke to at the Carmichael Estate called her "Daddy's little rich girl" … It could have been a birthday present. But why would they name the boat *The Léa-Camille*?'

'Maybe it's just a coincidence?' O'Reilly asks; he shakes his head. As much as he's tried to ignore Julia Harte, he's been listening over the last two days; where investigations are concerned, there are no coincidences.

The phone on Dan West's desk is ringing, but he's typing quickly, steadfastly ignoring it.

'Will you answer that!' Sadie Horgan demands, but he doesn't seem to have heard her, his eyes fixed on the screen in front of him. Armstrong steps over to his desk and stands behind him. 'What's this?'

'It's the report on Grace York's laptop.' He scrolls down a page of text with the mouse, leaning closer to the screen. 'It landed in my inbox just now. This case just keeps getting weirder …'

Horgan moves towards them and leans one hand on the desk, reading over his shoulder as Saoirse O'Reilly wheels her chair across to sit beside him.

'Are they newspaper articles?' she asks as he scrolls slowly through an array of saved pages. Each article looks similar; blocks of black and white text set under bold headlines and photographs of Julia Harte. Without looking at the year each article was published, it's clear they were saved in chronological order; the passage of time is captured in Julia's changing haircut and appearance. From youthful, uniformed Garda, to suited detective with a sleek dark ponytail at the nape of her neck, to retired author giving a lecture on criminology, her life is captured as though it's a photobook of her career.

'This is on *Grace's* laptop?' Horgan is unconvinced. 'There must be dozens of articles here!' West clicks through the rest of the files; next is an audio folder containing fourteen different saved podcast episodes with titles all referring to Julia. Armstrong reads the first one aloud: 'Fifteenth of April 2019, *Unravelling Her Secrets – Julia Harte & The Alias-Code*. What's this about?'

'I've no idea,' Horgan answers incredulously. The room is silent, save for the incessant ringing of the telephone on West's desk.

'That must be about that online craze a few years ago to decipher the pseudonyms she used in her book,' O'Reilly offers. The others look at her, stunned.

'There are radio interviews saved here too,' West says after a few more clicks of the mouse, 'going back ten years. And two RTÉ news interviews from back when she was a detective. But they were only saved recently; two years ago, six months ago, eight weeks ago. Hang on … it looks like they were accessed from the archives and saved into this folder over the last four years.'

'All right.' Horgan rubs the space between her eyebrows. 'Let's try to get our heads around this. And, Jesus, Dan, will you *answer that damn phone*!' Her face is flushed. 'It looks like Grace York had quite an interest in Julia Harte.'

'It looks more like an obsession to me.' Saoirse O'Reilly wheels her chair back to her own desk.

'Perhaps ... Neil, what are your thoughts?'

Armstrong doesn't answer ... right now, he doesn't know what he thinks.

'Well, she's studying criminology, isn't she?' Saoirse O'Reilly answers. 'Maybe that's it? She could be researching a project on Mrs Harte. We can ask her in a couple of hours when we interview her.'

Dan West clears his throat, the desk phone handset pressed to his ear. 'I don't know about that – Grace York has disappeared from her hospital room. She gave our lads the slip; they're looking for her and her mother is freaking out.'

Sadie Horgan looks over at Armstrong. 'Where did you say Mrs Harte is now?'

'She's back at the guesthouse, but—' He stops suddenly, his eyes on a Garda standing across the room. Lee Murphy. 'What *the fuck* are you doing here?' His shout booms around the room. 'You're supposed to be with Des Riordan's family on the Western Road!'

Lee Murphy's feet are rooted to the ground, his mouth opening and closing silently in the face of Armstrong's anger.

'I pulled him back!' Horgan's voice rises defensively. 'Once we had Ian Daunt in custody there was no need to leave a man there when he was more useful here!'

Armstrong can't speak – sheer frustration is vying with exhaustion inside his head and he can't form any words. His eyes meet Dan West's and the man nods, then starts speaking instructions into the phone. All Armstrong can do is tap Saoirse O'Reilly on the shoulder.

'With me,' he grunts, running from the room.

44

2024

It is twilight when Julia arrives back at the guesthouse. She wants nothing more than to stand under the heat of a shower until her skin feels clean, pour herself a large measure of brandy, and curl up in a chair with Mutt on her lap. She's exhausted.

Her phone and the stolen canister of pepper spray that she really must put back now that the investigation is ending, are in the pocket of another person's jogging pants, resting against her thigh. Grace York is alive, Ian Daunt will talk, and whoever helped him will be caught. If there *was* a connection to her, Armstrong and his team will figure it out – she's certain of it all. Within a few days, her car might be released and she and Mutt can head home.

It's almost over.

As she waves goodbye to the Garda that dropped her off, she thinks about the moment she found Grace. Embarrassment at how she introduced herself has stung her all afternoon.

'I'm Detective Inspector Julia Harte. Everything is going to be all right.'

It's what she said every time she rescued someone – the rank was different, of course, changing over time. But she can't understand why she introduced herself that way earlier – perhaps it was just the thrill of finding Grace York alive, the excitement of a great result. It's funny how she slipped so easily back into old habits.

Des will get a good kick out of it, she thinks, and she'll tell him too when she visits later. They had a great outcome this morning – she feels sure that positivity will extend to Des's recovery. Philip survived after all, and James Cox's attack on him was brutal. Where there's hope there's … what? She can't remember, it doesn't matter. She needs to get cleaned up and pull Mutt into her arms and get on with her life.

When she pushes open the front door to the guesthouse, Mutt runs towards her, a blur of white that barrels into her legs. She steps inside and pushes the door closed; the house is dark, the only light coming from the living room window off the hallway, and it feels cold in here, almost as cold as outside.

'Hello, little scruff.' She bends down to rub him, groaning at pain she wasn't aware of until now; she banged her knee hard on the floor inside the yacht. She notices Mutt is panting and his body is shaking; she gathers him into her arms and kisses the top of his head, pressing his body to hers. 'What is it? Are you cold? Where's Rosie?'

He whines repeatedly, his body shaking so hard it jerks in her arms. The tiny hairs on the back of her neck stand on end – she's never seen him like this before. She wonders why

319

he's agitated and why Rosie isn't with him.

'Have the Riordans left you behind?'

She had agreed with Rosie that when her father returned, she would leave food and water out for Mutt and put him in the kitchen with his toys and blanket before they left. And she assumes they *have* left the house because she didn't see Lee Murphy stationed outside. So why is Mutt so distressed?

She reaches out and flicks on the switch in the hallway. Nothing happens; the power is off. That explains the darkness in the house and the cool feel to the air inside here. Mutt licks her face, his touch shocking against her skin. Something is wrong. She blinks and breathes deeply, trying to keep focused. A dark house without power has been the substance of her nightmares for too long ...

The house is deathly quiet until suddenly a jolting cry pierces her. This could be the house in Douglas in 1994, it could be her home in Knockchapel where Cox came to kill her ... but it's not. It's a house where a young girl was waiting for her father to come back, and maybe she's in danger.

Because of Julia.

She eases open the nearby hall closet and pulls two coats onto the ground, gently resting Mutt on top, covering him with another, hoping it might warm him up. 'Stay here,' she whispers. She reaches behind the coats for a golf club tucked into the back. Next, she pulls a slim black flashlight from inside a man's boot – Riordan's, probably. Pulling her mobile from her pocket she dials Neil Armstrong's number.

He answers on the first ring.

'We're on the way. Are you inside the house?'

'Yes,' she whispers, 'the power is gone.'

'Get outside now!'

As she hangs up she hears a whimper of fear from the kitchen. It sounds like a young girl … it can only be Rosie. The front door is within touching distance but she knows she won't do it, she won't leave her. Memories flash and pull and she pushes them aside. Armstrong is minutes away, help is coming. But a lot can happen in minutes; she knows better than anyone that a life can be taken, a family destroyed. She won't let Rosie's life end because she was in the wrong place at the wrong time.

The golf club is cold in her hand, the flashlight in the other is steady. She closes the closet door, sealing Mutt safely inside, and moves quickly through the hall towards the kitchen. The beam of light in front of her rests on something by the entrance to the living room door; two feet splayed out on the carpet. She angles the light upwards, trailing up the legs and back of Rosie's mother. She lies face down on the floor, a red halo of blood around her head. Julia reaches out and presses the skin at the woman's neck; the weak pulse makes her sigh in relief. Pulling her phone out again she types a quick message to Armstrong: **Ambulance.** He calls her immediately and she silences the noise, pushing the phone back into her pocket.

A squeal of pain makes her jump to her feet. Mutt is barking loudly in the closet and she moves away from that noise towards the other.

In the kitchen, Rosie is standing rigid, facing the door, her neck stretched back as a blade presses into her flesh. Her eyes search the ceiling wildly, her mouth trembling. Metal glints against her skin. The torch beam swings over her and Rosie blinks, gasping. The shape behind her, the person pressing the knife into her skin so roughly that lines of blood drip down her neck, is too deep in shadow for Julia to make out who it is.

'You didn't recognize me – don't you remember me, detective?' They step forward, into the torch light. Julia staggers, grips the kitchen door. No ... this doesn't make sense.

Grace York's face is bruised and bandaged; she should be recovering in hospital or answering questions about her ordeal. She should be anywhere but here. But she smiles at Julia as she peers around the young girl held tight in front of her.

All the ghosts that haunt Julia in the dark of night are shrinking back now. This ghost is real, standing right in front of her.

'Because I remember you!'

45

2024

Grace York is panting with exhilaration, smiling in enjoyment.

Julia grips the golf club tight. Fear spikes her heart rate but the beam of her flashlight holds steady. She hadn't recognized the girl in the woman she found on the boat earlier; she'd been too distracted by another link to James Cox, *The Léa-Camille*. Her eyes had absorbed the blood and bruises on Grace's face but were blind to what should have been obvious – the look of satisfaction in the woman's eyes when Julia had spoken her name.

'It was all you,' she whispers, struggling to absorb the truth.

All the pleasure and excitement is stripped from Grace's face, as though she has been slapped. Suddenly her eyes are wide, fearful, and Julia is pulled into a fifteen-year-old memory ...

Three weeks into the search for five-year-old Grace Dunlea, they were desperate for any lead. Her disappearance was the beating heart of their team now, but for too long they'd been floundering with nothing to go on. Until one evening a call came in to the station that prompted a night-time operation.

'This is DS Julia Harte; you said you have information?'

'Well it might be nothing, but it's definitely strange. I saw my neighbour in Penneys this evening buying knickers for a child. He doesn't have any kids, I know that for a fact. It's just not right!'

Maybe it wasn't connected to Grace's disappearance in any way. But Riordan ordered four of them to call to the man's house immediately.

'Tell him it's a door-to-door enquiry. Suss him out.'

'If he's hiding something, I'll find it all right,' Jim Connolly muttered.

Riordan split the group in two; Steven Molloy and Garda Rachel Brennan would knock on the man's front door while Julia and Connolly would wait at the back of the house in case he made a run for it.

So they waited for the suspect, identified as Christian Thomas, to come home. Darkness descended while they sat in unmarked vehicles on his street, the day giving way to night. Ice had settled on the surface of the road and she could see it glistening as she shivered in the freezing air of the car, earning a derisive scoff from Connolly.

Before long, Thomas's car pulled into his driveway and they watched him walk into the house – he looked ordinary. Julia had learned by now that the more dangerous people always did.

Molloy and Brennan strode towards the house and up the driveway, the ruse of a routine house call in play. Julia and

Connolly stayed in the shadows at the side of the property and walked quickly around to the back. The glint of light from a narrow rectangular window near the ground caught her attention – this house had a basement. They heard the faint chime of the doorbell and Steven Molloy's deep voice reached them. Seconds later a man's voice joined in answer to his questions; it all sounded reasonable, no raised voices.

'What do we do?' Julia hissed as minutes passed without any escalation or sign this would go as they'd hoped. Connolly suddenly kicked at a refuse bin near the back door. It crashed to the ground, the sound booming in the quiet night. The voices at the front door rose, then higher still.

'Here we go!' he warned. 'Be ready!'

There was an audible commotion at the front of the house. Thomas argued that they had 'no right!' while Julia heard Molloy tell the man firmly to 'step aside!' There was a shout and, seconds later, the back door was yanked open as a man almost ran into them; Christian Thomas found himself face to face with Jim Connolly, who had been waiting too long for this moment. He grabbed Thomas by the shoulders and spun him around, pinning one arm high up his back. Thomas groaned in pain and fell to his knees on the hard concrete.

Julia stepped past them, pulling forensic gloves over her hands. The basement windows drew her like a beacon and in the kitchen she found a narrow door leading to a staircase. She ran down quickly, flicking a switch beside her on the wall, glad when a lightbulb sprang to life.

The basement was a workspace, with three desks loaded with computers and printers, high-tech cameras and lights

325

on tripods. She crossed to another door on her left, finding it locked.

'Shit!' she muttered. There was no time to search for a key. The light was dimmer here; pulling out her flashlight, she pointed it at the door and examined the wood. It was old, thin. She focused her eyes on a section of it and kicked at it as hard as she could, until the wood splintered and broke. Holding the flashlight between her teeth she pulled at the remains of the door until one long piece of wood came away. It had taken only minutes and the door yielded; she stepped inside another small room and felt like she had run into a brick wall. She was suddenly winded, unable to do anything but stand still and try to breathe. A small child lay on a single mattress in the middle of the room, dark hair falling over her cheeks, her body huddled, her eyes wide and fearful as she watched the door.

'Grace?' Julia sank to her knees beside the mattress. 'My – my name is Julia. I'm a guard. I'm going to bring you home to your mam, okay?'

The kitchen is cold, the plastic sheeting billowing in a draught that has invaded the house. The chill snaps Julia to attention. She steadies the beam of her flashlight on Rosie's chest, just below her neck, where Grace is still pushing the blade of a knife into her skin. Rosie has stopped crying but Mutt is barking incessantly; soft, muffled thumps tell Julia he's trying desperately to get out of the closet.

'I know you remember me,' Grace says, her voice hushed, reverent. 'It was a long time ago but I've never forgotten you.'

She has positioned Rosie like a shield between them. Only

326

half of her face is visible to Julia, the half that is bruised, with a hospital dressing over one eyebrow. Her eyes glance over the golf club. 'You can put that on the floor. Slide it over to me.' In the dim light Julia can see Rosie is growing paler.

Where is Armstrong?

She drops the golf club with a loud clatter onto the kitchen tiles and kicks it towards them, but gently, so it rests closer to her than to Grace.

'Yes, I remember you, Grace,' Julia says, trying to make eye contact. It's difficult to read her face in the near darkness. 'It was 2009 and we found you in Christian Thomas's basement. I've never forgotten you either.' *And even though we saved you, your face is one of the ones that haunt me when I'm trying to sleep*, she wants to add, but doesn't. At Thomas's name, Grace winces, Julia is sure of it. 'Why are we here? What's the point of all this?'

Grace shuffles forward, pushing Rosie with her. 'We moved house, you know, when Mam got married. Oh my God – you wouldn't believe the coincidences! Mam and Conrad bought a house in the Carmichael Estate. My stepbrother told me it was famous because a serial killer once attacked a guard there. So I looked it up. And there you were! Your face in every newspaper. And there's more! Our house is number thirty-six – just like the house where your partner was killed. Isn't that incredible?'

Grace sounds much younger than a woman of twenty; the knife at Rosie's neck vibrates as she talks. Her voice is cautious, her eyes never leaving Julia's face; Grace wants a connection, she wants Julia to feel what she feels.

'You and him and all the other people that were there in the house ... sometimes I didn't know if it was real or not, or who was good and who was bad … but I always remembered *you*.' She sobs suddenly, a sound that seems to burst from her throat. 'You were pretty and kind and you smelled so nice … sometimes, I thought …' Whatever she had been about to say makes her cry harder.

Julia steps forward a little, her unease escalating; there's something in the tone of Grace's voice that she's heard before. Cox sounded the same at the end, and others too, over the years. Not everyone's voice sounds so flat, only the ones that don't care if they live or die.

Grace wipes her eyes with one hand and gulps for air.

'But then you wrote a book about everything you were proud of and you left me out of it. I studied every word – even though you changed the names I knew none of your example cases referred to me. I followed all your interviews and all the podcasts and read all the magazine articles, but there wasn't one word about the cases you didn't include … I wanted to ask you about that – I mean, why would you do that? Why were some people less important than others?'

'It was an academic textbook,' Julia answers quietly; she has regretted this book for so long. 'The cases I included were to highlight certain investigative techniques or forensic procedures. Leaving your experience out wasn't personal.'

'Oh yeah? Well I think you're full of shit!'

'How's that?' *Keep her talking* … Julia knows Armstrong can't be far away. Watching Rosie's eyes roll, Julia feels a noose tighten around her own neck. She slips her free hand into the pocket of her borrowed jogging pants.

'It's all shit! All the credit you claimed in that book, and the people you *saved* …what about *me*? Why wasn't I in your stupid book? I'll tell you why!' Grace pushes Rosie

328

aside now and the girl crumbles to the ground, her head bouncing hard on the tiles. She lies still, unconscious. 'Because you *failed* me! Any self-respecting detective would consider it a failure to leave a child with that animal for *three fucking weeks!*' She screams her pain at Julia, who is happy to stand still and take it, happy to hear this, because she's always known it's true. Not every closed case was a success. She's not proud of every investigation she worked on, even when they got the outcome they wanted in the end.

'I'm so sorry, Grace,' she says, and she means it. She edges forward again, another small step. 'You're right. You're absolutely right. We did everything we could but three weeks was too long; we failed you. We all were crushed about it, but we found you alive. We hoped that counted for something.'

She can see Grace clearly now; she's a grown woman but Julia can still see the little girl curled up on a mattress. 'Have you done all this to punish me?' she asks.

Julia watches Grace's throat moving as she swallows, her chest rising and falling quickly, as though she's fighting panic. They are standing closer now, Grace's arms hanging by her sides, the knife limp in one hand as she struggles to compose herself. An armed woman losing control isn't something Julia can allow right now …

Keep the suspect engaged.

'Why did you kill Elena Kehoe and Hannah Miller?'

Grace blinks quickly, her eyes glassy with tears, and focuses on Julia's face. 'I … I didn't mean to. Your book was in one of our course lectures, and—' She looks into Julia's eyes, her face crumpling. 'I told them about us. They didn't believe me. They laughed at me.' Her voice is a brittle broken sound that dies on her lips.

'Did you drug them when you took them back to your house?'

Grace doesn't answer, her eyes are unfocused as she is momentarily lost inside her mind.

'You dragged them from your house over small stones … and you put your own skin under Elena's fingernails. You read about forensics in the books on your beside locker.'

Grace rubs at her bandaged forearm, the knife shining in the half-light.

'You painted antifouling paint on your skin and planted it, knowing it would lead me to Knockchapel. Just as you placed my book at the scene. It's *your* boat, isn't it? *The Léa-Camille.*'

Grace shakes her head from side to side. '*Stop!*'

Shouts and banging at the front door make them both jump; the difference between them is Julia is waiting for Armstrong to arrive and Grace is caught completely by surprise. She gasps and drops the knife; it bounces onto the tiles and she dives for it, just as Julia's foot kicks it away. The beam of her flashlight is pointing at the ground, glinting off the golf club; Grace's hands close around that instead of the handle of her knife.

The swinging arc of metal flashes in the air as Grace swings it with all her strength, and a searing rip of pain as it connects with her left shoulder brings Julia to her knees. She drops the flashlight. Grace swings again, makes contact; Julia's head explodes in agony. Her arm hangs slack against her body and blood runs down her face. As Grace raises the golf club again, Julia grips the kitchen island, knowing she must get to her feet, she cannot stay on the ground.

The golf club connects with her shoulder again. The tiled floor sways under her feet but she stays upright, leaning her body against the island. Grace is now a shape in the dark, a screaming, howling mass of pain, lashing out until the world around her stops moving. The banging and shouting at the front of the house continues.

'Grace!' Julia finds her voice. It's weak, but it's enough to still the woman, even just for a moment. Her eyes have adjusted to the dark; Grace is so close Julia can feel her breath on her face as she gasps with exertion. Julia's right hand closes around a slim canister; somehow, in the midst of their conversation, she has managed to pull the pepper spray from her pocket. She angles it to where she can see the shape of Grace's face and presses hard on the nozzle.

All she can do is hope and pray it reaches its target.

When Neil Armstrong runs into the room his shoes slip on the tiles for a moment and he catches the door to steady himself. Three dark shapes on the floor punctuate the almost complete darkness of the kitchen. The smallest shape isn't moving. Another is a writhing figure, gasping for air and clutching at her face. The third is watching him from a seated position against the island, panting.

'Neil, if you wouldn't mind fetching my dog from the closet, I'd really appreciate it.'

46

2024

In Julia's memory, in the parts of her mind where the ghost of her past life still lies, Des Riordan is a physical force, a whirlwind that both terrified and enthralled her. He was the man in charge, and when a case went awry or was completely derailed, he was always the one she turned to. Over the years, her mentor became her friend. He never replaced Adrian Clancy, but he came as close as anyone ever could.

When he walked towards her on the Shakey Bridge, she had marvelled at how time had taken the vigour from him; his hollowed cheeks, skin stretched too thin over his bones, his perpetually unsteady hands. Then she'd felt protective of him. When he had survived the assault on the day of the press conference, she had felt optimistic that he was stronger than he looked. But a heart attack a few days later shattered all hope. Now, she sits beside his bed, the plastic chair creaking underneath her, the noise of it lost among the steady hum of the machines that are keeping him alive. She grips his hand nearest to her; his skin is warmer than she had expected.

'Síle told me it's time to say goodbye.'

The words hover in the air around them; she shakes her head at the absurdity of it. She will never say goodbye to him, not really. Her right hand grips his tight, her left bound in a sling against her chest.

He was her first thought when she came around after surgery – was he still alive? In the aftermath of her confrontation with Grace York, she was aware he was two floors up from her in the same hospital. She knew he was fading, was in a coma in intensive care. But Riordan had always been stubborn and over the last few days, as he had continued to hold on, she had dared to hope. But the time has come; Grace York and the crimes she committed were their last case together.

'I'm glad I got to see you again,' Julia squeezes his hand, 'even though it was as bad as it was. I've been thinking that maybe I shouldn't have run away – let's face it, that's what I did. The book got out of hand and without my job, without anyone to stay here for, it felt easier to leave Cork and start over. But I've missed my life here. Or maybe I've just missed you, Des.'

The steady, rhythmic beat of the equipment beside his bed is almost soothing. She rubs her thumb over his hand, wishing he would speak to her. They should be thrashing out the case, dissecting Grace York's motive and wondering what signs they might have overlooked. She longs to hear his deep voice, his Northern Irish accent is still so clear in her mind; there is no comfort in holding his hand and imagining how he would have unpicked the case and what conclusions he might have made.

Julia leans over and presses her lips against the soft skin of his hand. Her boss ... her friend ... She had once stood on a kerb to meet his eyes, determined he wouldn't look down on her.

A long time ago, she realized he never had.

In the lift back to her ward, Julia looks at her reflection in the mirrored wall. The sutures at her hairline are hidden beneath a white bandage and bruises stain the skin around her temple. Her arm rests in a sling against her chest; these wounds will heal slower than the ones James Cox inflicted on her inside the Carmichael Estate. She had youth on her side then. Her eyes track each line on her face, marking every one of the years she spent rising through the ranks of the Gardaí. They made mistakes – and some of the people they tried to help paid a heavy price. Grace York is testament to that. But Riordan's team did a lot of good too and she was proud to be part of it.

The doors slide open and she walks back to her room. Sitting beside her bed, a woman waits silently, leafing through a paperback from a stack on the bedside locker. Even though more than five years have passed since they've seen each other, her face is a familiar comfort; eyebrows arched in amusement, lips lifted at the corners in a ready smile.

'Liz Begley.' Julia blinks in disbelief. 'I thought you were knee-deep in grandchildren these days.'

'And I thought you'd disappeared!'

She stands and they embrace awkwardly. Liz whistles softly as she holds Julia at arm's length.

'Christ, you always had a knack for running into trouble. So tell me, how do you get any rest around here, between the bodice-ripping novels and the sexy doctors with come-to-bed eyes?'

Julia can't help but grin, grateful her old friend is here. She feels less alone. The past she tried so desperately to run away from won't let her go, and for the first time in a very long while, she's okay with that.

47

2024

Des Riordan's funeral will take place on a crisply cold morning nine days after he was attacked.

Julia signs the last of her hospital discharge papers and nods in greeting to Neil Armstrong, who is standing against a nearby wall with his arms folded. She can tell he disapproves.

'Good morning, sunshine,' she greets him, 'thanks for collecting me.'

He pushes off the wall with a frown and picks up her small bag from the ground at her feet.

'This is a mistake. You're not supposed to leave yet, Julia!'

'I'm so glad you're finally calling me Julia!'

He ignores that. 'Isn't this a bit soon? You've had surgery. I'm not responsible if you fall and split your head open!'

'Oh relax, I'm as steady on my feet as I've always been! And I'm not missing Des's funeral.' Armstrong offers a quick nod of understanding. 'Mary Clancy said I can stay with them for a few days so you can drop me to her daughter's afterwards, if you don't mind.'

'Gladly. This is a really bad idea.'

'Noted. You need to learn when to relax, Small Step!'

He narrows his eyes at her and turns away, walking the route to the hospital car park in silence, although at a slower pace than usual so they are still side by side. Once inside the car he exhales wearily as he starts the engine.

'Something on your mind? Tough case maybe?' she asks. She hopes he has an impossible-to-crack case on his desk and is about to share the details, anything to take her mind off the day ahead.

'Aren't they all?' he mutters.

'Care to talk about it?'

'No I do not!'

'Yes, yes, I know – you don't need my help,' she says, 'but if you ever want to run anything past me, I'd be glad to look over it.'

His eyes slide to hers. 'Don't tell me you're coming out of retirement!'

'God, no!' Her thumb rubs the gold wedding band on her finger; it's been sitting in her hospital-room locker for over a week. She feels more like herself with it back on. 'Just thought you might miss someone looking over your shoulder ...'

The car idles, the heating on, and he watches her for a moment before saying, 'I'm glad to see your sense of humour is intact. And I'm even happier to hear you'll be going back to Cuan Beag soon.'

'Who told you where I live? Was it Shauna Clancy?'

Armstrong taps the side of his nose, a smirk playing

337

at the edges of his lips. Let him have his fun, Julia thinks; it's nice to see him smile. As she pulls the seatbelt across her body her head throbs in pain and the muscles inside her shoulder feel torn loose again. She gasps, then clears her throat to camouflage the sound before Armstrong can offer another reproach.

'I assume Mutt is behaving himself?' She attempts to divert his attention from the fact that she is probably still too weak to attend Riordan's funeral.

'That dog is being treated better than I am!' He turns out of their parking space. 'Mutt and I have reached an agreement. He doesn't shit in my house and I don't leave him on the side of the road.'

Julia's fingertips ruck at the black silk scarf at her throat; leaving Mutt with Armstrong was her absolute last resort.

'I'm not sure you'll get him back, actually. Aria and Rosie have him spoiled.'

Knowing that Rosie and her mother are healing well is something that has accelerated Julia's own recovery. The cut on Rosie's neck was superficial, the bump on her head nothing to worry about. Julia knows Rosie will carry the memory of the attack for the rest of her life, which was why she introduced her to Shauna Clancy. They have a lot in common.

'Have you confirmed where Elena and Hannah were killed?' Julia can't help seeking updates on the case. She has barely thought of anything else since her encounter with Grace in the guesthouse.

'Conrad York keeps an SUV in Cork for when they return home; it was found parked near the marina in Knockchapel. Blood inside it belonged to the victims. We're still working it all out, but the most likely scenario is that Grace killed them in her stepfather's vehicle and arranged their bodies where she knew they'd be found quickly.'

His lip curls in disgust. Julia presses on.

'Did you learn anything useful from your interviews with Grace's family?'

'Yes, actually. Her mother confirmed Grace was obsessed with you from a young age. I guess that's understandable, you were her saviour, the first face she saw after her ordeal. She talked about you non-stop. Then, once she had her own laptop, she followed you in the press. She saved every article – we knew that much already. There was an interview about seven years ago where you said you didn't believe in coincidences. Grace zoned in on that. When she realized you had a connection to the Carmichael Estate, and that the number of her house was also part of the same case, she began to speak about a bond between you, her and Cox. His death was some sort of catalyst that spurred her to kill. You had disappeared, and she desperately wanted to draw you back into her life.'

Julia closes her eyes briefly, sadness rushing through her.

Armstrong concentrates on navigating out of the car park as he continues. 'The report from Grace's psychiatric tests is still pending. I'm not sure prison is going to be the best place for her, but that's up to the judge. Daunt isn't saying a word without his solicitor this time. At least they're both somewhere they can't hurt anyone else.'

'Speaking of Daunt – what's the full story with him? Why was he at *The Léa-Camille*?'

'Just checking in on her, I think. He knew what was going on, but how deeply involved he was remains to be

339

established. He *did* attack Riordan – the forensic team have confirmed that. His relationship with Grace is a couple of years old. She reached out to him shortly after your book was released. She actually emailed every employee listed on your publisher's website. Daunt was the only one who replied. They struck up a friendship of sorts, and recently, they began sleeping together. She's a lot younger than him and way out of his league, but she used him. He was just another link to you as far as she was concerned. I think she convinced him to attack Riordan because she was staying out of sight. Daunt's heart wasn't in it, which is why Riordan survived initially. I'm not sure how Grace imagined this would end, and what part Daunt would eventually play.'

'She is in a lot of pain.' Julia's nights in the hospital ward have been haunted by the memory of Grace's eyes – the small girl on the mattress and the woman crying in Riordan's kitchen. In her imagined conversations with Riordan she asked him if this was their fault – could they have done more back when Grace was missing? Knowing he would have said no is not the same as hearing it.

'Yeah, well, so are Elena and Hannah's families.'

'Grace suffered, Neil, she—'

'She doesn't have the right to kill innocent people just because she's hurting!' Armstrong meets her eyes. 'This is about right and wrong. It's as simple as that.'

Julia thinks of Shay – James Cox – and the people he killed because the depth of his pain was too heavy to endure. She has felt revulsion, fear and anger towards him since then. He was a monster – does she think the same of Grace? She has learned that very few people are born evil;

340

for some, the circumstances of their life can twist them into a person capable of terrible things. Grace suffered horribly. But Armstrong is right, she doesn't have the right to kill innocent people because she's in pain.

Suddenly, Julia feels weak and exhausted. Armstrong turns the radio on and drives south, near the coast again, to the church funeral Riordan's family have arranged. Julia promises herself that within a few days she will be on the road to Cuan Beag, back to her life again, leaving this all behind.

When Armstrong helps her out of the car a little while later, he insists she wait while he finds a place to park. He'll escort her inside, still afraid she might collapse on his watch; she would argue with him, but she felt lightheaded on the journey here, each pothole in the road making her stomach lurch unpleasantly. She feels unsteady now on her feet, despite her earlier protests. Tears fill her eyes as she spots Síle and Rosie up ahead, near the entrance to the church, arms around each other in a tight embrace. Julia wipes her face and looks away.

Beside her, on a wilting rose bush, a spider has been busy; she reaches out and trails her fingers in the air over the spirals of a web that dazzle in the sunlight. After a moment, a tingle along her skin tells her that she's being watched. She turns her head and all the air rushes from her lungs.

It's been thirty years but she could never forget his face. His eyes are dark pools of light that seem to twinkle behind glasses she didn't know he needed. His hair is still thick and slicked back; what was shiny and dark is now salt and

341

pepper around his ears. He leans on a walking stick and smiles broadly at her. It's the smile he offered after every night shift, when he was flipping bacon at the stove and brewing up her tea, just the way she liked it. Philip's eyes roam over her face and rest on her arm, tight against her chest in a sling, exactly like the last time they saw each other.

'Hello, Julia.'

Acknowledgements

I am infinitely grateful to my wonderful agent Sara O' Keeffe for believing in my potential, and for championing this book. Encouragement is a powerful thing, and I am thrilled to have yours.

To the wider team at Aevitas Creative Management, including Vanessa Kerr, Augustus Brown and Tom Lloyd-Williams. Thank you all for your support.

To my lovely, insightful editor Kate Mills. Thank you for your enthusiasm for *The Dark Hours*. Thank you to Rachael Nazarko, Patricia McVeigh, April Osborn and to all the extended team at HQ, HarperCollins UK, HarperCollins Ireland and MIRA, HarperCollins US. I am grateful for your expertise and support, from edits to cover design, publicity, marketing and sales. I am truly excited to work with you.

Thank you to the publishing team at Piper Verlag, in Germany.

Thank you to the kind people who explained procedures, answered emails, and talked me through processes. I am so grateful for your time and that you were willing to share your knowledge and experience. Any mistakes are from my own misinterpretation.

Thank you to the Irish writing community who continue to be so supportive. Special thanks to Cork author Michelle Dunne. I enjoy reading your thrillers just as much as sharing coffee/bubbles and discussing all things books!

Thank you to book bloggers, book sellers and librarians – helping books to reach new readers is a wonderful thing, and I truly appreciate your support.

Special thanks to readers and book lovers – without you, I could not live this dream of creating stories and sharing them with people who love to be immersed in another world.

Thank you to my family and friends; I probably talk about books far too much! Know that I appreciate that I can share my passion with you.

I love living in Cork – the ever-changing weather, the beautiful coastline, the storytellers, the sense of humour. It will always be home. Knockchapel and Cuan Beag are fictional places weaved among real ones. They are based on villages in Cork that I have loved and, for several reasons, drawn both light and darkness from. They inspired parts of this story, but I hope Corkonians will forgive me for renaming them as fictional places. The Carmichael Estate doesn't exist, but is based on another creepy laneway leading to an old house, where I had adventures and where the shadowy gloom allowed my imagination to run riot.

I am thrilled to share this journey with my husband and children. Thanks for the encouraging notes and cups of coffee. You three own my heart.

ONE PLACE. MANY STORIES

**Bold, innovative and
empowering publishing.**

FOLLOW US ON:

@HQStories